*The perfect summer begins
with Jenny Oliver*

The Vintage Summer Wedding

JENNY
OLIVER

CARINA™

This edition is published by arrangement with Harlequin Books S.A. CARINA is a trademark of Harlequin Enterprises Limited, used under licence.

Published in Great Britain 2015
by CARINA, an imprint of Harlequin (UK) Limited,
Eton House, 18-24 Paradise Road,
Richmond, Surrey, TW9 1SR

© 2015 Jenny Oliver

ISBN 978-0-263-25414-3

98-0315

Harlequin's policy is to use papers that are natural, renewable and recyclable products and made from wood grown in sustainable forests. The logging and manufacturing processes conform to the legal environmental regulations of the country of origin.

Printed and bound by
CPI Group (UK) Ltd, Croydon, CR0 4YY

Jenny Oliver wrote her first book on holiday when she was ten years old. Illustrated with cut-out supermodels from her sister's *Vogue*, it was an epic, sweeping love story not so loosely based on *Dynasty*.

Since then Jenny has gone on to get an English degree, a Master's and a job in publishing that's taught her what it takes to write a novel (without the help of the supermodels). Follow her on Twitter @JenOliverBooks.

The Vintage Summer Wedding

For Lucy and Les,
Thank you

Chapter One

They arrived in the dark in a heatwave. As Anna stepped out of the car, all she could smell was roses. An omen of thick, heavy scent. A potent reminder of a well-buried past. She remembered being knocked off-kilter by a huge vase of them at the Opera House once – big, luxurious, peach cabbage roses – and shaking her head at her assistant, trying to hide her agitation by saying dismissively, *'No, they're not right. Swap them for stargazers or, if you can get them, hydrangeas.'*

'Wondered whether you two would ever turn up.' Jeff Mallory, the landlord of the new property, a man with a moustache and a belly that sagged over his dark-green cords, heaved himself out of the cab of a white van.

'Sorry, mate.' Seb strode forward, arm outstretched for a vigorous handshake. 'We would have been here earlier but—'

He left the reason hanging in the air. They both knew it was Anna's fault. Stalling the packing at every conceivable opportunity. Dithering over how clothes had been folded and obsessively wrapping everything in tissue paper, then bubble-wrap until teacups were the size of footballs.

11

'Not a problem.' Jeff shook his head. 'Just been reading the paper, nice to have a bit of time to myself if I'm honest. Nice little cottage this – you'll love it, just right for a young couple.'

Anna turned her head slowly from the view of the field opposite, the pungent smell of cowpats and hay and something else that she couldn't quite put her finger on that had mingled with the sweet roses and was drawing her back in time like a whiff of an old perfume. She let her eyes trail up from the white front gate, the wild overgrown garden, the twee little porch and the carved wooden sign that she knew would spell out something hideous like Wild Rose Cottage.

You have to try, Anna.

Seb did all the chatting while she opened the car door and grabbed her handbag.

'It's good to be back,' she heard him say, taking a deep breath of country air. 'Really feels good.'

'Well I never thought I'd see the day.' Jeff ran a hand along the waistband of his trousers, hitching them into a more comfortable position. 'Anna Whitehall back in Nettleton.'

She scratched her neck, feeling the heat prickle against her skin, wondering if by some miracle someone had thought to install air-conditioning in the crumbling cottage. 'Me neither, Mr Mallory,' she said. 'Me neither.' She attempted a smile, felt Seb's eyes on her.

'You know I played you at the village Christmas play the other year.' He nodded like he'd only just remembered. 'Best laugh in the house I got. Dressed

12

in a pink tutu I had to shout, "I'm never coming back, you losers. Up your bum."' He snorted with laughter. 'Brought the house down.'

Sweat trickled down between her shoulder blades as she huffed a fake laugh. 'I'm so pleased I left a legacy.'

'Too right you did.' He moved round to the boot of the car to help Seb with the other cases, hauling them out as his trousers slipped lower. Seb was smiling along, trying to smooth out the creases of tension in the air. 'Whole village has been waiting for you to come back,' Mr. Mallory went on, regardless.

Seb wheeled a case past her over the uneven road and let his hand rest for a moment on her shoulder. She wanted to cover it with her own, but not good with public shows of sympathy she shook his hand off, trying to keep her poise.

'Well I'm glad I gave them something to talk about.' *This won't be for ever*, she said to herself as she gathered some of the plastic bags crammed with stuff out from the back seat. *You can do it, I promise*.

'Gave?' Jeff laughed as he hauled another case out of the boot.

'Oh mind that—' She ran round and rescued the dress-bag that was being crumpled under the stack of suitcases he was piling up in the street.

'No past tense about it, Anna. Still giving, sweetheart. Still giving.' He laughed.

She folded the Vera Wang bag over her arm and took a deep breath. That was it, that was the smell that mingled with the rest. The unmistakable scent of small-town gossip. I bet they loved it, she thought. The great Anna Whitehall fallen from her perch. Rubbing their hands together gleefully, hoping she landed with a painful bump.

Well, she'd made it through worse. She may have promised Seb a year, but she was here for as short a time as she could manage. All she had to do was get a decent new job and, she stroked the velvety skin of the dress-bag, get married. The wedding may no longer be at the exclusive, lavish Waldegrave, and it may not have tiny Swarovski crystals scattered over the tables, a champagne reception, forty-four bedrooms for guests and a Georgian townhouse across the street for the bride and groom, a six-tier Patisserie Gerard chocolate frilled cake and bridesmaids in the palest-grey slub silk, but there was still this bloody gorgeous dress and, she looked up at the cottage, a bare bulb hanging from the kitchen window that Seb had clicked on, and took a shaky breath in, well, no, not much else.

They hauled in bag after bag like cart horses as the dusk dipped to darkness. When Seb handed over the cash for rent, Anna couldn't watch and, instead, peered into each room, flicking on lights and opening windows to try and get rid of the stifling heat. The air, though, was still like the surface of stagnant water, mosquitos skating over it like ice, buzzing in every room. She swatted one and instantly regretted it, the little squashed body oozing blood on the paisley Laura Ashley wallpaper. It was the same paper her granny had had. The memory made Anna's breath catch in her throat – of warm, cosy fires and freshly baked bread. Of her hair being stroked as she relished the sound of *Coronation Street* – half an hour of peace before her mum would come and drag her back. If her granny were still alive, still here, keeping the village in check, then none of this would be so bad. But she wasn't, and it was.

Looking out from the upstairs bedroom window, she could see Seb talking with Jeff in the street, their shadows as they laughed. She leant forward, the palms of her hands on the cracked, flaking windowsill, and watched as Jeff waved, clambered into his van and cranked the engine and imagined him pootling off to the King's Head, his pint in his own silver tankard waiting for him on the bar and a million eager ears ready for his lowdown.

'So what do you think?' A minute later she heard Seb walk across the creaking floorboards as he came to stand behind her, his hands snaking round her waist, the heat of him engulfing her like a duvet.

'It's fine,' she said, leaning her head back on his shoulder and feeling the rumble in his chest as he laughed.

'Damned with faint praise.'

'No, it's really nice. Very cute.' She turned and almost muffled it into his T-shirt so he might miss the lack of conviction.

'Yeah, I think it'll do. It could be much worse, Anna. I think we'll be OK here. Get a dog, plant some vegetables.'

She bit her lip as her cheek pressed into the cotton of his top, swallowed over the lump in her throat and nodded.

He stroked her hair. 'We'll be OK, Anna. Change is never a bad thing. And you never know, you might love it.'

'I might,' she lied with as much enthusiasm as she could manage. Pulling away from him and going over to the big seventies dressing table she unclipped her earrings and put them down on the veneer surface. The reflection in the big circular mirror showed Seb's profile – wide eyes gazing out across the fields of wheat that she knew from her quick glance earlier was accented with red as the moonlight picked out the poppies. She couldn't miss the wistful look on his face, the softening of his lips.

She wanted to say, 'One year, Seb. Don't get any dreamy ideas.' But she couldn't bear the idea of wiping that boyish smile off his face. And anyway, she wasn't in any position to lay down the rules. The fact that they currently had nothing was her fault. The dream she had been pushing had broken, now it was Seb's turn to try his. The feeling was like having her hands cuffed behind her back and her smile painted on her face like a clown.

He turned to look at her. 'Think of it like a holiday,' he said, his eyes dancing with teasing laughter.

She thought of her vacations, two glorious weeks somewhere with an infinity pool, cocktails on the beach, restaurants overlooking the sea, basking in blazing sunshine. But then again, there had been schlepping round Skegness with her dad in the rain as a teenager. Anything was better than that.

'I'm going to have to shower, I'm too hot,' she said, peeling off her silk tank-top, wondering whether if she just hung it by the window, the little dots of sweat would dry and not stain.

The bathroom was tiny, the grouting brown, the ceiling cracked where the steam had bubbled the paint. She pulled back the mildewed shower curtain and found herself perplexed.

'Seb!' she called.

'What is it?'

'There's no shower.'

'No shower?'

'No shower.'

He stood in the doorway and laughed. 'You're going to have to learn to bathe.'

'Who doesn't have a shower?' she whispered, biting the tip of her finger, feeling suddenly like a pebble rolling in a wake, her façade teetering.

'Primrose Cottage, honeybun.'

Oh she knew it was going to be called something dreadful like that.

'Home sweet home.'

Chapter Two

'I couldn't sleep for ages last night and do you know what I could hear?' Seb was standing at the end of the bed in just his boxer shorts, speaking as he took gulps from a glass of water.

'What could you hear?' Anna was still half asleep, hoping that maybe when she opened her eyes it might all have been a dream.

'Nothing.'

'Nothing?'

'Nothing. Not a sound. Just total and utter silence. And then I got up to look out the window and do you know what I could see?'

'Nothing?' Anna said as she started to push herself up from the bed.

'Exactly! It was black. Pitch bloody black. I couldn't see my fingers in front of my face.'

'Hang on a second—' Anna slipped her arm into her silk dressing gown that was hanging from the post of the bed. 'Is this a good thing?'

'I thought the countryside was meant to be being ruined by motorways and lorries and flight paths.'

Seb gulped down the last of his water as she wandered groggily to the mirror. 'But there was nothing, Anna,' he said. 'It was amazing. Like being a kid again. I haven't slept this well for years. I literally feel like I did when I was ten. You know, boundless energy. Anna, I have boundless energy.'

She looked at him over her shoulder, one brow raised. 'You're not going to make me go for a run or something are you?'

Seb laughed. 'Anna, darling, I would never dare make you do anything.' As he strolled over to the bathroom he added, 'Except get dressed because I have been shopping – d'you know the corner shop is still there, Anna, still selling slightly out of date stuff – and I have made breakfast and it's downstairs waiting for you.'

Anna smiled. She realised then she could smell the bacon he'd grilled. As she watched him pause by the bathroom door and lick his finger and try and stick down a bit of peeling wallpaper with his spit, she allowed herself a tiny weeny second to think about their old place in Bermondsey – the clean white walls, the huge windows, the wooden floors she padded across to make a breakfast of yoghurt, seeds and plump, juicy blueberries.

'Come on, get dressed, you'll be late for work otherwise.' Seb was holding a tub of Shockwaves, running the wax through his hair as he watched her daydreaming.

'Where did you get that stuff, Seb? It's for teenagers.'

19

Seb narrowed his eyes at the tub of hair wax and thought for a second. 'I think I confiscated it off one of the kids at school.' Then he shrugged and went back to check his reflection in the mirror.

Anna rolled her eyes. While Seb adored his career and had landed his dream job of teaching at Nettleton High, getting back to his roots as he put it, Anna was about to begin a new career working in a little antique shop that her dad had pulled in a favour for. If her memory served her correctly, it was the same dark, dusty place that she had had to sit in as a child while he haggled the price of his wares up before he took her to ballet lessons. It was going to pay her six pounds fifty an hour.

'Come on, if you're lucky I'll take you for coffee in the village before I have to go to school.'

'Do you think there's a Starbucks here yet?' she asked, brow raised.

'I checked this morning. No Starbucks, I'm afraid. There is a petition against a Waitrose though, which I thought might make you happy,' Seb replied. 'The Waitrose, not the petition.'

'Do you know actually, a Waitrose might make it all a bit more bearable.' Anna agreed. 'Petitions never work, do they?'

Seb leaned against the doorway of the en-suite. 'I signed it, in the greengrocer's.

Anna made a face.

He shrugged, smiled, and said, 'Gotta become part of the community, Anna. Gotta try.' Then he smacked her on the bum as he strolled out of the room, 'Come on, breakfast's ready and it's a beautiful, beautiful day.'

Anna groaned. 'Why must you be so goddamn cheery?'

'Because I have such a lovely, sweet, adoring fiancée,' he said, deadpan.

As she watched him retreat down the stairs, whistling a tune he'd clearly made up, Anna thought about the look on his face when she'd told him that The Waldegrave had gone into administration. That all their money was gone. Everything. That even just the loss of the fifty percent deposit was actually the whole shebang. That she hadn't been exactly truthful about the extent of the cost and now they had nothing. Barely more than the money in their wallets.

And he had turned to the side for just a fraction of a second, clenching his face up, all the muscles rigid, shut his eyes, taken a breath. Then he'd turned back, eyes open, squeezed her hand in his and said, *'It's OK. It'll be OK.'*

It was his kindness, his patience that had got them through this. She knew full well that it wasn't hers! And for that she had moved here, had packed up her life, left her friends, headed back to the place where pretty much the entire population hated her, and, while her whole body felt squashed and heavy with the fear that this was it, she was going to try.

'Anna. Anna! Come and look at this. There's a cow in the front garden!'

She looked in the mirror and shut her eyes. For Seb's sake she was going to try.

Driving to the village, Seb had trouble with the narrow lanes, bramble branches flicking into the window as he had to keep swerving into the bushes as Golf GTIs and mud-splattered Land Rovers hurtled past on the other side of the road, beeping his London driving.

'It's a bloody nightmare,' he said, loosening his tie, knuckles gripping the steering wheel. 'You just can't see what's coming.'

'I thought you always said you knew these roads like the back of your hand.' Anna straightened the sun-visor mirror to check her reflection. She'd been told by Mrs Beedle, the antiques shop owner, on the phone to wear something she didn't mind getting mucky in. Anna didn't own anything she minded getting mucky. Her wardrobe had predominantly consisted of Marc Jacob pantsuits, J Brand jeans and key Stella McCartney pieces. The only memory of them now were the piles of jiffy bags that she had stuffed them into and mailed out to the highest eBay bidder. At a loss, she'd ended up borrowing a pair of Seb's khaki shorts; that and a black tank-top she wore to the gym.

'I did. I think they've planted new hedgerows since my day.'

Anna laughed and said, 'I think that's highly unlikely, Sebastian,' before pulling her sunglasses down from the top of her head, closing her eyes and trying to imagine herself on some Caribbean beach absorbing the wall of heat, about to dive into the ocean, or settled into the box at the opera house to watch the dress rehearsal, sipping champagne or a double vodka martini.

'Eh voilà,' Seb said a minute later, cutting the engine and winding up his window.

She opened her eyes slowly like a cat interrupted from sleep.

There it was.

Nettleton village.

The sight of it seemed to lodge her heart in her throat. Her brow suddenly speckled with sweat.

'OK?' Seb asked before he opened the door.

Anna waved him away, 'Yeah, yeah, fine.' She unclicked her door and stepped out onto the cobbles. Unfurling herself from their little hatchback, she stretched her back and shoulders and surveyed the scene as if looking back over old photographs. Through the hazy morning mist of heat, she could see all the little shops surrounding the village square, the avenue of lime trees that dripped sticky sap on the pavement and cars, the church at the far end by the pond and the playground, the benches dappled with the shade from the big, wide leaves of the overhanging trees. Across the square was the pharmacy, its green cross flashing and registering the temperature at twenty-seven degrees. She looked at her watch; it was only eight o'clock. The window still had those old bottles of liquid like an apothecary shop, one red one green, it could have been her imagination playing tricks on her but she thought she remembered them from when she was a kid. Next to that was the newsagent, Dowsetts. A bit of A4 paper stuck on the door saying only two school children at a time. Now that she did remember. Three of them would go in deliberately and cause Mrs Norris apoplexy as they huddled together picking the penny sweets out one at a time and pretending to put them in their pockets. Then, when her friend Hermione locked Mrs Norris in the store cupboard one lunchtime, it earned them a lifetime ban. Her granny had said Anna deserved it and hoped it had taught her a lesson, but also agreed not to tell her mum. Did that ban still stand, Anna wondered. Would she be turned away if she dared set foot inside? Or was it like prison? Twelve years or less for good behaviour?

Nettleton, she thought, hands on her hips, there it was, all exactly as she remembered it.

Seb came round and draped his arm over her shoulders, giving her an affectionate shake. 'Isn't it lovely?'

She gave him a sidelong look. 'Nothing a Waitrose wouldn't fix.'

He grinned as they strolled over towards a bakery coffee shop, its yellow-striped awning unwound over red cafe tables and chairs, a daisy in a jam jar on each. 'You'll have to sign the petition. Whether you like it or not,' he said, then paused, pointing to the cakes in the window. 'Well isn't this charming?'

Anna thought back to when she'd picked the wedding cake in Patisserie Gerard. The slices the chef brought over on little frilled-edged plates and metal two-pronged forks, watching as she placed the delicate vanilla sponge or chocolate sachertorte into her mouth and sighed with the pleasure of it. How he had suggested that she had to have between four and six layers, less was unheard of for weddings at The Waldegrave; two chocolate with a Black Forest-style cherry that would ooze when cut and soaked through with booze, heavy and dense. Then a light, fluffy little sponge on the top, perhaps in an orange or, he suggested, a clementine. Just slightly sweeter. The guests would be able to tell the difference. They'd definitely be the type to appreciate such delicate flavours. She'd known it was too expensive for them, that he catered for celebrities and royalty and was way out of her price range. But as she'd nodded along, pretending that she could taste the difference between orange and clementine, she'd started to get swept up in her own façade. Without warning her mother's voice had popped into her head. *We never had a wedding, Anna, and it was a sign.* Anna hadn't seen the prices written tiny on the brochure, just imagined instead her mother telling people proudly that the very same cake had appeared in *Hello!* magazine. *Pregnant with you, Anna, and standing in some crummy registry office with a couple of witnesses he'd dragged in from outside. I didn't even get a new dress. And in those days you didn't have pregnancy clothes, Anna, not the flashy things you have now. Oh no, I had a big hoop of corduroy pleated around my belly like a traffic cone. There were no photos. Thank God. But when I think about it now, I know it was definitely a sign. He wanted to gloss over it. A wedding is more than just a day, Anna. It's a statement of intent.*

As she stood in front of the little bakery, consumed by her memories, Seb pulled out a chair, stretched his legs out in the morning sun and said, 'So you never told me what your mum said.'

Anna perched on the seat opposite him. 'When?'

'She rang yesterday didn't she? I'm sure I saw her name on your screen.'

'Oh.' Anna shook her head as if it was nothing. 'She said that she'd give us the money to get married. All of it.' Seb sat up straighter. Anna licked her lips and pulled her sunglasses down over her eyes. 'As long as I don't invite Dad.'

Seb spluttered a cough. 'You're kidding? No way. What did you say?'

She brushed some of the creases from her top. 'I said I'd think about it.'

'Anna, you can't not invite your father.'

'Why not? What difference would it make? At least it'd solve my problems.' She paused. 'Maybe then I wouldn't have to invite yours either,' she joked, pushing her sunglasses back so he could see the glint in her eyes.

Seb raised a brow in faux admonishment. 'My parents would be there whether you invited them or not. They'd camp outside. Anna—' He paused. 'You can't not invite your dad.' He raked a hand through his hair. 'She's manipulating you. She's being a bitch.'

Anna sat up a bit straighter. 'Don't say that. She's not, he just hurt her. God, it's so hot.'

'It was a long time ago, Anna,' he said as she fanned herself with a napkin.

Anna glanced to the side, away from looking directly at Seb and, in doing so, caught a glimpse of the girl behind the counter.

'Oh God, it's Rachel.' Anna whipped round so fast her sunglasses fell off her head and landed with a clatter on the metal table.

'What? Who?' He stuck his nose right up against the glass. 'No it's not.'

'It is. You're so obvious.' She pulled him back by the arm.

'Well what's wrong with it being Rachel? I liked Rachel.'

'Urgh, that's because you were a big old square at school just like her.'

'I don't think people say things like that any more. Not when they're grown up.'

'God, I bet she's loving this,' Anna said, picking up her glasses and sliding them on to cover her eyes. 'Me back here with my tail between my legs. I bet that means Jackie's somewhere about the place as well.'

'Of course she is, Anna, she's a teacher at the school, she helped me get the job.' Seb shook his head at her pityingly.

'Oh great, that's all I need. Come on, we have to leave.'

'Anna, stop it. You're being ridiculous. You're going to see people you used to know.'

And they'll think, *Stupid Anna, now it's our turn to laugh at her,* she thought. They'll think, *What's Seb doing with her? Have you heard, she lost all their cash? Spending outside her means. Running off to London to be a prima ballerina, ha, we all knew it was doomed. Never made it though, did she? Very few do, it's a tough industry to break into. Did you hear she lost her job at that fancy opera house as well? Tough times though, isn't it? Or the time to cut loose dead wood?*

'I can't sit here.' She started to push her chair away.

'Anna!' Seb chuckled as if she was acting crazy. 'Anna, calm down. Sit down.'

'No, I'll see you later. Have a good first day,' she said, grabbing her bag from where she'd slung it over the back of the chair and run-walking away in the direction of Vintage Treasure. She heard him call her name again but couldn't turn round. He'd be thinking she was mad but she couldn't help it. Something inside her had snapped. It was like stepping back into her past and all the teenage emotions that went with it. She caught sight of her reflection in the window of the old gift shop, Presents 4 You, and tried to regain some of her infamous poise. As the sun sizzled behind her, she retied her hair and slipped her sunglasses on, exhaled Pilates-style and even did an odd little laugh. As she was finding her composure her eye caught a T-shirt draped over a stack of gift boxes, the writing on it read *Paris, Milan, New York, Nettleton*. In their dreams, she thought, incredulous, in their dreams. Who would ever want to end up back here?

'How do you like your tea?' a woman's voice called as soon as the bell over the door of Vintage Treasure chimed.

'I'm fine, thanks,' Anna said, her eyes widening at the catastrophe of objects piled around the place. On her right was a shambles of dusty antiques, on her left a rail of tatty clothing and a mannequin draped in snakeskin bags. Ahead of her was a cracked glass counter, dull jewels catching the dim light. It smelt of damp, mothballs and baked potatoes.

'That's not what I asked.'

She heard a clinking of teaspoons and the air-tight pop of the lid coming off a tea caddy, and frowned at the woman's tone.

'Have you got any Lapsang Souchong?'

'No.'

'OK, well just white then please. Skimmed milk if you have it.'

'I don't,' the voice snapped.

'Oh. Just white's fine.' Anna made a face and carried on her journey into the dingy Aladdin's Cave, relieved to be out of the scorching heat and the fear of gossiping voices, but having to stifle a nervous laugh that this was her new office, and this terrifyingly gruff woman, her new boss.

Inside, dust swirled in the beams of sunlight that forced their way through the dirty windows and shone like spotlights on such delights as a taxidermy crow, its claw positioned on an egg, a chip in the left-hand corner of the glass box; a dark-green chaise longue, the back studded with emerald buttons and a gold scroll along the black lacquered edges; an old black lace dress with beads hanging off torn threads; a dead-badger fur stole with little feet wrapped round the neck of the tilted mannequin; a looming Welsh dresser stacked full of plates and cups and a line of Toby jugs with ugly faces and massive noses.

If there was one thing Anna hated, it was antiques and vintage clothes. Anything that wasn't new, anything with money off, anything that had to be haggled for or marked down.

All it did was remind her of being wrapped up against the cold, having her mittens hanging from her coat sleeves, her dad bundling her up at five in the morning in the passenger seat of his van, a flask of hot chocolate and a half-stale donut wrapped in a napkin that she ate with shaking hands as he scrapped the ice off the inside and outside of the window of his Ford Transit before trundling off to Ardingly, Newark or some other massive antique market. She had inherited her mother's intolerance of the cold. The fiery Spanish blood that coursed through her veins wasn't inclined to enjoy shivering in snow-crisp fields, her fingers losing their feeling, her damp lips freezing in the early morning frost as she trudged past other people's mouldy, damp crap for sale on wonky trestle tables.

As she edged her way through the maze of a shop, a woman bumbled out of the back room with a plate of gingernuts and two mugs of stewed tea clanking together, their surfaces advertising various antique markets and fairs.

'Right then, Lady Muck, see if you can bring yourself to drink this,' she said, pushing her glasses up her nose with her upper arm as she plonked the tea onto the glass counter.

Mrs Beedle. How could Anna have forgotten? Huge, dressed in a smock that could have doubled as a tent, round glasses like an owl, white shirt with a Peter Pan collar, red T-bar shoes like Annie wore in the film, a million bracelets clanging up her wrist and pockets bursting with tape measures, pencils, bits of paper and tissues. Her greying hair pulled back into an Anne of Green Gables style do, the front pushed forward like a mini-beehive and a bun held with kirby grips.

'Anna Whitehall, now look at you.' She leant her bulk against the counter, took out her hanky and wiped her brow. 'Still as much of a pain in the arse as you always were, I imagine.'

'Hello, Mrs Beedle,' Anna said, running a finger along the brass-counter edge.

Mrs Beedle narrowed her eyes as if she could see straight inside her. 'Mmm, yes,' she murmured.

Anna licked her lips under the scrutiny of her gaze.

'Now, remember, I'm doing your father a favour, I don't want you here. Got that?' She took a slurp of tea. 'And why he wants you here, I have no idea.'

Anna didn't say anything, just pushed her shoulders back a bit further.

'To my mind, you're a jumped-up, spoilt brat who's caused more harm than good. But, I'll tolerate you. As long as there's none of your London crap, or—' She picked up a gingernut. 'Any of that attitude.'

'I'm not sixteen any more, Mrs Beedle,' Anna said with a mocking raise of one brow.

Mrs Beedle's lip quivered in a knowing smile. 'That's exactly the attitude I'm referring to. Ditch it.'

Anna ran her tongue along her top teeth, bristled but didn't say anything.

'Good.' Mrs Beedle half-smiled. 'Now we understand each other.' She dunked her biscuit into her tea and sucked some of the liquid off it, before saying, 'You can tell me what you can do.'

What could she do? Anna thought back to the opera house. She was very good at mingling at parties, casually introducing people, she could calm down an overwrought star with aplomb, she could conjure a masterful quote out of thin air for any production, she could throw a pragmatic response into a heated meeting. And her desk was impeccable, perfect, spotless. A place for everything and everything in its place, her mother would say. 'I'm very organised,' she said in the end.

Mrs Beedle snorted. Then, clicking her fingers in a gesture that meant for Anna to follow, she pulled back the curtain behind her to reveal Anna's worst nightmare. A stockroom filled with stacks and stacks of crap, piled sky-high like the legacy of a dead hoarder.

Anna swallowed. She had imagined spending most of the day sitting behind the desk reading *Grazia*. 'What do I do with it?'

'You organise it.' Mrs Beedle laughed, backing out so that Anna was left alone in the chaotic dumping ground and settling herself down in the big orange armchair next to the desk, a thin marmalade cat appearing and twirling through her legs. 'I've been meaning to do it for yonks.'

Anna opened her mouth to say something, but Mrs Beedle cut her off. 'You know,' she chuckled, 'I think I might actually enjoy this more than I thought I would.'

There had been a time, Anna thought two hours later, as she carefully plucked another horsebrass from a random assortment box and put it into the cardboard box on the shelf she had marked, BRASS, that she had had an assistant to do all this type of manual work in her life. In fact, she'd had two. One of them, Kim, she'd rather forget. She had given her her first break and, in return, the ungrateful brat had stolen her contact book and then promptly resigned and was now clawing her way up the ballet world while Anna was holding what looked like a Mexican death skull between finger and thumb.

Anna had had people to move boxes and post parcels and send emails to the people she'd rather avoid. It was only as she stood there now deciding

33

whether a brooch with half the stones missing was jewellery or trash, that she realised quite how much her status had defined her, had made her who she was. She liked the fact she had her own office with her name on the plaque on the door. She liked the fact people came in to ask her advice or crept in in tears and shut the door to bitch about some mean old cow in another department. She liked the signature on the bottom of her email and the fact that she didn't follow most of her Twitter followers back.

She patted the beads of sweat from her face with a folded piece of tissue she'd got from the bathroom and blew her hair out of her eyes. The room had heated up like a furnace and she felt like a rotisserie chicken slowly browning.

She had been somebody. And it didn't matter that at about three o'clock, most days, she had stood in a cubicle in the toilets holding a Kleenex to her eyes after catching a glimpse of the dancers rehearsing and thinking, *that should have been me*. Before blowing her nose, telling herself that this was just life, this is what happens, this feeling is weakness and you're not weak, Anna Whitehall. Then calling up Seb, all bright-eyed and smiling voice, asking if he wanted to go for cocktails after work, her treat. It didn't matter because more often than not she lied to herself that it had never happened – back at her desk her daily cry was swiftly erased from her memory.

Anna lifted up another jewelled brooch: a revolting glitzy number shaped like a horse-shoe, and thought of her old air-conditioning unit, her ergonomically designed chair, the fresh-cut flowers in her office, her snug new-season pencil skirt and a crippling pair of beautiful stilettos.

Turning the tacky gem over in her fingers she wanted to grab her old boss by the shoulders and shout, Look at me, now! *Look what you've made me become, you stupid idiot! Why did you have to scale down the PR department? Why couldn't you see how valuable I was? Why?*

'Everything all right back there?' Mrs Beedle had pulled back the curtain and was watching Anna as her lips moved during her silent tirade. The cat was curled up under Mrs Beedle's arm, nestled on the plump outline of her hip. A wry smile was twitching the woman's lip as she said, 'Christ, you still stand in third position.' She shook her head.' Well I never, you'll be doing pliés in here next.'

Anna, who hadn't noticed how she was standing, moved immediately and leant up against the stack behind her.

'Haven't got far, have you?' Mrs Beedle peered at her work.

Anna frowned. 'I thought I'd done quite a lot. Look. I have boxes for all the different items. Here—' She waved her hand along one of the lines of shelves. 'Necklaces, brooches, figurines, brasses, decorative plates, medals…'

'Maybe.' Mrs Beedle said with a shrug. 'I'm going for lunch and, as it's so quiet, I'm going to shut the shop and make a couple of deliveries. I'll be back, what? Three-thirty? Four?'

'What should I do?' Anna asked, her forehead beading with sweat, her shorts dusty, her fingers rough with dirt, her Shellac chipping.

'Just carry on as you are. No point stopping now,' Mrs Beedle said and backed out, shaking her head at the marmalade cat. 'She has a lot to learn about work this one, doesn't she? A lot to learn. Always the little princess.'

Chapter Three

'That's it, I hate it here.' Anna was sitting opposite Seb in the King's Head. She'd been home and had a bath, scrubbing the dirt and the sweat from her body in an attempt to block out the memories of the day.

The pub was as she remembered. Flock wallpaper in red velvet and gold, and a deep-maroon carpet worn threadbare by the end of the bar where the regulars stood. The bar top was dark mahogany, shiny under the low glass lamps and dappled with patches of split beer. Silver tankards hung from hooks around the lip of the bar top, swinging below the spirits that were mostly different types of whisky. One side of the room was booth seats, and a smattering of round wooden tables. At the back was a dining room that had placemats with hunting scenes or ducks flying.

'Here, drink this, it'll make you feel better.' Seb put a glass of yellow wine down in front of her.

She held it up between finger and thumb, inspected the colour and laughed. 'I very much doubt it.'

Seb tried to hide a smirk. 'It can't have been that bad.'

'I don't think I can talk about it.' She sighed, taking a sip. Then, unable not to, said, 'She made me clear out the stockroom. I don't think anyone's touched it for years. It's literally inches thick with dust. Personally, I think just chuck it all away.'

'You never know, Anna, there could be something worth about thirty grand in there, like on *The Antiques Roadshow*.'

'I think I can pretty much guarantee that there's not. Oh God, look at this, sing-along piano tonight. I can't believe they still do this. Do you remember when my gran got up on the table and did "Knees Up Mother Brown"?' She picked up a flier that was resting between the mustard and tomato ketchup bottle on their table.

Seb took a sip of his pint and read over the list of songs. 'It's still there. Look, "Knees Up Mother Brown". You could carry on the tradition.'

Anna coughed into her wine. 'Yeah right. Can you imagine the looks on their faces?' She glanced around the pub and then sat back in her seat, toying with a coaster. 'I did a really bad job.'

Seb looked puzzled. 'When? Have you actually sung "Knees Up Mother Brown"?'

'No, you doofus. At the shop. I did a really bad job.'

'Why?' Seb asked, frowning.

'Because I didn't want to do it.'

'Anna.' His brow creased. 'You kind of need this job. We seriously don't have any money and if you want a wedding…'

'Sebastian.' She leant forward. 'I get six pounds fifty an hour. Whether I have this job or not, it's not going to cover a wedding.'

Seb studied his pint.

Anna tapped the coaster against the table top. 'I'm going to have to get back to London, I have to do some serious looking.'

'Come on. You know there's nothing out there at the moment, and the commute will really cost.' He traced the beads of condensation down his glass. 'You're just going to have to get on with it.'

'What if I can't?' she said, and he shrugged like she didn't really have a choice. The shrug took her by surprise, she'd never seen it before. This wasn't the way their relationship worked. Seb adored her. He laughed at her jokes, he consoled her when she was down, he bought her Vitamin B6 when she had PMT, he stroked her hair when she cried. He looked after her. That was their dynamic. It had been since the moment she had walked out of Pret a Manger with her sushi and can of Yoga Bunny and he had walked straight into her, fresh from his interview at Whitechapel Boys' School, fumbled his briefcase and said, 'Wow, God, Anna Whitehall. Didn't expect to bump into you of all people. Wow.'

Really all she wanted now was for him to hate being back as much as she did.

As the fan in the corner of the pub whirred away like it might take off, circulating the stale beer-soaked air, they sat in silence for a second. Murmurs of laughter drifted in from the tables outside the front that Anna hadn't wanted to sit at in case she got bitten by mosquitoes.

'So how was your day?' she said in the end.

Seb held his hands out wide. 'Now she asks!' he said with a smile. He was good at changing the atmosphere, at not holding a grudge. His aim in life was for everyone to get along, not like Anna who could stagnate in a sulk like nobody's business. But, as usual, she felt herself get sucked into the lines that crinkled around his eyes as he smiled and winked at her across the table.

She rolled her eyes. 'Did you save any poor, badly educated children?'

Seb was back in Nettleton to make a difference. To give back. To do for the new Nettleton generation what their teachers had done for him. Anna could barely remember a teacher, let alone anything good they'd done for her. She could vaguely summon a memory of being whacked with a lacrosse stick accidentally on purpose by Mrs McNamara for calling her a lesbian. And the satisfaction she'd felt when she'd handed her a note from her ballet teacher exempting her from all school sport because it clashed with her training and the development of her flexibility.

No, lessons and Anna hadn't gone hand in hand. What she'd learnt had been predominantly from sitting at her granny's kitchen table while she leaned over Anna's shoulder and went over and over her homework, patiently rewording the questions so

40

that Anna would get an answer in the end. She never shouted, just told Anna how bright she was and how much potential she had. Anna only believed her when she was sitting at that kitchen table, though. And when Anna moved to London and schoolwork took a backseat to ballet she did all that was necessary to scrape by. She was going to be a dancer; what was the point of algebra?

'I made a huge impression,' Seb joked. 'And young minds across the village are rejoicing that I have arrived as head of year.'

A female voice cut in next to them, 'I'm sure they are, Seb, no doubt about it.'

'Jackie, hey, how are you? Come and join us.' Seb edged along his bench seat so Anna's high-school nemesis, Jackie, could sit down.

'Anna,' Jackie said by way of greeting, with a distinct lack of emotion.

'Jackie.' Anna replied with similar flatness. Their relationship was such that they'd spent much of their youth circling each other, snogging each other's boyfriends and generally pissing each other off without ever fully acknowledging their mutual dislike.

'So how are you?' Jackie ran her tongue along her lips, then grinned. 'Never made it to New York, then?'

'No.' Anna winced a smile, cocking her head to one side and then saying sweetly, 'I see you didn't either. Ever make it out of Nettleton?'

Jackie shrugged. 'Everything I need is here.'

Anna blew out a breath in disbelief.

'Whereas you…I mean, what was it we were meant to see? Your name in lights at the Lincoln Center? Wasn't that always the dream?'

Anna pushed a strand of hair out of her eyes. 'I grew too tall to be a dancer.'

Jackie sat back and crossed her legs. 'Shame.'

As the air between them hummed, Seb clapped his hands and said, 'So, what does everyone want to drink?'

As Jackie said she'd die for a gin and tonic, Anna hitched her bag onto her shoulder, stood up and said, 'I'll get them.' Just to get away from the table.

She stood, tapping her nails on the bar. *Her name in lights at the Lincoln Center*. It was like a jolt. *If I hadn't got pregnant,'* her mum had said, holding up an advert listing the New York City Ballet's winter programming in the paper, *'I'd have made it to the Lincoln Center in New York, that's where I would have been. That's where I would have ended up. Imagine dancing on that stage. Anna, that's the pinnacle.'*

When she heard laughter behind her, Anna swung round thinking that it must be about her, but saw instead a couple in the corner enjoying a shared joke. She blew out a breath and tried to relax, but she was like an animal on high alert, poised and ready. At her table Seb and Jackie were looking at something on Jackie's phone and giggling. Anna found herself envying Seb's effortless charm, the ease with which he slipped back into relationships. The way he could be so instantly, unguardedly, involved.

'What's going on?' she asked as she pushed the tray of drinks onto the table.

'Jackie is educating me on the world of internet dating,' Seb laughed.

'It's nothing.' Jackie waved a hand. 'Just Tinder.'

Anna nodded, not sure what she was talking about but, rather than ask, pretended that she wasn't really that interested. She felt herself doing it on purpose, fitting into the role Jackie expected.

'The website. No?' Jackie said, taking a sip of her gin and tonic, as Anna obviously hadn't been able to hide her blankness as well as she thought. 'Well I suppose you wouldn't know, not being single. It's meant to be the closest thing to dating in the real world,' Jackie went on, leaning her elbows on the table. 'You know, you rate people on what they look like, it'd be right up your street, Anna.'

Anna narrowed her eyes.

'Look—' Seb leant forward, Jackie's phone in his hand. 'If you like them, you swipe them into the Yes pile and if you don't, you swipe them into the No. Isn't it amazing? I just can't believe it exists. It's so ruthless, like some sort of horrible conveyor belt of desperation.'

'Thank you very much, Seb.' Jackie sat back.

'I didn't mean you. I meant them.'

Forgetting her act for a moment, Anna inched her head closer, fascinated, as she watched men appear on screen and Seb swipe them into the No pile as easily as swatting flies.

'Hang on.' Jackie snatched it off him. 'Don't waste my bounty,' she laughed.

Seb leant over her shoulder and said, 'I mean, look at this guy.' He stabbed the shadowy profile picture on the screen. 'Why put that picture up? Why wear a hat and a scarf and take it in the dark? Surely all it does is say that you're weird and ugly. That's an immediate no from everyone, because weird, ugly people know the trick because they'd do it themselves, and everyone imagines if they were weird and ugly that's what they would do. He's a fool.'

Jackie laughed and swiped the shadowy image away.

'He's quite nice though.' Anna edged closer as a picture of a snowboarder popped up, all tanned, chiselled cheekbones and crazy bleached hair.

'Never fall for the snowboarders or surfers. Believe me, without the get-up they're all pretty average and all they talk about is how great they are.'

'I take it you've been on quite a lot of dates.'

Jackie shrugged. 'A fair few. Before this it was eHarmony and Match. I've done them all.'

Seb crossed his arms over his chest and sat back against the wooden slates of the booth. 'It's interesting isn't it, the idea of being paired by a computer?'

'I wonder if you two went on something like eHarmony,' Jackie said without looking up from her swiping, 'whether they'd match you.'

'I doubt it,' Seb guffawed.

Anna tried not to show her shock. 'You don't think?' she asked, as neutrally as she could.

'Oh come on. You're always going on about how different we are,' he laughed, taking a sip of his pint.

Anna felt her mouth half open, saw Jackie glance up with a wicked look in her eye.

'Well you are!' Seb said, as if he knew suddenly that he'd said the wrong thing. A slight look of worry on his face.

'Yes.' Anna nodded. 'Yep, I am. Yeah, they'd probably never match us,' she said casually and sat back with her wine, her legs crossed, trying to set her face into a relaxed expression.

Seb looked away from her, back to the phone screen and she felt a shiver over her skin despite the stifling humidity. This was a man who used to look at her like she was made of gold, who saw a goodness in her that she barely saw herself, who saw the softness beneath the plating.

She suddenly felt like her dusting of glamour was wearing off.

'Actually, Anna,' Jackie said, handing her phone to Seb, 'I wanted to ask you a favour.'

'A favour?' Anna felt herself stiffen.

Seb paused momentarily and glanced up.

'Well it's just—' Jackie licked her lips and Anna wondered if she was nervous. Wondered how long she'd been sitting there, laughing and joking, building up to asking whatever it was she was going to ask.

'There's this, this dance group. In the village. They're only little – you know, eight to sixteen. No one's older than sixteen. And well, they always perform in the summer shows and they put on little routines and stuff and everyone really loves it. Well, they've been working towards a *Britain's Got Talent* audition.'

Anna snorted in disbelief at the idea of actually wanting to go on *Britain's Got Talent*.

'They're really excited. I mean, really excited. And I know they're not the best but well, the whole village is kind of behind them.'

They never got behind me, Anna thought, surprised to feel such envy. Wondering suddenly how different it might have been if they had got behind her. Made her banners and cards and wished her well on her quest for stardom.

She glanced at Seb who was looking away with disinterest but clearly just pretending not to listen.

'Anyway.' Jackie shifted uncomfortably in her seat. 'They've been working super, super hard and well, Mrs Swanson's au pair was teaching them but her visa ran out a fortnight ago and she hadn't told anyone, so now, well, she left on Wednesday. There's um, no one to help them.'

'I see.' Anna did a quick nod, rolling her shoulders back. She could see where Jackie was going with this and just hoped that she might bottle out before she got to asking the favour.

Someone wedged the front doors open and the sounds from outside got louder, the laughter and

46

chatting, but the heat stayed where it was, like a wobbling great blancmange.

'You could do it,' Seb said, jumping into the silence, unable to keep his mouth shut.

Great.

'I don't think I could, Seb,' Anna glared at him.

'Well yeah, I mean that was exactly what I was going to ask. You see, it's been me and Mrs McNamara—'

'She's still there?'

Jackie nodded.

Anna blew out a breath of disbelief. 'It's like time literally stood still here.'

'Neither of us are particularly good dancers. I mean, I can hold my own at a party but you know, I don't exactly know enough to teach them and well, we all know McNamara's not exactly a lithe mover. I just don't want to let the kids down.'

Anna didn't answer. Instead she tried to find something to distract herself, and rummaged in her bag for her lip gloss. Anna didn't dance. Anna hadn't danced in ten years. She hadn't set foot on a stage, hadn't warmed up, hadn't looked out at the glare of the spotlight or felt the hard floor beneath her feet. Anna's name had never been in lights.

Anna didn't dance.

'God, it's so hot. Why does it have to be so goddamn hot?' She could feel Seb watching her.

'Some of them aren't the best kids and it's really good seeing them involved in something—'

'Jackie, I'm really sorry,' Anna cut her off. 'God, it's just insufferably hot.' She pulled her top away from her stomach. 'I'm not going to do it. It's just a definite no.'

'Could you just think about it? We'd pay you?'

'No.' She shook her head again, reaching for the sing-along song sheet to fan herself with. 'All the money in the world and I couldn't do it.'

'Well, that's not strictly true,' she heard Seb add and shot him a look.

'OK,' Jackie shrugged. 'It was worth a try.'

'I'd be terrible with the kids,' Anna added.

'That's true, actually,' Seb said, sitting back with a grin on his face. 'She really would be bloody awful teaching kids.'

Anna narrowed her eyes. He raised a brow. Was he deliberately being mean, she wondered. Like this was almost her punishment – for hating Nettleton, for spending all their money, for not trying hard enough.

'It's really OK.' Jackie shook her head, picking up her gin and tonic and taking a sip. 'I just thought I'd ask.'

Anna rubbed her forehead and felt the heat prickle over her body. Jackie looked away, pretending to glance at the menu chalked up on the blackboard. The fan whirred on above the din of chat in the bar, a low hum beating out the seconds of their silence. Anna watched a fruit fly land in a spilt drop of her white wine and wondered whether to challenge Seb about his lack of belief in her imaginary teaching ability. Before she could say anything, though, Seb shouted, 'Holy shit!' and almost leapt from his seat.

'What?' Both Jackie and Anna said at the same time, equally desperate for some distraction after the dance snub.

'It's Smelly Doug.'

Jackie pulled the screen her way. 'God, it is as well. And look, he has a Porsche, he's photographed himself leaning against it. Oh no.'

'I don't know who you're talking about,' Anna said, confused.

Jackie took another sip of her drink. 'You know, Smelly Doug. Never washed his hair, trousers too short, huge rucksack…?'

Anna only had a vague recollection. 'Was he in the year below us?' Everything to do with school, pre-London, pre-the English Ballet Company School, was a bit of a blur. All she could remember was coming back for a few summers to stay with her dad and despising every minute of it.

'This is fascinating,' Seb said, as he clicked to look at more photos. 'There's one of him in Egypt. Doing that point at the top of the Pyramids.'

'You should go on a date with him, Jackie.' Seb nodded at her over the rim of his pint.

'No way.' Jackie shook her head.

'Go on. It'd be a social experiment. Catch up, see what he's up to. Find out how he could afford a Porsche. It's a fact-finding mission. I'm putting him in your Yeses.'

'Don't you dare,' Jackie laughed. Anna watched them, feeling stupid for feeling left out.

'Too late.' Seb sat back, smug, and Jackie snatched the phone back, incredulous.

As Seb went to take a final gulp of his drink, his eyes dancing with triumph, Anna toyed with her coaster again, pretending not to be jealous of their laughter.

Then a shadow fell across the table, and Anna heard a familiar voice drawl. 'Seb, darling, I thought you were going to pop round as soon as you arrived.' Hilary, Seb's mother, was standing at the end of their table, one hand on her hip, lips pursed. Anna looked her up and down, took in the carefully set hair, the diamond nestled in her creped cleavage and the loop of pearls round her neck, the trademark cream silk blouse with gold buttons and the handbag, like the Queen's, hanging in the crook of her elbow. Hilary had had the same angry look on her face, and been wearing the same outfit, when Seb had first introduced them. And it had been clear from that moment that she didn't believe Anna was good enough for her son.

Seb glanced between the two of them. 'Sorry, Mum, yes we were going to pop round. Arrived late last night though.'

'Hi, Hilary.' Anna stood up as much as the table would allow against her legs.

'Hello, Anne.' Hilary said, glancing over briefly and then turning away as Roger, Seb's father, ambled in to stand by her side.

Hilary always called Anna the wrong name. It was always Anne, and if either she or Seb tried to correct her she'd frown as if Anna had somehow done it deliberately. Every time she met Seb's parents, they made her feel like she wasn't enough. Like Seb had trailed his hand in the Nettleton mud one day and pulled out Anna. The list of problems was endless. Her parents' divorce, their messy break-up, her father's job, her mother being Spanish, like her immigrant blood would pollute the famous Davenport gene pool. They must rue the day their lost, London-shell-shocked son had bumped into Anna Whitehall on her lunch break in Covent Garden. They must look back and wonder why they didn't do their weekend orienteering round London rather than the Hampshire countryside. That way Seb would have been savvy and street-wise, not like a lame duck ready and waiting for her fox-like claws to swipe him away. And now, of course, despite getting their precious youngest son back under Nettleton lock and key, the reason behind it had been her fault. Her inability to keep her job. Her fault he left his position at the elite Whitechapel Boys' School. Nothing to do with him hating bloody Whitechapel, all the boys who just put their iPhone headphones in during lessons and said things like, *'My father pays your salary, Sir. Which kind of means he owns you, doesn't it? He paid for that suit you're wearing.'* While she knew Seb wasn't thrilled she'd lost their savings, he certainly wasn't upset that she'd lost her job because that meant he could teach at the kind of school he wanted to teach at, where he could make a difference. But of course, because he was as terrified of his mother as Anna was, he was happy to let them believe that the move was more her doing than his.

'So what's happening with this wedding, then? It's very unusual, this limbo,' Hilary sighed. 'On hold? Everyone's been ringing me up, asking what it means. People like to be able to make plans, Anne. They have to book hotels. You must understand. I mean, is the save the date still the date? I have it in my diary but, well, should I rub it out?'

Anna shook her head. 'No. We are sorting it, Hilary.'

'Well that's all very well for you to say, but it doesn't look like you are. As far as I can see, you have a dress and a hotel that's gone into receivership. And when people ask me what's going on I simply don't know. I know you've lost money, but what about what we gave you?'

Anna could feel herself getting hotter again. Wanting to shoo Jackie away so she didn't witness her humiliation at the hands of Hilary and Roger.

When she'd told Seb how much she'd paid and, as a result, how much she'd lost, the main point he'd kept repeating was: just don't let my mum and dad know.

'It's young people and the value of money, Hilly.' Roger mused. 'I just can't believe you didn't pay for it on a credit card. Everyone knows you pay on credit cards. Instant insurance.'

Anna swallowed. The credit cards she'd kept free to pay off the rest of it, month by month, to syphon off from the salary that she no longer had. 'I've applied to the administrator, I'm doing everything I can.'

Roger snorted. 'As if that will do anything at all. You won't see a penny. You're just a generation who thought they could have, have, have. I blame Labour. All you *Guardian* readers thinking that the world owes you another pair of shoes. What's that woman in that ghastly programme?'

'Sexy in the City,' Hilary sighed.

'Yes, just like that. Well, it's come back to bite you.' Roger tapped a cigarette out of a silver case that he always carried in the top pocket of his shirt, put it between his lips but didn't light it, just sucked on the raw tobacco.

Jackie at least had the decency to absorb herself in her phone, Anna noticed, as Hilary leant a hand on the table and said, 'You need to sort it, Anne. Can't fail at your first job as a wife. That wouldn't do at all.'

Tell them to stop, Seb, she thought as they carried on. Tell them to stop.

But he said nothing, just looked at his glass.

The conversation swirled on around her until she heard Jackie say, 'I know, I've been trying to persuade her to put her phenomenal talent to use back here in Nettleton. Razzmatazz are heading towards a big *Britain's Got Talent* audition.'

'And Anna—' Hilary frowned. 'You're not doing it?'

'I just—' Anna made a face, glanced at Jackie and thought, with grudging respect, *that was a sly move.*

'You really should, Anna. I would have thought you'd jump at the chance of extra money. Seb, what do you think?'

Tell them that you think it's a terrible idea. Tell them. Tell them because you know, more than anything, I don't want to dance.

Seb licked his lower lip and said, 'I think it's Anna's decision.'

Chapter Four

Anna's ballet teacher pulled her mother aside when she was eight and told her she had talent. Real, proper talent. Talent that she couldn't really do justice with her own teaching. Anna's mother had wanted to whisk her off to London there and then, but it had been her father who'd said no, who'd said a child should enjoy their childhood. So the compromise had been summer, Easter and Christmas holidays spent at The Yellow House, a precursor to the English Ballet Company School.

But the second her father had been caught in bed with Molly, the local auctioneer, he forfeited, in her mother's opinion, any rights to Anna's future. And, quick as a flash, they were speeding down the M3 to London, towards an audition for a full-time placement at the English Ballet Company School.

As the sun edged its way over the Hammersmith flyover, her mother had said, *I should have left him years ago. I should have just gone back. I should have gone straight back to Sevilla. What is there keeping me here? There's nothing, nothing for me here.*

55

The feelings of the springs in the back of the car seat jutting into her back and whether she'd ever see their cat again were Anna's predominant memories of the trip. Which distracted her from the fear of her audition and the possibility that she wasn't quite good enough. That everyone else there had started when they were six, and weren't chastised every lesson at summer school for their lack of flexibility. That if she did get in she'd suffer the humiliation of being in classes with younger kids, that she'd be described as a 'late bloomer'.

You. Her mother had looked over from the road, the sleeves of her black fur coat flopping down over her hands on the steering wheel, and said, *You're the only thing keeping me here, darling. You. You're going to be a star. I can just see it. You're going to be a star and we'll wear Chanel and we'll go back to that bloody village and we'll show them that we're better. We're better, Anna.*

Anna was lying in the bath when Seb popped his head round the door to say that he was going out with his brothers, then added an eye-roll, as if it was more of a chore than a pleasure.

Anna gave him a look of sympathy. She knew he'd be forced to drink shots and go to some hideous club on an industrial estate out of town that they'd gone to when they were sixteen. An image of his siblings with their middle-aged One Direction haircuts made her wince. She knew they called her a stuck-up cow and blamed her for the loss of Seb's apparent sense of fun. But once again, she'd been the scapegoat, Seb's excuse to get out of their invitations to visit. When she and Seb had been firmly ensconced in London she hadn't minded, but now they were back and all Seb's little white lies were coming back to bite her.

As he leant over and kissed her on the top of the head, Anna found herself saying, before she could stop herself, 'Why didn't you stand up for me in the pub the other day?'

Seb turned and leant against the sink. 'I don't know what you mean.'

She looked at the bleeding cuts on the backs of her hand where she'd been lugging boxes around all day, her chipped nails with dirt underneath them, her bruised legs. 'It just feels a bit like you're punishing me.'

'Don't be ridiculous.' He shook his head. 'Anna, I was unhappy in London. I'm not ashamed to admit it. We both made mistakes, we both lived outside our means, the wedding was just the icing on the cake. I promise, I'm not punishing you. By no means am I punishing you. I suppose I just want you to try.' He paused, his fingers thrumming on the edge of the porcelain basin. 'Also, I wonder if maybe you weren't as happy as you think you were.'

Anna guffawed. 'I was happy!'

Seb shrugged and nodded, then turned and opened the bathroom cabinet, fishing about for some aftershave. 'I saw the vicar today,' he said after a moment.

Anna paused, popped a bubble in her bath.

'He said we were welcome to use the church for the service. Said that it would be nice you know, to go full circle, since I was christened there. I thought that was nice. You know, a nice thing to say. He didn't have to say anything, did he? But I thought that was nice.'

'You're rambling.'

'It's because I'm nervous about telling you this. Nervous of what your reaction is going to be.'

'If you know my reaction, why are you telling me?' She suddenly wanted to be out of the bath, dry and dressed and having this conversation at eye-level.

'Because I think it could solve quite a lot of problems. And if we use the village hall it'll be one hundred pounds. That's it, Anna. One hundred pounds. That's nothing.'

'The hall I did Brownies in and ballet lessons and choir practice and sat with my dad at the antiques fairs? That hall, you mean?'

Seb nodded again, a little less vigorously.

'The hall where all the old people have their weekly bridge sessions and that smells of cabbage and boiled potatoes afterwards?'

'That's the one.'

Anna nodded.

Seb bit his lip and seemed to close his eyes for slightly longer than a blink.

'And the vicar who counselled my mum to stay with my dad even though he'd been having an affair for two years? That one? Still the same one?'

Seb did a really small nod, almost imperceptible.

'That it was her duty to stay with him even though he had no intention of giving his mistress up? That the sanctity of marriage meant turning a blind eye.'

'I had actually forgotten that bit—' Seb swallowed.

Anna breathed in through her nose and slowly exhaled like they used to do at her Bikram yoga class that she couldn't go to any more because there was only one in the next village and it was twenty pounds a class. In Nettleton all she'd seen was an advert for Zumba pinned to a chestnut tree.

The bubbles on her fingers glistened in the drooping sun, pearlised pinks and blues like sequins. Twinkling on white, reminding her of the first costume hand-stitched just for her. The individual silver sequins flickering on netting under the heat of the strip-lighting in the shabby costume department. The material as it was ruched and pinned, the corset as it was nipped and tucked, the patterns traced with tiny seed beads and embroidery against her chest and up over her shoulders in trails on fine gauze.

The flat that her mother had rented just off the Charing Cross road was horrible. A dingy little place that lit up bright blue when ambulances and fire engines screamed past at all hours of the night.

They'd had nothing but a couple of suitcases of clothes, some pots and pans and a massive heap of bitterness. There was one bedroom, which Anna slept in, where a lamp in the shape of a white horse sat on a stack of old *Hello!* magazines left behind by the previous tenant, flickering from a dodgy connection in the plug. And it was cold. The kind of cold that made the blankets damp and kept toes frozen. That first night Anna had lain staring at the ceiling doing everything she could not to cry and, as if her mum could sense it, she came in from her own makeshift bed on the sofa, a red crocheted blanket wrapped round her and snuggled up next to Anna. She had stroked her hair away from her face and said, *We'll be OK. You, you'll be fabulous!*

Then she had leant over and grabbed a *Hello!* from the pile. *When I was a child we used to make scrap books*, she'd said as she'd started flicking through the glossy pages. *We'd stick in pictures and postcards of places we wanted to go or people we wanted to be. I had a big picture of the ceiling of the David H. Koch theater at the Lincoln Center. It's paved with gold. Did you know that? A gold ceiling. That's the best you can get, isn't it? And then I had a picture of Buckingham Palace, can you believe it! Still, we've never been.* As she talked, she let her finger trace the outline of the big chandeliers, the Caribbean super-yachts, the million-pound stallions in stately home stables, and Anna watched silently as the moisture collected in the corner of her eyes. *I stuck in all the things I'd ever wanted and dreamt of.*

From that night they sat up together in bed and went through the *Hello!s*, one by one, staring at pictures of Princess Grace of Monaco, Ivana Trump, Joan Rivers' daughter's wedding extravaganza, Caroline

Bassette-Kennedy on the arm of John Jnr, Princess Diana photographed by Mario Testino, Darcey Bussell in *Swan Lake*, Claudia, Naomi, Cindy and Kate draped on the arm of Vivienne Westwood or Jean Paul Gaultier. Houses that dripped in gold, taps shaped like dolphins with emeralds as the eyes, satin sheets and heart-shaped beds, wardrobes that cantilevered to reveal rows and rows of shoes like coloured candy, chandeliers that hung like beetles glinting in the camera flashlight, oriental rugs as wide as ballrooms and mirrors trimmed with gold and giant porcelain figurines. This was a world of faces turned a fraction to the left, a tilt of a smile, a waft of arrogance and confidence. This was a world that made her mum smile when she looked at the pictures, that would forever remind Anna of being tucked up together in that cold, damp bed.

That's who I'm going to be, Anna had thought as the light flickered in her bare bedroom and the noise of an ambulance howled past along the street below. *In this enchanted world they have everything*.

The next day she had started her own book, one that until a week or so ago was crammed with scraps of every picture, article, photograph, postcard, ripped-out catalogue page she'd seen over the last however many years.

The book that went everywhere with her. The book that housed pages and pages of her dreams. The book that, when they had packed up their beautiful Bermondsey flat, she had left in the bin on top of her old ballet pointes.

61

'The thing is, Seb,' Anna said, staring at the bubbles, 'I think I'd rather not get married than get married in Nettleton Village Hall and be married by that man.'

Seb ran his tongue along his bottom lip and then replied, 'Isn't it about us, Anna? I understand about the vicar, but isn't it about us, rather than where it is?'

She looked from her bubbles back to him, she thought about her book, about the stupid, simple promises she'd made to herself all those years ago. Then she shook her head. 'I can't. It's not enough for me.' She couldn't really believe what she was saying but it felt like she had no other option. These ideas, these rights and wrongs, hopes and dreams, were so firmly ingrained in her being that she couldn't just walk away from them. To do so felt too much of a compromise. However skewed that was, she knew that anything else would be living a lie. 'I'm sorry.'

'Christ.' He shook his head. 'I don't know what to do then. We don't have the money for more. I don't have the money. I honestly don't know what to do.'

She leant over the bath, her movements languid still by nature, arms crossed gracefully on the rim, water dripping from her skin. 'We'll work something out, Seb. I promise,' she said, then nodded furiously to try and convince him and made her eyes go all big and persuasive.

He shook his head and she saw him start to smile, then he pushed away from the sink and took the few steps over to her and kissed the top of her head. 'Maybe.'

As she heard the sound of the front gate clicking shut through the open window she had a sudden memory of Seb's phone ringing as she was cutting up her credit cards in their London living room. It was the call to offer him a place at Nettleton High. *Amazing. Brilliant. Yes, I can start straight away. Get to know the kids before the start of the new school year. Perfect. Thank you. Thank you. Yes.* Anna had listened quietly, realising that she'd never heard Seb so enthusiastic.

So we're really going? she'd asked, her Visa card snapping in two as she spoke.

Trying to hold in a beaming smile, Seb had nodded and said, *I'm not sure we have any other options. What we have here, Anna, it's not real.*

At the time, they had both assumed he was talking lifestyle.

Chapter Five

The next day was another spent in the sweatshop stockroom but Anna was slightly more prepared. She had on a green headscarf to protect her hair and a pair of plastic gloves that she'd nabbed from the petrol station dispenser when she'd filled up the car.

'You're not handling priceless antiques, you know,' Mrs Beedle noted as she clocked the gloves while ambling into the stockroom to make the tea.

'Oh I'm well aware of that,' Anna muttered under her breath, staring unimpressed at the mound of junk before her.

'I heard that! You mind your mouth, young lady,' Mrs Beedle said sharply, 'I know your trick, do as little as possible and still get paid. Well if you're not careful, I'll start paying you by the square foot you clear. That'd get you moving, wouldn't it?'

Anna glanced at what she'd done so far and realised if that became the case she'd have earned about £2.99.

Mrs Beedle pushed her glasses up her nose and watched as Anna upped her pace a touch. 'Have you been to see your dad yet?'

Anna paused, then turned round, a collection of handbags up her arms and a tatty box of hats in her hands that she tilted forward to show Mrs Beedle. 'Where should I put these? With the clothes or do they warrant a space all of their own?'

Mrs Beedle narrowed her eyes. 'I take it that's a no about your dad.' She shook her head. 'Still a selfish little madam, I see.' When Anna made no move to reply, she sighed and then said, 'Put the hats in a box of their own, sort them because I think some are probably past it. The bags, leave aside because we need to clean the leather. I have to look at a cabinet in Ambercross, it'll take me what?' She looked at her watch. 'Forty minutes. Do you think you can handle it here on your own or should I lock up?'

Anna scoffed. 'Yes, I think I'll manage,' she said. 'I'm not sure.' Stubby fingers on her hips, Mrs Beedle stared at Anna and then the counter behind her, contemplating the safety of leaving her behind, while Anna tried to remember if a customer had actually come in on the occasions she'd been in the shop.

'It'll be fine.' She waved a plastic-gloved hand. 'I'm good with people.'

It was Mrs Beedle's turn to scoff. 'I find that very hard to believe. OK, I'll try and make it half an hour.'

'Fine.' Anna had turned away and focused on the next box to sort through, which seemed to be mainly necklaces, all tangled up into one giant ball of gaudy, shimmering beads. She thought they were best suited to the bin, but instead made a show of carefully unpicking the mess, one strand at a time.

As soon as the bell over the door tinkled closed, however, she was out of that room, gloves off, Lapsang Souchong in hand, sitting in the threadbare orange armchair and switching the TV to *Murder She Wrote*. Then she picked up the shop's phone and called her friend Hermione.

'Darling.' Hermione's cut-glass accent boomed out of the receiver. 'Hang on, I think there might be a pause, like you're calling long distance.'

'You're hilarious.'

Hermione made a noise between a snort and a laugh at her own joke. 'I try. How is it there? Have they driven you out of town with pitchforks yet?'

Anna snuggled down in the chair. 'They're just sharpening the prongs.'

'Tines.'

'What?'

'They're called tines. The prongy bits.'

'Not on pitchforks.'

'I think they are. Google it.'

'I'm not Googling pitchforks.' Anna took a slurp of tea.

'So I laughed out loud at my desk when I got your email about having to hang out with Jackie. I can't believe she's still there. What's wrong with people?' Hermione's voice clinked in her ears like champagne flutes touching. 'But, you know what, I was so intrigued I've joined too.'

'Joined what?'

'Tinder.'

Anna sat up straight, a smile spreading across her face as she imagined Hermione sitting in her penthouse disparagingly scrutinising the poor unsuspecting Tinder men. 'And have you said yes to anyone yet?'

'Christ no, they're all dreadful. All from bloody Milton Keynes. Ugly and poor.'

Anna covered her face with her hand. 'You can't say things like that.'

'Of course I can, who's listening? I just thought though, why should I sit at home in a bloody heatwave and not go on some dates. Especially if even Jackie's doing it. But I've set my lower age limit to forty-five just so I don't get Smelly Doug,' Hermione went on.

'Well no wonder you don't like any of them,' Anna said, absentmindedly flicking through an antiques magazine on the counter.

'I'm waiting for a silver fox. I quite fancy a sugar daddy,' Hermione drawled. 'I'm looking at them now, there are so many that are so dreadful. You should join.'

'What?'

'Just to keep me company while we're on the phone.'

Anna ignored her and kept on flicking through the magazine. 'I think you should say yes to some even if you aren't sure, Hermione. Just to warm up.'

Hermione snorted. 'I'm warm enough thanks, Anna. I don't want just anyone to think they could have me.

I'm not having some old duffer in the pub bragging that Hermione Somers-Brown said yes to the catalogue photo he decided to upload instead of a picture of himself. Go on, join, it'll give us something to talk about, otherwise I'm hanging up because I don't really want to hear any of your depressing Nettleton news.'

Anna shut the magazine and looked around the shop. The idea of being stuck there on her own with nothing to do except sweat buckets in the stockroom and no one to talk to was enough to make her log onto the Vintage Treasure WiFi and download the Tinder app.

'It links to your Facebook,' she said after a minute, 'I can't do that.'

'Oh who goes on Facebook any more?' Hermione waved away her concern.

And as soon as Anna was up and running, any niggles were soon replaced by the sheer joy of happily discarding so many over-eager looking men.

'Oh Jesus!' she heard Hermione say, as she was swiping away a snowboarder doing a double thumbs-up for the camera.

'What?'

'Your dad's on here.'

'No!' Anna made a face of horror.

'Shall I put him in my Yes pile?' Hermione laughed.

'Don't you dare.'

'He's a silver fox if ever I saw one. You know, I'd forgotten how handsome he is.'

'Hermione, you're talking about my father.'

'I know and he's a dish. Perhaps I could have a torrid fling with him.'

'Hermione, don't even thi—' Anna paused, her hand hovering over the screen of her iPhone as her attention was caught by the new picture that had just popped up.

'What?'

Anna didn't reply.

'What? What's happened?'

She stared at the face on her screen, thick dark hair all messy and lightened at the tips from too much time in the sun. Desert camouflage fatigues, huge white-toothed grin, pale lips cracked, face tanned around goggle marks. 'Nothing,' she said to Hermione.

'Don't give me that. Who is it? Who have you seen?'

'Luke.'

'Luke Lloyd?' She could hear the delight in Hermione's tone. 'The delightful Mr Lloyd back from saving the world and looking for sex. How marvellous. You must Yes him.'

Anna shook her head. 'I'm not going to Yes him. I'm not Yes-ing anyone.'

'Why not? You should meet up with him, show him what he's missing. Show him what a glamour puss you've become.'

Anna looked down at her dirty cargo shorts and made a face at the idea of ever being referred to as a glamour puss again.

'I couldn't do it to Seb.'

'Seb schmeb,' Hermione sighed. 'He doesn't even have to know. Email me a screen shot so I can see Luke.'

A few minutes later, after some convoluted and irritated instructions from Hermione teaching her how to take a screen shot and then how to email it, they were both staring at the same image.

'He was always a delight. Always. And so exciting. Nettleton would have been unbearable if he hadn't been around. You should do it, just meet him for coffee.'

'Hermione, I'm engaged.'

There was a pause. 'Anna. What did you do today? In fact, don't tell me, it'll make me ill. Just think what you would have done had you been here. What are you doing now? Let me tell you what I'm imagining and you can tell me where I'm wrong. Stop me anytime.' There was a clinking noise as she assumed Hermione was taking a sip of her drink. 'You're holed up in that crummy shop and, day to day, maybe one, two people come in. No one buys anything and if they do it's a ghastly side-table or flea-ridden fur coat. Tonight you'll go home and sit in the garden, the scrap of lawn has possibly been trimmed recently with a Flymo or some other suburban tool. There are bedding plants in various arrays of life and death. Perhaps a fruit tree at the far end, which makes you convince yourself that you'll make jam at some point and become a domestic goddess when really you'll get fat and never eat the fruit because it will get some kind of disease or the apples will be too sour. I imagine there are birds tweeting and cows mooing which is all very lovely if you ignore the smell. I know that smell, Anna, I lived with that smell for eighteen years. And I bet your fence is just low enough for some busybody neighbour to stick her head over and say hello, bitch about someone in town or tell you that her colicky baby had her up all night. You haven't stopped me yet, Anna. Let me think about you. The wine in your fridge is the only white wine you could find in the town, perhaps a Hardys or, if you're lucky, an Oxford Landing. It's warm because it's so fricking hot that you can't keep it cool enough, and, oooh I know, I bet you'll lie on one of those ghastly sun-loungers that has brown and orange flowers on it and spiders that live in the metal fold-out posts while Seb watches the rugby or plays on his PlayStation. Am I close?'

Anna had shut her eyes. 'He sold the PlayStation.'

'Thank fuck for that.' Hermione snorted a laugh.

'Shall I tell you what I'm doing? Anna, I'm sitting on the balcony of my flat, the Thames looks beautiful, the sun just catching the water. I can see the Houses of Parliament and the wheel, the sky is red. Actually red, like someone's squashed a handful of cherries and smeared it over the sky.'

'That's very artistic.'

'Well I don't work at Sotheby's for nothing, darling. I am sitting on an Adirondack chair and I have my feet up on the glass wall of my balcony. And I have next to me a bottle of Bollinger in a cooler and a glass that I am topping up little by little so it doesn't warm. And, later, my darling, don't get jealous, I am popping to a party on the top floor of the Gherkin where the alcohol will be free and the Michelin-starred canapés my dinner.'

'OK, that's enough, thank you.' Anna watched the marmalade cat perk up as the bell rang above the door and someone came in, nodding a greeting as she glanced over.

'Put him in your Yeses, Anna. Seb doesn't have to know. You need to grab yourself a little excitement while you still can. Before you forget, Anna. Before your waist starts thickening and you think getting 50p off your cappuccino because the milk wouldn't froth is a bargain.'

'No.' She shook her head, looking back at the photo of Luke and trying to ignore the feeling that his crazy, action-packed existence conjured inside her, the taste of adrenaline and adventure in her mouth, the idea of slipping into something new, something chic and expensive and strutting into some bar and making him realise what he had given up in search of Sandhurst officer training and army fatigues. To show him what she had become since their teenage years snogging on park benches whenever she was back in the village. To see that glint in his wicked blue eyes, the cocky arrogance, to feel the shiver that ran through her just because he'd sauntered over to where she had been preening next to Hermione.

Then she shook her head to make the image go away. Feeling an instant rush of guilt about how just the idea of Luke Lloyd made her feel.

The customer was moving around the shop and Anna did a quick check to see they weren't listening in on her call, before cupping her hand over the receiver. 'Stop winding me up, Hermione, I know what you're doing,' she hissed.

'Tempting though, isn't it?' Hermione said, gleefully. 'It's just a shame you've become so dull. If anything, just for us to have something to gossip about that's not you getting married in the stinking cabbage hall.'

'How did you know about that?' Anna straightened up, forgot about whether the customer could hear her or not.

'Seb phoned me to ask what I thought. And I told him it was a dreadful idea and that he should forget about it ASAP.'

'He called you?' Anna closed her eyes. 'But he knew, he knew I wouldn't want to do it.'

'He's a simple man, Anna. He wants a simple solution.'

'Why would he have asked you before me and then still asked me? How do you know me better than he knows me?' She thought about their conversation the night before in the bathroom. Thought how she would always, forever, now be on the back foot. Always trying to be forgiven. Always seeming spoilt if she didn't agree with something that would make their life easier. Thought of the future and saw an endless wheat field stretching out ahead of her.

'Look, Anna, Hermione is always right. Listen to me. What have you got to lose? Fucking hell, what are you expected to do, just stay cooped up in the country all your life, staring at cows and becoming the little wife? No. You need to live. People become boring in the country, it's a proven fact. I mean, you never know, you think it's Nettleton that makes you unable to breathe, but it could be the thought of marriage. Often I find that what we think is wrong in our lives is rarely what is. I'm not saying running off with Luke Lloyd is the answer but live a little, do some casual flirting, it's fun. It'd make you feel better – you've been through a shitty time recently – it'll make you feel more alive. And that can only be a good thing, Seb'll notice the difference. And, he'll never have to know either. If he did, he'd probably advocate it anyway – wasn't that his rationale about Smelly Doug – a social experiment?' Hermione paused and Anna could almost hear her brain thinking of a new tack to take. 'And anyway, you should come up to London, set up some meetings. Did I tell you I bumped into your little assistant the other day, the one who stole all your contacts? What was her name?'

'Kim,' Anna said, nodding vaguely at the customer as they did another lap of the shop.

'Oh yes. Well, she said you should have a catch-up. And, look, listen to this, it says on Wikipedia that a pitchfork has long, thick, widely separated, pointed tines. Tines, Anna. Tines. See, always right, Anna.

Hermione is always right.' She snorted a laugh down the phone.

The bell tingled over the door again and Anna heard the familiar out-of-breath panting of Mrs Beedle. 'Look I've got to go, H,' she whispered, scrabbling to get herself together.

'Only if you swipe that man into your Yeses, Anna. Swipe him,' Hermione carried on regardless.

'OK, fine.' She fumbled to pick her iPhone up from the counter and, swiping Luke Lloyd into her Yeses, quickly shoved it into her pocket. 'I've swiped him. Happy? Now I have to go.'

Anna cut Hermione off, but kept the telephone to her ear as Mrs Beedle came towards her. 'Yes,' she said to the dial tone, 'absolutely, we have a range of different antiquities, something for everyone, and if there's something specific you require, we can have it in mind as we scour the markets across the country and across the channel. Oh yes, many of our pieces are from France.'

As she hung up, she noticed that Mrs Beedle was smiling, which never happened.

'You sold the Russian clock?' she said, dumping a shopping bag of milk, custard creams and an antiques magazine that Anna remembered her father getting delivered, down on the counter.

'No.' Anna shook her head. 'I haven't sold anything.'

Mrs Beedle paused and then looked out into the street. 'I just saw a man leave with it.'

'Not from here.'

'Anna, it was from here.' Mrs Beedle huffed back to the front door but there was no one in the street. Anna could see her standing on the pavement with her hands on her hips, looking right then left, calling to the group of men sitting on the bench on the other side of the square who shook their heads in response. When she finally came back in, she was rubbing the crease marks of her frown. 'Bother,' she sighed.

Anna straightened her shoulders. 'He must have bought it from somewhere else.'

'I got that clock as part of a repossession auction of a Russian oligarch. Anna, it was the only clock of its type west of the Ukraine. Don't tell me that wasn't my clock.' Her cheeks started to flush. 'Clearly he didn't buy it at all. See over there—' She pointed to a cabinet that had a dust-free square on the top about the size of a shoebox. 'That's where it was when I left.'

Anna glanced over at the shiny, polished square of emptiness and bit her lip, then pushed a strand of hair from her face and said, 'Was it expensive?'

Mrs Beedle closed her eyes and sucked in her top lip before muttering, 'You could say that.'

'It wasn't my fault,' Anna said, almost without thinking.

'I'd rather you didn't say that, Anna.' Mrs Beedle opened her eyes, she looked sad and tired and old suddenly, and glanced from Anna over to the CCTV monitor that was currently rolling the closing credits of *Murder She Wrote*.

Anna felt herself inwardly cringe as Mrs Beedle squeezed past her, took the remote down and flicked the TV back to the security monitor, then took her bag of shopping into the stockroom.

Anna yanked off her gloves and covered her eyes with her hand. All her usual defence mechanisms kicked in straight away. It wasn't her fault. It could have happened to anyone. And even if she had been watching, what would she have done, tackle him to the ground? She leant against the counter top and gave it a bit of a polish with an old rag to look like she was doing something, anything rather than go into the back room with Mrs Beedle. As she polished and listened to the kettle being flicked on and saw the cat scamper underneath the curtain, her eyes kept being drawn to the dust-free patch on the top of the mahogany cabinet. She could actually remember the clock, and she knew it was probably the most expensive item in the shop. Gold and magnificent with two lions holding up the dial and an eagle on the top, its wings spread wide. A square base with claw feet like talons. She had remembered admiring it as quite a gem amidst the taxidermy, the assorted crockery and the jumble of chairs that blocked the back half of the shop.

When Mrs Beedle came out with her tea, Anna leant back against the counter and mumbled, 'I'm sorry.'

Mrs Beedle paused as she brought the mug up to her mouth. 'That's not really much use to me.'

Anna frowned. Why would no one forgive her? It had been a mistake. 'It could have happened if you were here or not—'

'Anna.' Mrs Beedle locked her with a look that cut her off immediately. 'Don't make excuses to me. It wouldn't have happened if I was here, I know that, because this shop is my life and the things in it are my life. To you they may be nothing, but to me they are my livelihood and I respect them. I have given you a job when a lot of people here wouldn't and all I ask in return, is you show my possessions just a little respect. That's it. That's all I ask,' she said, her lips taut, her jaw as rigid as it could be in her round little face.

Anna opened her mouth to reply, but chose instead to say nothing, just nodded.

'I don't need you here. In fact, I'd rather you weren't here. But your father has been my friend since I was at school and he asked for a favour. I'm not putting up with your shit, Anna Whitehall. I see through you. And, quite frankly, I'd say it's about time you grew up.'

At five on the dot, Anna grabbed her bag and sloped out so that Mrs Beedle wouldn't see her, and once outside she'd never been happier to feel the scorching heat of the afternoon sun on her face.

Pausing for a moment to sit on one of the chairs outside the French bistro, she leant her head against the wall and took a deep breath. She'd spent the rest of the afternoon flitting between humiliation over her telling off and guilt over the clock theft. Why had this had such an effect on her? It was just a crappy antiques shop, but it felt like the culmination of everything. The conversation with Hermione had rattled her, shaken her foundations. Her relationship with Seb felt like it was being prised apart by a huge Nettleton crowbar, and now she had the big, sad, watery eyes of Mrs Beedle's disappointment to contend with.

'I don't care,' she whispered under her breath. 'I do not care.'

As she was repeating the mantra to herself, the owner came out of the bistro where Anna had taken residence of one of his chairs. He was very good-looking in a dark, Gallic way she thought as he started watering the pots of red geraniums with an old glass bottle. 'Bonsoir, mademoiselle. Can I get you something to drink?'

'Oh no sorry, I was just sitting.' Anna pushed herself up. 'I'm just going.'

He shook his head, pouring the last of the water into one of the gnarly pots. 'There is no hurry. You can sit as much as you like.' He winked, shook out the drops from the bottle, and then disappeared back inside. Was that a marketing trick, she wondered, letting her sit for free so she'd come back sometime and spend money? She looked through the window and saw him glance up from polishing wine glasses and smile.

Maybe he was simply being friendly?

Be careful, Anna, she thought, looking away. *Don't get sucked back in. They don't like you here. You don't like them. Remember that.*

Standing up, she hauled her weary body across the cobbles, the sun burning on her back, the group of old men sitting on the bench staring, hands resting on their bellies, the old sheepdog at their feet turning its head away as she passed. She felt like everyone knew about the stolen clock.

I don't care, she said again under her breath. But then why was she so riled?

As she neared the bakery, she saw Jackie and Seb sitting on the chairs outside, laughing together over chocolate cake. She could see Rachel inside, behind the counter, wrapping up bread and scooping chocolates into gold boxes. The window had changed again, piles of jellied sweets shaped like strawberries and green apples, orange slices and bobbly raspberries glistened in the afternoon sun. Scattered nasturtium flowers fluttered like butterflies, shots of bright vermilion and dazzling cerise. And hanging from ribbons in the window were tiny glass test-tubes, each with a sweet pea drooping from the weight of its pastel petals. A photo of the display would have been worthy of her book, if she hadn't thrown it away.

'Anna!' Seb called with a wave.

Jackie was still sniggering as she approached. Again Anna felt like the outsider.

'Jackie was just asking me whether you'd ever change your mind about coaching her dance group,' Seb said, as if by way of explanation for the giggling.

Why was that funny? Anna wondered.

'Seb said that you didn't really do things for other people,' Jackie said over a mouthful of chocolate cake.

'I didn't say it like that.' Seb shook his head, waving a hand to try and make her disregard Jackie's comment. 'I just said that you weren't, you know, community-focused.'

Anna didn't say anything, a thousand possibilities of what Seb had said swirling through her head. She watched the two of them, their eyes dancing with the remnants of their shared joke. Back in London, after work was her time with Seb. She'd call and arrange to meet him in a swanky bar, but he'd often catch her just before she went in and pull her into a sweet, family-owned tapas place where they'd get free sherry with their chorizo, or make her stroll down the Embankment to look at the river in the twilight and the blue and white lights threaded through the branches of the ragged trees.

When they'd first met she'd led him round London like a pro, pointing out various landmarks and over-egging her knowledge of the history, but he'd stopped her with a raised brow when she'd said that it was a rule that you had to have more than two people in a London Eye pod in case you had sex in there, and he'd said, 'You're full of shit, Anna Whitehall.' And she had turned, ready with a quick retort but had seen the twinkling in his eyes and realised that he was laughing at her. No one had really laughed at her before, no one had ever looked beneath her surface and realised that they could, and she had loved it.

But now, this laughter that he was sharing with Jackie was a different type. One that excluded her and made her feel foolish, out of the joke.

Jackie sat back in her chair, took a sip of her espresso and said, 'Don't worry about it. You probably don't have the skill set to do it anyway, Anna. Teaching kids, it's hard.' Then after a moment's pause she added with a wink, 'It'd make prancing about on stage seem like a walk in the park.'

Refusing to be riled, Anna closed her eyes for a second but instead of nothingness she saw sequins and feathers and Swarovski crystals. Powder on a white puff, flicks of eyeliner and the sparkle of shadow. Tights with a hint of shimmer, pointes worn down to the box, ribbons frayed around her calf, the hoops of sweat on her leotard, the vomit in her mouth the split-second before the curtain went up, the thrum of the orchestra, the darkness of her eyelids as she waited, one deep breath after another until she could feel the warm, engulfing heat of the lights. The steely determination, the poise, the held-back tears, the constant scrutiny, the shouting, the pushing to be better, the *'do it again'*, the *'once more'*, the *'physiologically you don't need a day off'*, the in-built stubbornness that fired like the strike of a match as soon as anyone questioned whether she was good enough, whether she could do it, whether she wanted it or not.

'Tell me what time they rehearse,' she heard herself saying as she pulled on her sunglasses, deliberately not looking at Seb. 'I'll be there.'

Chapter Six

The Nettleton village hall was at the far end of the square, red brick with a parapet and a white key stone with the date, 1906, carved into the masonry. It was flanked on either side by plane trees, their prickly seeds swaying like hedgehogs, the leaves shading the front steps with spots of dancing light breaking through like rain. By the looks of the noticeboard, the building was used for everything, from old people's tea dances to after-school clubs. From the outside, Anna could see the windows decorated with paper-plate suns and pipe-cleaner daffodils.

She could feel her hand shake as she pushed open the heavy wooden front doors and was almost blown backwards by some hideous pop track as it blasted in her face like a roar.

Perfect, she thought. It was like her once only venture to Glastonbury. Same annoying-looking teenagers, same painful music, same hippy-dippy niceness and only one toilet she could find that flushed.

Jackie and Mrs McNamara were standing at the front of the stage chatting while a bunch of spotty juveniles bounced around like malcoordinated maniacs on stage wearing tracksuit bottoms, oversized T-shirts and crop-tops. One, she noticed, was actually wearing a onesie with a tail. That would have to go.

'Anna!' Jackie called, clearly delighted to see her for the pure fact she could now pass the buck of this terrifying shambles.

The hall was stuffy and Anna felt completely overdressed in tight leather-effect leggings, flimsy blue tank-top and a gossamer MaxMara cardigan. The heat, mixed with the nerves of coming back into this type of situation, of drawing on skills that lay happily dormant, made her wonder if she might faint.

'This is the dream team, Anna Whitehall,' Mrs McNamara shouted, and Anna's name on her lips catapulted her straight back to gym class. Huffing and puffing across the lacrosse pitch in the freezing cold. *Come on, Whitehall, none of your ballet flim-flam out here!*

Anna gave her a tight smile, and then they all stood side by side for a second and watched the debacle on stage. The horror of what she was watching quickly gazumped her fears.

'OK, Matt,' Jackie shouted. 'Turn it off a second.'

A pale, loping teenager flicked off his iPod on the stand and Anna felt like she'd experienced a miracle.

'Everyone, this is Anna Whitehall. She's here to put the final touches to the routine. Iron it out before the big audition.'

'I'm sorry,' Anna whispered, perplexed. 'Was that the routine?'

'Yeah, what about it?' a girl with a bright-orange Amy Winehouse beehive shouted from the stage, a tiny nose stud glinting as she sneered.

Anna just waved a hand. 'Nothing,' she said, but could feel herself about to get the giggles. As her attempts to stifle her laughter mixed with the adrenaline of her nerves, it must have done something strange to her expression because another girl sprang forward, this one with a platinum fringe flicked like Farrah Fawcett, and said, eyes narrowed, 'What's wrong with it?'

'Well, it's just—' Anna glanced at Jackie and Mrs McNamara for back-up, but they both just looked at her with blank expressions. 'Well, it has no steps,' she sniggered, as if it was obvious. She was the first to admit that this style of dancing wasn't her forte, but it didn't take a genius to see it was just a hotch-potch of random jumping about the place.

'It's got fucking steps.' Matt, the iPod owner said, running his hand through his dirty-blond hair and frowning, his freckle-smattered nose runkling.

'OK, Matthew, don't swear,' Mrs McNamara cut in.

The flicky-fringe girl pointed a finger at Anna. 'What would you know, anyway?'

Anna raised a brow, was the girl baring her teeth at her? Christ, it was like being in the zoo. Anna shook her hair and straightened her back in an attempt to maintain her hierarchy. 'I'm a professionally trained dancer—' she said, and was about to add her qualifications; that she was a goddamn expert in everything from classical ballet to jazz and contemporary to bloody mime, when Jackie cut in, 'Lucy, Anna was going to be a *star*!'

Anna turned to see if she had deliberately said it like that to belittle her, and from the slight tilt of Jackie's lips, realised that that was exactly what she'd done.

'But you weren't? You never made it?' Lucy's lips pulled into a smug smile and a couple of the others giggled.

Anna swallowed. 'I grew too tall,' she replied quickly and too defensively. 'I would have done. But I was too tall,' she said again, slightly slower and with a hint more poise.

'You don't look very tall to me. Darcey Bussell is tall.'

Anna rolled her eyes. 'TV makes you look taller.'

'What's your excuse then?' some little wavy-haired shit called from the back and they all laughed.

'Billy!' Mrs McNamara said with a warning tone, but even her lips twitched.

Anna ran her tongue along her bottom lip, furious. As they all eyed her with delight, she just managed to stop herself from retaliating. She was better than this, she reminded herself, glancing up at the ceiling. There was no marble ceiling rose here, no golden cherubs carved into the plaster, no fleur-de-lis in the arched moulding, no giant spotlights or even a lighting rig, no royal box with duck-egg-blue furniture and velvet drapes. No, this was nothing.

She surveyed the motley crew, all attitude, Beats headphones round their necks and low-slung tracksuit bottoms. She thought of her stars at the opera house – their elegant grace, their long limbs like gazelles as they stretched, their fluid beauty as they poured themselves into yards of net and tulle that shone and frothed and flickered as they danced. She thought of sitting in the stalls, watching with her notepad, pen poised for notes about the opening night gala dinner, swallowing down the giant lump of envy, of failure, of disappointment, lodged in her throat.

She didn't have to do this.

She glanced across the row of them as they flopped down on the edge of the stage, at the spots, the barely there stubble and the Wonderbras, and shook her head as if to say that they were lucky to have her, and then made the movement to turn and walk away but, as she did, she saw the chin jut out of Farrah Fawcett Lucy and was catapulted back further, to exactly where she hadn't wanted to go: to her interview at the English Ballet Company School. Her hands shaking and sweaty as she'd passed the state-of-the-art, air-conditioned studios, head down, eyes glancing furtively to the left and seeing only the unwavering confidence reflected off the faces of the dancers in the three-sixty wall of mirrors.

'You will give your life, Anna, and most probably fail,' Madame LaRoche had said, her black cigarette pants and spotty scarf making Anna feel like Audrey Hepburn was sitting crossed-legged in the chair in front of her, cigarette dangling between her red lips. *'Less than one percent make it, Anna. And you are*

already old. Already you will have to catch up. One percent.' She held her fingers close together to show the tiny amount. *'Are you in that one percent?'*

Anna hadn't answered.

'Of course she is.' Her mother had crossed her hands over her Chanel bag, the only designer item she owned, that she pulled out of its tissue paper at the bottom of the wardrobe to impress at moments like this.

'Anna?' Madame LaRoche had fixed her in her beautiful, beady gaze. *'Are you in the top one percent? Do you have the hunger?'*

And Anna had swallowed. She thought of the auditions, of the classes she had watched, of the girls who might be thinner, harder, cleverer, tougher than her. Girls who didn't blink when they looked at her. Who danced through stress fractures, twisted ankles, who pushed themselves till they were sick on the floor, vomiting blood they'd worked so hard. Toes bound and crushed and bleeding; blistered, swollen feet frozen in ice. The constant, gruelling quest for perfection, the hours at the barre, the gnawing hunger. Knees strapped into place, tiredness that seeped into the bones like lead, weighing you down like an astronaut suit. Did she have the hunger?

In Nettleton, Anna was the top one percent. Here. Here she felt suddenly tiny, soft, fragile, breakable, scared, nervous, terrified. She could see her father watching them leave, cheeks wet, begging her mother to stay, that he was sorry. She could see the eyes in the street as they sped out of the town. She glanced momentarily at her mother, saw her rigid jaw, her defiance, her determination.

'For goodness' sake,' her mother huffed, *'stop asking her. Of course she is.'*

'Anna?' Madame LaRoche had asked again.

And Anna had done that pose, the Farrah Fawcett Lucy pose. She had swallowed down all her fear, she had locked it up tight, jutted out her chin and thought of all the girls she would have to battle to take down. *'Yes,'* she said, unblinking. *'Yes. I'm better than the top one percent.'*

And then she had fought like a stray dog in that place, the black-haired, olive-skinned girl amidst a sea of alabaster blondes who would walk past in the corridor whispering things like, *'Bet she doesn't even know what a passé is.'* By the time she had to come back to Nettleton for holidays, she was a tough little ball of conditioned attitude and steely defences.

'Anna?' Jackie said again, nudging her on the arm this time.

'Yes.' Anna spun to face her, tearing her eyes from the girl on the stage. 'Sorry, yes. Erm.' She rubbed her forehead. 'OK, look, maybe I wasn't watching clearly.' She took a step back, ran her eyes back over the bunch of reprobates. 'Why don't you come down off the stage, I'd like to see it here, on the floor. You shouldn't be on the stage yet, you're not ready.' She pulled off her cardigan when she realised that she was sweating and would have killed someone for a glass of water.

'Come on,' she called as none of them moved. 'Jackie, Mrs McNamara, it's fine, I'll take it from here.'

'I'm not sure that's a good idea,' said Mrs McNamara dubiously as she watched the kids schlep sullenly down the stairs to the vacant space in the centre of the hall.

'It's fine.' Anna waved a hand. 'It'll be better without you.'

Jackie raised a brow and smirked. 'OK, if you say so.' The two of them then made a show of slowly gathering their bags and walking out of the hall, pointedly glancing over their shoulders to check that order hadn't slipped to chaos.

Razzmatazz lined up sulkily, facing Anna, but none of them meeting her eyes. Ten-year-old Billy, thick wavy brown hair, too long and swept to the side like a miniature Justin Beiber, who seemed to just come on stage to be thrown about the place, scowled at her like she was the devil.

'OK, no music. I'm going to clap the beat,' Anna said as they stared at the floor.

'No fucking music? We can't do it with no fucking music,' Matt shouted.

Anna saw Jackie pause at the door and open her mouth, but she jumped in before she could say anything. 'No, you probably can't,' Anna said, with a sardonic raise of her brow. 'That's my point. If there are steps, you won't need music.' She eyeballed Matt. 'At the moment all you have is *fucking* music. Shit music at that.'

Billy sniggered.

'We can all swear,' she went on. 'I'd just prefer it if from now on we didn't.'

'And why the FUCK should we do what you say?' Lucy goaded.

'Well,' Anna paused for a second and then shrugged. 'You know those montages on *Britain's Got Talent* of all the worst acts, the really, really bad ones, that they play over and over again?'

No one said anything.

'At the moment that'll be you,' Anna said with a wry half-smile, cocking her head to the side and watching as all the kids looked at the floor. 'Right, let's go.'

An hour later, Anna wondered if some of them had sweated for the first time in their lives. And she had to congratulate herself for the fact that they were now at least moving their feet in time with one another on occasion.

Seb was waiting for her outside, leaning against the side of the car reading a book. Anna was feeling good, not that she'd admit how good to anyone, but it felt like she'd achieved something. Not a massive amount, but more than sorting antiques into boxes and getting job application rejections.

The feeling made her see Seb differently too. Blond hair caught in the early evening sun that was just dipping behind the spire on the church, eyes down, concentrating on the book, lips moving ever

91

so slightly, long fingers turning the pages. His tie was loosened and top button undone. He wasn't the enemy. He was hers, she remembered, like an object she'd put in a cupboard or on a shelf and forgotten about, something she'd seen so often she no longer saw it.

Pulling on her cardigan, she crossed the road and when she was by his side kissed him on the cheek.

'Oh!' He looked up, startled. 'What was that for?' he said, as if such casual shows of affection weren't something they'd done for a while.

She shrugged. 'I just, you know—' Suddenly a bit embarrassed for being so free. 'Nothing.'

'How was it?' he asked, glancing from her to the door of the hall.

'Yeah, good.' She nodded. Wanting to say more, to let everything trip off her tongue about how she'd whipped them into shape, how in one fell swoop she'd stopped the swearing and made them focus on the job in hand. How it had felt using skills that she had let hibernate for so long. 'They're terrible and there's just so much work to be done, but it was a good start. I think we're all pleased.'

Seb nodded, incredulous but impressed. 'And you like them? You were OK with them?'

'I wouldn't necessarily say I like them, but I think we respect each other. I think they're grateful that I'm here.' Shielding her eyes from the sun, she gave him a casual smile and breathed in the sweet smell of the evening sunshine.

Seb closed his book and draped his arm over her shoulder. 'Well congratulations.'

She liked the feeling of his surprise, of his appreciation. 'Yeah, it was good,' she said, pushing her shoulders back, flicking her hair out of her eyes. 'I like to think I made a difference.'

'Well I was certainly wrong, wasn't I?' He squeezed her shoulder.

'Yes you were!' she said with a laugh, bashing him on the chest playfully. 'I think I was pretty good. Made them realise the work something like this takes, how they need to apply themselves.'

'Good work, Anna. See, not so bad here, after all.'

She almost agreed. It was almost there on the tip of her tongue…

But then the doors in front of them were kicked open with a bang, and they both turned to see the kids start to amble out of the hall, bags slung over their shoulders, make-up redone, sweaty tops changed, Coke cans in their hands and packets of Hula Hoops.

'That was shit,' Lucy said, with a flump of her freshly backcombed hair.

Two at the back turned to look furtively in Anna's direction while Clara, with the flame beehive, said lazily through a yawn, 'It was total crap. And I'm fucking knackered. I'm done.'

'It's like Nazi youth camp,' Matt said.

'Hey, we should tell Mr Watson next History.' A fat boy Anna had ignored threw his head back with a cackle.

Matt laughed. 'We could put her up as an example of modern dictatorship.'

'I'm done as well,' Billy piped up and kicked a stone that Matt caught with the side of his trainer and booted miles ahead.

Clara swiped him round the head. 'You have to go, Mum wouldn't let you quit.'

'That's just unfair,' he whined and they all laughed.

After a pause, Lucy added loudly, 'It's cos she's such a fucking bitch.' And gave a casual flick of her fringe as her eyes skated sideways to lock with Anna's.

As Anna's lips parted, her mouth just dropping open a fraction, the others giggled but, noticing Seb, their new geography teacher, pulled their heads together as if he wouldn't be able to single them out individually if they became one giant organism that scuttled off like a crab along the pavement.

Anna sucked in a breath. The word bitch hit her hard in the stomach. She wanted to go over and grab bloody Lucy by her bloody fringe and tell her she wasn't allowed to call her a bitch. She swallowed, thought of what she'd said to Seb, of how she thought they had been hanging off her every word. Her little victory popped.

She felt Seb's hand on her shoulder and wanted to shake it off. The last thing she could face was his sympathy.

I don't care, she repeated to herself. *I don't care*. Call her a bitch. That was good. It was good not to be liked. All those teachers with canes and detentions in the past, good old-fashioned discipline, they didn't care if they were liked. In fact, it was better this way. Hate her. Yes. That was much easier.

'Are you OK?' asked Seb.

'Yeah,' she shrugged, nonchalant. 'Fine.'

He paused and she could tell he was debating whether to say something else.

'Anna—' he started.

Here we go, she thought.

'The thing is, with kids you have to connect with them. You know, you can't just tell them what to do.'

'Thanks for that, Seb,' she muttered. Codswallop, she thought. You want something, you work damn hard to achieve it.

Seb sighed and shook his head, then gave her shoulder another squeeze before she straightened herself up tall and pulled on her sunglasses.

'Shall we go home?' she said, as if the whole previous conversation hadn't happened.

If people sense your weakness, Anna, they take advantage of it. She remembered her mum saying that as they walked back to the pokey flat, the vintage Chanel clutched in her hands, beige nail varnish shimmering. *If you have any problems, you talk to me, not them.* Anna remembered nodding, wondering how she was going to be able to ring her dad to let him know that she'd got into the ballet school. The phone was in the living room where her mum slept. *If you're injured, you dance through it, we'll fix it. If they know, you'll be marred with being weak for ever, Anna. And no one associates winning with weakness.*

They drove home in silence, the countryside streaking past the window in bright lines of green, red and yellow, but Anna stared ahead at the grey Tarmac.

'Look, don't worry about the kids, Anna. It'll get better,' Seb said as they pulled up outside Primrose Cottage.

'Too right it will,' she said, glancing at him briefly before opening the car door. 'Because I'm never helping those little brats again.'

She felt him put his hand on her thigh. An image of her kiss on his cheek just ten minutes ago made her wonder if she could put her hand over his where it rested on her skin but her body wouldn't let her. Instead, she stepped out of the car and walked over to drag open the rusty garden gate, lifting it on its broken hinge. As she walked up the path, the thorns on the big fat yellow roses caught her top, the stems sagging even further under the weight of their grotesque petals and heady aroma. 'These bloody flowers,' she shouted, ripping them off her before storming up to the door.

At the end of her first year at the EBC School, they had staged a performance of *Swan Lake*. Anna had felt a rush of triumph when cast as one of the four in the *Danse Des Petits Cygnes*.

Linked with three others, Anna? Is that what you want? her mum had said, glancing up only briefly from a minestrone soup she was stirring. *It's a good start, but I'll come and watch you when you're The Swan Queen, Anna. When you're Odette.* The soup bubbled in the pot and when she flicked the spoon to rest it on the side, it sprayed drops of red against the white tiles. Anna had watched them trickle down, holding her breath and keeping her eyes wide so she wouldn't cry.

I'm not saying this to punish you, Anna darling. I'm saying it to make you better. Don't settle for what they tell you is good. You decide what is good, what is the best. If you believe in something enough, and you're determined, you'll get it. I want to spur you to do better, she had said, taking a sip of the soup at the same time as ripping off a piece of kitchen towel so Anna could wipe her eyes. You have to go out and grasp what you want.

The photo of the girl, two years above, playing The Swan Queen had been glued neatly into Anna's book.

She paused at the shabby door of the cottage, the rose scratches just welling with blood on her arms, the air burning her lungs like a sauna, and thought, I don't want this. I'm better than this. You have to go out, Anna, and grasp what you want, she reminded herself, before thrusting the key into the lock.

I have to go out and grasp what I want.

Chapter Seven

As forecast, the temperatures continued to soar, with no end in sight for the excruciating heat. Predictions of record temperatures, warnings of elderly people dying and sun-worshippers frazzling covered the front pages of the papers that Anna read over commuters' shoulders as she sweltered on the London Underground.

Her face pressed close to a stranger's sweaty armpit and her body squidged between the door and three Russian tourists and their luggage, she closed her eyes and tried to stay calm and relaxed. She was meeting her ex-assistant, Kim, at Zédel in Piccadilly. After the disastrous Razzmatazz rehearsal, Anna had emailed her to ask if they could meet up to discuss her 'options'. Kim had emailed back within three minutes: *Honey, Hermione said things weren't great. Would love to chat strategy. Meet me Tuesday. We'll have some champagne.*

The day after, she'd been woken at midnight by a text that left her lying in bed, eyes open as the muggy heat enclosed her like hot soup, the monotonous thrum of the fan like the incessant drone of a fly suffocating her senses, feeling like she was opening doors that should remain firmly closed. Feeling like the girl in *The Red Shoes,* with the feet that couldn't stop dancing.

Anna Banana. Long time, no see. Heard on the grapevine Pleb Davenport snapped you up. Clearly should have taken him out at school when I had the chance. Intrigued why you're on Tinder. Intrigued enough to meet up and find out. Luke Lloyd.

She had deleted it without replying, ignoring the deadly, intoxicating thrill she had felt on seeing his name.

And now she was shuddering along on the burning Piccadilly Line dressed in last year's Céline pencil skirt, Stella McCartney flesh-coloured tank-top and the metallic green Jimmy Choos she kept in their bag in their box, under her bed. The heels were a little too high for *Grazia* to approve this season but when she looked down at them, just visible under the Russian tourists' luggage that she had had to shuffle right up to, they made her smile.

When the Tube doors opened, she saw posters for films that she hadn't even known were coming out, books she might want to read had she known about them, gallery exhibitions she had let pass her by. Drinking in the advertising as she rode the escalators, she felt a cool breeze flutter her tank-top away from her skin and allowed herself a second to exhale. Calm and relaxed, she repeated. Were her hands sweating from nerves or heat, she wondered.

And then she was out – out in the light. Out into London. Beautiful, packed, busy, loud, bustling, hectic, crystal clear, effervescent, pushy, rude, loud, boiling, steaming London.

Wow. She took a moment to stand in the corner of the pavement by Lillywhites and just stare at the statue of Eros, his little winged feet and bow poised ready for aim. I heart London, too, she thought watching him. She gazed up at the huge advertising boards that gleamed with lights and reflected the blinding sun as pictures of McDonald's and Burberry macs blasted out at her. And the buses, big and red and lined nose to tail in traffic like red ants marching forward. Oh and pigeons, how she'd missed the pigeons, pecking about at chewing gum and takeaway wrappers. She had never been so grateful to see such grubby, deformed birds before in her life. No big, plump Nettleton wood pigeons for her, she would always be faithful to their scrawny London cousins that hung onto their existence by whatever means possible.

Her hand resting on the brickwork, she took a breath in and inhaled the toxic taxi fumes and burger smoke air. People barged her shoulder, stopped in front of her to consult their maps, shouted into their phones next to her. No one sat serenely on benches and gazed at the wide blue sky. No one stopped for a chat outside the local coffee shop nor walked their fat, groomed dog and perused the Sunday papers over a brioche here.

This was London. My London, she thought, gulping in the sounds, the heat, the smells, the pollution, the noise, as if jump-starting the battery inside herself that had been slowed to a Nettleton crawl.

She was so excited that she turned around and took a selfie of herself with Eros in the background, then deleted it and took another, better, one and posted it on Instagram. When someone smashed into her ankle with a suitcase, she shouted 'Ow!' loudly and they told her to piss off. Even that made her smile.

Crossing the road, she trotted past the wooden awnings of a shop refit, pushed through crowds around a stall selling tourist tat, made a note to pop into Nespresso and perhaps peruse Wholefoods later, and then beamed a smile at the stunning Zédel doorman who tipped his hat and smiled as she strutted her way in in her sky-high heels feeling every bit the London woman about town rather than mucky country antique worker.

She was walking into her future.

This was where she belonged, she thought as she skipped down the stairs and glanced at herself in the corridor of mirrors, checked her hair and her nude lipgloss, brushed down her skirt and popped her clutch under her arm. Not too shabby, she thought.

'Anna Whitehall! Over here.' Kim's brash Anglo-American drawl called from halfway across the restaurant.

The waiter led her over to where tiny, petite, fiercely ambitious Kim was already seated with a glass of Prosecco and a bottle of mineral water.

'Love this place, hun.' Standing up, Kim air-kissed her from where she stood, then waved for Anna to sit down and proceeded to fill her glass with bubbles. 'Did you find it OK? Not quite Brambly Hedge, is it?' She bellowed a laugh that made other diners turn and look their way.

Anna had to quash the fact that she had been the one to bring Kim here on Kim's first day working for her, and instead smiled through a sip of Prosecco.

'Drink as much as you can, hun, we're totally on expenses.' Kim lifted her glass in a cheers and drank a gulp. 'God, I remember that skirt from the Céline show, wow, I haven't seen that for ages.'

It was then that Anna noticed Kim's outfit. Her Aztec-print shirt, cigarette pants and flat patent loafers. Her own clothes suddenly felt the season or two out of date that they were – her skirt three inches too long, the heels on her Choos too high, her sharp-edged clutch bag not casual enough. Damn it, she thought. She looked like she was trying too hard. She looked like she was out of the loop.

'So, hun, I heard about your redundancy. What a bitch. Highest salary always goes first...so unfair. I mean, I never thought it would have been you though. You must have been gutted. And with the wedding on the horizon. The Waldegrave.' She made a sad face. 'You didn't lose too much, did you? Who'd have seen that collapse coming? What's happening with the world?'

Anna gave a tiny shake of the head. 'I'm in talks with the administrators, it's fine.'

'I heard the invitations were fabulous.'

She inwardly cringed that Kim hadn't been sent one and wondered what the gossip was behind her back. Did they discuss how she would have afforded such a wedding at such a place? Did they wonder how she would top it now?

She remembered her lovely invitations. How she had always thought she'd want a proposal at the top of the Eiffel Tower or in a gondola in Venice, but Seb had proposed in Hyde Park. Sitting at a picnic table, daffodils just opening. He'd dropped something on the floor and said, 'Hey, Anna, check this out.' And she'd bent down to look where he was pointing under the dark, cobwebby table and scratched into the leg of the table was, *Seb Davenport wants to marry Anna Whitehall.* Under that table, like kids playing, she'd felt carefree and without expectation. His penknife-carved graffiti had been photographed and sent out on glossy paper to all the guests.

Kim had carried on talking as Anna was swept off with her memory. 'And it's shit out there. There are no jobs. Sweet FA in the arts. No one's moving. And, to be honest, it's hard when you've been let go because people, you know, they wonder why you. I'm not saying that's what they're saying about you, but there's always that worry.' Kim smiled and then glanced down at the menu as the waiter came over and hovered by the table. 'We're not ready,' she said, without looking up, and Anna gave him a beaming smile to try and counteract Kim's curtness.

Poise, Anna repeated to herself as she looked at the menu but didn't take anything in. Poise. Shoulders back. Just keep cool and calm and don't get riled and think about the fact that she may be your one chance to get out of Nettleton. Poise, poise, poise.

'So, what have you been doing with yourself? I have visions of you in *Oklahoma*!, singing at the top of your voice while riding a horse through fields of corn,' she snorted.

'I'm, erm, I'm in antiques at the moment. High-end antiques.'

'Oh I love it, like Sotheby's?'

'Yes, something like that,' Anna said, brushing down the napkin in her lap, straightening her blouse, and not quite meeting Kim's glance.

'Amazing.' Kim clicked her fingers for the waiter and he was back in an instant. 'So I'll have the carottes râpées, then the salmon tartare and a green side salad. And we'll have another bottle,' she said, tapping the neck of the Prosecco. 'Anna?'

Anna hadn't even looked. Her eye had been caught by her green metallic shoes glinting in the overhead lights. It suddenly occurred to her that her whole outfit, her whole spiel, was like her mum's Chanel bag. Kept neat, clean and precious in the cupboard and brought out for special occasions when she wanted to impress, to be who she thought she deserved to be rather than who she was. 'Oh, the carrot for me too, and then, erm…' She rushed over the menu. 'The sea bass.'

I am the Chanel bag, she thought.

'So I have something that I think you'll be really interested in.' Kim leant forward, elbows resting on the table, fingers steepled and tapping so that her blood-red polish glinted glossy in the light. 'Really, really interested in.'

'You do?' Anna took a nervous sip of Prosecco.

'Uh huh.' Kim nodded, and Anna realised that she wasn't just going to tell her, she was going to have to work for it.

'I'm all ears,' she laughed, hearing the simpering in her voice and inwardly cringing.

'You are?' Kim sat back and crossed her legs, her lips spreading wide in a teasing smile. But then the waiter brought over two plates of carottes râpées and Kim squealed with delight. 'This is my absolute favourite, it's to die for.' And then proceeded to scoop up the carrot with her fork, moan about the flavour and then start to talk about what mutual friends in the industry were up to.

Anna was on the edge of her seat, desperate to bring the conversation back to whatever it was that Kim was about to dangle in front of her nose, but realised that she was going to have to wait. This was all part of Kim's fun. Knowing that she was squirming in her two seasons-old skirt.

The carrot was cleared away, more Prosecco was poured and they were finishing up their fish by the time Kim lounged back, crossed her legs, sucked on her e-cigarette and said, 'So there's a job. In New York.'

Anna's eyes shot up and locked with hers. 'You're serious?'

'Deadly,' Kim drawled. 'If I wasn't doing so well here, I'd take it myself.'

'And you think it would suit me?'

'Hun, it's right up your alley. PR and marketing based, New York Dance Academy. I think it's a year's minimum commitment. They tried to recruit in the US, but no success. People aren't moving. Salary isn't as competitive as it could be but, for someone like you, it would be the perfect way to get your name back out there. They have someone over here recruiting next week, I think. I've mentioned your name. They'd like to meet.' She took another puff on her e-cigarette and then let her red lips stretch into a big wide smile as she delighted in Anna's shock and obvious excitement.

'Wow,' Anna said, hardly able to take it in. New York, that was the dream. *That's the pinnacle.* That was where she was meant to end up. God, her mum would go silent on the phone if she told her, she'd be so damn delighted. Her name wouldn't be in lights, but she'd at least be in the Lincoln Center, sitting in the seats of the David H. Koch Theater, looking up at that ceiling paved with gold. She'd be strutting up Fifth Avenue, shopping in Saks, lounging in Central Park after work. She and Seb could practise their baseball swings and stroll arm in arm around MOMA.

Seb.

The thought of him brought her back down to earth.

'Dessert, ladies?' the waiter asked as he cleared their plates.

'I'm totally dieting but, what the hell, the tarte tatin, of course. What else would you have here?' Kim rolled her eyes.

'And for you, Madam?'

Anna had promised him a year in Nettleton. A full year. That had been the deal. If she went to New York, she went on her own. She knew that, she knew he wouldn't leave this new job. Could she go on her own? Would she do that? When they were meant to be getting married? Would she pass up an offer that would put her back on track? The excitement of starting again, Stateside?

'Just a coffee.' She shook her head at the offer of dessert.

'Oh well, I can't have dessert if she's not having it. Scrap the tarte tatin, I'll just have an espresso,' said Kim.

'No, have a dessert,' Anna said, 'I just didn't feel like it.'

'I'll only have one if you have one,' Kim pouted.

'OK, fine.' Anna skimmed the menu feeling like she owed her the calories in exchange for the job news and said, 'I'll have the profiteroles,' without thinking.

Seb had taken the job at Whitechapel Boy's School, she knew, mainly to stay in London near her. She had taken him to Zédel to celebrate, running in from the pouring rain; she'd said it was her treat but, on her salary at the time, she could afford only wine and dessert. And they had sat giggling in the fancy restaurant sharing profiteroles, swiping their fingers across the plate to lick up the last of the chocolate sauce and eking out the wine till the waiters were clearing up and they were turfed out into the drizzle.

'Good girl, Anna.' Kim smiled and reordered her tarte. 'So, New York. Fun, hey?'

'Yeah, definitely,' Anna nodded.

'Will Seb mind?' Kim probed.

Would Seb mind? This was the step she was meant to take. This was the next rung up on the ladder. This was part of her life plan. New York. Would Seb mind?

Seb would be livid.

'Probably.' She laughed, as if it was nothing, and Kim guffawed wickedly. Then the waiter appeared with their rich desserts and poured thick chocolate sauce over Anna's profiteroles and the whole thing made her suddenly feel a little bit sick.

As they walked out into the glaring sunshine and headed back towards Piccadilly Circus, Anna felt woozy from the Prosecco, not to mention the idea of broaching NYC versus Nettleton with Seb. Kim lit a normal cigarette, chucked her soft slouchy bag over her shoulder and moaned, 'Jesus, it's so goddamn hot, all the time.' Then she kissed Anna on both cheeks, waving the fag dangerously close to her hair, and said, 'I'll be in touch, or someone will be in touch re: New York. Try and play the redundancy down, or at least make sure they know you were over-qualified.' She snorted a laugh. 'They'll just want to see ambition. Hunger.'

Do you have hunger, Anna? 'I have hunger,' Anna nodded.

'That's my girl.' Kim winked, walking backwards and then turned and disappeared into the crowds of tourists.

'Jesus Christ.' Anna exhaled a breath, in a bit of a daze. She walked on, with no particular direction in mind, and then paused, leaning up against the wall of the Nespresso shop. 'Do I have hunger?' she said to herself and then laughed. 'Too right, I have hunger.' She nodded, and stood up taller again, shoulders back. 'I have bloody hunger and I'm going to go to New York and be amazing again.' *I'm going to be a star.* If she went to New York, she wouldn't come even close to being the Chanel bag. It would be real. It would be better. It would be who she *wanted* to be. 'Nettleton, schmettleton.' She laughed again. 'Thank you, London,' she said, looking up to the sky and blowing it a kiss. Then she tucked her bag under her arm and went to buy little pods of coffee.

As the glass doors of the Nespresso shop slid open, her phone beeped in her bag. She paused, wondering if it would be Seb asking how the chat went. As she opened her clutch, she wondered what she could tell him. How she could spin it. She could persuade him. Seb was persuadable. Seb would do anything for her. Wouldn't he? The thought went through her mind that *once* he would have done anything for her. Would he still now, now that the glamour was slipping?

The text, however, was from a number she wasn't expecting…

I'm around the corner from you. Luke.

She stared at the screen. Her mouth suddenly seemed dry.

How do you know? she wrote back.

I followed you on Instagram. I'm sitting outside Wholefoods. In fact, I can see you.

Shit.

Chapter Eight

There he was, lounging on a green mesh chair like a young Tom Cruise. Large nose, eyes so blue that it was like they weren't meant to be on a human face, wild black curls and a laughing smile, that all came together to be far more impressive than the sum of its parts. That had always been Luke Lloyd's thing: startling attractiveness that one couldn't put one's finger on.

'Looking gorgeous, if I may say, Anna Banana.' He sat forward lazily and pushed himself up so he could lean over the table, rest a hand on her shoulder and pull her towards him for a kiss too close to her lips. Falling back into his seat, he grinned around the gum he was chewing and her face burnt where his lips had touched her. 'Christ.' He nodded again as she stood, not quite sure what to do. 'You've always been so damn good to look at. Take a seat.'

As he bit his smiling bottom lip and watched her, she knew that the appropriate action was to shake her head and say, 'I'd love to but I can't, sorry. Gotta rush. Good to see you though.' And he would say, as she walked away, 'Hey, what were you doing on Tinder?' And she would pause and smile over her shoulder, 'Just messing about with Hermione.' And wink and sashay away. In her mind she would remember what Luke's gang were like at school. She would see the look in poor Seb's eyes when he pretended to laugh about the stupid things they'd done to him. The silly things that really meant nothing at all. How they'd unpacked all his possessions on the geography field trip at school and laid his baggy white Y-fronts out on all the girls' beds. How they had turned his desk upside down, locked his locker with ten different padlocks, thrown his books, one by one, out the window. And she would think of the worry on Seb's face when they first started dating and he would say, *'So you and Luke, you've definitely split up? Even if he hadn't joined the army, you wouldn't still be together? You don't still have feelings for him?'*

But Anna didn't walk away. She didn't smile over her shoulder. She pulled out a matching green mesh chair and folded herself into it, laying her bag down on the table and when Luke smiled, stood up, rested a hand on her shoulder and said he'd go and get her a coffee, she did a little casual shrug, preening herself because of the quiet thrill that shot through her.

When he came back out, she was on her phone, reading her emails and about to text Seb to let him know that she might be a bit late back.

'Texting him indoors to let him know you're out with the enemy?' Luke laughed.

'Not at all.' She put her phone down on the table. 'We don't keep tabs on each other.'

'I'll bet.' He narrowed his eyes and grinned.

She took a sip of her latte and felt him assessing her. 'So what's the great Anna Whitehall up to? Taken over the world of dance yet? I imagined you, you know, dressed like this – all power-suited up – strutting into meetings and deciding the fate of little dancers everywhere.'

Anna flicked her hair out of her eyes and said, 'I've just been offered a job in New York, actually. I've just had the meeting.'

He nodded, impressed, and she sat back, crossing her legs and felt herself getting into her role. She was lying and embellishing simply so that he would think she had made it, that she was a success. So that she could walk away and, for once, not feel the burden of being such a failure. 'Yes, I'm not sure if I'll take it or not. Want to keep my options open.' The metal of the chair was hot against her back and she felt the sun beating down on her scalp. He seemed unruffled by the heat, probably all that time in the desert, but she felt her skin prickling, like a warning telling her she shouldn't be sitting out – neither in the sun nor opposite Luke.

He stretched his arms up in a yawn and said, 'Always the high-flyer.' Then he took a sip of his coffee, glanced to one side, and said without looking at her, 'But what about your fun, Anna? Who's giving you that?'

'I have fun,' she retorted, forcing a laugh that came out high-pitched and annoyingly fake.

He looked back her way and said, 'We used to have fun, didn't we? I think I brought a hell of a lot of fun to your life.' He nodded, as if he didn't need an answer. 'That was my gift to you. Loosened you up, undid some of the damage.'

'Damage.' She rolled her eyes. 'You wish. It was me that brought the fun.'

'That's true, actually.' He licked his lips. 'You were like a wildfire when you came back, just intent on causing trouble.'

'I wasn't that bad.'

Luke snorted into his coffee, 'You were like this stunning whirlwind who just whipped into town every holiday and blew the roof off every house in the place.'

She laughed at the idea of it, shook her head.

'Do you remember we'd go to that crappy club with my brother's ID? What was it called? Ritzy's, was it? Something like that. We'd drink that luminous-pink drink, do you remember?' He sat back, hands locked behind his head. 'We could move on that dance floor, baby.' His eyes flashed and she had to laugh.

'We did dance.' She smiled.

'Damn well.' He leant forward, his grazed, scratched elbows resting on the table, a tattoo of a snake coiled round his right bicep. 'How does Pleb dance?'

114

It was a well-known fact that Seb did not dance. Never had, never would. He wouldn't even sway. She had a sip of coffee in her mouth when he asked the question and found herself pausing a moment too long before she swallowed. Luke sat back and clapped his hands together delighted. 'I knew it! Ha, so no more dancing for Anna Banana.'

She shrugged, coughed over the coffee that felt like it had gone into her lungs by mistake. 'I don't really have time to dance any more. And where the hell would I dance? I hardly go clubbing nowadays. I'm not seventeen.'

He raised a brow. 'Excuses, excuses.'

'Let's change the subject.'

'Whatever you want.' He grinned. Then there was a pause where her mind went completely blank and all she could think about were the little victory ticks that Luke probably had bursting out of his brain right at that moment.

In the end, it was Luke who spoke, 'So I don't know what game you were playing, but I've got to tell you I was pretty smug when I saw you'd Yesed me.' He ran a hand through his hair, making it stick up all on its own, and she noticed the rugged roughness of his hands, the scratches and scars and general army wear and tear. 'I think about you sometimes, when I'm out there. I look up at the stars.' He laughed again. 'Do you know how many goddamn stars there are in the desert? More stars than sky. It can make a man think about his life.' He unfolded the Wayfarers he had hooked onto the neck of his T-shirt and slipped them on, covering his eyes. 'I have to admit that I think about you, quite a lot.'

The unexpected confession startled her. He'd always been adamant about leaving and that he wanted to do it unencumbered. 'I would imagine that's just the effect of the stars,' she laughed, trying to brush it off. 'Running about the place with guns and all that macho-bonding, I doubt you give a second thought to what you gave up.' She glanced over her shoulder after she said it, suddenly aware that someone might spot her, like Hilary and Roger popping up after a day's sightseeing.

'I do, Anna. I look at the guys getting their letters and Skyping their wives and kids and I think, Christ, we could have had some good-looking kids.'

She snorted into her coffee. 'Steady on.'

'No, I mean it,' he said, his face serious for a second. 'It's not often a bloke can admit he was wrong.' As he looked her way, she could see herself reflected in the dark lenses of his shades.

She felt annoyingly uncomfortable and it wasn't just the heat. It wasn't the worry of being caught. It was the feeling of someone taking her life that was already a muddle and giving it a good hard shake. Like she was in her own personal snow globe.

The tightness of his lips brought back the memory of lying next to him in the single bed in the crummy flatshare she had taken in London. When everything had ended and her mum had left in a fury to go back to Seville. When she had nothing. When she was working in a bar to pay her rent. Luke had said that life wasn't fun any more. He wasn't enjoying himself, and had decided that the army was the career for him. She had said that she could be more fun. But he had rolled towards her and said he'd applied and been accepted to Sandhurst. He had never asked her once about herself, about what had happened, and she had never felt more alone in her life. She pitied her old self now when she remembered sitting up in bed and looking down at him, with his hands behind his head, and saying, pleadingly, 'What can I do to make you stay?' And he had looked up at her with that same expression he was using now, and said, 'Nothing.'

Looking at him now, she suddenly realised that there was the same degree of something not quite right about his look now as there was then. She couldn't put her finger on it. Like it was the expression of an actor acting serious rather than a look of genuine emotion.

As if the atmosphere had got too intense for him, Luke's face shifted back to its relaxed, mischievous grin, leaving Anna feeling one step behind, still caught in a memory. He whipped off his sunglasses and said, 'So, tell me about Pleb, how's he getting on? Tell me everything, I can't bloody believe the two of you ended up together. No wonder you're on bloody Tinder.'

'Don't call him that,' she said, catching up to her present. 'It's not funny. Call him Seb.'

Luke crossed his arms in front of his chest and chuckled, tipping his head back in delight. She shifted in her seat and altered the direction of the conversation towards his career and army life, which touched the right nerve and he proceeded to rhapsodise about the helicopters he'd jumped out of, the rapids he'd canoed, the sandstorms he'd battled, the times his parachute hadn't opened or his rifle had jammed.

Anna carried on with the conversation, but she was only half there. The other half of her had stood up and was wandering round the table observing, thinking: golly I was envious of him, of his adventure, of his excitement. He, too, was going away to be a star. He, too, was going away to make it.

But as he talked, as the pedestrians strutted past him on their iPhones and a tourist interrupted them and asked him for directions that Luke couldn't give, she realised that he was as lost as her. Outside the army, outside the regime, the excitement, what did he have? She understood then that he had the memory of a relationship that ended years ago.

I'm his touchstone to reality, she thought.

What is he to me?

She crossed her arms and looked at him, watched his mouth move, watched his eyes crinkle as he sniggered at his own jokes.

Just a damn good-looking memory, she thought, and the relief was palpable. Luke was a fantasy detached from all the shit that was currently bundled onto her relationship with Seb like barnacles on an oyster shell. Luke was devoid of her feelings of guilt over the wedding money. Her frustration over losing her job. Seb's sweetness to her when she knew she may not have been so sweet to him had the situation been reversed. The niggling feeling that perhaps she would have punished him.

For the first time, as she sat back in her chair and finished her now-cold coffee and felt the heat of the sun dip as it started to get dusky, she dreamed of Nettleton. Of getting out at the station and walking across the sun-warmed cobbles of the square and the dappled light of the lime trees sprinkling shadows that danced over the pigeons, the wooden benches and the fountain that turned off abruptly at nine o'clock every night. As Luke spoke and cracked more average jokes and she smiled along with him, she was back on the walk that Seb had made her take on one of their first Nettleton mornings to prove that it wasn't so bad, when it had been too hot to sleep so they had strolled through the fields, ears of wheat drooping over and brushing their skin, poppies delicate and perfectly still in the misty early morning, the odd lazy bee bouncing into them and butterflies pausing in their path. They had sat on a stile and Seb had poured coffee from a Thermos and she had mocked him for owning a flask and he had pushed her so she'd almost tipped backwards and struggled to keep her balance. When she'd laughed, he had kissed her and put his arm around her and said, *'Look, look at that,'* as the sun beamed down at them and the sky was so blue it was like the sea, and the view was old oak trees, thatched cottages and ears of wheat as far as the eye could see. *'How could you not love that?'*

Anna glossed over the fact that she'd then been bitten by a horsefly and they'd had to go home and Seb had driven to the pharmacy for some cream but it was shut, while she'd tried to have a bath and the water had run brown so, in the end, she'd had to sit on the back porch with a cold flannel on her massive bite, biting her lip against the throbbing pain and cursing the countryside.

Her overriding thought was that she had to get back. That the image of Seb and the stile and the view was getting further away, receding like the mouth of a tunnel. Fading as the dusk settled.

'I have to go,' she said suddenly, cutting off some story Luke was telling mid-flow.

'You can't go,' he smirked. 'We're catching up. I thought we could go for a drink, maybe get some dinner. I'm not in town for long, Anna Banana.' He pushed his sunglasses up into his wild hair and his grinning eyes creased at the corners.

'No, really, I have to go. I'm sorry to leave you here, but I have to go home.'

'Running back to Sebastian?' He shook his head. 'He's got you under lock and key, hasn't he, Anna?'

'No, not at all, it's just…' She shook her head, trying to think of something to say. Seeing suddenly that the sum of the parts of his face didn't always add up to better. That sometimes, like right now, they added up to looking a bit cruel. 'I'm not feeling that well. I think it's the sun. Look, it was really nice to catch up. I mean it. Enjoy your evening. Sorry. Bye.'

She picked her bag up and thrust it under her arm, taking a couple of steps backwards as he watched her through narrowed eyes, then raised a hand in a salute goodbye.

'Bye,' she said again, and turned to make a tottering dash for the Tube, barely pausing to look at Eros again, or the buses, or Regent Street, or to smell the air and absorb the heady bustle. But her eye caught one looming building, its gothic spire thrust up into the sky, the mullioned windows dark and lifeless, the big metal doors locked tight. The Waldegrave, in all its magnificent, bankrupt glory, now just a ghost of a former life.

As she got to the stairs of the Underground, she started to jog, holding onto the banister to steady herself in her heels. The tourists were suddenly an annoyance, blocking the path, not getting out of her way, messing up their Oyster card transactions so she had to wait in line, tapping her foot.

All she could think was, I have to get home. Whatever happens with the job, I have to go home. Seb cannot find out about Luke. It was a mistake to see him. Sitting across the table from him, as he talked about Tinder and her relationship, felt suddenly like the worst betrayal, one she wished she could suck back in.

Sitting on the Tube, she counted the stops, it wasn't moving quickly enough. By the time she swapped to a train, she was tapping her fingers on her bag in her lap. She flicked through the free newspaper, but couldn't concentrate, so stared out the window willing it to move faster until finally, finally, they rattled into Nettleton Station. The familiar wooden-slatted station building with its intricate white cornicing, the closed ticket office with its blind pulled down, the little coffee stand – an off-shoot of Rachel's bakery – locked up for the night, baskets of petunias, geraniums and pansies, carefully tended, hanging along the platform.

Just get home, her mind was chanting. Her feet were raw now from the Jimmy Choos and crying out for her to stand still, but something was making her feel like she was running out of time.

There was no taxi in the rank, just a phone on the wall that would connect her directly to the cab company.

'Bruce is five minutes away, Anna. He'll be right with you,' said Pam from Pam's Taxis. How she knew who Anna was, Anna had no clue.

She took her shoes off and stood on the patch of grass in front of the station, waiting for Bruce who, when he pulled up, got out of the car to open the door for her.

'Lovely evening, isn't it?' Bruce mused from the driver's seat as he snaked his way to her house at a fifteen mile per hour crawl. 'Been anywhere nice?'

'Just London.'

'I don't get to the city much. The wife does, loves the theatre. Sees everything. How's your dad?'

'Fine, I think,' she said, drumming her fingers on the leather seats, then throwing five pounds fifty at him as he was still pulling up outside her indecently drooping roses and legged it barefoot up the path.

'Hi, honey. Seb?' she called to what seemed like a strangely empty house. 'I'm home. Sorry I was late. I—'

Seb was sitting on the sofa in the living room, tie off, collar undone, glass of something clear on the table. From what she knew they owned, it was either water or vodka and it was lacking the off-white colour of their tap water. His hands were clasped in front of him.

When he looked up, his eyes were flat and hard and she felt like one of his pupils hauled into his office, not sure what their crime was but running through a list of excuses in their head, ready for any eventuality.

'Luke rang,' Seb said, his voice bland.

'Who?' As soon as she said it, she rolled her eyes at herself.

'Seemingly your date for this evening.'

Anna licked her lips.

'You left your phone. In your hurry to get home, you left your phone at wherever it was you'd arranged to meet.'

'We didn't—'

'He wanted to check that you were OK, not too ill.'

'I erm—' She ran a hand over her now-feverish forehead.

Seb rubbed his hand over his face, then picked up the glass and slumped back, his legs spread wide. 'He had a great time, Anna. Great time telling me all about

123

Tinder, your date, how he admired that I let you stay free to casually date. How he always knew I'd work out a way to keep a woman. He fucking loved it.'

'It wasn't like that.' She stayed where she was. Felt every muscle in her body tighten, her shoulders go back, her chin rise, her spine instinctively arch.

'No?' He glanced up. 'Doesn't really matter how it was, does it? He got what he wanted out of it. I imagine you did too. You look very glam. Did you get your fix? Did you have a good laugh about boring Pleb dragging you back to the country? Because I'm assuming it was all my fault? No Anna blew every penny we had and then lost her job? No both of us having too good a time that we couldn't afford it any more? Couldn't afford the lifestyle and the holidays? He said you were really sick, Anna, he said you were having such a good time reminiscing that you must have been really sick to have to run off.'

'He was winding you up, Seb.'

'Yeah, and fucking good at it he is too. Did you say Yes to him on Tinder?'

He was talking with a really flat voice, like the recorded voice at the station. Like, *'You have arrived at Nettleton. Bad things will happen here. You have been warned. You will ruin your relationship. Are you sure you want to get off?'*

'Kind of.'

'Yes or no?'

'Yes. But you know what it's like. I was bored, Seb. It's boring here. We don't do anything because there's nothing to do. I was chatting to Hermione, and it was just another experiment. It was something to do.' She squared her shoulders. 'I don't have anything I want to do here.'

'Oh fuck that, Anna.' He took a gulp of what she'd now decided was definitely vodka from the gloopy shine in the glass. 'Hermione, of course. She'd have loved this.'

'It was an experiment. You encouraged it before. With Jackie and Doug.'

'Give me a break. This was behind my back, and with—' He closed his eyes. 'Luke Lloyd, of all people, Luke Lloyd. Why would you do that to me?'

Anna picked at the stitching on her bag.

'You just blatantly lied. I mean, who else have you been dating that I don't know about?'

'No one,' she scoffed. 'And I didn't lie. I just…' She searched for a word. 'Omitted.'

He paused. She could feel the blisters on her heel burning. She wiped away the dampness that was appearing on her face, the heat that had been building in the room all day engulfing her like a huge, flumpy duvet.

'Like you omitted your swanky new job in New York?' he said, looking up at her under half-closed lids.

She was too surprised to reply.

Seb stood up, knocked back what was left of the glass and scooped his jacket up off the back of the armchair. 'Good luck with that by the way, sounds right up your street. I assume, from the sounds of it, that you'll be taking it? New York City or cornfields. Pretty hard for me to compete.'

She opened her mouth to speak, but was silenced by the look on his face.

'Who are you?' he asked, bemused, before walking past her, swiping his money and keys off the table by the door and walking out, but still carefully closing the door behind him so as not to rattle the stained-glass panel that was loose.

Chapter Nine

When Seb hadn't come home by ten o'clock and Anna had exhausted every range of excuses about why this wasn't her fault, practised speeches that she would make in apology and imagined herself just throwing herself at him in an out-of-character, movie-inspired leap that would have them whirling through the house knocking vases off sideboards with gay abandon, she went to look for him.

He wasn't in any of the places she thought he might be sulking in isolation – the stile in the corner of the field opposite, the allotment shed that his grandfather owned, the bench in the village square – nor was he sitting stubbornly in the car, so finally she went to look for him in the pub.

In London, Anna made a point of going into pubs alone because she was determined not to inherit her mother's hang-up about walking in and believing the whole place took a collective in-breath of horror at the idea of a woman alone in a public house. But in Nettleton, that was exactly how it felt. The almost-familiar faces at the bar did seem to pause, the sound did seem to drop as she stood alone on the threshold, she thought she saw a woman in the corner nudge her partner on the arm.

When she spotted Seb's brother, Jeremy, at the bar, it was almost a relief.

'Look what the cat dragged in,' he smirked, propping himself up in a casual lean. 'Isn't this a bit beneath the great Anna Whitehall?' he asked, sweeping a hand around the place while his mate smiled into his pint.

'Hi, Jeremy.' She sighed, wishing that perhaps she wasn't wearing the cashmere lounge pants that Seb said made her arse look like a ninety-year-old's. 'Have you seen Seb?'

'Why, have you lost him?' Jeremy's eyes twinkled.

'No, he's just not answering his phone.'

'Had a row?'

'No.'

'Why isn't he answering his phone, then?' Jeremy raised a brow as he sipped his bitter.

'I don't know.' She sighed again, hand on her hip, tongue pressing against the back of her teeth.

Jeremy shook his head and drained the rest of his pint. 'These are not good wifely answers.'

A couple walked up to the bar and as the man nudged her out of the way so he could have a look at the beers on tap, she took a stumbled step forward and said, exasperated, 'Can you just tell me if you've seen him.'

'Have I seen Seb?' Jeremy mused as if it was a great philosophical question. 'Now you come to mention it, I may have seen him earlier with Jamie.'

Anna pounced on the news. 'You did?'

'Maybe.' He cocked his head and she felt him toying with her.

'Where were they going, Jeremy?'

'Wouldn't you like to know?' he smirked, tapping his nose.

She sighed and he grinned. 'D'you know what?' she said after a second. 'No, actually I wouldn't. I just wanted to know if he was alive or not.' She pulled her hair back from her face into an elastic band and started to turn and leave.

But then Jeremy said, 'Oh, he's alive all right. Very, very alive. Most alive I've seen him in years.'

She waved a hand in dismissal. 'I don't want to know.'

'No? You sure? I'd want to know if it was me.'

She took a step back. 'I'm not playing this game, Jeremy.'

'Suit yourself.' He chuckled and turned back to the bar, pouring a handful of peanuts into his mouth and laughing with his friend as she started to walk away.

Just as she got to the door though, she paused when she saw someone familiar sitting in the booth on the far side of the bar, white hair swept back from a dirty-tanned face, thick black horn-rimmed glasses, his paper held low so he could see her. She looked at the door and then back at the booth. After a second's hesitation she started to walk towards him, down the opposite side of the bar where she had been chatting to Jeremy, past the woman who had nudged her partner and was now pretending not to look up as if some Z-list celebrity was in the vicinity. Anna decided they must have been to school together, she looked about the right age.

But then the woman stopped her as she saw Anna coming closer and said, 'You're Anna Whitehall, aren't you?'

'Yes. Yes, it's me, I'm back.' Anna held her arms wide. 'Gawp all you like. Yes, it's me. I'm Anna Whitehall. Yes, I was forced to come back. No, I never made it big. Yes, I'm here.' She sighed, almost about to give a twirl, ready to say more and involve the whole pub, but the woman cut her off.

'Well, I hope you're proud of yourself. My kids are in Razzmatazz or, I should say, were in Razzmatazz.' She looked at the man sitting next to her. 'She's the reason they're not doing it any more. Just went in and told them they were all crap and then quit.'

Anna, shocked by the revelation that this woman didn't know her from Adam and inwardly cringing at her spiel, opened her mouth to reply but the woman wouldn't let her.

'I was told you were a top dancer. We trusted you to teach those kids and now—' She held her arms out wide as if there was nothing. 'Shocking. Shocking behaviour,' she said and turned her back on Anna who mumbled an apology and scuttled to the corner where the man was still watching over his paper.

'Hi, Dad,' she muttered, sliding into the seat opposite him.

'Still causing trouble wherever you go, I see.' He folded the paper and smiled. 'About time you said

130

hello to your old dad.' Then he did a surreptitious check over towards the door.

'Are you waiting for someone?'

'No, not at all. What are you doing here on your own?'

'Looking for Seb.'

'Why, have you had a row?'

'Oh God! No.'

He took his glasses off and folded them into his top pocket. 'I like Seb.'

'So do I.'

'He's gentle, kind. I like him. Don't mess it up.'

'Why would I?'

'I know you.'

'Clearly you don't.'

Her dad leant back, folded his arms across his chest and laughed. 'Always the same. Always quick with an answer. You are allowed to relax, Anna.'

'How am I meant to relax when the first thing you say to me is not to fuck up my relationship?'

'Don't swear, you sound like your mother. And calm down. Relax.'

'I am relaxed.'

'You're not, you look ready to bolt. Sit back. Go on, sit back, lean against the wall. Slump. That's more like it!' He laughed as she curled herself back awkwardly and tried to suppress her own smirk. 'Now, what do you want to drink?'

'Nothing.' She glanced over at the bar. 'The wine tastes like cat's pee.'

Her dad ignored her and called over to the blonde behind the bar. 'Babs...'

'What can I do for you, my lovely?' Barbara leant over the edge of the bar, wafting a cloud of Rive Gauche their way.

'A Guinness and she'll have a dry white wine,' he said, gesturing to Anna. 'And, Babs, the good stuff, not the old crap you've got behind the bar.'

Barbara raised a brow, clearly dubious about wasting the good stuff on Anna, but her dad winked and handed Barbara three crisp fivers saying, 'And have one for yourself while you're there.' Which seemed to soften her.

When it arrived, the wine was sharp and crisp, a New Zealand Sauvignon that tasted like liquid gold. 'Very nice.' Anna said after one sip.

Her dad looked up over the rim of his Guinness and grinned. 'You see, honey, you've just got to know how to ask.'

'Or to be an old alcoholic regular,' she said, a brow raised.

'Never have been good with people, have you? Never seen the subtleties.'

Anna made a face and went back to her wine.

'But it's there,' her dad carried on. 'I've always known it is.'

'What?' she asked.

He leant forward as if whispering a secret. 'Your soft side. The bit you got from me.'

132

'Oh shut up.' Anna rolled her eyes and crossed her legs to the side so she could survey the pub rather than have direct eye contact with her dad.

'You mark my words, it's there.' He did a little laugh and then his phone beeped a text that distracted him for a moment. While reading it, he said at the same time, 'Go easy on those kids. That little group. I saw them perform last year in the square. They made your granny laugh, God rest her soul.'

'I'm not doing it any more, so it doesn't matter.'

Her dad wasn't listening. 'She always liked watching you dance when you were a kid. Wasn't such a fan of all that pressure, mind you. She'd pull me aside and say, *Patrick you be careful, Mona is going to ruin that kid.*'

Anna swallowed and tried not to listen. There weren't many people that she remembered adoring, but her granny was up there at the top of the sparse list. They'd make Eccles Cakes together when her mum needed a break or her parents were rowing and she'd be marched up the road and deposited at the yellow front door of her granny's house with its curling paint and knocker shaped like a lion's head. Anna would stand on a stool and squash the fruit into the rounds of pastry with her little hands while her granny would pinch them shut and she'd watch as she scored the tops. They'd eat them piping hot and burn their chins when the fruit rolled out, while her granny would get her knitting out and Anna would curl up next to her and just smell the warmth and the safety. And when Anna said things like, *'I'm going to be a prima ballerina when I grow up. Just like Mum,'* her granny would pause and say, *'You know I always like watching the corps de ballet. Like seeing them move in unison.'*

'Do we have to talk about this now?' Anna put her wine down on a frayed coaster. 'I haven't seen you for six months and you're straight in with this.'

'And I'd say, no, it's OK, she's OK. She loves it,' her dad went on. 'And she'd say, she loves the *idea* of it. Very perceptive, your grandma. You should have seen her more before she died.'

Anna found she suddenly couldn't get air in further than her breastbone so had to look to the ceiling to try and take a breath. She felt her dad watching her, felt like her emotions were under scrutiny, so she glanced back his way and said defensively, 'Mum says she'll pay for the wedding only if you don't come.'

She fired the words at him like arrows. Ping, ping, ping, bullseye. You have won this round, Anna, congratulations. Your prize is the fleeting look of devastation in your father's eye.

'Well, well,' he said after a second to compose himself and another sip of his drink. He coughed. 'She never fails to surprise me. She's a wily old cow, my God.' He ran a hand over his mouth, rasping over a couple of days' worth of white stubble. Then he held both hands up as if in surrender. 'And I certainly don't have the cash to match that offer. What are you going to do?'

Anna hadn't expected to feel quite so dreadful. She suddenly wished the words were on a fishing line and she could just reel them back in. 'I don't know. I haven't decided.'

He nodded. 'You should do what you can to get the best. She can give you the best.' He smiled softly and took another sip. 'And you always have liked the best.'

Anna twirled the stem of her glass around in her fingers. 'It's not getting the best, Dad, it's getting something. There's no other way.' An image of Nettleton village hall did a little dance in front of her eyes.

Her dad paused, then leant forward and said, 'There's always another way, sweetheart.'

Anna glanced away, her cheeks flushing pink and, just as she did, she saw Hermione Somers-Brown strut into the pub.

'Hermione?' she said, shocked.

Now Hermione was someone for whom the whole pub paused. Paused to drink in the skin-tight snakeskin trousers, the fluorescent-yellow silk vest, the loops of Chanel pearls and the beautiful, caramel blonde hair piled into a candyfloss blob on top of her head.

A model-like pout on her lips, Hermione sashayed through the onlookers, one red wedge mule in front of the other.

'What are you doing here?' Anna asked, a feeling not unlike relief that her friend had realised how in need she was and travelled from London to the sticks to see her.

'She, darling, is here for me,' she heard her dad whisper across the table.

'You're what?' Anna looked between them, at the slightly guilty quirk of Hermione's lips and the absolute smug delight on her father's face. 'Urgh, no way?' Anna sneered.

''Fraid so.' Her dad laughed and then, giving Hermione a quick peck on the cheek, disappeared to the loo while Anna just stared at her friend, horrified.

'Er, hello! What the hell are you doing?'

Hermione flicked a strand of hair out of her face and shrugged. 'He was on Tinder.'

'So? So what? Are you dating?'

Hermione thought about the question for a second and then drawled, 'I wouldn't call it dating as such.' Then she smirked the corner of one slicked-red lip. 'How's Luke?'

'He's shit. Don't change the subject.' Anna glanced over her shoulder to see her dad coming out of the bathroom. 'What is it, then?' she hissed.

'It's just—' Hermione paused, smoothed down her acid-yellow top. 'Sex.'

'Oh Jesus Christ. You booty-call my dad?'

'If you want to put it like that.' Hermione sniggered. 'Yeah, I suppose that's pretty much hit the nail on the head.'

'Ready, my darling?' Anna's dad appeared next to them, his hair slicked back with water from the tap, his black shirt unbuttoned to his chest like some movie mogul, white chest hair poking out, cream chinos that Anna hadn't noticed before and were unusually smart for her father, but still wearing his black flip-flops.

'Always. I'll call you tomorrow, Anna,' she said, blowing her a kiss.

'Don't bother, I've lost my phone.' Anna slouched back in her seat sulkily.

'Well, let's lunch maybe later in the week. Ta-ta.' Hermione was already sauntering back out of the pub, as if the air was so distasteful she could only stand a short burst.

'Bye, honey.' Her dad gave Anna a quick peck on the cheek and said, 'Don't forget what I said about Seb. Whatever's happened, don't be too proud to apologise.'

Chapter Ten

Seb never came home that night. Anna lay on top of the sheet, staring across at the whirring fan, listening to the old bed creaking as she turned over, restless, and then the silence of the night change to the sound of birds waking in the fields as the pitch black softened with the faded light of early morning.

She wondered, if she did accept her mum's money, who would give her away. She cringed at the idea of Seb's dad Roger, or her mum's thirty-year-old gigolo, Eduardo. But why pick another father when she had one of her own to strut proudly down the aisle with her?

Would he be proud? She'd always thought it was her place not to be proud of him, to look down at his bad behaviour and choices, but what had she ever done to make him proud?

Anna rolled over, pulled the sheet up over her ears.

What had she ever done to make him proud? He'd come to her shows dressed in an old Barbour, tatty trousers, holey woolly jumper and cravat and she'd pretended that she didn't know him. He had come whether she was The Swan Queen or not, and at the time she had thought that that made him weak – the fact that he would come and see her just for her.

She had no problem introducing her mother to the school director, dressed in her fur coat and clutching her Chanel, but she'd gloss over the subject when it came to her shabby old dad. And her granny…

She buried her head in the pillow.

Oh God, she remembered watching him wheel her outside after Anna'd lied and said that the champagne reception was for sponsors only. She'd made them all sit in a tiny Jewish cafe round the corner and eat salt beef sandwiches and drink lemon tea while her granny said what a shame it was that they weren't allowed the bubbles. She wished now that she'd visited the old people's home where she'd spent her last couple of years and showered her with magnums of champagne. But, actually, she couldn't remember if she'd been more than once to see her. She'd told herself that the sight of all the old people in the grey room eating apple puree with a ninety-inch TV blaring in the background was all too much but, really, Anna had spent all that time wrapped up in herself.

As she listened to the birds outside and the odd car driving past, the heat lying heavy on her body like a blanket, she remembered her father looking round the ornate decoration of The Waldegrave, raising a brow at the Moroccan-tiled spa pool, the trays of espresso martinis lined up on the edge of the sunken bar, and the doormen in red jackets and top hats. How he had made some comment about it all being too grand for him, how he would have to wait outside and chat with the staff, and she had ushered him out before the wedding planner could have heard.

Anna stared up at the crack in the ceiling and prayed for sleep. She felt like Scrooge at the mercy of the ghosts: when would the nightmare memories end?

As she crossed the square to the shop the next morning, the air was like soup. Thick and gloopy and moving through it was like groping through hot fog. Anna was exhausted, there were big dark smudges under her eyes that were too much even for Touche Éclat, and she felt like she lacked the energy to push her way through the insidious heat that crept into her lungs and forced short, choppy breaths like being in a sauna.

She almost didn't see Jackie jogging past her, headphones in her ears, nose in the air, seemingly deliberately determined to ignore Anna.

But Anna was still suffering from the haunting nightmares of the previous night and the idea of Razzmatazz making her granny laugh. 'Wait!' she called.

Jackie either didn't hear, or pretended to ignore her.

'Wait, Jackie.' Anna called again, taking a couple of quick steps forward, her hand outstretched, and this time Jackie did slow and turn, jogging on the spot while pulling one earphone out.

'What?' Jackie snapped. 'I've already heard that you've dumped them. I can't talk to you about it,' she said, then paused and took a step closer to Anna. 'Do you realise how much they've done on their own? They put that group together. They practise because they want to. They meet because they want to. There are no groups here because there's no one to bloody teach them and no one to drive them all to bloody London so they can go to fancy ballet schools—'

'I was just going to say that I'll do it,' Anna said, cutting her off. 'I'll do another rehearsal.'

'Too late. We don't want you.' Jackie shrugged. 'You've missed your chance.'

'Oh. Right. OK.' Anna pulled her bag up on her shoulder, feeling a strange sense of disappointment. Surely this rejection should have been a relief, she'd tried to make amends but hadn't been needed. Woo-hoo, she was off the hook. But how would she let people know? That woman in the pub, for example, who thought her so dreadful, how would she tell her that she'd tried? Or her dead granny, who might have missed that precise moment as she watched from above.

Anna shook her head, her dead granny watching over her? Really. Don't start getting sentimental, Anna, she chastised herself. The tiredness and the soupy heat were clearly affecting her. Backing away from Jackie, who had started jogging on the spot, she reminded herself that this was a good thing. Woo-hoo.

'Just kidding,' shouted Jackie. 'There's a rehearsal tomorrow. Don't be such a bitch to them this time.' Then she laughed to herself and, putting her earphone back in, trotted off in her purple Lycra, disappearing into the mist.

Anna was left momentarily taken aback, alone in a pea soup of hot fog. Bugger, she thought, her granny had better damn well be watching because otherwise she was suddenly teaching this bunch of misfits again for no reason other than a bit of Nettleton-inspired guilt. That was where sentimentality got her.

'Goodness me,' said Mrs Beedle as Anna walked up to the shop. 'Isn't this a surprise? Early.' She locked her sludge-green Morris Minor Traveller and pushed her massive owl sunglasses up into her grey beehive, then went round to the boot and fiddled about with the rusty lock until it clicked open. 'Is that a guilty conscience about my clock, Anna Whitehall?'

'No,' she said quickly, shaking her head.

Mrs Beedle laughed, hauling open the boot with one hand. 'So like your father.'

The words made Anna shudder. Especially with the Luke debacle and not knowing what had happened to Seb. Was adultery hereditary, she wondered, then scoffed – adultery! It wasn't adultery. One meeting didn't equal a two-year affair with the local flame-haired auctioneer that ripped apart a little family and left her mother with the burden of a lifetime of revenge, and Anna with a lifetime of having to find different ways to agree with her fury.

What's that, Anna? What's that necklace you're wearing? Did he buy you that for your birthday? With her money, I suppose. He has no money of his own, Anna. She'll have paid for it. Or if he does have money, he's hiding it from me. Buying you that with what? If it's his money why are we living in this...this dump? My family had a lot of money in Sevilla, Anna. We were important people. I was from an important family. And now look. Look around. Look at that plasterwork? Look at that sink? Look at that oven? And these...baked beans? I didn't even know what a baked bean was in Spain. Now look at them. I will die drowned in baked beans. If you want to wear that, Anna, don't wear it in front of me.

'Come on then, we have work to do.' Mrs Beedle rested a hand on the boot of her car and beckoned for Anna to come over and join her. 'Picked this up from a dealer yesterday, needs work but look at that craftsmanship.' She traced her podgy hand over the wooden inlay and carving along the edge of a shabby chest of drawers wedged into the boot of her vintage van. 'Don't look at it like that. Sand, paint and varnish and it might make a dent in the profit lost on that clock.'

Anna was about to say something, offer an apology or add something in her defence when she looked over and saw the smirk on Mrs Beedle's lips.

'Now, let's see if you've still got any muscles. Help me get this thing into the shop.'

When was it, Anna thought, as she lumbered across the road with the wooden chest, that she had lost her strength? She was yoga-fit, but if she looked at her back in the mirror there would no longer be the sinew lines of muscle. She wondered if her calves would even support her on her pointes, how good her line

143

would be if she tried. As she put her end of the chest down on the carpet, she had a momentary pang for the self that used to untie her shoes and compare the blood-blackened toes and blisters with the girl next to her. To inspect the wounds in all their gory detail.

'Shall I make the tea?' Anna asked, backing away towards the counter as Mrs Beedle put her overalls on and started wrapping sandpaper round a block of wood.

'If you want. Or you could just help me with this?' she said, looking up over her glasses.

'No.' Anna shook her head. 'No, I think I'll make the tea and then keep on sorting.' She indicated the stockroom. Today felt like a day for hiding.

'Suit yourself.' Mrs Beedle shrugged and started pulling the drawers out of the dresser and laying them on a sheet of clear plastic. 'Oh God, there's clothes in here.' She held up an old woollen dress, a fringed Spanish shawl, a flowered house-coat and a cream satin slip with lace along the edges. 'You can add this lot to the stuff out back. Some of it's not too bad,' Mrs Beedle called and bundled the discarded clothes up into a ball that she threw across to Anna.

As she caught it, a couple of the items fell to the floor. Anna bent down and scooped up the slip and the bright turquoise shawl then, as she pushed the stockroom curtain to one side, she glanced back. She thought she had sensed Mrs Beedle watching her, but her head was down, concentrating on taking the first layer of grime off the top of the chest.

A few minutes later, when Anna plonked a stewed-orange mug of tea down on the counter top with some gingernuts, she went to go back into the hot-box stockroom but, instead, found herself staying where she was. Watching.

Mrs Beedle had propped open the front door. Cloudy light was streaming in, carrying with it the smells of dewy pavement warmed in sunshine, freshly watered geraniums and the sharp tang of cut grass. The cat was basking on the front step. She could see the hazy outline of a couple standing in the square laughing, the sound just audible over Classic FM, which was playing on an old paint-splattered radio, and the steady, monotonous noise of the sandpaper rubbing.

Anna found that she'd pushed herself up on the counter and was sitting, legs swinging like when she was a girl in her dad's outhouse, watching him drilling and sanding and sawing, pausing to ask her to hand him a wrench, a screwdriver or hold the nails in her cupped hands that he would take with his rough fingers while shouting the answers to some radio quiz and getting cross with the contestants for getting the answers wrong.

Anna sipped her Lapsang Souchong but tasted instead the Coca-Colas her dad kept stacked in bottles in the corner that, if she was good, she could have one with a straw, while he gulped his back.

In summer sun as dense as today's, while her mum would try to defy the muggy clouds and top up her tan in the garden, Anna remembered trailing after her dad round car boot sales. They'd drive there with the top down on his vintage Merc, she'd wear her red shorts and an old Lacoste polo shirt, with white Green Flash trainers. If her dad saw something he could make a profit on, he'd walk on and get Anna to go back, briefed with how much to pay and some sob story about only having the motley selection of coins she had in her hand. Before she'd go, he'd stop her and say, 'Show me.' And she'd pull her sad, forlorn orphan face and he'd say, 'Good girl. Excellent.' And invariably they'd fleece the stallholders from here to the London suburbs of every piece of antique furniture they owned.

When she laughed, caught off-guard by the thought of it, Mrs Beedle looked up and allowed a momentary smile to toy with her lips before putting her hands on her hips and saying sternly, 'I don't pay you to sit there, Anna. What are you going to do?'

'I don't erm…' Anna didn't want to go back out to the stockroom where it was hot and lonely and full of boxes of old jewellery. Where there was a danger of other memories clawing their way to the surface. She might, for example, think about the holiday she'd gone on later with her dad and the mistress, Molly. Where she'd lain on a sun-lounger, massive sun hat covering her face and refused to speak directly to Molly the entire trip. Talking to her through her dad. Her aim to be as vile as possible so she'd never have to come again. She cringed as she thought of some of the awful things she'd said…*If she wants me to do that*

*she's going to have to ask me in a much nicer way.
I'm not going with you if she's going to wear that, it's
embarrassing, it's far too young for her.*

'I could dust.' Anna offered.

'Dust?'

'In the sunlight everything looks very dusty.'

Mrs Beedle watched her for a moment, narrowed
her eyes and to Anna it felt like she too was seeing the
little seven-year-old who would come in with her dad
and sit playing with the cat while they laughed over
incredulous business deals and eventually settled on a
price that left one of them hand on heart saying, *'I've
been robbed.'*

'OK, Anna, you dust.' She seemed to be holding
in a smirk as Anna pushed herself off the counter
and scrabbled around to find some Pledge and an old
yellow duster. She started by the left-hand window
and wiped down every one of the jewelled brooches,
pinning them to the mannequin rather than putting
them back in the box. Next she folded up the horrible
badger stole and replaced it with the beautiful fringed
shawl that had come in the chest, bright red flowers
embroidered onto the turquoise material and tiny
blue birds dancing along the edges. Picking some of
the belts from where they sat on a shelf up high she
wound them round the waist of the dummy, snakeskin
overlapping leather and gold chain-mail. Then she
reshuffled the collection of bags, finding amongst the
tatty heap an exquisite crocodile-skin clutch which she
rested at the front in all its glory.

Then she moved over to the right, polishing the little enamel boxes that sat on top of a large mahogany chest of drawers and wiping down a bronze lamp with cherubs on the base. But instead of putting it back where she had found it, she turned it over in her hands and inspected it, thought how gruesome the fringing was on the lampshade and how dated. She glanced over at Mrs Beedle, who seemed absorbed in her sanding, and when she was certain she wasn't looking, pulled all the tassels and the strip of braid off the edge of the shade to make it look more contemporary and less old-granny, then put it back on the edge of the chest rather than on the odd three-legged table where it had been sitting, incongruously, at knee height.

Next she moved onto a stack of plates covered in lily of the valley and bluebells. After dusting them down, she arranged them one by one on the Welsh dresser that loomed on the side wall adjacent to the mahogany chest. In between the two was the emerald chaise longue coated in cat hairs. Wiping them off into a nasty furball, she walked round the shop gathering up every cushion she could find and plumped them up along the backboard – rich black velvets sat next to blood-red satins and jostled for space next to ornate blue toile, tartans of dense wool in soft greys and creams and beautiful gold and navy brocade – the green sofa suddenly becoming more like a throne fit for royalty. Along the armrest she draped the blankets that Mrs Beedle had stacked in a dark corner – patterned purple lambswool in similar plaids to the cushions and so soft that if it wasn't so damn hot she would wrap herself in one and curl up to sleep. Rest her exhausted eyes.

To set a proper scene, she pulled over a white, shabby-chic standard lamp that was sticking out from a heap of junk at the back and placed it between the chaise longue and the Welsh dresser, before draping the hooks with the sparkling diamente necklaces she'd found in the stockroom and a collection of French christening mugs with tiny porcelain flowers and gilded script. Finally she repositioned a huge gold mirror on a nail above the chaise longue, hung a strand of black pearls from one corner and stood back to survey her work.

All polished and gleaming, it was like the kind of room that drew you in and back to a warm, cosy past of hot chocolate and log fires or, as it was now, dancing with morning sunlight and inviting someone to lift the whole collection up as it was and place it in their front room.

'Very nice.' Mrs Beedle was suddenly standing next to her, taking in the newly organised quarter of her shop.

Anna turned to see if she was being sarcastic but, from the look of calm surprise on Mrs Beedle's face, she was hiding it well if she was. Then Anna shrugged and said, 'I am quite good at organising.'

'So I see.' Mrs Beedle stepped forward and lifted up one of the cushions. 'I forgot I even had these.'

'I saw them, you know, in the back.'

She nodded. 'Yes. Yes, they cost me a fortune. They look good.'

Anna paused. 'Thanks.'

Then Mrs Beedle gave her a quick tap on the arm before going back to her sanding. 'Not as much of a waste of space as I thought.'

'Is that a compliment, Mrs Beedle?'

'If you want,' she shrugged and Anna found herself beaming as she watched the old woman walk away.

But she didn't get to bask in the feeling for long because, when she looked back to admire her handiwork, the bell on the shop door tinkled and, while Anna didn't look up, she felt the mood change. Then she heard Mrs Beedle suddenly gather up all the dirty mugs and say, 'I think this one's for you,' before disappearing out the back to wash up.

Anna glanced around to see Seb standing in the doorway, silhouetted in the murky sunlight but then, as he walked closer, she felt herself frown at the look of him. Face covered in stubble, shirt tails hanging loose, no jacket, sweat streaking the blue of his shirt. Had he been to work looking like that, she wondered. His hair was sticking up all over the place, his eyes were bloodshot and his lips pale. There was a sheen of sweat over his brow that made her wonder if he'd slept at all or if he was just crazy hungover.

'You look terrible,' she said.

'So do you.' He stood by the chest of drawers, his hand tracing the outline of the newly sanded carving.

Anna thought of the movie-inspired leap into his arms that she'd rehearsed in her head. The idea of it seemed so preposterous now it almost made her laugh out loud, which, given the look on Seb's face, would have been highly inappropriate. 'Where have you been?' she said instead.

Seb ran a hand through his messy hair and then grabbed a bunch of it, looked to the ceiling and almost shouted, 'Why did you have to make everything so complicated?'

Anna stiffened where she was standing. 'I didn't.'

'Yes you did. You always make everything so hard. Why can't you be simple? Why can't you let life be simple?'

'I don't think you'd like me if I did that. I think that's why we're together.'

'Oh you think so? Really. Christ, Anna, I could handle a bit of simplicity.' He put both hands on the wooden surface and braced his body against them. 'You know what would be my dream? A cheese fucking sandwich. Just that nothing else, just cheese. A simple cheese sandwich.'

'OK, Seb, well you can have that any time you like.' She made a face like he'd gone mad.

'I can't. I can't have that because we only have posh cheese. We don't have Cheddar, we have brie and Stilton. And I want that bread, the crap stuff that looks like polystyrene. I want crap bread and crap cheese.'

Anna didn't say anything; Seb was pacing, small steps up and down as he listed his sandwich. She wondered if Mrs Beedle was listening out the back. She could hear the tap running, so hoped that might block his insanity out.

'I spent the night with Melissa Hope,' he said mid-pace, turning to look at her with an expression of utter exhaustion.

'You did what?' Anna leant forward, trying to place the name and suddenly remembering some blonde girl with huge boobs from the year above them who was friends with Seb's brother, Jeremy. She angled her head slightly towards him, hoping that he might say it again and she'd hear differently if her ear was closer to his words.

'I spent the night with Melissa Hope. I didn't have sex with her, but I kissed her and I slept in her bed and I have no idea why I did it and I didn't want to do it but, Jesus, you made everything so complicated.'

Anna held up a hand. 'You can't blame me for this.'

'I can.' Seb nodded helplessly. 'I can because this isn't me. I don't do this. I live a normal, simple cheese sandwich life and now suddenly I'm waking up in the bed of the girl who shagged the whole rowing team at school.'

'She works in the pub sometimes, doesn't she?' Anna said.

'So?' Seb had his hand back raking through his hair, and turned to glare at her.

'Nothing.' Anna shook her head. 'It just means I have to see her, that's all.'

'That's all? That's all you can think about? That you'll have to see her? Anna...I have slept in the bed of someone else when we are meant to be getting married. Don't you think this is odd? Don't you think you're missing the point?'

She took a step closer from where she was standing and bit her lip, looking at him in his dishevelled clothes. 'Don't you think maybe I'm trying to miss the point?'

'See—' He held his arms out wide. 'See, that's exactly my point. Complicated. Fucking complicated,' he said and stalked away. He got as far as the doorway, rested one hand on the frame and turned around to look at her. 'I—' he started, then swallowed. 'I was really drunk. I think I just wanted a bed to lie down in. But I'm sorry. I'm really angry, but I'm sorry.'

Anna didn't reply, wanted desperately to do her run and jump. Wanted to throw herself at him and say that none of it mattered. That they should get on a train to Gretna Green and to hell with the rest of them. But something kept her stuck to the spot where she was standing. There would be no running into his arms. Years of conditioning made her just run her tongue over her lips instead. She pushed her shoulders back and raised her chin just a fraction, her feet defaulting to third position almost as if locking her armour into place.

She heard her dad saying, *Don't be too proud to apologise.*

That, though, was swiftly gazumped by an overwhelmingly more powerful and more familiar voice that urged, *Better to stay aloof, darling. Never apologise, never explain. It keeps you one step ahead. It's always worked for me. Aloof poise, there's no way to better it. If no one can break you, Anna, then they can't hurt you. Do you understand?*

Yes she understood. This was the mantra she had lived by. This was the one ingrained into the fabric of her being.

As Seb strode out and his figure faded into the mist, Anna found herself suddenly braced over the edge of the chest she'd just polished, her forearms on the cool mahogany, her head bent over, taking deep breaths that when she exhaled fogged up the shiny surface so she couldn't see her reflection.

When had it worked for her mother? was all she could think. What example did she have? Her father had had an affair and she'd never forgiven him. Now she dated young Spanish men and had too much Botox. His rejection was still a parasite eating away at her from the inside out. *Aloof.* Anna wondered if, as she watched the mist of her breath disappearing, aloof just meant bottling everything up. Her mother was still champing for revenge twenty years later.

When she stood up straight, Anna felt Mrs Beedle walk out of the stockroom, heard her put fresh mugs of tea down on the counter and then come to stand next to her. After a second she heard her say, 'Why don't you help me?' Then she nudged a block of sandpaper in Anna's direction like you might with a stray cat and a saucer of milk.

Anna felt herself stare at it for a second, her eyes blurring in and out of focus then felt her fingers inch forward to trace over the rough grain of the paper, felt the shuddering rasp of her nails as they grazed over it. Picking it up, she felt the solid weight in her hands and, for a moment, forgot about the conversation seconds before.

Mrs Beedle didn't say anything else, just went back to the chest and began rhythmically sanding, as Anna took a few tentative, trance-like steps forward. Once there, she rested her hip on the edge of the chest and, bending her knees slightly, took one downward swipe with the sandpaper, watching the dust sprinkle satisfyingly to the floor. Then she changed her grip on the block so she had it firm and could really apply some pressure and started to really rub the bloody chest of drawers, sanding it down so that the layers of old paint and varnish in the grooves disappeared and nothing but bare, beautiful oak was left behind.

They worked together on it silently, on the framework and the drawers until the whole thing had been stripped back and there was barely a trace of paint. The air swirled with balls of tumbleweed paint dust and there was a smell like burning from the sanded wood. Great drops of sweat fell from Anna's forehead like she was purging everything from inside her. As she stood up, her back felt like it might snap in two, reminding her of a particularly gruelling session with Madame LaRoche. *Down through the ball of your foot, and lift your arabesque higher, Anna, up toward the sky from your hip socket, higher, into penchée. This leg pushes the body down. It cannot do it by itself, Anna. OK, no, it's not right, back to the barre.*

Mrs Beedle straightened her back and took her paint-dusted glasses off to give them a wipe on an old rag. 'Very nice. Good work. Good for someone who once didn't want to chip their nail varnish.'

Anna scoffed. 'I don't mind about my nails.'

Mrs Beedle raised a disbelieving brow and swiped a hand over the surface of the roughened wood. 'What a beauty. What a beauty they were hiding.'

Anna helped her put the drawers back in and they both stood and stared at it. 'Someone didn't know what they had, did they?' Anna said in the end.

'No. No they didn't, which is often the case with the world.'

Anna looked away, wondering if somehow the chest was becoming a metaphor for her life and not wanting to acknowledge it in case Mrs Beedle was expecting some kind of emotional breakdown that would see Anna clasped to her bosom sobbing her eyes out. When she looked back however, Mrs Beedle said, 'I'm going to microwave my tea, do you want me to do yours?' Clearly not remotely in tune with Anna's overactive imagination.

Anna shook her head. Mrs Beedle paused before she went out the back. 'You did well, it looks good.'

'I don't think my side is as good as yours.'

'That was a compliment, Anna. You should just accept it.'

'Well I just…' She shrugged, embarrassed. 'I think I was more enthusiastic than skilled.' She tilted her head to one side. 'Look, here—' She pointed to a bit where the paint was deep in the groove still. 'I don't think I'm very good at it.'

As Mrs Beedle swept through the curtain, she said in a voice just loud enough for Anna to think she may have misheard, 'You were good enough, Anna.' And it was then that she realised Mrs Beedle didn't deal in metaphors or hidden meanings, she just said exactly what she thought, and Anna felt herself stiffen in surprise at how much the sentence seemed to affect her. 'Now go home.'

Chapter Eleven

But Anna couldn't go home. The idea of it made her feel quite ill. She had images of Seb shouting in the shop, the wild panic in his eyes at his own behaviour, the mental pictures of him touching some other woman's body like the cutaways in *9½ Weeks* – all breathy, soft-focus and intense – and, like a dog with fleas, she had to shake her head to make it all go away.

As the afternoon had worn on, the mist had started to lift, replaced by a hanging humidity that left her skin feeling moist. When she pushed her hair off her face it stayed there, tiny droplets of moisture slicking it into place. The square was deserted, too hot for anyone to even sit outside the cafes. Rachel's bakery was closed, as was the bistro, and the gift shop was just turning over its closed sign.

Paris, Milan, New York, Nettleton. She paused in front of the T-shirt in the window. They had no problem believing Nettleton was as good as New York.

She didn't stop walking when she got to her hatchback, instead she took the alleyway down the side of Dapper, a clothes shop that had a three-piece suit in the window, complete with riding crop and top hat, the arm of the sleeve draped around a mannequin wearing a cream-and-blue flowered blouse, matching knee-length skirt and wide-brimmed hat. A banner with, *Just right for Ascot* had been stretched across the window. At the end of the alley was a small cottage-lined road that forked one way into more houses, and the other way towards the fields. Instinctively, she went right. The way she had gone for years after school, down the road, past a cluster of apple trees where Hermione claimed to have lost her virginity, over a wooden fence with the same *Keep Out Private Property* sign dangling off an electrical tag and into a field that stretched out with raspberries as far as the eye could see. What felt like miles and miles of bushes with their little red fruits glistening, plump in the heavy humid air.

It was a Pick Your Own field and Anna and Hermione had worked there one summer term, every afternoon after school for a week, when they were about nine. Mr Milton had paid them in fruit and they'd eaten so many raspberries that Anna puked bright-red sick all over herself. She'd arrived home looking like *Carrie* and everyone had laughed when she'd pretended she was dying some grizzly death.

Now she walked through the canes of green leaves, plucking the odd fat fruit and eating it without thinking, walked knowing exactly the route, finding it strange that her school bag wasn't on her shoulder and her shoes weren't Doc Martens and her clothes weren't her school uniform – the marl-grey sweatshirt and dark-grey worsted wool skirt she had to wear.

She trudged on and on, midges collecting in clouds around her head, her ankles itching from patches of long grass, her skin slick from the cloying warmth. She thought about Seb, about the look on his face in the doorway, about New York, about sitting on the floor in their Bermondsey apartment and sobbing when they had realised how much debt they were in, the humiliation of calling everyone to let them know the wedding was on hold, of sitting for hours on the phone to the administrators getting more and more frustrated and shouting until a woman on the other end cut her off, of hearing her redundancy speech and walking out of her job with all her things from her desk crammed into her Michael Kors tote, a spider plant trailing over the edge, of leaving her scrap book on the bin and not looking back, of standing in the shower and watching the water as it rolled off her, knowing then that the world that she had constructed was built on sticks. It was her own personal Kerplunk, and too many had been pulled out for her to save it. She had been living on sticks since the day her mum had driven her from Nettleton and her dad had leant in through the car window and said, 'No matter what, I lov—' but her mum had floored the accelerator so he'd had to stop mid-sentence and jump back or else face decapitation. And her mum had said, *'Love? Useless bugger doesn't know the meaning of the word. The only person he loves, Anna, is himself.'*

Ahead of her, through the rows of raspberries, she could see the sky start to change, the fuzzy white tendrils of mist left over from the day were getting thicker – clumping together like marshmallows. The heavy blue of the sky was darkening, like dirty paint-water that eventually always turns grey. The smell in the air was changing, from hot and sticky like warm bread to sharp and tangy, like fresh-cut grass and dew in the morning. A flock of black birds darted up from among the bushes and flew away en masse, deserting the field. Anna pushed her hair back from her head and paused for a moment, knowing exactly what was coming. Knowing that in a second there would be a crash and she would be engulfed in a wall of rain and she would be standing in the middle of a field with as much distance behind her as in front of her. She had no raincoat, no umbrella, no cafe to dart into. She was going to get wet.

And then someone tipped over a bucket in the sky.

Rain cascaded in sheets all around her, shaking the little raspberries off their stalks, shuddering leaves, pounding on the dry, cracked earth at her feet, and pouring down her face like tears. She stopped and put her head back and shut her eyes and let herself get soaked. Soaked until her feet were sloshing in their shoes and her clothes were stuck to her body and her hair clumped and dripped water down her back.

Then she ran. Her feet were squelching so she took off her shoes and ran barefoot, splashing through the pools of mud, jumping from the thunder. Ran so the wet earth flicked up on her calves and pushed up through her toes, ran with her arm outstretched so it flicked the dancing leaves, ran so the water blinded her eyes and blurred everything ahead of her.

At the far side of the field she was confronted by a much more impressive metal gate than the one she'd scaled to get in. Looking up at the rows of bars, dripping with rain, she knew her only option was to start climbing. Wiping her palms on her sodden top, she took a deep breath and hauled herself up. Scaling her way up the gate as it wobbled precariously under her weight, she paused to straddle the top rung, made the mistake of looking down and, distracted by how high up she was and how far she could see, her hands slipped and she slid halfway down the other side, bumping on the rungs and landing in an ungainly heap.

'Shit,' she muttered, picking herself up from the mud and inspecting the grazes on her elbows and knees. A far cry from her primped and perfect opera house persona, she felt like her nine-year-old self, mud-splattered, grazed, carefree.

But then she turned and saw, across the road, the house that she'd grown up in and was fast-tracked back to the present reality. Full of cares, worries, debts, hurt feelings and damaged pride.

Swiping the dirt away, licking her hand to clean her cuts, she darted across the road, up the wonky path and sheltered under the porch of her childhood home. Her dad's vintage cherry-red Mercedes in the drive, the rain bouncing off its beautifully waxed exterior. She hadn't been here for years. It took her a second to summon the courage to ring the bell.

'Hang on!' she heard after so long had passed that she'd assumed no one was home. 'Anna!' Her dad answered the door in his dressing gown.

'Who is it, Patrick?' she heard Hermione call.

'Oh, you've got to be kidding me. It's the middle of the afternoon.' Anna shook her head, and took a step back.

'Anna, wait, come in. It's pouring.' Her dad beckoned for her to come closer.

'No way.' She shook her head and backed out into the deluge.

Anna marched away through the warm rain that bubbled now in puddles on the street and, blocking her ears to her dad's shouts, wondered where the hell she was going to go. She wasn't sitting around with those two, post-coital, in their dressing gowns. And there was no way she could get back over that fence.

The rain lashed in warm fat droplets, her knee stung as the water rolled over the cut. The road ahead looked endless.

'Anna?' she heard a female voice say behind her. 'Anna, what are you doing here? Are you OK?'

Anna turned to see Rachel from the bakery cycling up the road, a big, red waterproof cape on that covered practically the whole bike as well as herself.

'You look like Little Red Riding Hood,' Anna said, because they were the only words that would come to mind.

Rachel laughed, looking down at herself in the pouring rain. 'I suppose I do.' Then as she hopped off her bike and crossed in front of Anna to open the gate to her wisteria-draped cottage, she said, 'You're soaked. Do you want to come in?'

Anna paused, looked from Rachel standing with her bike to the beautiful white cottage with a tabby cat sitting in the window and the huge purple flowers bunched like big, juicy grapes over the front door and she realised suddenly that it wasn't Hermione that she had got the job picking raspberries with, it was Rachel. And she hadn't gone to her own house, but here, to Rachel's parents', that was why no one had got cross with her about the raspberry juice because Rachel's mum had taken her clothes and washed and dried them before she'd gone home. It was Rachel's mum who'd laughed at her *Carrie* impression. And as the tumble dryer spun, Anna had sat in Rachel's dressing gown while Rachel's mum had laid out a Victoria Sponge, plump with cream and jam and dusted with icing sugar, and home-made lemonade that clinked with ice cubes as it was taken out of the fridge. When the big chunks of lemon had tumbled into her glass, and she had watched as Rachel had heaped in a teaspoon of sugar, Anna had said with a touch of panic, *I'm not allowed sugar. I can't have it, it's part of my training.* Rachel's mum had looked at her like she'd never felt so sorry for someone and Anna had tried to smile. Without saying anything, she'd swapped the lemonade for a glass of tap water and then sliced the smallest sliver of Victoria Sponge, rested her hand on Anna's shoulder and said, *I reckon this won't do too much harm.* When Anna had eyed it nervously, Rachel's mum had sat down and cut a massive slice for herself, winked at Anna and said, *Don't worry, we won't tell, will we, Rache?*

But, after Anna had left for London and only come back to Nettleton for holidays, she had found herself cutting all ties to Rachel for exactly that reason – because she held nothing for her except memories of those fun, carefree days. And for Anna, who dreaded coming back to stay with her father, resenting him so much that she armoured herself up as best she could – brittle and defensive – she couldn't still frolic in fields or sit on high stools and drink lemonade and eat Victoria Sponge. It was all too much, all too confusing, the two worlds juxtaposed too much. So she had just severed their friendship without a word. She hadn't even sent a card when Rachel's mum had died.

Now, as Rachel was standing with her hand on the gate, Anna said, completely out of the blue, 'I was really sorry to hear about your mum.'

Rachel tipped her head and looked slightly puzzled, then nodded and said after a moment's pause, 'That's OK. Thank you.'

'I really liked her,' Anna said as the rain lashed down between them.

Rachel laughed. 'Me too.' Then, as the pouring water seemed to get heavier and the thunder rolled in closer, Rachel said. 'Just stay till it stops raining if you like, Anna?'

And, in the face of such gentle kindness, Anna did the one thing that she never thought she would do in front of anyone ever, especially not in front of Rachel of all people. She cried. Big, heavy tears that merged with the rain and would have been disguised had Anna not let out a sob when she opened her mouth to say, *No, I'll keep going thank you*. But she hadn't said that because Rachel had let go of the bike and run over and put her arm around her shoulders and led her inside the picturesque little cottage and closed the door on the rain.

'But I do not understand. Why would you go on the Internet dating if you have already found a person that you want?' Philippe, the dashing French bistro owner and seemingly Rachel's husband, lounged back in his chair at the head of the kitchen table. 'I would be glad that I didn't have to go on the Internet.' Then he sat forward, his brow furrowed. 'You put people into Yeses and Nos?' He blew out a breath, 'It is like the animals, non? Too fat, too skinny, too ugly to eat.'

They were seated around a big farmhouse kitchen table, its surface soft from use, the raw wood scratched and beaten. Anna felt like she'd been gathered up in warm blankets as she blew her nose on a big, soft Kleenex and sipped from a steaming mug of tea, perfectly brewed and in a chunky white mug with uneven edges, hand-thrown on the potter's wheel. On the table was a bunch of hydrangeas in a jug, big and pink like footballs on sticks. Philippe was opposite her, drinking a glass of red wine and cutting furiously into one of Rachel's fruit tarts, kiwi and crème patissiere falling onto the little plate. When she had walked in all wet and red-faced, he had looked her up and down and said, 'It is the antique girl who sits at my table and orders nothing.' Then he smiled and she had done another humiliating sob. They had both been so sweet to her that, in a moment of unfamiliar vulnerability, she had recounted her whole sorry tale.

'Tindle,' Philippe said through a mouthful of pastry.

'Tind-er,' Rachel had corrected.

'*Amadou*,' Philippe nodded.

'What does that mean?'

'In French tinder is *amadou*. The dry wood, for the fire.'

'Dead wood.' Anna blew her hair out of her eyes. 'How apt.'

'Luke Lloyd.' Rachel sucked in a breath. 'Of all people.'

Anna had to look away. She remembered, suddenly, not just axing Rachel as a friend but as part of her defence mechanisms actively building her up as an enemy, so clearly aware of the heart she wore on her sleeve. Her kindness and sweetness had been something easy to disparage. One of Anna's more despicable moments had come after Hermione had stolen Rachel's diary and they'd found Luke's name surrounded by hearts. Anna had persuaded him to sit by Rachel in the square, lean in for a kiss and, as Rachel closed her eyes ready, to walk away. She shut her eyes when she thought about it now, too embarrassed to look up. She cut into her own little tart, blackcurrants and figs delicately arranged in slices on top of the dense, wobbling crème and pastry that snapped sharp in two as she pushed the side of her fork down into it. The taste in her mouth was like summer, reminding her of sitting round the table at the back of Rachel's mum's bakery eating warm chocolate croissants that her mum would make before their eyes and drinking thick, gloopy hot chocolate out of mugs with no handles so that they would grasp them with both hands like a bowl and drink till only the lump of unmelted goo at the bottom remained. That was before Mrs Hall their ballet teacher had pulled Anna's mother aside, before she had been told to dream of higher things. Of a path speckled with diamonds. Before her family had cracked down the middle. Before Rachel's mother, who had watched the moment with Luke through the window of the bakery, and seen her little girl left flustered as Anna and Hermione giggled behind a plane tree, had turned to Anna and said, *'You were a lovely little girl once. I hope you're ashamed of yourself.'*

Hermione had done a disparaging snort while Anna had pretended to sneer, but had felt her insides shake with self-disgust.

The doorbell rang as Anna was chewing the fruit tart and Rachel went to answer it while Philippe continued to muse over the story. 'And Seb, he has slept with Melissa Hope. Rachel…do I know this Melissa Hope?'

'Philippe!' Rachel hissed. 'You can't ask things like that.'

He shrugged. 'Why not? It is the facts, *non*?'

'Melissa Hope?' Anna's dad's voice echoed from the hallway. 'Who's slept with Melissa Hope?'

'Who hasn't slept with Melissa Hope?' Hermione sneered as she strutted in, wearing plain skinny jeans and a marl-grey vest but still managing to look like a catwalk model.

'Seb,' said Philippe. 'Seb has slept with Melissa Hope.'

'Can you stop saying that?' Rachel snapped.

Hermione nearly choked on her own surprise while Anna's father sighed and said, 'I knew it. I knew it, what did I tell you, Anna?'

'Oh sod off,' Anna said with a shake of her head. 'And don't lecture me when you're shagging my best friend.'

Philippe snorted. 'Ah, *très* bon, the English countryside, it is full of the sex and scandal, *oui.*'

'Philippe!' Rachel thwacked him on the shoulder to get him to pipe down, then turned to the group in front of her and said, 'Would anyone like tea?'

Philippe blew out a breath. 'I think it is time for wine.' Then, as Anna's dad nodded in agreement, Philippe collected a varying array of wine glasses, some tall, some short and squat and sploshed out the rest of the vin rouge. 'Ah, Melissa Hope. I know who she is now. She is the one with the bottom?'

Rachel did a tiny nod, as if hoping that might be the end of it.

Philippe blew out a breath. 'It is huge. Huge,' he said, spreading his arms wide. 'It is like the rhinoceros. She could kill someone with this bottom.' He handed out the wine and then raised his brows at Anna. 'You are lucky he is still alive.'

Hermione guffawed. 'Marvellous. I like this man.'

Anna shot her a look. 'Maybe you should have sex with him, too.'

'Anna!' her dad said sharply.

'Please don't,' said Rachel, as if Hermione could just snap him up with effortless ease. Anna glanced between them and realised how incongruous it was to have them all in the same room together. Sweet childhood friend Rachel and Hermione, who had fitted Anna's teenage criteria perfectly, a wicked combination of terrifying confidence and complete disinterest in anyone but herself. She would ask Anna nothing simply because if it wasn't happening right at that very minute, if she couldn't kiss it, drink it, wear it or sneer at it, she wasn't interested.

Philippe waved a hand. 'No one is having the sex. Well, except Seb, and I don't know what is going on between the two of you—' He pointed towards Anna's dad and Hermione, as Rachel shut her eyes like it was all so unBritish that she had to try and block it out.

'He didn't have sex with her,' Anna muttered.

'Sounds like New York might have come just at the right time, darling.' Hermione took a sip of her wine and rolled it around in her mouth. 'This is divine.' She beamed at Philippe who waved a hand and said, '*Naturellement.*'

'You're going to New York? You're leaving?' her father said, and the tone of his voice, one of more disappointment than shock, took her by surprise.

'*Non*, you cannot leave. It would be running away.' Philippe shook his head and rolled down the corners of his lips.

'You left a relationship that wasn't working,' Rachel said to Philippe, inclining her head and playing devil's advocate.

Philippe stood up and went over to the window, throwing it open to let in the post-thunderstorm air. He took a deep breath and said, 'Ah, the smell of English summer, *la belle* Nettleton. Yes, I left my first marriage but we tried for a long time to make it work and there was no love. Whereas here…' He waved a hand in Anna's direction. 'Here I think there is love but they play this crazy game. Here there is madness.'

'I agree.' Her dad sat back in his chair, crossing one leg over the other. 'A marriage can never last when the love's gone…'

'Oh don't you start.' Anna swung round. 'Don't try and justify your failed relationships. You certainly didn't try for a long time to make it work, you ran off with the first woman you saw as far as I can tell.'

'Anna—' he warned.

'Well it's true. If you hadn't bloody run off with that woman, none of this would have happened.'

She saw his jaw clench. 'You can't blame me for what's happening in your life now, Anna. At some point you have to take responsibility for your own actions.'

'Like you have? You ruined her life. That was it. She couldn't do anything after that.' Anna shook her head.

'Anna, it was never going to work with your mother and me. We wanted completely different things. We were completely different people. We probably should never have got married, and she should never have left Spain.'

Anna stared at the hydrangeas on the table. The hundreds of small flat flowers making up one great ball, if she squinted her eyes she could merge them all into one. *When we live in Sevilla, Anna…*had been her mum's favourite saying when Anna was a child, and her dad had always shifted uncomfortably in his seat when she'd said it. Anna had known they were never going to live in Spain even when she was tiny and she had always wondered why her mum hadn't realised. It was like a fantasy life just around the corner.

Her dad knocked back his wine and said, 'She should have just said that she married the wrong person, made a mistake and gone back, but appearances have always been too important to your mother.'

She saw Rachel look down into her lap and Hermione shift uncomfortably in her seat.

'You don't have to make her mistakes. Our mistakes, Anna,' he said, running his hand over his stubble and sighing. 'You make your own history.'

There was a pause where even Philippe seemed to be at a loss for what to say. The fresh, rain-scented air was circling through the room as they all sipped politely on their wine. Anna kept her eyes fixed on the hydrangeas.

'OK,' Philippe said in the end. 'Let us look at what is happening. You have gone on the website because you are bored here. *Oui*. And you are maybe testing your relationship?'

'I actually encouraged her to do that,' Hermione piped up proudly. 'I sometimes think she could do better.'

'Better?' Philippe put his hands in the air. 'Better what? Better sex? Better money? Better clothes? What is better? And is it better for you or for Anna?' He blew out a long breath of frustration. 'This is the problem. We should not get involved in other people's relationships because we are all looking for different things. You, you think you are looking for sex, *non*? But maybe it is something else. Maybe it is that you are afraid to commit?' Hermione pouted and sat back, unable to answer. 'What do you think is the problem, Anna? Do you think maybe you are a little afraid, too?' he asked.

'No!' Anna huffed, and then looked around at the group, embarrassed by the very idea of it.

'I think maybe you are a little afraid,' he said, twirling the stem of his glass.

'Of what?' Anna rolled her eyes.

'You tell me.' Philippe shrugged.

'Maybe of missing out?' Hermione chipped in, leaning forward and crossing her arms languidly over her knees.

'I don't think so.' Rachel shook her head. 'I think maybe it's just all the stuff with the wedding. You know, the uncertainty of the venue.'

173

'I think she's afraid of failing.' It was her father who said it, who didn't sit forward or say it in a questioning tone but rather just a matter-of-fact statement. 'I think it stems from something your mother would have told you. Something she'd have drummed in over and over again.' He paused for a second and studied her. Then he said, quietly, 'If you're looking for her approval, then just stop. It's pointless. Anna, you'll never get it.'

Anna swallowed, felt her bottom lip quiver slightly and bit down on it to keep it still. 'I'm not afraid of failing' she said stubbornly.

Her father shrugged and shook his head.

'That is good, because you hardly winning at the moment, are you, Anna?' Philippe raised a brow and Rachel hit him on the leg for being so inappropriate.

After the wine was finished and the conversation had moved from Anna's turbulent love life to polite small talk, everyone filed out into the now cooler evening air. Hermione strutted next to Anna's dad, glancing over her shoulder at Anna, who was dutifully ignoring her, Philippe was leaning in the doorway swirling the remains of the wine in his glass round in his hand, while Anna followed Rachel who was going to lend her her bike to get home.

As Rachel lifted the bright-blue bicycle from where it leant against the fence, she apologised for Philippe's bluntness, but Anna laughed it off. 'Don't worry, it was good for me. I enjoyed him.'

'Well, he's an acquired taste,' Rachel smiled.

'You're lucky.' Anna smiled back, taking the bike and liking the feel of it in her hands. It had been a while since she'd pedalled down country lanes. 'God, I don't think I've ridden since…' She paused to think about it. 'Probably since with you.' Two little girls riding as fast as they could down hills and through fields, hair streaming, knees bleeding from where they'd fallen off, daring each other to keep their mouths and eyes open as they hurtled through clouds of midges.

Anna's mum had given her bike to the neighbour's kid when her ballet teacher had advised against cycling and the contradicting forces on the muscles in her back.

Rachel tapped the handlebar. 'Well, as they say, you never forget how to do it.'

Anna nodded, but thought how easy it was to forget everything else. Rachel had been her friend as a kid and she had just wiped that out. Her only aim when coming back to Nettleton – to try and stop her dad pushing for her to come and visit again. If she was bad enough, then she could just stay at the EBC School and close the door on that part of her life. On the faces that had peered through windows as her mum had thrown all his clothes out the window, and the people who had watched in the square as her mother had faced up to Molly, the auctioneer, and stood as close as she could get to spit, You are proud of yourself, you little slut? *You have sex in my bed, did it feel good? Destroying my family?*

'Why are you so nice to me?' Anna asked Rachel as they stood there with the bike. She could see Hermione out of the corner of her eye, pausing on the threshold of her dad's house. She knew she'd be watching and wanting to know what they were talking about.

'Why wouldn't I be?' Rachel shrugged, ducking away as a huge bumblebee bobbed past.

'You know—' Anna said. 'Because I was such a bitch to you. If I was you, I'd be gleefully watching in the corner now.'

Rachel nodded her head from side to side, undecided, and said, 'It was obvious that you were just so upset back then. We all knew it.'

'It was?' Anna thought she'd handled it all quite well – donning her mask of emotionless uncaring every time she stepped foot back in the village. It was unnerving to think that anyone might have interpreted this so easily as weakness.

'Yeah. Definitely. And I suppose I liked being your friend. I liked you and while, yeah, you were a cow, I think there was part of me that just wanted you to want to be friends with me again.' Rachel shrugged. 'Sounds weak, doesn't it?' Anna shook her head, kicking the wet grass with her toe, as Rachel went on. 'I was a bit jealous of you as well. I wanted to be in London living this glamorous ballet-star lifestyle.' Rachel laughed. 'We were stuck here doing gym with Mrs McNamara. And then you came back all cool and strong and, while my mum would tell me it was a front, I was terrified of you.' She laughed again. 'You were pretty damn scary.'

'Really?' Anna made a face, although looking back on it she could imagine being a bit scared of herself if she met her now. She thought of the look on the face of Farrah Fawcett Lucy in Razzmatazz.

'When everyone would say that you were going to be a star, I would secretly wish that you weren't. Sorry, I shouldn't say it, should I? I just wanted you to come back and it all to go back to normal, but it never did.'

'I'm really sorry for how I was. I'm ashamed to look back on it,' Anna admitted. The relief of saying it was like shrugging off a big, old, heavy coat.

Rachel smiled. 'It's just nice to see you now. You don't forget do you, your childhood friends.' As Anna shook her head, Rachel added with a cheeky grin, 'And I think maybe you've got your Luke Lloyd comeuppance.'

Anna rolled her eyes, then got on the bike and walked it out backwards through the gate. 'Yeah, that's true,' she said as she straightened up and started to pedal, the bike leaning precariously to the right making her brake straight away. She laughed. 'Oh God, now I've got to remember how to ride a bike!' Then tried again and tilted again. 'This may take me slightly longer than I anticipated.'

'You'll get there.' Rachel leant her hands on the fence and Philippe came up to join her.

'She is not very good on the bicycle,' he said.

'But I'm getting there!' Anna shouted over her shoulder, unable to turn around now she was sort of pedalling and the bike was sort of moving, more

177

wobbling, and she was braking too hard every time she picked up any speed. 'I'm getting there,' she shouted, and then laughed and they watched her get smaller and smaller as the endless road stretched out ahead of her.

Chapter Twelve

The first thing Anna noticed as she pedalled up to Primrose Cottage was that the roses had gone. Shorn off at the base of the stem, the bush was now bare. The second thing was Seb, sitting on the front step, his arms draped over his knees.

She wheeled the bike up the path and he looked up and said, 'I'm moving out.'

Anna paused. 'Right,' she said after a second, nodding.

He looked up at her, his face rigid.

'Where are you going?' she asked.

'Into the shed.'

Anna snorted a laugh, unable to help herself.

'I don't think it's very funny.'

'No.' She shook her head. 'But you can't live in the shed.'

'I've swept it out. I've put up a camp bed and there's an old camping stove, a radio and I'll come in if I need the loo.'

'Sounds cosy. Like a man cave,' she said, trying to find some neutral ground where they might crack the surface and remember that they liked each other. 'Maybe you'll quite enjoy it.'

'No, Anna. It isn't a bloody man cave, it's a shed. I won't enjoy it at all.'

'Why are you doing it, then?'

'I thought you'd want me to.'

'Shouldn't you have checked with me first?' she asked. There was a pause.

'Maybe *I* want to,' he said. 'Your phone arrived this afternoon. Could you do me a favour and delete that app?'

'You really think I'd keep it?' she asked, incredulous.

He looked stubbornly down at his hands.

Tell him you're sorry.

I can't.

'Well, fine, enjoy the shed,' she said, wheeling the bike to the side of the house and locking it up to a drain pipe. 'I'm sure you'll be very happy there. Your parents will be delighted to hear about this turn of events.'

'I'm not telling them,' he replied as she walked back round to the front door.

Don't ask why not.

'Why not?'

'Because I don't want them to have anything else against you.'

Tell him that maybe you are afraid, Anna. 'How chivalrous. Especially considering you're the one who stayed out all night with Melissa Hope.'

Seb pushed himself up off the step. 'I think the horse had already bolted by then.'

Laugh. 'Please don't use one of your dad's sayings at a time like this.'

'See you, Anna,' he said as he walked away in the direction of the shed.

Follow him, Anna. Follow him and live in the shed with him. Are you winning?

No. No I'm not.

But years of training, years of that infamous poise, kept her standing exactly where she was.

Chapter Thirteen

As Anna walked into the Razzmatazz rehearsal, she was tired. Looking out the window at the little light in the shed all night would do that to a person.

She was wearing the clothes she'd worn all day in the shop, a dusty pair of safari shorts and a grey vest, and as she pushed open the door of the hall she noticed how the temperature in the cavernous room had dropped alongside the thunderstorm. It was dark and cold and the shafts of sunlight coming in through the high windows seemed to be doing nothing but illuminating the dust and glitter from the children's nursery as it swirled like snow.

She rubbed her hands down her arms and looked around to see where everyone was. Three kids sat on the steps to the stage, heads down, arms slumped on their knees, shoulders rounded.

'Where is everyone?' she asked, checking her watch because she was sure she was quarter of an hour late.

It was ten-year-old Billy who looked up. Matt kept his head bent, red Beats headphones over his mop of hair. 'I think they're making a stand, Miss.'

'Anna.' she said. He looked confused. 'Anna,' she said again, 'Not Miss.'

'Oh, OK, Miss.'

'A stand about what?' she asked, shivering slightly as she went to look for a light switch.

Billy sighed like she was stupid. 'About you, Miss.'

The brunette who sat on the step below the two boys and who Anna didn't really remember from the previous rehearsal, glanced up, a look of nervous terror on her face at the exchange. As if somehow maybe this all might get back to a real teacher.

Anna paused with her hand on the switch and, before throwing light on the great hall, said, 'So why are you lot here?'

'My mum made me.' Billy rolled his eyes. Then he added, more quietly, 'She thinks I could be a dancer.'

Anna looked at him, head tilted, eyebrow raised in surprise, as she asked, 'Do you think you could be a dancer?' She flipped the light switch and the room blinked with bright, fluorescent light.

Billy squinted. 'Dunno.'

'Do you enjoy it?'

'I didn't enjoy the last class. With you.'

'But that's what being a dancer would be like,' she said, walking closer to the three of them.

Billy narrowed his eyes and said, 'Well I don't want to be one then.'

The look on his little face suddenly didn't sit comfortably with Anna. It was like the feeling of a Daddy Long Legs landing on her bare arm, that once brushed off could still be felt, still make her shudder at the thought of it.

Was that what being a dancer was like? Had it been like that with Madame LaRoche? It had been hard, it had been painful and sick-making and exhausting and she had been shouted at and pushed and pushed beyond her limit and her body had ached and her feet had been battered and bruised and her muscles had shaken with pain, but then there were times when it had been amazing. Like being sprinkled with fairy dust, like the sweat and the ache and the thirst and the fear had fuelled her hunger, her adrenaline, her skill, her determination and when it had come together and been perfect she had flown. And she had loved it.

When had she last felt that adrenaline?

'What about you?' She nodded towards Matt and said loudly so he might hear over his music. 'Why are you here?'

He raised his head a fraction of an inch, bright-blue eyes blank, and shrugged a shoulder like he couldn't give a shit whether he was there or not.

Billy sniggered. 'Cos he fancies Lucy.'

Anna glanced around the room, looking for that massive fringe. 'But Lucy's not here.'

'Yeah, but he didn't know that, did he?' Billy snorted.

Anna felt her lips twitch as Matt blushed scarlet and swiped Billy across his carefully swept to the side hair.

'And you?' Anna nodded to the girl.

'Mary,' she said, playing with her split ends.

'Why are you here, Mary?'

Mary paused, looked down at her feet. 'I felt sorry for you.'

Anna opened her mouth to huff but didn't, instead she straightened her shoulders and tried for poise but as she lifted her nose a little higher in the air it suddenly seemed completely pointless. Taking in her surroundings, and the disgracefully poor turn-out, she thought, d'you know what, sod it, and walked over to the stage, sliding herself up onto the wooden slats.

'OK, fine. We'll work with what we have.'

'You're kidding, right?' Billy made a face.

'No,' she said more sternly than she had intended and she watched the three of them bristle. 'No,' she said again, softer. 'No, we'll just practise. Billy and Matt, you had a good connection from what I remember, and your lifts were good, but you're not focused enough, you aren't aware enough of what your bodies are doing. We'll work on posture today and that should lead to balance. It's here—' She put her hand on her stomach. 'Got any muscles there?' She snorted at the idea of it.

Matt bashed Billy. 'He's got no muscles.'

'Oh, and you have, I take it?' Anna raised a brow.

Matt hooked one finger under his T-shirt and lifted it to reveal a cracking set of abs.

'Blimey!' Anna was caught totally by surprise and realised she was blushing.

'Like what you see, Miss?' Matt winked.

Her instinctive reaction was to brusquely tell him no, but instead she found herself laughing. 'Well, that's a hell of a set of muscles,' she said. And, as Matt grinned for the first time that she'd seen, and even Mary sniggered under her curtain of hair, Anna felt her shoulders soften.

'Come on, let's warm up. We'll do some Pilates, just to get your muscles loose.'

'Pilates is gay,' Matt sneered, glugging down some Coke. Billy sniggered.

'Oh good God.' Anna shook her head. 'Even top footballers do Pilates, you idiots. Come on, it'll make you better with those tumbles. And swap the Coke for water.'

'Why?' Matt took another glug.

'Better for your muscles. Better for your bodies, less sugar.' She paused. He eyed her dubiously, seemingly waiting for some kind of order or reprimand.

'But, it's up to you.' She shrugged, pretending that she didn't care if he carried on drinking Coke or not, when really she wanted to tell him that he was wrong and she was right.

After a quick Pilates warm-up, they then paced through what they could of the basic steps. Billy hurled himself into the air whenever the chance arose, back-flipping like an elastic band, then running off to sit on the sidelines until his next portion of acrobatics. It turned out, however, that, as they practised the moves for their slightly bizarre street dance, disco and now ballet-infused routine, Mary and Matt were actually quite a duo. Mary, who, when she tied her hair back and was pulled out of the shadows, her sleeves

186

pushed back on her jumper, could seemingly move. And not just move but move really damn well.

'Mary, why don't the two of you try the Hustle in the mid-section. Stand in for Lucy.'

'I don't wanna do it with Mary,' Matt sulked.

'Just try it,' Anna urged.

'But I want to dance with Lucy.'

'Yeah,' Mary added, quietly, 'I don't want to be Lucy's part.'

'She's not here!' Anna said, exasperated. 'Just give it a go.'

And so Mary took a reluctant step forward from where she'd been standing on the edge while Matt made a face at Billy and Anna gave him a look to try and stop him being mean. The step was a version of the disco, Continental Hustle, that Anna had attempted to teach them last time round.

'Remember, it's based on six counts not four,' Anna said as they stood awkwardly together, Mary barely able to touch Matt's hands.

On the first go Mary wrap-turned to the left instead of the right and ended up in completely the wrong direction, treading on Matt's toes and leaving Billy smirking on the edge and Matt sighing with his hands in the air. 'It's not going to work,' he said, immediately stepping back.

'Give it another go.' Anna tipped her head to the side. 'You may as well, there's no one else here. Otherwise it's just a waste of the rehearsal.'

Matt sighed, Mary looked at the floor.

'Mary, stand up straight. The most important thing is communicating with your partner. Look into his eyes. Look at each other's expression. You have to assume the personality of each dance.' And so they went again, and again, and gradually they looked at one another and Anna felt herself smiling inside at the pinking of Mary's cheeks as she stopped turning the wrong way and instead stepped in time with Matt and the two of them started to really move as Billy whooped from where he had perched himself on the top of the piano. 'Lovely. Love it. Enjoy yourself, Mary,' Anna shouted, and Mary went even pinker.

When they stopped, Anna found herself doing a little clap. 'See! Now that's what I call a step!' She laughed and Matt wiped the sweat off his face and deigned to allow a tiny smile while Mary looked back down at the floor and nodded.

A car horn beeped outside and Mary said, 'I think that'll be my dad.'

'OK, let's call it a day.' Anna nodded as the three of them immediately darted off to grab their stuff. 'By the way,' she said, wondering if any of them were listening when they didn't look up. She swallowed, not actually sure what she was going to say, and then blurted out quickly, 'That was good. You were good.'

Matt, who was already near the door, just shrugged a shoulder.

'Erm,' she went on, 'next rehearsal…Will the others come, do you think?'

Billy and Matt exchanged a look. 'Depends what we tell 'em, Miss.'

She paused for a second before asking, 'What will you tell them?' As she said it, she realised that all her muscles had tightened in expectation of the answer.

As Billy and Mary trooped past her, Billy turned to walk backwards, his rucksack strap looped over his forehead, 'We'll tell them to come, Miss.' He grinned, a little dimple appearing in his cheek.

Anna breathed out, unable to believe quite how much that meant to her. 'Thank you,' she said.

'Whatevs,' Billy called, turning his back to her and holding his hand in the air in a wave as he jogged out of the room.

Her bubble of pride was short-lived. It lasted as long as it took for her to get in her car, drive home and walk into the house. As she flopped down onto the sofa, Seb walked past her from the kitchen, a bowl of pasta with tomato sauce in his hands.

'Hi,' she said, tentatively.

'Hi,' he replied. 'I just – I had to come in because the gas stove wasn't working.'

'Oh, right.' She nodded, sitting forward on the couch. 'That's fine. Come in anytime.'

'No, I'll get it fixed,' he said, his voice flat and unfriendly, then carried on towards the door.

She thought how ridiculous they must look, Seb taking his pasta out to the shed.

'Bye,' she said then.

'Bye,' he muttered, without turning round.

When he came in late that night to wash up his plate and use the bathroom, Anna stood on the upstairs landing in her nightie, listening to the sounds of the water running and lights turning on and off. She leant on the banister and peered over but he didn't look up and she didn't say anything.

Chapter Fourteen

Since the thunderstorm, the weather had become quite erratic. Cool in the mornings, scorching in the afternoons and then suddenly cloudy with bursts of rain. Even the forecast gave up on solid predictions – the jet stream seemingly as volatile as events in Anna's life.

Since Anna had rearranged the furniture, Mrs Beedle had sold nearly half the cushions, three crocodile-skin handbags and the giant gilt mirror. Anna had watched as she'd almost flogged the chaise longue but the guy had said he needed to think about it, which Mrs Beedle said was the kiss of death for a sale. As a result of this sudden flurry of interest, Anna had spent the last few days working her way around the front of the shop, re-hanging pictures and carefully arranging jewellery, vases, bags and trinkets. But all the time she was aware of the big pile of chairs and junk that sat piled high in the far corner of the shop. If she stood with her back to the front door, the counter and the curtained stockroom on her left, to the right was a portion of the shop floor that resembled a post-modern vintage sculpture and made her feel a little queasy every time she saw it. Just visible through a mesh of mismatched chairs was an old shop sign, a tangled collection of beaded tiaras, a moth-eaten theatre set of Manhattan, a fairground fortune-teller with a missing eye and some precariously stacked boxes.

When she asked Mrs Beedle what she was going to do about it, Mrs Beedle shrugged and sat down in her armchair next to the counter, her back to the rubbish heap saying, 'That, my dear, is exactly why my chair faces this way.'

But for Anna it was like an itch that needed to be scratched, and while Mrs Beedle told her there were other, more important, things to be getting on with – like clearing the stockroom, polishing the good stuff that was out the front already – Anna would spend a surreptitious half hour each day while Mrs Beedle napped in her chair, tugging bits free from the complicated maze and either adding them to her sorting boxes out the back, or positioning them unobtrusively round the shop. The oil painting of a young girl with a white dog at her feet that was now hanging where the gilt mirror had been, for example, had been before plucked from the heap and Mrs Beedle had paused next to it the day before, narrowing her eyes as if trying to decide where in the hell it had come from.

At the end of the day, Anna had just freed a box of glassware – little jugs with cut-glass edges, a set of six champagne flutes etched with delicate gold stars and a vase of deep-purple and blue faux-marino glass that shone when she held it up to the day's fickle sunshine –

when she saw a couple of Razzmatazz-ers troop past
the shop on their way to the hall.

She checked the time and realised this was it, this
was when she'd find out if they'd OK-ed her. The
idea made her brow start to bead with sweat. The
possibility of victory at this rehearsal made other
victories possible – perhaps next she'd be able to have
a proper conversation with Seb.

Pushing the box of glass onto the Welsh dresser, she
went out the back and grabbed her bag and sweatshirt.
Then as she stood at the door of Vintage Treasure and
looked over at the hall, she felt her hands starting to
shake. If none of them came, what would that mean?
That, once again, she had failed? *Hold yourself tall,
Anna. Poise. Never apologise, never explain. Never let
them see your weakness, Anna. No one puts winning
with weakness, Anna.*

She realised then that, nowadays, she spent so long
protecting herself from the possibility of failure, that
she never put herself in a position that came with the
possibility of winning.

But as she walked across the sun-dappled square,
past the lazy sheepdog and the pecking sparrows, her
mother's voice was silenced by a louder one in her
head, one that she hadn't heard for a long time that
said, *I do mind. I do care. It does matter if they are
there or not. Please. I really want them to be there.*

Her own voice.

Pushing open the big double doors and stepping into
the darkness of the hall that smelt of glue, sandwiches

and orange squash she paused before looking up. Breathed in through her nose before raising her head but, when she did finally glance up, she felt her whole body fizz like it was filled with bubbles. There, sitting along the edge of the stage like birds on a telephone wire, was the whole motley crew of them.

'We're all here, Miss,' Billy shouted.

Anna glanced across the faces that she didn't really recognise, the wary expressions, the hair pulled high on top of heads, the T-shirts with a faded Razzmatazz written across them, the trainers banging against the wood, the Twixes and packets of Hairbo, the acne, the fat fingers, the thin fingers, the greasy skin, the powdery foundation, the streaky fake tan, the faces engrossed in iPhones, the headphones, the tipped-over school bags, the mess, the scowls and the half-smiles. And she found her own mouth stretch into an involuntary grin.

'Except Lucy,' Mary added, quietly 'She doesn't want to do it any more.'

'Why not?' Anna asked, realising then that she'd actually been searching for the Farrah Fawcett fringe.

'Because you gave Mary her part,' Billy said, while curling himself over into a bridge from where he stood at the foot of the stage stairs then, as he kicked up into a handstand, got stuck halfway so Matt kicked him and he fell in a heap on the floor.

'But I didn't give Mary her part, she just stood in for her in that section.'

Matt jumped down off the stage and gave Billy a hand up, while muttering, 'We think it's better this way round.'

'That's because Lucy has a new boyfriend,' cut in a pale-faced, fat boy who was sitting at the end of the line.

'Fuck off it is, Peter. It's because it's better.' Matt glared at him and Peter snorted a laugh.

'OK, OK fine, look don't worry about it.' Anna waved her hands to settle them down. 'We'll talk about Lucy later, let's just get warmed up.'

'I'm pretty hot already, Miss,' one of the guys called out and the others laughed.

'I'm sure you are,' Anna raised a brow in his direction and then turned to Billy. 'Do you want to lead the warm-up?'

'No way I'm following him,' muttered Peter as the ten-year-old bounded to the front of the hall.

At the same time as he said it, Anna was distracted by a movement of the doors to the side of the room. 'Well—' she said, her attention caught by who she thought it was. 'All I can say, is go home then.' She shrugged and felt Peter glare at her as she jogged towards the doorway. She might be trying to be a little nicer to them all, but that didn't mean she had to put up with their every whim and sulk. 'You need to all work together. It shouldn't matter who leads the warm-up,' she called as she went.

Just before pushing the doors open, she glanced back to see Peter slope into the middle of the group and start a shuffling, half-hearted attempt at the warm-up. She also saw Matt pause to take a sip of Evian before turning the tune up loud and that made her smile.

Out in the corridor, she glanced both ways and just caught the swish of a blonde ponytail ahead of her. The girl was walking fast, but perhaps not fast enough to want to go unnoticed.

'Lucy?' Anna called, and the girl paused but then carried on.

'Lucy!' she shouted again and started to jog after her. It crossed Anna's mind that she could just leave her, that it would probably make her life easier if she let her go. But when she finally caught up with her, just in front of the fire exit that led out the back to the bins, and put her hand on her shoulder which Lucy, spinning round, shrugged off quick as a flash, it wasn't the Farrah Fawcett flick that Anna saw. Instead her mind seemed to see brown hair, centre-parted with a long fringe, a cropped New Kids on the Block T-shirt over a black leotard and leggings, eyes narrowed like a cat's, perma-frown of aloofness and an almost rigid poise in her body. When the girl turned, Anna almost had to take a step back at the accusation, temper and annoyance on the pursed lips. She wasn't face to face with Farrah Fawcett Lucy but with mini-Anna.

Anna swallowed and said, 'Do you want to come inside?'

'No.' Mini-Anna scowled and went to walk away.

'Wait, hang on.' Big Anna pressed her hand against the bar on the fire exit door to stop her from opening it. 'Wait.' Why was she suddenly finding it so hard to breathe? She'd only jogged down the corridor. 'Wait. It's OK. Come back,' she said. 'Please don't throw this away, you enjoy it.'

'How would you know?'

Anna frowned, 'I just think you do. I think that's why you're here, watching. Because you enjoy it. Because you're good at it.' She paused, saw mini-Anna's jaw lock, saw the fury on her face. 'It doesn't matter about being the lead part or anything like that, you do it for you.' She tried to will her to listen to her. 'It's about you being good at something and letting your—' When she saw the trembling of mini-Anna's chin, she tried to keep her own steady. 'Letting your talent shine whatever position you're in. About doing it for you,' she said again, more quietly.

Anna kept her hand firm on the fire exit bar, unwilling to let this girl escape now that she had her, thinking of how much more she had to say, when suddenly mini-Anna fizzled away and Farrah Fawcett Lucy's voice snarled, 'But you think I'm shit.'

Anna sighed, turning to rest both her hands on the doorframe behind her to steady herself. 'I don't think you're shit at all,' she said, trying to hide her disappointment, her bewilderment at seeing her former self so clearly. 'To me, Lucy—' She coughed, buying herself some time to get her thoughts in some kind of order.

'To you, what?' Lucy muttered.

'To me you were one of the leaders of this group,' Anna said, drawing on her PR experience and trying to compensate for the turmoil of emotions that she felt must be visible in her eyes. 'And, as a leader, that doesn't mean you always go up front, Lucy. It can mean that you lead by showing others. All those who look up to you and think you're good can then see that it's OK to be anywhere. You lead by being part of the group—' Anna paused, realised this was almost the exact same talk she'd had with her boss when her annoying colleague Beatrix had got the promotion she'd been coveting. She hadn't listened at the time, just sulked and fumed at the idea of being kept down. It was only as she was repeating it that it now seemed like reasonable advice. It sounded like something her dad might say…No, something that her granny would have said and her dad would have repeated, passing the wisdom off as his own. That thought made her laugh, completely inappropriately given the circumstances, so she stifled it into a sort of horse-like snort which made Lucy raise a brow, like Anna was gross and old and couldn't manage her bodily noises.

'Lucy, you are a leader, and you need to acknowledge that every one of you in this group is a star.'

Were they stars? If Anna hadn't been a star, could she allow this rag-tag bunch to think they were stars? As she considered it, felt ridiculous and childish for making such a petty comparison, she suddenly questioned what this word was that she had clung to and placed so much emphasis on. What would she have had to do to finally take a bow and say, I am a star?

'You're stars,' she said again, 'for trying. And what would make you personally stand out would be by doing what's best for the whole group, because you want your whole team to succeed.' Anna added a small smile of encouragement at the end.

Lucy kicked the floor. 'You should have told me about Mary.'

'How could I have told you? You didn't come to rehearsal.' Anna shook her head.

'It's a small village. You've seen me about. I see you about.'

'You do?' Anna couldn't imagine even showing up on Lucy's radar.

'I had to find out from Billy, little shit.' She pushed her big fringe back and sighed.

Anna realised that she had probably seen her, hanging around outside Rachel's bakery, or sitting on the bench in the square with her friends, that she could have walked over and maybe mentioned what had happened in the rehearsal. If she'd put herself in Lucy's position, she would have realised that that was what she should have done. If she'd remembered that that narrow-eyed swagger wasn't something to be daunted by but something to just push through, a wave to duck under. She of all people should know. 'Yes, I should have told you,' Anna nodded.

Lucy licked her lips and looked away down the corridor.

'I'm sorry,' Anna said.

199

Lucy glanced back, eyes glinting. 'What was that, Miss?'

Anna rolled her eyes. 'I'm sorry,' she forced out a second time.

There was a pause between them, and then Lucy grinned and said, 'That works for me.' Then she laughed. 'Jesus Christ, Miss, never thought I'd hear you apologising.' She laughed and then strutted away in the direction of the hall, leaving Anna trailing behind thinking exactly the same thing.

Back in the hall, Billy and Matt were attempting to show the others a couple of the steps Anna had run through with them at the previous rehearsal. The rest of the group were lined up behind them watching and awkwardly attempting to follow. It wasn't very pretty. Peter stumbled over his Nikes while Mary retreated back into herself on the back row and Billy's sister Clara, her luminous dyed-orange hair curled in neat fifties-style rolls on top of her head, just stood at the side with her hand on her hip saying, 'That's just stupid. It's impossible.'

Anna crossed her arms in front of her chest and tried not to wince. Lucy looked from the group back to Anna and made a face. 'I don't want to be in the bad bits on the TV, Miss.'

'No.' Anna shook her head. Shit. OK. She was out of her league. Anyone she'd worked with at least had a semblance of rhythm. How did one teach non-dancers how to dance? She tried to picture Seb at the dance lessons they'd gone to before their wedding. His grimacing face as he'd stood in the bright studio and Pepe, their Brazilian instructor, had tried to get some sway into his rigid hips. He'd got him to visualise a hula hoop round his waist like he was a kid in the playground and in the end had managed to get Seb to relax, even laugh, which was way more than Anna had ever been able to do when dancing at weddings. At the time she hadn't found it funny at all, she'd stood to one side looking aloof. Secretly she'd been consumed by her own panic – the rigidness of her body when she thought about having to dance, wondering if she would be able to put one foot in front of the other, the sickness it caused in her stomach as she lay in bed the night before the session. It hadn't occurred to her to confide her fears in Seb. That maybe a marriage was the exact place that secrets could be shared and kept safe. Instead she had said something unforgivable about cancelling the first dance because it would be a disaster. Hiding her own fears at Seb's expense.

She was brought back to the scene in front of her when Peter stumbled and knocked a skinny kid with freckles who, in turn, pushed Mary who tripped and fell on her bum while Clara patted her hair and blew a bubble and Billy sighed loudly before throwing himself into a double back-flip just for something to do and everyone started swearing and shouting.

'OK, OK, let's stop for a minute.' Anna held her hands up.

'Lucy!' Matt said surprised when he saw her standing next to Anna and then blushed luminous red.

'I'm back, yeah.' Lucy strutted over and took a place between Peter and the skinny freckly boy. 'I'm leading from back here, with my crew.' She smirked.

'We're like *Step Up 2*,' Clara laughed.

'In your dreams.' Billy raised a brow and Clara gave him the finger.

'Or *Dirty Dancing?*' Anna added and they all looked at her like they had no idea what she was talking about. 'You haven't seen *Dirty Dancing?*'

'No!' Clara looked horrified. 'It's from like the fifties.'

'The eighties,' Anna said. 'It's not that long ago.'

'For you maybe, Miss,' smirked Billy. 'I was born in 2004.'

'Jesus!' Anna shook her head.

'Yeah, you're old.'

'OK, that's enough, thank you. For your homework you should all watch it.'

'You can't give us homework.'

Anna rolled her eyes. 'Just watch the film. It's probably on Netflix. OK, listen, I just wanted to say that I was wrong the other day when I said you didn't have any steps. You do have steps, it's just that some of them get a little lost and some of them could be...' She searched for a word. 'More refined.'

'It's not ballet, Miss,' Lucy shouted.

'No, I know it's not but, look, I'll call it and we'll go through really slowly and it doesn't matter if anyone treads on anyone else's toes.'

'OK, Peter?' Matt laughed.

'Piss off.'

'OK, so from the beginning,' Anna shouted and they all shuffled into place. 'Clap left, clap right, left arm goes in front of the body, Mary, yep, and hips forward. That's nice. You're looking for simplicity. Let the music do the work.' Anna walked along in front of them as Lucy, Billy, Matt and Mary came forward and the group split into its front and back row. 'Very nice. Look at your arms, Peter, like a wing. Like wings, everyone. That's better. And now you're on the spot, leg up and OK, pause. Hang on a minute. This bit is where the back row, you're getting lost.' She leant against the piano and they all stared at her, waiting.

For a second she thought about going to stand with them and doing it herself to show them where they were going wrong, to run through it quickly and they could watch, but her body froze at the very idea. Instead she said, 'Maybe you need to think about it differently, maybe imagine you're pulling your boots on, so it would go...knee up, body over, welly boots pulled up.'

'We don't wear welly boots, Miss.'

'Well imagine watching someone who does.'

'My mum has a pair,' the freckly skinny boy shouted.

'Great,' said Anna. 'Imagine, sorry, I don't know what your name is.'

'You're so forgettable, Scotty,' Matt laughed.

'We're all thinking about your mum, Scotty,' Peter chimed in.

203

'Yeah? Well no one wants to think about your mum, Peter,' Scott snarled.

'OK, no one's thinking about anyone's mum. We're thinking about wellington boots.'

'Can we think about another type of boot? Like I could think about my Uggs?' Clara offered.

'Yes.' Anna clapped her hands. 'Think about whatever boot you like. Or even think about socks. Right, let's go from there. So your left boot—'

'Sock!' someone yelled.

'Shut up.'

'Right boot, lovely. Now you're going to jump, feet apart, left arm reaching up, it's a punch in the air, less violent, Peter, think about maybe picking an apple, that's better, and then clap either side, yes, clap up… no, up! Like, I don't know, like you're squashing midges. Yes. Very nice. Good. And we'll go from the top.' Anna stopped clapping. All the kids stopped and waited with their hands on their hips. 'OK, so when we go again I'm just going to shout wings, boots, apples, midges. Yes?'

And they all did it again, and then again, and then they wanted to stop for a break but she made them do it again, and Peter swore and Lucy glared at him, and then they did it again and this time no one stepped on anyone's toes and the sun streamed in through the little windows, and while there were still some dubious looks they did it in perfect time, with perfect posture and perfect movements.

'Brilliant. Brilliant.' Anna clapped, quite taking herself by surprise by the euphoria of seeing them move as one giant unit.

'Miss,' Lucy said as they peeled apart and had a drink. 'Can we add some twerking?'

'I don't know what twerking is,' Anna narrowed her eyes, 'but I'm not sure I like the sound of it.'

Forty minutes later, they were all sweating, red-faced and aching but the looks of desperate concentration had turned into smiles, and Anna's niggle of a guilty conscience for axing her from the main role had led to Lucy managing to get her own twerking solo just after the Matt and Mary Hustle. It was just as she was in full twerk, gleeful that she'd managed to get her own way, that the back door opened and slammed shut loudly. Lucy stopped, straightened up, and Anna turned to see Hermione strutting towards them, kitten heels clipping on the parquet floor, sunglasses pushing caramel hair back like velvet, dressed in minuscule green shorts and a black-and-white print vest that billowed out behind her.

The boys stopped staring at Lucy's bottom and instead watched, paralysed, as Hermione sashayed over.

'Hello, darlings,' she drawled. 'Anna, I've brought you some refreshments.' She held up a can of gin and tonic and, setting down her Fortnum's cool bag, pulled out two little glasses with ice and a slice. 'Is that outfit meant to be ironic?' she asked as she straightened up, taking in Anna's old leggings and sweatshirt.

Anna crossed her arms self-consciously over her baggy jumper and then said, her voice clipped, 'I can't drink while I'm teaching.' She didn't really want Hermione there. They hadn't talked properly since Hermione had started shagging her father and Anna couldn't help but one hundred percent disapprove.

'Sure you can. I don't think one can be a teacher and not sneak a snifter on the sly. What's this I hear about Seb sleeping in the shed?' Hermione asked as she cracked open the can.

'Mr Davenport's sleeping in the shed?' Peter asked, incredulous.

'Of course he's not sleeping in the shed.' Anna rolled her eyes.

'Did no one ever teach you not to eavesdrop, you little shit?' Hermione sneered at Peter. 'Go on, go back to your Backstreet Boys.'

'It's not bloody Backstreet Boys.' Peter curled his lip but Hermione just raised one perfectly arched brow and he seemed to shrink back into the gang.

'Thanks for bringing that up about Seb. I'm sure he'll be thrilled when they ask him about it at school,' Anna hissed.

Hermione just made a face and sipped her gin as Anna clapped her hands and shouted, 'OK, let's go through it one more time, I'm not going to call unless you get stuck and we'll try it with the music this time.'

Billy made a face. 'I don't know, Miss.'

Hermione sniggered at the word Miss.

'It'll be OK and, if it's not, it doesn't matter.'

206

'How very pragmatic you're becoming,' Hermione said, as she pulled up a stool and perched on the edge to watch.

'Ready? Matt, music,' Anna called.

'He's a delight, isn't he?' Hermione purred.

'Shh, just watch.' Anna said, really hoping that they would look amazing. But as the music blared out it seemed to catch them all off guard so they weren't together when they started. Peter was one step behind the whole way through and, at one point, turned the wrong way into Lucy who gave him an angry shove. Billy, distracted by the pushing, launched into a back-flip too early and thwacked his sister in the face. Lucy then stopped and shouted, 'This is shit.'

'Keep going,' Anna urged, but they'd lost the timing and only got it back after Matt and Mary did their solo which Anna had a sneaking suspicion they'd been practising in private because they were much better than they had been and Mary could now hold his eye contact for almost the whole time.

When they finished, the group out of breath and dejected, pointing and blaming each other, Hermione leant over to Anna and whispered, 'That was dreadful.'

A week ago, Anna would have agreed but now she felt herself bristle. 'They're getting there,' she snapped and Hermione snorted into her G&T.

'It's fine, it's fine.' Anna turned to the group. 'Don't worry, you're OK. It's OK. You can't expect to be perfect all the time. It's going well.'

They all glared at her, panting and sweating.

'I promise,' she said. Then paused at the use of the word. Did she promise? And if she did, how much sway did her word hold nowadays? Even she knew she'd diluted its worth. 'I promise it'll be OK,' she said again. 'We'll do it again tomorrow and the next day and the next until it's perfect all the time. Yes?'

There was a varying degree of nodding as they dispersed to get their bags and disappeared out of the hall.

Anna walked out with Hermione, pulling off her sweatshirt as they stepped into the square, the temperature warmer than it had been all day.

'They can't go on TV like that,' Hermione said once they were outside.

Anna just shrugged. 'Like I said, we'll just make sure it's perfect.'

'You might have been good once, Anna Whitehall, but you're not a magician.'

'Thanks for the vote of confidence,' Anna said as they sat down on a bench under a plane tree and Hermione poured her a gin and tonic, the ice cracking as the liquid bubbled over it.

'I just think there are some things more worthy of your energies. For example, I went into your little shop this afternoon, very nice, I think you've done a marvellous job, that fat woman was telling me all about it.'

'You think it looks good?' Anna asked, more tentatively than she'd expected.

'I even bought a lamp,' Hermione nodded, taking a sip of her drink. 'Hideous old thing with cherubs on the base but I think it'll look very eclectic in my hallway. I saw one just like it in *Elle Decor*, but that one was two grand. I paid fourteen pounds fifty. And then I saw Seb as I was putting it in the car. Looked like he hadn't slept for a week which, if he's in the shed, I imagine he hasn't. See, darling, that's perhaps where you should be focusing your energies.'

Anna ran her tongue over her lips. 'Hang on, you always go on about how boring he is with his rugby and PlayStation, how normal, and how I shouldn't be marrying him.'

Hermione made a face. 'Darling, I say everyone's boring and normal. That's my schtick. If I said people were nice, then I'd be boring.'

'Oh no, don't give me that. You've spent years chipping away about how you think I shouldn't settle, should test all possible options, and whatnot.' Anna swiped her hair out of her eyes.

'Well OK, fine, yes, I admit I did think that, but you know I'm beginning to see the positives of settling. And actually I've been to two rugby games with Patrick and they weren't too bad—'

'Give me strength.' Anna knocked back the rest of her drink and rummaged in the cooler for another can as she tried to rise above Hermione calling her dad Patrick.

'Anna, don't be upset about me and him.'

'Hermione—' Anna turned her head to face her. 'There is no you and him. You're having sex. He doesn't commit to anyone and neither do you. There is nothing there.' She waved her hands in the air as if to emphasise the void. 'Nothing. You'll both get bored and, anyway, he's my dad. It's disgusting.'

Anna watched as Hermione lowered her eyes down towards her lap, examined her perfect nail varnish and swept a finger down the back of her beautifully moisturised hands, then rummaged in the cool bag without saying anything, just fussed around searching for her own second can.

Realising she had perhaps been a touch too harsh, Anna sat back and shut her eyes, hoping the subject might change if she didn't say anything more and let the dappled early evening sun dance on her closed lids.

'Do you know, my divorce was the worst few years of my life,' she heard Hermione say into the silence. Trying not to show how shocked she was by the fact Hermione had brought the subject up, Anna remained in exactly the same position, rigidly trying to look relaxed. 'We were so goddamn horrible to each other,' Hermione went on. 'And I would look at him as we were arguing over tiny things and think, to think I used to love you. But it was like all memory of that had gone. And I'd wonder if I was lying. If I ever had loved him.

'Sometimes I'd stare at our wedding photos and the look in my eye and I would try and see what I felt. I would see happiness but I couldn't tell if I could see love.' She snapped open the ring-pull of the gin and tonic and instead of pouring it over the ice in her glass, took a huge gulp straight from the can before saying, 'It's a terrible thing to realise that you've been lying to yourself. That you have the ability to be so wrong in the choices you make and that someone else has the ability to hide so fundamentally who they are until it's too late. I was haunted by the bloody thought that, if I just kept going, it'd be OK.' Hermione crossed one long leg over the other and looked out over the concourse, at the birds bathing in the fountain and a couple walking their dog. Anna stared straight ahead of her and watched as Rachel came out of the bakery and started to wind the awning in. 'I just thought, week after week...' Hermione sighed, 'if I keep going, I can make it better.'

Anna rolled her head along the bench to look at Hermione, who had an expression of open vulnerability on her face that Anna had never seen before. She had never heard her talk about her divorce, in fact, as far as Anna knew, he'd just walked out one day and Hermione had gone to the Maldives to get over it and come back right as rain.

'We had this almighty row over some Hungarian painted furniture,' Hermione went on. 'We'd seen it on our honeymoon and he'd bought it in this wild, extravagant gesture. There was a bed, a wardrobe and a bureau. Beautiful stuff. It was green and painted with tiny flowers, red and yellow, and beautiful. It must have been hours and hours of work. Well we never thought of shipping costs, which I ended up paying and were the bloody same price as the furniture.' She took another gulp of her drink. 'So when it came to dividing up our stuff he said it was all his – he bought it. And I was like, bugger that. He's not getting away with that, it's in the country because of me. That was our greatest battle. Months we fought over it, it was like *The War of the Roses*, except we didn't die at the end.'

'I haven't seen that film.'

'Well,' Hermione laughed. 'Now you know what happens.'

'Did you win?' Anna asked. 'Did you get the furniture?'

'What do you think? Of course.' She smirked, almost indignant, then said a little more quietly, 'I just wanted you to know how bloody miserable it was. I don't think I've ever told anyone. And I suppose I'm telling you because I don't want you to take this thing from me. I know he's your dad, and it's probably all midsummer madness but, at least, all his baggage is there for me to see! I'm having fun, Anna. Just let me have it for a bit.'

Anna bit the inside of her cheek, watched the people start to fade away in the square, the lights in the bakery flick off, the dog walkers disappear down the lane, and said, 'It's just, why did it have to be my dad?'

'I don't know. Because we can't help who we fall for?' Hermione shrugged. 'Anna, all that Hungarian furniture is in my garage. Has been for six years under tarpaulins. I can't have it in the house. It just sits there, rotting probably. I think there might be mice in one of the wardrobe drawers. It was all such a waste of energy.' She shook her head. 'What I'm trying to say is, if you have something good you should fight for it.

If it's bad, give it away. Walk away. I wish now that I had just walked away.'

Anna thought about her weekly phone calls with the administrators of The Waldegrave, the angst and emotion they left burning inside her, the constant reminder of her balls-up.

Were some mistakes just better left where they were made?

The idea of simply cutting that thread, letting the whole thing loose like a broken kite string, walking away rather than fighting, as Hermione said, held such unexpected appeal that she almost caught her breath.

'And, as Philippe said, we can't judge other people's relationships – yes, don't look at me like that, I did listen and I took it in – we have to live and let live. I shouldn't have wound you up about Seb and I really hope one day you'll be OK about me and Patrick. Christ, as you say, it'll probably be over next week, but I'd really like us all to hang out. I think it could be fun. He misses you.'

Anna sighed and Hermione seemed to realise she was pushing that thread a little far. 'Anna, if you look at Seb and you still love him and can see why you love him, then there's a chance you're about to throw something away that you won't realise the value of till it's gone.'

Hermione paused. Anna saw images of diamonds and precious jewels floating away on the same breeze that her broken kite was soaring away on, saw the little lines around Seb's mouth when he smiled.

'This is all very emotional for you, Hermione,' she said in the end.

'Well I know,' Hermione guffawed, lounging back on the uncomfortable wooden slats. 'As I said, it's all midsummer madness. Maybe I'm in love.'

Anna coughed into her drink. Hermione raised a languid hand and fluffed her hair up. 'Don't waste it, darling, there's only six more cans in the bag.' She leant down and rummaged through the bag. 'Oh and a bottle of Dom Pérignon.' She laughed, pulling out the champagne that dripped with bubbles of condensation. 'We're like your little teenagers, getting smashed in the park. Just much classier.'

'And older,' said Anna.

'Would you go back to that age?'

'Yes,' she said, without hesitation. Yes she would go back and try it again, do it differently, work harder, hit the heady heights, take her bow of stardom but, just as she said it, so determinedly, she paused, confused. If she did it all again, achieved the dream, then she wouldn't have anyone living in the shed who, as Hermione said, she wouldn't have the chance to realise the value of until he had gone.

Chapter Fifteen

The front door was unlocked when Anna got home. She pushed it tentatively and shouted, 'Hello?' But there was no answer.

Getting a glass of water from the kitchen, she thought she heard noises upstairs. Glancing out to see if Seb was in the shed which, judging by its dark lifelessness he clearly wasn't, she took some hesitant steps up to the upstairs landing. 'Hello?' she shouted again.

There was banging from the bedroom and she had a sudden vision of Seb in bed with Melissa Hope. Of him touching her skin and maybe her draping her arm protectively over him as they slept. The thought made her shudder, her shaky hand spilling some of the water in her glass on the carpet.

'Hello?' she whispered this time as she pushed the bedroom door open, her eyes half shut in anticipation of what she might see, of who she might see.

But the bed was as she had left it that morning, beautifully made with the flowery Zara Home sheets pulled back and the big peacock-patterned cushions she'd splurged on from Liberty propped up by the iron bedstead. The noise was coming from the bathroom. 'Seb?' she said, as she took a step forward and saw him bent over the bath, a wrench sticking out of his back pocket, Gap boxers revealing a bit of a builder's bum, sweat down the back of his T-shirt, a tool-box open on the floor with the contents cascading out over her white fluffy bathmat. 'Seb?' she said again, a little louder, and this time he jumped back in surprise.

'Shit, you scared me,' he said, hand holding a power drill on his heart.

'Sorry, I didn't know you were here.' Nor did she know that he owned a power drill. 'Is that yours?'

He looked at the Black & Decker. 'Yeah,' he nodded. 'I bought it today. I thought, you know, it was maybe the kind of thing that I would need. You know, in life.'

'Right.' She nodded, looking slightly confused around the bathroom that had been half covered with clear dust sheets.

'I wanted to do the shower, you know. I thought you would need a shower,' he said, looking away to point at the new taps and shower hose that he was fitting and the instructions crumpled out over the floor.

As she looked at him then, in his ripped T-shirt, slightly red cheeks, messed-up hair, dusty face and visible awkwardness, she realised that her image of him in bed with Melissa Hope had been completely wrong. There would have been no touching, just him probably staring up at the ceiling, desperate for somewhere to lie down, aware he'd made a terrible mistake and unable to go home.

'It looks like a really good shower,' she said.

'Well, you know, just B&Q,' Seb shrugged.

'Still really good. Thank you.'

He looked back to his instructions and there was silence between them. Anna, resisting the urge to pull her bathmat out from under the tools, watched as he smoothed out the paper and rummaged for whatever was needed. 'It's been a nice day, hasn't it?' she said, gesturing out of the porthole window next to the bath.

'Yes. Nice now the weather's broken a bit,' Seb said without looking up. 'I won't be that much longer in here, I just have to tighten a couple of bits.'

'Take all the time you like,' she jumped in.

There was the silence again. She could hear birds singing outside and the low rumbling of an aeroplane.

Seb sat back on his heels. 'My mum rang again about the wedding. What we're doing.'

'What did you tell her?' Anna asked, holding her breath for his answer, as if they were deciding their future over veiled, polite chit-chat.

'I said we were still undecided.' He shrugged, and leant back over the bath to tighten the shower fittings.

'Are you?' she asked, turning away from him, picking at some cracked paint on the door frame. 'Undecided?'

She heard him exhale. 'I don't know, Anna.' He clanged around with the bathroom fittings, and then he paused. 'It doesn't feel like we're a couple on the verge of getting married, does it? I don't even know if we like each other any more.'

Anna stuck her finger under a flap of paint and flicked it up, watching it crack and fall to the floor. The birds carried on lightly chirping outside. She stared at the spot of dry wood she'd exposed. 'I like you,' she whispered, maybe too quietly.

He didn't reply. Just busied himself pushing all his tools back into the box and closing the latches.

As he pushed himself up, he flicked on the tap and water gushed out of the shower head. 'There you go, one shower. That should make your life a bit more enjoyable.' He nodded.

'It's brilliant. Thank you.' She gave a small smile. 'Mr Mallory will be pretty pleased as well, you know, for the next tenants, it'll add value.' As she said it, she wished she hadn't, wished that she'd just pretended that it was for them only, made no reference to their transience here, and just thanked him for the gesture of doing it for her.

Seb shrugged, flicking the tap off again. 'I'd better go,' he said, squeezing past where she was standing and out the door. She could smell his sweat and the familiar scent of Seb that reminded her of cosying up next to him and feeling like everything in her head was calm.

As he walked away, she thought of Hermione and the precious jewels scattering away on the breeze, the rubies, the diamonds, the emeralds just floating away out of reach. 'You could...' She swallowed. *Say it, Anna. Swallow your pride, your poise and just say it*. 'You could stay for dinner if you like. I don't know what it'll be, nothing fancy. Just dinner. If you wanted?' She hesitated, the sleeves of her tatty old sweatshirt pulled over her hands.

'I don't think so, Anna.' Seb hoisted his tools up into his other hand. He paused and looked at her, then down at the carpet. 'Nothing's changed. Has it?'

She didn't reply. She didn't even really hear. For her the invitation to dinner was the equivalent of stripping naked and laying herself bare. It was her olive branch. She had opened herself up and been rebuffed. 'Absolutely. You're right, yes, nothing's changed. It was just food, nothing more than that, but yeah I totally see how that might be misconstrued.'

'Anna—'

'No, seriously, thanks for the new shower, Seb.' She felt her cheeks start to flame, she was mortified. The house itself seemed to be mocking her with its twee, smug country cottage ways. 'You know, actually, I think I might have left something at the erm...at the shop. So, yeah, I think I need to go and get it.' She moved past him where he stood in the centre of the bedroom. 'Feel free to use the kitchen and stuff. I'll probably be a while.'

It was only as Anna cycled on Rachel's bike down the lanes, mentally ticking people off that she couldn't stay with, that she realised she had nowhere to go. Hermione was at her father's house which ruled both of them out, it felt too pally to go and knock on Rachel's door, and she'd had too much to drink with Hermione to drive back to London, where her friends would ask too many questions about why she was on their doorstep at ten o'clock. She pedalled into the square and looked around. It was pretty much deserted, there was low-level noise coming from the pub but no sign of anyone. The bistro had a couple of diners but it looked like they were finishing up their coffees. She knew she couldn't go home. Couldn't lie in that house and look at her new bloody shower and know that he was right.

Nothing had changed.

When it came down to it, she still didn't want to be there. She still felt the snapping at her heels of something more.

Locking the bike to a lamppost, she paused on the edge of the square and wondered what to do next. Where to go. She flicked the bike keys over in her hand and, in doing so, saw the other keys that were attached. The ones to the shop. The ones she had been given only a day or so ago when Mrs Beedle had gone on a buying mission to Ardingly Antique Fair. She had placed them in Anna's hand and said, *Don't let any more clocks go missing! Yes.* And Anna had nodded, feeling like she had passed some kind of test. Like she was worthy of being trusted with something precious.

As she unlocked the door, deactivated the alarm and flicked on a couple of lights at the back so as not to draw attention, she felt the initial trepidation and spookiness of being there alone at night disperse into a sort of excitement. Like sneaking into a sweet shop as a kid. All the familiar objects – the portrait of the young girl, the mannequin draped in jewels, the beautifully restored chest of drawers, a row of porcelain ornaments – seemed to move closer, to wink at her in clandestine excitement. She felt like Bagpuss waking up while all the little toys yawned from their day asleep.

Walking around in the dusky light, Anna let her fingers trail over glittering brooches she'd polished, crystal glasses she'd wiped, velvet cushions she'd flumped. The eyes of the taxidermy birds watched her as she went. The thumping noise of the cat jumping down off the counter startled her.

'What are you doing in here, still?' she said, looking down at him as he twirled in and out of her legs. Then, quite unexpectedly, found herself reaching down to give him a tentative pat on the head, their first ever friendly encounter. 'It's just you and me, cat,' she said, before going through the curtain to the stockroom in search of food.

When she curled up in the armchair and ate a dinner of Marmite on toast while flicking through the only terrestrial channels available, it felt like coming home from school when she was tiny and having nothing to think about bar whether to watch *Home and Away* or *Blue Peter*. Time was suspended. Her thoughts pushed to the back of her head like the mountain of

221

chairs and crap at the back of the shop, to be dealt with another day. But as soon as the toast was eaten and the TV descended into absolutely nothing to watch, the thoughts loomed again. Threatening to pick up their endless loop of confusion.

So she did the only thing she could think to keep them at bay. She stood up, walked round to the back of the shop and gave the first chair in the haphazard mesh sculpture a tug. Three came away at once and another crashed to the floor. The cat scarpered. The Welsh dresser seemed to shrink back with a sigh.

An hour later, the stack was dismantled and lay in its various pieces round the shop like an odd, mismatched musical chairs. Half a set of mahogany antique dining chairs sat next to cult Conran design classics, a pile of wrought-iron garden chairs were stacked alongside a crappy wooden stool that was inextricably interlocked with an old French upholstered nursing chair, while a rattan sixties bucket chair was lounging next to what she thought, if she was lucky, might be an original Eames lounge chair.

With the stack cleared, she pushed her way further into the sea of junk and found an old apothecary cabinet spilling out with multicoloured buttons like Smarties, swirls of ribbon, silk ties, battered leather purses and feather fascinators that, when she put one on, wobbled on her head like a bird. Next she unearthed vacuumed bags of clothing, stacked one on top of the other, the squished fabric catching the light – tantalising glimpses of satins, silks and beadwork.

She felt a sudden compulsion to unzip the plastic. Second-hand clothes had never been her thing, a hang-up of always being dressed from charity shops and jumble sales as a kid, Anna liked everything new – wrapped in tissue and carefully slotted into a chic cardboard bag with rope handles – but the delicate beauty of the detailing she could see on the squished material had her reaching forward guiltily, checking that no one was watching, to set the clothes free. As she unzipped the bag, air streamed in and the fabric plumped almost with a sigh.

Inside was a rainbow of Versace, Gucci, Ossie Clark, Biba…beautiful material, silky and bejewelled, but all flawed, imperfect in one way or another. Poorly kept and destroyed by age. A skirt of fine cream net embroidered with rows of antique sequins was ruined by rips and tears so it resembled Cinderella's rags, a jacket in a watery aquamarine jacquard smelt of mould, sundresses and thick crepe trousers were peppered with moth holes, a black cotton kaftan was decorated with scrolls of unravelling gold, a slinky gown with a pearl choker had come apart at the seams. There was even a Versace sweatshirt with a house and fields embroidered on it and a hot pink pencil skirt – both stained with what looked like red wine. Holding the sweater up, Anna found herself laughing at how marvellously terrible it was and, as she was on her own and no one would see her, she pulled it on, careful not to snap the fascinator, and smoothed it down as it hung, baggy to her mid-thigh.

It reminded her of sneaking upstairs to glimpse inside the chest that housed all her mum's old ballet costumes. Corsets of peacock feathers, delicate red silk dresses, the dusty pink satin of her most cherished *Romeo and Juliet* tutu. Anna would finger the neatly folded fabric and feel within it the expectation of her own future.

The contrast of the huge Versace sweatshirt made her laugh to herself and she felt the fascinator wobble.

Pushing further into the space her foot kicked a black lacquered box that, when she lifted the dusty lid, was crammed full of jewellery – gold engraved bracelets, pearls on broken string, gaudy cut-glass rings and dangly earrings of amber and mother-of-pearl. In one of the teetering cardboard boxes she found a stack of top hats, in another vintage enamel jugs with blue rims, a mismatch of teapots, more cushions – beautiful ones with intricate patterns block-printed on velvet – a gold carriage clock and a whole stack of dusty Kilner jars. It was all stuff that must have been brought in from various car boot sales and auctions, then forgotten about as more and more was acquired and less and less sold.

As Anna lugged the boxes into the stockroom she found she had cleared enough room to prop up the old, battered stage set of Manhattan. In doing so, she knocked the glass of the one-eyed fairground fortune-teller who flung forward and back in its seat and croaked, 'Fortunes told here.'

'Shit!' Anna jumped back and had to stand for a second to get her breath back. The machine seemed to settle back into place as she looked at the scraggy, moley chin of the witchy fortune-teller and the moth-eaten purple robes she was wearing. Hand-drawn instructions pointed to a slot where Anna should place her hand and another to a wheel that she should wind.

She glanced around the shop, and everything seemed to slink back into place, like it had all been leaning forward, straining to see what would happen next. Only the birds in their glass boxes stayed watching as she wound the wheel and the craggy old witch sat up straighter. A light came on above the slot for her hand, and Anna tentatively reached her fingers in. A second later, a stamp slammed down hard on the back of her hand making her jump, 'Jesus!' she shouted, wondering if any of her little metacarpals had been shattered by the impact.

At the same time, the witch raised a broken finger from the desk and said, what sounded to Anna like, 'Do not mistake temptation for opportunity.'

'Great.' Anna shook her hand in pain and watched as the fortune-teller slumped back down into nothingness. 'You could have said that before I met up with bloody Luke Lloyd!' But, her attention piqued, she was intrigued enough to wind the machine a second time, keeping her hand clear of the stamp, and listened expectantly as the voice said, 'You are never too old to learn,' while the mechanics of the old woman's mouth took a couple of seconds to catch up.

Anna rolled her eyes, thinking how her father would be nodding in agreement and then raising his brows pointedly at Anna. But rather than dismiss the comments, as she carried on hacking through the jungle of mess, the advice from the woodworm-riddled fortune-teller seemed to echo in her thoughts.

She *did* see herself as too old to learn. She saw her life and her choices as very much cemented and immovable. Pausing when she caught a glimpse of herself in a sliver of window pane, dressed in her hideous sweater, she wondered if it *was* possible to change. To carve new paths in directions different to the old, familiar ones. If she was honest she'd assumed she'd stopped learning years ago. Precisely the moment she opened her A-level results. The very idea that perhaps *this* didn't have to be it was astonishingly liberating.

It was only as she was staring at herself, at her new Versace-clad reflection, that she realised what she was actually looking at. What she had always assumed was a wall was really floor-to-ceiling French windows. She felt behind all the boxes propped up against them and found a light switch which she flicked, bringing a tiny courtyard patio sparkling to life with strings of coloured outdoor bulbs. It was all cobbled stones, a mess of dandelions and higgledy-piggledy with pots. Vines trailed across the back wall, up over a wooden trellis that jutted out from the top of the windows. She stood and stared, her breath steaming up the windows. It was like watching magic.

Twisting the latch and pushing the doors open, Anna stepped out into air scented sweet with buddleia and lavender and the papery yellow petals of evening primroses crumpled and ghostly in the moonlight. The strings of lights swayed, caught by the corner of the French doors, and beams of blue, yellow and red danced on the cobblestones. The cat wove its way out between Anna's legs and she followed, walking once around the small plot, her legs catching occasionally on brambles, her arms swiping through old spiders' webs. 'Wow.' She said to no one. 'This is amazing.'

And it was then, as her mind already saw her sawing through branches, trimming vines without a thought for her nails, deciding which table and chairs would look best out there, arranging the enamel jugs with big bunches of purple lavender and drooping sprigs of buddleia and setting the scene with candles and delicate cups and saucers, that she wondered if there was an inkling of a chance that she was happier here, in this stuffy little shop, than she had been in her job at the opera house. The heart-breaking pressure of quashing her jealousy every day that she worked with the dancers, watching as other people realised her dream, clinging desperately onto a world that had chewed her up and spat her out – the daily reminder of her own failure – was more exhausting than she'd thought.

Perhaps, she wondered, her unceasing determination to climb to the top, her need for the best of everything, hadn't been ambition but escape.

She paused to pluck a grape off the vine and, squishing the purple juice between her fingers, thought how much she actually wanted Razzmatazz to succeed.

227

That she didn't watch them from velvet theatre chairs, legs crossed, stiletto swinging, half-consumed with envy. That her smile today had been real. Dressed in her crappy jumper and leggings.

Today she had been the Primark bag rather than the Chanel and she had loved every minute of it.

Chapter Sixteen

'What the bloody hell have you done to my shop?'

Anna darted awake at the sound of Mrs Beedle's voice.

'Have you spent the night here? Why have you spent the night here? And on the chaise longue. Blimey, Anna, that must have been uncomfortable. Oh my goodness, my garden...' Mrs Beedle paused, giving Anna a chance to work out where she was, why she was wearing a jumper that smelt of mothballs and had fields embroidered on it and to acknowledge that her back killed, and her hand had swollen up into a big red lump.

'My little garden,' said Mrs Beedle again. 'Oh, Anna, look what you've found.' It sounded like there might be tears in her eyes.

'I'm sorry I was here. I just—'

'Anna, my dear, if this is what you want to do with your time, then far be it from me to stop you. Isn't it glorious?' She walked over to the French windows and peered out. 'Oh my little garden. How I have missed you. Anna...' Mrs Beedle turned to look at her, her hand over her mouth, her big watery eyes magnified behind her owl glasses. 'Anna, I had forgotten it was here.' She laughed. 'I had forgotten,' she said again.

Anna watched her from where she sat on the chaise longue. Her desire to yank off the jumper and fascinator overpowered by the surprisingly lovely sight of watching Mrs Beedle's delight. Anna watched as she walked round trailing her hand over the same wild, overgrown flowers that Anna had. Watched her mouth quiver in a smile. Realised that Mrs Beedle had given her a chance when no one else would and this seemed like the perfect thank-you. In the comfort of this nest of a place, with no one watching, judging behind her back, Anna Whitehall had been sanded back, stripped of her layers of crap and was possibly, just maybe, beginning to reveal the original, beautiful, rough around the edges, raw wood underneath.

They ate breakfast sitting outside on the white wrought-iron chairs, the backs patterned with curling leaves. In front of them a marble-topped Singer sewing table was laden down with croissants that Mrs Beedle had dashed excitedly out to Rachel's bakery to buy, flaky pastry crisp with almonds and squishy with chocolate still warm from the oven. She'd even forgone her orange tea for take-away cappuccinos, the froth foaming thick over the rims, the bubbles bursting under the weight of cocoa and cinnamon dusted on top. Anna had poured orange juice into two of the gold-leaf glasses she'd found the night before, the edges so thin it felt like they might shatter to the touch, and laid out flower-patterned side plates for the pastries. A bunch of dandelions flopped erratically out of a jam jar in the centre of the table as wasps buzzed lazily around the vines.

'I meant to say the other day how much I like your friend, Hermione, is it?' Mrs Beedle said, before tearing off a chunk of croissant.

'Really?' Anna said, surprised.

'Yes. An interesting character.' Mrs Beedle nodded, holding her hand over her mouth as she spoke. 'She's going to sell me some Hungarian furniture.'

Anna sat up a little straighter. 'Is she? When did she decide that?'

'I was in the pub with her and your father last night. You know I don't remember her at all growing up here.' Mrs Beedle shook her head. 'They make a nice couple,' she added, as if she was pointing out something as pleasant as a sunrise.

Anna made a face. 'Oh they're dreadful. It's awful,' she muttered over a sip of cappuccino froth. 'They'll never last and the whole thing is disgusting. He's old enough to be – well – her father. It's embarrassing and it's never going to last. Ever.'

Mrs Beedle sat back and Anna could feel her watching her. The cat jumped up on her lap and Anna was tempted to boot him off, his affection seemed too revealing, too telling of her mood the night before.

'I wouldn't be so sure, Anna,' Mrs Beedle said, looking like she might be holding in one of her knowing smiles. 'I think she's quite good for him. He needs a firm hand.' She took a sip of her own coffee, froth coating her upper lip. 'I was watching them and I thought,' she licked the bubbles away, 'I think he's finally growing up.'

Anna guffawed. 'He's sixty-eight!'

'Well, some men mature at different rates,' Mrs Beedle laughed.

'I just think it's totally wrong.'

The bell above the front door tinkled and they both turned to see a woman walk in carrying a Dachshund under her arm.

'Anna,' Mrs Beedle sighed. 'There is no right or wrong. When are you going to get that through your thick skull! There's just...*how it is*. You can't make everyone fit into your view of the world.'

'I hardly think disliking my friend shagging my dad is a particularly obscure view of the world,' Anna snorted.

Mrs Beedle shrugged. 'Or you could see him as an adult who has had a lot of terrible relationships and perhaps finally found one that fits. You've been the spoilt daughter, Anna, you've made him pay. You can't keep it up forever.'

Anna glared up at her. 'I don't know what you mean.'

'Really?' Mrs Beedle raised a brow in challenge and Anna found herself looking away, at the big swathes of purple buddleia, butterflies hovering around each drooping flower, and tried to hold her cool, her feeling of rightness.

232

The customer cut into the silence asking, 'How much is this bird?' and pointing at the taxidermy crow.

Mrs Beedle stood up, now chuckling at Anna who'd jutted her chin out in defiance, and said, 'That one, my love? Let me see.' Pausing to drain her coffee cup before going over to the counter to search for a price.

Anna, who after hours of dusting, polishing and repositioning, knew everything in the shop and its retail value probably better than Mrs Beedle, sat with the price on the tip of her tongue. But she didn't do the selling, she'd decided that quite firmly. That part of the job wasn't for her. Yet as she sat there watching, saw Mrs Beedle run her finger slowly down her price list, she was suddenly struck by the flashes of memory that had been darting in and out of her consciousness since she'd started working in the shop. There she was in her red shorts, ponytail swinging, going to the antique fairs and car boot sales with her dad. All their little scams and schemes flooding back, the haggling, the stifled giggling and the belly laughing, the rush of a good bargain, the pat on the head when she pulled off a brilliant deal, an ice cream melting in the heat, the smell of frying onions from the burger vans. The chill of frost-bitten fingers warmed by hot chocolate and mittens in winter and sunburnt cheeks slicked with luminous lotion in summer, the shouts and insults and the stories about old coins and postcards that went on forever, the little dogs that curled up on the front seat of vans and the big dogs that barked when she walked past, the smell of cut grass or the slide of icy concrete.

The thrill of taking the crumpled notes that he would strip off the wodge in his pocket and give her at the end of the day if she worked hard enough. The fine line between right and wrong that they were acting out every time they went in for a deal. The worry of whether it would work. The breath-holding wait. The knowing winks, the knowing that everyone was doing it. Everyone was screwing each other for a bargain. And then driving home, the Thermos in the van, the crack across the windscreen, the day's spoils on the roof bungied on at precarious angles.

Memories more fun, more precious, than she had allowed herself to believe.

'I'll take this one, Mrs B,' Anna said, jumping up. And Mrs Beedle paused, her finger hovering over the price list, then smiled as she walked willingly back to her seat at the table.

'Nice, isn't it?' Anna said to the woman with the sausage dog and they both looked up at the bird. 'A real beauty. We haven't had him in long.' She thought about the beady little eyes of the fortune-teller watching her the night before, remembered the throbbing of her stamped hand.

Now, what did I teach you, Anna? Go in high. Why knock off fifty straight away when you can add it on straight away. See what I'm saying? That way you all leave knowing you got the price you want. And they think they got a deal.

'I've got it on for a hundred and fifty.' Anna heard Mrs Beedle suck in a breath and pause to lean on the window frame and watch as the woman walked round either side of the glass cabinet.

'And can you do any better?' the woman asked without looking up from the bird, its iridescent feathers catching the sunlight and sparkling blue, green, pink.

Everyone wants what they can't have, Anna.

'I'll have a look but I know I don't have a lot of room to move. There's so much demand for these. They're in and out the shop like that—' Anna clicked her fingers and took a couple of paces forward. 'Very desirable.'

The woman traced her finger round the edge of the case.

Anna watched her, watched her lick her lips, watched her glance out to where someone was waiting for her in the car, watched her hand hover over her bag, watched her look into the glass case again and then step away, unsure. Anna waited, walked over to the counter, pretended to study an invoice. She felt like her eight-year-old self. Her dad would be nodding, just out of sight. *Wait, Anna. Not too quick. Wait, patience, wait, wait. Let the desire build, wait, wait, and now... now reel them in. Catch them off guard. Slice it down and they'll be putty, Anna, putty.*

'Best I could let you have it for is a hundred,' Anna said in the end, without looking up from the invoice. 'And that's pretty much cost price for me. I have someone coming in at the end of the week wanting similar, so...' She glanced over her shoulder, held out her hands. 'It's up to you.'

'You take cards?' The woman asked, a fraction too quick, taking a step back to glance casually at the bird from a different angle.

What was it the fortune-teller had said? That she was never too old to learn. Perhaps, more importantly, she was never too old to remember.

Anna tipped her head to one side and smiled. 'Of course.'

As the woman backed out of the door clutching the stuffed bird in its case against her chest, the dog trotting beside her, Mrs Beedle wandered in from outside. 'So she is her father's daughter after all.'

'I don't know what you mean,' Anna said, feigning a total lack of comprehension.

'Why knock off fifty when you can add it on straight away? I've worked with the old bugger long enough to recognise his tricks anywhere, Anna.' She laughed.

Chapter Seventeen

Razzmatazz got steadily better. She wouldn't have said they were perfect, not by a long shot, but they were beginning to move in real steps with real timing. Long gone were the bumbling random jumps and wiggles that had made up the performance when she'd first seen them.

Matt and Mary had started arriving together, heads down, barely looking at one another but giving the occasional murmuring laugh as one of them muttered something while the other might allow a playful nudge.

'Look, Miss, they're in luurve,' Billy goaded, making Mary scuttle away in a pretence of changing her shoes.

Matt blushed and Anna heard Lucy, who was sitting next to her, shout, 'More than you'll ever get, Billy. Who's going to ever fancy you?'

'Don't need to pretend, Luce, I know you want me.' Billy swaggered over and Lucy threw her head back in a mocking laugh of disdain.

'Come back to me when you've hit puberty, you little runt.'

As they wound each other up, Anna watched Mary take a couple of steps out of the shadows of the sidelines and nearer to where Matt was standing. She was struck for a second how simple their love triangles were, how sweetly naive. Maybe all she needed to do was sidle up to Seb and offer him a Haribo and all would be well again. Maybe that was where she'd been going wrong.

Gradually, the others started to arrive, Peter sloped in, Scott loafed about by the piano and Clara appeared, dressed in black-and-white leggings and a ra-ra skirt, cramming half a sandwich in her mouth, and they took their places.

'Two days to go, Miss,' Peter said as she walked to stand in front of them.

'I know.' She nodded. 'How are you feeling?'

'Shit-scared,' Lucy shouted.

'No, you shouldn't be scared. You should be excited,' Anna laughed. 'What are you afraid of?'

'Getting it all wrong,' Peter bellowed.

'Well, because, Miss, we used to be shit and we knew it. And, well—' Lucy looked around at the rest of them who seemed to be in agreement. 'Now it's like we know we're OK, so there's more to worry about. If we think we're good and then actually we're shit, then that's embarrassing, d'you know what I mean? It's more serious, isn't it?'

Anna watched Mary nodding and felt a mix of pride and frustration. 'That's got to be a good thing, surely? Think how good it will feel if it goes well,' she said, feeling her brow furrow as she looked along the rows of them.

'Maybe, Miss.' Matt shrugged.

'It's just we probably want it more now, if you know what I mean? It feels like something we could maybe have, maybe get on the TV in a good way, kind of.' Lucy shrugged. 'Or Peter'll just fall over and we'll all go home.' She cracked a smile and the subject was over.

Peter swore while they sloped off the edge of the stage and took their places to start. Matt led the warm-up while Anna watched in silence, her mind rolling one thought over and over…

She had given them hope. And with hope came the huge possibility of disappointment.

It was midway through a second run-through, this time to music that was so loud the windows seemed to bow outwards, that the door slammed its now familiar booming thwack and the sound of a number of pairs of stiletto heels seemed to puncture the thumping track.

Peter stopped mid-move and said, 'Bloody hell, Miss. Your mates are supermodels.'

Matt stumbled to turn the iPod off while the rest of the group just stood and gawped while Anna swivelled, uncertainly, round in her seat.

Striding towards them, heels clipping on the wood, wasn't just Hermione this time, but her ex-assistant and now job-pimp Kim, her slicked-red lips beaming around an e-cigarette and the towering platforms on her shoes wobbling precariously with every step as she waved a vigorous hello.

And who was that next to her? Anna wondered. She knew her, she thought, was sure she recognised her. The need to place the face overcame the fact she

239

herself was wearing leggings, a plain white T-shirt and plimsolls, her hair, in need of a wash, was scraped back and her cheeks flushed from shouting instructions at the group.

'Anna Whitehall,' the stranger drawled. 'Well, I never thought this is where I'd find you.'

'Anna.' Kim sidled up next to her. 'I bumped into Hermione at just the most divine little launch party the other night and I asked where you were, and she told me about this lovely little village and I thought, where better for Lucinda to chat to you than here, in picturesque England. It's perfect. Hello!' She waved at Razzmatazz, who just stared back in silence.

Lucinda.

Anna thought for a moment.

'So, do you recognise me?' Curly flame-red hair, skin so white it was like she'd been cast from cream, taller than Anna by one inch exactly, eyes that sloped down at the corners, a mouth that curled up just on one side when it was satisfied it had got what it wanted.

'Lucinda Warren,' Anna breathed.

'Great to see you again, Anna. I've been looking forward to it, what's it been, ten years?'

'Eleven,' Anna said.

'Eleven. What's a year between friends?' Lucinda laughed.

What's a year between enemies. Anna held her mouth taut.

'Miss, we're running out of time,' Lucy shouted and all four women turned and looked at her as she flicked her Farrah Fawcett hair and then tapped her watch.

'This is what you're doing now?' Lucinda drawled, walking forward a couple of steps so she was beside Anna. Anna tried not to look at the group through the eyes of these newcomers. The various shapes and sizes, the ramshackle assortment of clothes, trainers, hairstyles, the hall that smelt of cabbage after the lunchtime Whist-drive, the booming Rihanna track. 'It'd be awesome to see them dance.'

Hermione leant round and whispered, 'I'm not sure it would actually.'

'Oh, Hermione!' Kim coughed on her electric cigarette. 'They're Anna's. We all know what magic Anna can spin. I bet they're fabulous.'

Anna licked her lips.

'You want us to go again, Miss?' Matt said, quietly.

'He's my favourite.' Hermione snorted a laugh.

No I want you to go home, Matt, Anna thought. *I'm embarrassed by you and I hate myself for being embarrassed of you.*

In her last year at the English Ballet Company School it had been announced that the company itself were staging a production of *The Nutcracker* that would start at the Royal Opera House in Covent Garden and then tour some of the greatest venues in the world, including the David H. Koch Theater at the Lincoln Center. The event would mark the fiftieth anniversary of the English Ballet Company and the decision had been made to open one role up to a dancer from the school.

The opening night would see the industry glitterati nestle into the audience, sip copious flutes of Bollinger, munch on canapés of sour cream and caviar croustades, and narrow their eyes at the performance of this fledgling ballerina, whispering witty criticisms or gasping in delight. It was a giant step towards a ticket to stardom.

By this time, under the tutelage of Madame LaRoche, Anna had begun to flourish. The more she grew, the more dedicated she became, the more she avoided her father and the less she went back to Nettleton, the longer she stayed behind so she didn't have to go back to the flat and her eternally furious mother, and she rose through the ranks to the heady, coveted position of unofficial favourite. She wasn't the best dancer technically, not by miles, but she had what Madame LaRoche would spread her arms wide and call spirit.

Trampled over, beaten, almost destroyed in her first two years and left hanging by a thread, frayed and terrified, as she went from Nettleton top dog to bottom of the London pack, worn down by the unrelenting competition at the school and constant questioning from her mother every night she came home about who she was better than, who she'd worked harder than, Madame LaRoche had leant over her at the end of one session, knelt down so her eyes were level with Anna's tired, bloodshot ones and said, *To become the top one percent, Anna, you have to look here* – she put her hand on her heart – *and not here*. She spread her arm out across the rest of the room. *You focus on this, you go to the devil. Natural talent may have got you here, Anna, but it is not enough to keep you here. Remember that.*

Anna had stared back at her, thinking, *please* throw me out, please, expel me, let this end. But Madame LaRoche had simply walked away, and Anna had hauled herself up and when the music started once more, for the first time she didn't see the others around her, she saw only herself, her beating heart, her gaze fixed and unwavering. And it had worked. She had started to get parts that weren't the starring roles but ones that allowed her to try, to experiment, to show her so-called Spanish spirit – the Mediterranean blood that pumped through her veins and imbued her with the fight, the passion, the determination to succeed against all odds. The same spirit that had turned inwards in her mother and was eating away at her bit by bit.

By the time *The Nutcracker* was announced, Anna's star was shining bright. Graceful and glittering. She would add the perfect amount of shimmer to the Waltz of the Snowflakes. It was there, the opportunity, dangling, ripe from the tree.

But then, poof, Lucinda Warren walked in. Flame hair slicked back, thick liquid eye-liner flicks, black mesh top over hot-pink leotard and matching leg-warmers. Fresh from a transfer from New York, no mere star, but a boiling, raging, beaming ball of sun.

'Miss, should we go again?' Billy stepped forward.

'Erm.' Anna scratched her head. Could she get Lucinda out of the room? 'Did you want to chat about the job? Should we go outside?'

The job. New York. Her ticket out of here.

'Oh no, honey.' Lucinda's mouth curved up. 'I came for the total experience. I want to see what these kids can do.'

Anna glanced back at the motley little crew. The pin in the balloon of her New York dream.

Kim scraped a chair over from the side and sat, legs crossed, puffing on her cigarette, while Hermione made an awkward face of apology at Anna and Lucinda strutted over to the piano where she leant gracefully against the closed lid, legs crossed at her perfectly sculpted ankles, and watched.

'OK.' Anna sighed and nodded to Matt to hit the music. If it was going to happen, they may as well get it over with. 'Let's go,' she said, her voice sounding tinny and bland. Then she saw Lucy shoot her an odd look and felt an immediate stab of guilt. She was taking their hope and she knew it and she couldn't help herself.

The music boomed out, Anna felt herself shudder, Lucinda tapped the lid of the piano, a smile playing on her lips in anticipation, but then Lucy missed the first step which meant her arm was outstretched as Peter turned her way and her fist connected hard with his cheek making him reel back, clutching his face in pain. Matt glanced over his shoulder to see why Peter was swearing, which meant he lost his timing and then tripped over his shoelace which stumbled him back into Clara, who, never one for keeping going, pushed him back and said, 'Get out my fucking way.' Mary tried to stay in time but was on her own, as the rest of them clattered about around her. Lucy, flustered, tried to save it with some spontaneous twerking, which made Hermione burst out in a laugh. And then, after the whole thing fell apart and Peter had skulked off to the side, Billy slapped out of a handstand cracking down onto his hip. Matt swore, his jaw locked rigid, and Lucy stalked off to sit on the edge of the stage while Mary looked guiltily at Anna from under her fringe.

'I did warn you,' Hermione sighed.

Anna couldn't look at anyone, just stared down at her hands. She could feel both Lucy and Lucinda watching her.

When Lucinda Warren danced, she blinded people, hypnotised them with energy, grace, confidence and perfection. Anna's spirit – her passion, her quirk, her style – crumbled next to this girl who danced as if the world had been created just for her. Anna was no stranger to falling from a height, but this was by far her greatest drop. She landed awkwardly, uncomfortably, stripped of her new confidence, like Cinderella at midnight, as the spotlight of favourite refocused on this perfect redhead.

And Anna, who had got used to the warmth of the limelight, didn't respond well to finding herself in a shadow. She would watch with fury boiling inside her as Lucinda practised, precision personified. She changed the way she danced to try and be better. She stopped laughing, stopped sleeping, she lived off adrenaline, off jealousy, off determination, wired by a desire to be better. To be the best.

Anna glanced over at Lucinda, who had walked round to the front of the piano and was engrossing herself in the keys and the sheet music, clearly embarrassed. Hermione and Kim were whispering next to her. She could feel the boring gaze of Lucy straight ahead of her.

'That was shit, Miss, wasn't it?' Lucy whispered.

Matt skulked over to stand next to Mary, who looked like she might be about to cry.

'Probably quite a good thing though, Miss, isn't it?' Lucy carried on. 'To know we go to pieces in front of an audience. Takes the edge of the nerves.'

Anna looked up and met Lucy's narrowed eyes, her brow raised in challenge, her heels banging on the stage.

Anna's mum had said, *This is what it's all been for, Anna. This is it. Don't waste this. There's nobody better than you, do you hear me? If you believe that, you'll get what you want. No – I don't want to hear it, it's just excuses. Anna, I mean it, I don't want to hear it. Anna! Fine, if you don't get it, don't come back. How's that for an incentive?*

'I just have to—' Anna pointed out to the back of the hall. 'Just take a minute, everyone. I'll be one minute.' She could feel her brow sweating as she turned and jogged to the doors at the back of the hall. Pushing through them she stood outside in the warm, sun-drenched air and leant her head back on the brickwork, closing her eyes and remembering the feeling of standing on the edge of that *Nutcracker* audition. They had all waited in the corridor to audition in front of a panel of Madame LaRoche, Mr Hadley, director of the EBC, and the resident choreographer, Barnaby Adams.

Anna's diet had consisted of protein and Prozac for that last pre-audition month, her hands shook so she sat on them as she waited, her skin was sallow, her muscles trembling like a bull wound up ready to fight, her cheeks hollow, her hair thin, her tired eyes sore, but her audition so perfect, so practised, so focused that she could have danced anywhere, slice her feet off and they would have kept on dancing. She had sat staring at a spot on the floor, a black dot of dirt on the white linoleum, looking at no one, nothing, just fixed, doing all her breathing techniques for calm, for focus, for confidence. Her body straining at the bit, ready. Her mind was visualising walking through the flat door that night, seeing her mum, waiting, trembling, apprehensive, and Anna would smile and her mum would leap up and hug her and she could finally exhale.

Leaning against the wall, she tried to search her mind for those relaxation techniques now. To lean forward and turn the dial in her mind that would release her endorphins and adrenaline, that would focus her and cut out the chatter.

247

But instead she saw her face making its biggest mistake. Saw it peering through the round window in the door just before she was called in for her audition. Saw it watch Lucinda glide across the space like she was made only of air, saw the muscles in her back ripple as they arched, saw the slick of red across her lips as she smiled, saw that this was hers. That whatever Anna did, she couldn't compete, she had lost before she had begun. And, as she watched, her adrenaline seemed to trickle out of her, her muscles held so tight just loosened and gave up, the exhaustion that was hidden by determination threaded through her and left her limbs like lead. So, when she walked into the room, she was already defeated. She had never felt so tired in all her life.

Across the square, Anna could see Mrs Beedle outside the shop taking in the chairs and other bits and pieces that had been arranged out the front. She saw her look up, shade her eyes and glance over in the direction of someone walking across the square. Anna's father. He took off his sunglasses and the two of them stood chatting, laughing. She watched him pick up a side-table and help carry it inside.

Before *The Nutcracker* audition, he had told her a story over the phone of a girl he'd seen on TV. A violinist. She'd picked up the instrument at four years old and been announced a prodigy. But, at twelve, when she'd started moaning about practising, her father had made her give it up. Made her put the violin away and told her that if she picked it up again, she picked it up for her. For no one else. No more moaning at him. And, four months later, she had opened the case and played and never stopped. Her father had told her the story and then paused and Anna had said sarcastically, *'I take it you're trying to tell me something.'* *'No,'* he had said, *'I was just making conversation.'*

'Miss?' Mary pushed open the door next to her, 'Are you coming back in? It's just no one's quite sure what to do.'

Anna turned her head to look at the mousy-haired girl, unable to look up from the floor mere weeks ago. She looked at her baggy T-shirt, leggings and the Converse hastily pulled onto her bare feet. 'Why do you do this, Mary?' she asked.

Mary did a little snort-like giggle. 'I don't know, Miss. I just do.'

Anna pushed herself off the wall and stood facing her. 'No. No, there's a better answer than that. Why do you come here?'

'I don't know, Miss.' She pushed her over-long fringe behind her ear. 'I suppose because I couldn't do it at school…'

'Why not?'

'They do ballet but they told me I wouldn't fit their criteria.' She did a self-conscious giggle. 'They've all been doing it for years and, well, I just didn't fit.'

'And here?' Anna asked, watching as she tugged on her T-shirt, clearly embarrassed and wanting to get back to the safety of the hall.

'It's just an opportunity. You know…to dance.'

Anna licked her lips, watched Mary shrug. 'How does it make you feel, Mary?'

Mary paused, swallowed, glanced down at the floor, at the sandy gravel and then back up at Anna, the tips of her cheeks pink, and said, 'It makes me feel beautiful, Miss.'

Anna was caught, she opened her mouth to reply but realised she had no answer.

'Can I go back in now, Miss?'

'Yes. Yes. Of course. Thank you, Mary. I'll be one minute and we'll go again.'

'OK.' The girl stepped back. 'Is that what you wanted to know, Miss? Was that the right answer?'

'There was no right answer,' Anna said, and laughed. 'There's just how it is.'

She had no memory of losing the part. Of actually being told. Her memory was only of unlocking the door of the flat and walking in and the whole place being filled with roses. Hundreds of them, every colour under the sun, yellow with pink trim next to heady white blooms and vibrant orange flowers in vases with deep, deep scarlets, ones so dark they looked black and others so pale they were like skin, crawling with dark veins, and almost see-though in the light. And the smell…dense and heady, overly sweet like bathing in burnt sugar, encroaching on Anna's battered senses and making her woozy. *Darling.* Her mum had stood, arms outstretched. Arms that had fallen in slow motion and at the same time knocked the closest vase, white porcelain smashing across the wooden floor, water splashing up on her mum's skirt, and yellow roses, heads heavy and useless, slapping to the floor.

The panel had asked her why she danced. She had reeled off her practised answers. The privilege, the buzz, the feeling of perfection when every movement she made was made and held identically to the person's next to her. It was in her heart, in her blood. It was her passion. My dad would tell me that I'd go to bed clutching my ballet shoes, she'd laughed.

Why did she dance? As she leant back on the warm bricks again, she thought it had been because she loved it, but one reason more than any other gnawed at her. *I wanted to make her proud.*

In the blue expanse above her, Anna watched a gull swoop lazily, buffeted on the warm air and thought, but how do I make me proud?

Her dad and Mrs Beedle were laughing, he had his hand on her shoulder, really guffawing at something. The sunshine was thick in the hazy air, clouds dotting shadows on the pavements.

On the other side of the square was the T-shirt in the window of Presents 4 You. *Paris, Milan, New York, Nettleton*. New York. Where was the flutter in her tummy when she thought of it?

The noise of her dad and Mrs Beedle's laughter echoed towards her and she found herself smiling at the sound. Because, in that moment, she realised, like the girl's violin, she had picked up Razzmatazz for her. However crap they were, they were hers. She had made the decision to give them hope, and bloody hell, she wasn't going to be the one to take it away from them. She knew what it was like to have someone ashamed of you, what it felt like. And she wasn't going to fill a room with roses and then smash them to the ground.

Taking a deep breath, smoothing down her T-shirt, Anna turned away from the square, pushed open the doors, strutted as confidently as she could to the front of the hall and said, 'It wasn't shit, it just started off badly. It's nerves. We all get them, we've all messed up because of them, now just be damn well grateful that it didn't happen at the audition. Get up, get into place and do it again.'

The whole group just sat there, glaring at her. Anna planted her hands on her hips. 'GET UP!' she shouted.

'Why should we?' Lucy sneered.

'Because you care,' Anna said, her voice sharp. 'Because…' She paused, looked along the row at them, at their flushed faces, big eyes, tight lips, and said a touch more quietly, 'Because I care.'

Mary looked down at her hands. Anna felt her heartbeat pulse in her temple. 'There are people here who want to see just how good you are. Now you either piss this chance away or show how much bloody work you've done. Now!'

She watched as heels bashed against the stage, watched as lips muttered and shoulders stiffened, felt the gaze of Hermione, Kim and Lucinda at her back, and then she caught a glimpse of Lucy's mouth as it tilted up into the vaguest of smiles.

'OK, let's go,' Lucy said, with a flick of her Farrah Fawcett fringe, and jumped up, bashing Matt on the arm who gave a bit of a shrug and then loped over to the iPod.

And Anna closed her eyes for a millisecond and thanked God, and then turned and walked back to her seat as if this was all completely normal and as it was meant to be.

'I thought that was awesome. Totally awesome.' Lucinda clapped her hands, strutting over to stand next to Anna. 'Just the best. I've never seen so many styles in one routine. I was super-excited.'

Anna found her lips twitch in a smile as the group tried to hide their pleasure.

'You thought it was OK?' Lucy said, from beneath her fringe.

Lucinda swept her bright-red curls back and said, 'I thought it was the best. Some technical errors but,' she waved a hand, 'it made me smile, and that's gotta be the aim, yeah?' She looked at Anna.

'Yes.' Anna nodded. 'I suppose it is.' The whole idea of Lucinda Warren talking to Razzmatazz was too surreal.

'There's nothing like grass-roots dance. Nothing like it,' Lucinda beamed. 'And everyone should have access to it. That's one of our objectives, Anna.' She turned to look at her. 'It's part of the New York job.'

Anna caught Hermione's eye behind her, who was making a face like they'd won the lottery.

The group were breathing heavily, sweating but still poised, hanging on for whatever Lucinda might say next.

'I did think, guys—' Lucinda nodded her head from side to side, 'that while the routine is super-rad, it might need something bigger for the finale. You know, a show-stopper. A final moment of full-on wow.'

'Yes!' Hermione chimed in. 'I thought that too, actually. I was waiting for a lift you know, like in *Dirty Dancing*.'

Anna shook her head. 'I don't think we have time for a lift, it's in two days.'

'And there's no bloody great lake to practise in, is there?' Hermione snorted.

'No, I suppose not.' Lucinda rubbed her finger along her lips. 'Shame.'

'We watched it, Miss. *Dirty Dancing*,' Clara called from the back row, her compact out so she could check her make-up was still firmly in place. 'Everyone came round ours and we watched it. It *is* in the fifties, Miss.'

'You did?' Anna was struck for a moment by the fact that they had all got together in their own time and watched the film that she'd suggested. Thought of them all crammed on the sofa bonding over *Dirty Dancing*.

'They can do it, you know,' Lucy said, nodding in Matt's direction.

'Shut up, Lucy.' Mary flushed beetroot.

'Do what?' Anna asked.

'The lift,' Lucy smirked, clearly enjoying herself. 'They can do it. We made them do it in the garden after we watched it.'

'Lucy, you promised,' Mary whispered.

254

'Oh get over it, it's for the good of the team.'

Hermione clapped her hands together with glee. 'Oh come on! Show us, we're dying to see.'

'Matt?' Anna ventured. 'Mary?'

'I don't want to.' Mary's lip trembled.

'Don't be so pathetic!' Lucy shouted.

Mary looked at the ground. Anna walked over to stand next to her and said in a low whisper, 'You don't have to do anything, but I think you'd be amazing if you did. I want people to look at you and go, wow.' She smiled. 'You have a lot of talent, Mary. Just don't worry about what anyone else is thinking or doing and keep the focus inside yourself, do you understand?'

Mary gave a little nod.

'The trick is to enjoy yourself, and then the job's half done.' Anna smiled.

Kim exhaled a puff of e-cigarette steam. 'Is this happening or not? I could totally handle a *Dirty Dancing* moment but, equally, I'm kind of crying out for a martini.'

Mary glanced at Matt and Matt winked at her and said, 'It's happening.'

And as Mary did a flying run and jump and Matt hoisted her effortlessly up in the air, and the muscles in her stomach wobbled as she laughed, and Hermione whooped and Lucy held her arms out as if she told them so, and Lucinda turned to Anna and winked, it seemed that they had their finale. And Anna realised she'd never been so proud in all her life.

Chapter Eighteen

'Ladies, I give you the best table in the house.' As they sashayed into his bistro, Philippe greeted them with a lazy smile and a confident click of his fingers to the waitress to make sure she got the table re-laid and ready for them. 'Champagne?' he asked as they settled themselves down in the wooden chairs, shaking the napkins out and laying them in their laps.

Kim guffawed,. 'Oh my god, I can think of nothing I'd like better than a good glass of champers.'

'Yes, thank you, Philippe,' Anna nodded, pulling her old cardigan round her and feeling decidedly under-dressed compared to all the designer outfits of her companions.

He winked at her and sauntered off to select the best champagne.

'So, Anna, this place is darling.' Lucinda looked around. 'I love it.'

'Well, it's no New York.' Anna tried to sound casual. They had mentioned the job briefly on the walk over to the restaurant and she found the reality of it suddenly terrifyingly daunting. A pipe dream of escape was completely different to the real thing.

'And those little kids. They're so cute. I was watching them thinking, god do you remember when we were their age? I'd broken three toes and had keyhole surgery on my knee already.'

Philippe came over with four flutes of champagne and the rest of the bottle in an ice bucket. 'Enjoy, ladies.'

Lucinda raised her glass. 'We should have a toast. I feel maybe it should be to something really inclusive, like to enjoying yourself. I liked seeing them enjoying themselves today. I was jealous of their buzz.'

Anna looked across at Lucinda as Kim boomed loudly, 'To enjoying ourselves. Fab idea.'

'You didn't enjoy yourself?' Anna asked. 'When you were dancing.'

'Oh, don't get me wrong, I loved it, but I don't think I'd ever say it was fun. I was just working so F-ing hard all the time.'

Anna sipped the champagne and all the bubbles went up her nose, making her almost sneeze. 'Sorry,' she said, wiping her face with her napkin.

Hermione looked up as if she couldn't take Anna anywhere, and then started to talk to Kim about where she'd bought her top.

Lucinda went on, 'I just think we were so damn young. If I did it now I think I'd be in more control, I'd know better what I wanted to fight for, which choices I'd make.' She flicked her hair and pouted her lips. 'All I wanted then was to win. Like you.'

'Like me?' Anna questioned.

'Yeah!' Lucinda laughed, half-studying the menu. 'Ooh, confit of duck, my favourite. Yeah.' She rested the card on her plate. 'I needed someone like you to fight against. It was exhilarating. I was terrified of you, but my god it pushed me.'

'But I was terrified of you,' Anna said, wondering whether Lucinda was remembering correctly. 'You were incredible. You just came in and wowed everyone.'

'Bullshit, I just tried to be as good as you. And goddamn Madame LaRoche would be like, *Look at how Anna does it, isn't Anna perfect?*' She laughed as she did a terrible French accent.

'No.' Anna shook her head. 'No it wasn't like that.' She saw Hermione glance up. 'It was, look at Lucinda. It was you. Not me.'

'Are you kidding me? Jesus, Anna. I had to sleep with that guy to get *The Nutcracker* part.'

This time Anna's champagne went everywhere. All over her side-plate, her face, her T-shirt. Kim leant over and patted the table with her napkin as Anna wiped the bubbles off her face a second time and then leant a little closer to Lucinda and said, 'You did what?'

Lucinda rolled her eyes. 'Mr Hadley. I seduced him in his office. Can you believe it? I can hardly believe it when I look back, but I would have done anything to get that part. To be young and ambitious, hey!' She smiled, clinked Anna's glass and went back to her menu.

Anna was dumbfounded. Her mouth wouldn't move. When Philippe came over to take their orders she just said, 'Me too,' to whatever Hermione had ordered.

'You slept with Mr Hadley?' Anna whispered, an image of him popping into her head – old and white-haired with a moustache and one front tooth longer than the other. Thin and wiry but with a strange belly that hung just over his belt like a bum-bag.

Lucinda made a face and then said in her best British accent, 'I shagged him on his desk. I would have done anything, Anna. There was just no way I was going to lose. I play much cleaner now, I promise.'

Anna swallowed.

It hadn't mattered. It hadn't mattered that she had looked through that window and watched Lucinda dance and lost her nerve. She could have flown into the room like Darcey bloody Bussell and she wouldn't have got it. What would her mum have made of that?

'But enough of that. It still makes me feel a bit sick when I think about it. You know, that vomit in your mouth feeling.' Lucinda shuddered.

Philippe brought over their starters. It appeared that Hermione had ordered tripe sausage. Which meant Anna had ordered tripe sausage.

'Hermione, why did you order this?'

'It's Patrick's favourite.' She grinned. 'Why did you order it?'

Anna didn't reply. Her dad's favourite food was tripe?

'Try it. It's really very good.' Hermione cut a piece and savoured the taste. Kim leant over, intrigued and sawed a bit off for herself, put it in her mouth and then, lifting her napkin, spat it out with as much dignity as she could.

'That, honey, is dreadful. Hello!' She waved a hand in Philippe's direction. 'I need something to take the taste of that out of my mouth.'

'Mademoiselle—' Philippe smiled. 'I have just the thing, if you think you can handle it.'

'Oh, I can handle anything,' Kim smirked.

Philippe came back with a bottle of clearish liquid that looked distinctly home-brewed, with a hand-written label on which was written Eau de Vie.

'And what does that mean?' Lucinda asked.

'It is the water of life. It puts the fire in your belly.'

'Well, I like the sound of that.' Kim took the little glass he proffered.

Philippe sloshed some more out and passed the thimble-full glasses round. 'I will drink with you. What are you toasting?'

'Well, it was to enjoying ourselves, but I can't think about that with that horrendous taste in my mouth. So think of something else. Anna – how about New York? Should we toast to you in New York?' Kim asked.

'Yes, Anna, should we toast that?' Lucinda cocked her head and looked at Anna, as if waiting to see if she was going to accept.

Anna paused, stared at the little glass in her hand. She could feel Philippe's eyes on her.

'If I may, ladies,' he cut in, 'I would prefer to toast to you all being here in Nettleton. Forgive me, but I do not want to toast a departure.'

'Hear, hear,' said Hermione.

'Well then.' Lucinda held up her glass. 'To Nettleton.'

'To Nettleton,' said Anna softly, knocking back the drink, the liquid hitting the back of her throat like fire and burning its way through her whole body in an instant.

Chapter Nineteen

Two days later, a parcel arrived on Anna's doorstep. It was a massive cardboard box that the delivery man struggled to get up the path.

The card read, '*Anna Whitehall, about* The Nutcracker*...I've never been so relieved to tell someone something. You wouldn't believe! The job is yours if you want it. I'd like to work with you, Anna. Think about it seriously. In the meantime, I thought your group could do with these...Lucinda x*'

She sliced open the top of the box and peered inside to find a stack of carefully packed costumes, all with the tags still on from the NYC Academy. She was holding up a cropped luminous-yellow T-shirt and red spangly leggings when Seb came out of the shed wearing his pale-grey suit.

'Very nice,' he said. 'They'll suit you.'

She smiled. 'Yeah, it's my new look.'

'It'll certainly get you noticed on the streets of New York.' He laughed like it was a joke he was comfortable with, grazing a hand over his cheek.

She looked down at the bright-red sequins, 'It'll more likely get a bunch of teenagers noticed on *Britain's Got Talent*.'

'Oh God, is that today?' he said, startled, seemingly annoyed with himself for forgetting. 'How are you getting there? Do you need me to drive anyone?'

'No.' She shook her head. 'Matt's dad, he's hired a minibus.'

They stood awkwardly for a moment, watching each other. Beside him she could see the space where the roses had now been taken over by a rhododendron bush, its flowers big trumpet-like bursts of vivid-pink, and, next to that, the recently pruned honeysuckle, filling the air unashamedly with its sugary sweetness while bees buzzed, drunk, from flower to flower. She tried to think of something to say.

She wanted to walk up and say, I'm sorry that you felt I drove you away. To say, I wish you hadn't slept in a bed with Melissa Hope. I want to be able to hold your hand and say thank you for cutting the roses that were clearly beautiful but made me sick. I want to straighten your collar. Ask when you cut yourself shaving. See if you need anything for the shed. Hear you laugh about all the spiders living in there and how you wake up at two a.m. to the sound of the foxes and get a bit scared but lie there trying to be macho and not care. I want to ask if you'd come back to sleep in my bed.

But instead she watched as Seb gave a quick nod and then turned, his sleeve brushing past the honeysuckle, the scent drifting softly her way as he opened the gate. He paused on the threshold, she saw his shoulders rise and fall as he took a breath and then he turned back and said, 'Good luck today, I don't think I've said it, but I'm er...' He paused, plucked a leaf off one of the spindly white flowers. 'I'm really proud of you.'

As he closed the gate behind him, Anna felt her fingers tighten around the red sequinned material as her heart seemed to batter itself against her ribs like a puppy left at home by its owner.

The minibus trip to London was like they'd raided an American Apparel. When she'd presented the group with the box of goodies, she'd never seen faces light up with such delight. The boys were yanking out pairs of tracksuit bottoms in electric-blue, turquoise, red and there was even a white pair that Billy took a particular liking to, all with the NYC Academy logo stamped on the thigh. There were baggy T-shirts, baseball tops with coloured sleeves, hoodies and truckers' caps with big embroidered NYCA emblazoned across the front. The girls fought over sequinned leggings in every colour of the rainbow and gold lamé leather-effect skin-tight trousers that Anna rather fancied for herself. There were crop-tops in hot-pink and blue leopard-print, luminous vests, fluffy headbands, wristbands, big chunky white socks and, at the bottom, was a shocking purple and yellow tutu, its layers of net jutting out like the ones Anna had worn at the EBC. As Anna let her fingers run across the fabric, Lucy snatched it and held up high like a bridesmaid catching the bouquet. 'This is mine!' she whooped and pulled it on over the top of her gold lamé leggings.

It seemed to Anna, at that point, as they were all pulling on their clothes, laughing at each other, back-combing their hair, pulling caps down low, that if the bus broke down and they never made it to London, this would have been enough.

'If you could take a seat somewhere on the left and wait for your number to be called.' A girl in a black T-shirt and trousers with a clipboard directed them into a holding pen like an aircraft hangar at the back of The Oval. 'The producers are running late, so I can't give you a time,' she said, before moving onto the next in the queue.

'The producers?' Anna said, making a face. The room smelt of other people's snacks, sweat and dirty carpet.

'That's who the audition is in front of, Miss.'

'What, not Simon Cowell?'

'No.' Lucy rolled her eyes, flumping up her back-combed top-knot. 'You've got to audition to get to him.'

'But I thought that was the point.' Anna scowled. 'I thought we were going to meet Simon Cowell.'

'Do you fancy him, Miss?'

'No!' Anna said, blushing.

'Miss fancies Simon Cowell. Wait till we tell Mr Davenport. He'll be well jealous.'

Anna laughed, then she thought of Seb's face that morning when he'd told her he was proud of her and she almost spontaneously burst into tears. Looking away from the group, shielding her eyes as if the shaft of sunlight from the windows was too strong, she stood up and said, 'I'm just going to…to the loo.'

'He's not here, Miss. You won't find him,' Billy joked.

Anna feigned a smile, feeling the water collecting in her eyes and nipped away to find the loo, where she blotted her face and blew her nose, trying not to think of Seb – the smell of honeysuckle, the flaring pink rhododendron flowers, the hazy sun, the shaving cut on his chin. She took a couple of deep breaths and focused on the moment. On her colourful little group.

On the way back to the waiting area, she caught a glimpse of one of the auditions. Another dance group, all arms and legs in perfect sync. She took a step closer and peered through the gap in the hoarding that separated the audition space. They were amazing. She bit her lip and watched as they tumbled and jumped, as their music morphed and their costumes changed and their whole routine flipped into a new realm.

Shit.

She could feel her heart beating.

'All right, Miss?' Lucy looked up as she returned to the group.

'Fine. Fine,' she said. But all she could see was their little hearts getting broken.

266

'We saved you these,' Lucy said and chucked over a pair of gold lamé leggings. 'We reckon Mr Davenport would like them.' She winked and Anna blushed.

'Razzmatazz?' A young brunette with a clipboard said. 'Number 15031?'

'Yes, that's us.' Anna held up a hand and the girl motioned for them to follow.

'Ready?' Anna asked, standing up and watching as the smiles turned suddenly to looks of absolute terror. 'Don't worry. Whatever happens, you'll be amazing.'

As they walked along behind the woman in silence, Billy an odd shade of whitish-green, Anna thought of all the things she wished her mum had said to her when she'd gone in for that audition. Of all the things she wished she'd said after every performance. But when they were gathered, waiting in the wings of the audition pen, after she had run through some of the key things to remember, checked that the music was ready, given each person something specific to focus on, she could think of only that one thing that she would have wanted her mum to have said.

'Just enjoy it.' She smiled. 'Whatever happens...' Her voice hitched in her throat. 'I'm really, really proud of you.'

The audition space was bleak, the carpet grey with red triangles, the boards at the back a dirty shade of blue, and the spotlights beamed down harsh and unforgiving into the nothingness. A panel sat at one end, headphones on, Starbucks cups littered the table alongside cans of Red Bull and packets of Wrigley's Extra. One girl was on her phone and barely looked up. The main guy sitting in the middle, thin-lipped and grey-haired at the temples, had lines on his face from where he looked like he'd had a nap in the break-room. Anna just wanted to run in there and do it for them. To clap her hands at the faces of the judges and shout for them to pay attention, to sit up, to take notice.

As the music boomed, the girl put down her phone, the grey-haired man rubbed his face. Razzmatazz danced like she'd never seen them dance before. Big beaming smiles on their faces, steps almost identical, sequins glistening as they caught the spotlight, a writhing, exuberant mass of primary colours. Billy's jumps were a foot higher, his tumbles a turn tighter, Lucy's twerking had the hard-faced, bored panel smiling, Matt and Mary hustled like pros. Their fingers stretched high, their toes pointed, their hair swished, their bodies finally moved as one, and Anna found herself on the sidelines, her fingers steepled over her lips, willing them on, her stomach in knots like she might vomit on the spot, every move, every turn, every twist, seemed to be in slow motion and then, finally, when Mary stood to the side and ran, flinging herself at Matt, she had to shut her eyes, just in case it all went horribly wrong, just in case he didn't lift her with effortless ease and hold her till Rihanna's final note. But she opened her eyes just in time to see that he did and they did. And then it was over.

Razzmatazz were smiling and sweating, doubled over in delight, clapping themselves, while Anna cast her eyes over at the producers who were conferring with unemotional faces and she pleaded with whoever was listening that they would get through. Pleaded that, while they weren't the best, they might get through on enthusiasm alone. That they would see what she now saw. That they would see their spirit.

'Thank you,' the main man said, glancing down at his clipboard and then back up again. Anna held her breath. Razzmatazz were all hugging and waiting. He cleared his throat. 'Some nice stuff there. Thanks for coming to show us, but it's a no this time, guys.' He nodded and Anna gasped, then watched, heartbroken, as they all nodded back, their heads low as they exhaled big breaths, and started to troop off the stage. 'OK, next act ready?' the grey-haired man said through a microphone on his desk. 'We need to get this moving, guys. We're way behind.'

As she followed them out, Anna knew then what it was like to care. What she had been avoiding for so long. What it was like to want something so much that it made her ache.

She watched their little slumped shoulders, waiting for tears. Waiting for the sense of failure to wash over them and the feeling of not being good enough, the dissection of what they could have done better. She wanted to turn back the clock to the euphoria of the minibus and the picking of the costumes.

She held her breath. She rehearsed a speech.

She waited.

But it didn't come.

'Shit, I felt like a star!' Lucy burst out a laugh once they were out in the open space of the foyer. 'Like a princess or something. Like fucking Miley Cyrus.'

'Has anyone got any change for a Coke?' Matt asked, rummaging in his pocket and finding only copper change.

'My money's in the bus,' Peter said, bending over to take a breath, his chubby hands on his knees, a rim of sweat on his cap. 'I'm knackered. Seriously sweating. Miss, can we go to Burger King on the way back?'

Anna felt her brows pull together in confusion. She watched as Billy, seemingly hyped-up on adrenaline, started doing Michael Jackson moves on his own at the side, Clara had broken away from the group and was lingering at the back, fluttering her false eyelashes at a lone guitarist about to audition, Mary was looking through her purse for change for Matt.

'Is everyone OK? Do you want to talk about what just happened?' Anna asked, tentatively.

'What's to talk about?' Lucy looked up from inspecting her tutu. 'We didn't get through.'

'I know,' Anna said, as if that was her point.

'We knew we weren't going to get through, Miss,' Matt said, a half-smile hitching its way up his face.

'There was no way we were going to get through,' Billy called from where he was moonwalking just to the left of them. 'But we did it pretty well.'

But it wasn't enough! Anna wanted to say. Why would you even try if you're not going to win?

'We didn't embarrass ourselves, Miss. And it was really fun, I'm buzzing.' Lucy held up her hand to show that it was shaking. 'I've never felt like this before. Ever. I thought we totally did amazingly,' she added and Mary nodded, 'Oh I did, too,' she said quietly, her cheeks flushed pink.

Anna glanced across at them, all their eyes staring at her like she was the one who might need their sympathy.

'You didn't seriously think we were going to get through, did you, Miss? You were the one who told us we didn't have any steps!' Matt laughed, checking whether he'd scrounged enough change.

Why would you do it, she thought again, if you didn't think you had a chance of winning?

But then she looked at them again, really saw them. All kitted out in their NYCA clothes, strutting about like royalty. Matt's arm slung over Mary's shoulders. Quiet Mary who she knew wouldn't naturally have been friends with this lot but had sat smiling earlier as Clara had slicked on eye-liner flicks and bright-pink lipstick, Mary who did this to feel beautiful. Mary who looked beautiful.

'Shall we go, Miss? I'm starving, I haven't eaten all day. I thought I might be sick everywhere if I did.' Lucy began walking towards the door.

As Anna started to follow, Billy came up next to her and said, 'You shouldn't take everything so seriously, Miss.' She looked down at him and he looked back up at her from under the peak of his cap. 'You saved us from that crap people video.' He laughed, then ran over to get in step with Lucy.

Anna was left walking alone, shaking her head at the very idea of it. Of not entering to win. Of not taking everything so seriously. Of doing it simply because it was fun.

'Hope it hasn't put you off for next year?' Matt shouted over his shoulder to her as he jogged over to the Coke machine.

Next year.

New York year. Fifth Avenue dressed in Chanel year. Where she would start living again.

Why then did the colourful backs in front of her, the bobbing top-knots and sweaty truckers' caps, seem so much more alive than anything else her imagination would conjure up? Could she really accept, she thought as she climbed into the minibus that smelt of hairspray, damp and salt and vinegar crisps, unable to hold in a laugh at some crap joke of Peter's, that this might be living?

Chapter Twenty

The bus pulled into Nettleton square just as the afternoon was fading into evening. A bin bag full of Burger King wrappers sat by the sliding door, feet were up on headrests, heads lolling back asleep so they had to be woken by a shriek from Lucy to see the banner across the square.

'Nettleton's Got Talent!' Was daubed in red paint on a piece of cream tarpaulin and had been hoisted across the plane trees, the lettering not yet dry and dripping down along the edges.

'Whoop!' Lucy shouted, sliding back the window as they all clamoured to stick their heads out and wave to the crowd that had gathered, waiting for their returning heroes.

'We're so proud.' Billy's mother was wiping away a tear as she grabbed him and Clara into a hug. 'Just look at you, little stars.' She laughed.

Jackie was waiting with champagne and popped the cork as soon as everyone was out of the bus, pouring it into plastic mugs and handing it out to grasping underage hands. 'Congratulations!' she shouted, holding the bottle in the air. 'Bloody brilliant. Well done! You'll have to do a performance for us.' Then she shook up what was left and sprayed it over all their giggling faces.

All their parents were there, arms round them, wanting to hear all about it, delighted with their effort, congratulating Anna, thanking her for teaching them, letting her know how much they've loved it, how much they've grown, how they've been really impressed.

Anna, who still couldn't quite believe that anyone could get quite so excited about not winning, found herself nodding, shaking people's hands, thanking them for the invitations to dinner, agreeing when they talked about how she'd have to come up with a new routine for Razzmatazz's part in the Christmas play, feeling slightly perplexed when they said how much the kids liked her, respected her, talked about her.

A glass of champagne was thrust into her hand and a sticky jam tart from a huge platter whipped up by Rachel. The warmth in the air was just right, just the perfect temperature, like the suffocating heatwave had finally decided to relinquish its hold and it was hard to imagine hot being too hot. The last of the afternoon sun was just enough to warm her flushed skin, to carry the sounds of laughter and the sharp tang of the gnarly geraniums in cans around the square.

'So I hear it went well,' she heard Seb's voice say behind her.

'Mr Davenport, it was amazing,' Billy shouted. 'And we got Miss some sexy gold leggings' He winked.

'I'm glad to hear it, Billy.' Seb nodded a smile, an eyebrow raised, and turned back to Anna. 'How was it?'

She found herself suddenly shy. 'It was good.' She nodded. 'They didn't get through but it was good.'

'Yeah?' he asked, his head tilted slightly to the side, as if watching for tell-tale signs of more. 'And you're OK with that?'

'Of course.' Anna made a face. 'They did their best.'

Seb blew out a breath. 'They did their best, eh? Blimey. What's happened to Anna?'

She took a sip of champagne, looked up and then away from the crinkles round his eyes. 'She's learning,' she said into the bubbles.

Seb nodded, mouth curling down like he was impressed.

Just then, she was hustled forward and knocked on the arm as someone else bustled through, 'Anne, my dear...' Seb's mother, Hilary, drawled. She was wearing a pleated skirt and matching blouse in a shade of rice-pudding cream, a big orange necklace of oversized stones hung round her neck like fishing floats. 'So your little group seem very pleased with themselves. Are they going to be on the television?'

'No.' Anna shook her head. 'I'm afraid they didn't make it that far.'

'Oh dear.' Hilary surveyed the throng. 'What a waste of energy.' She sipped from her own glass of champagne. 'But I suppose it kept you off the streets!' she said with a snort.

At that point Roger joined them, cigar clamped between his fingers, one hand tucked into the pocket of his cords. 'See your father's got himself a new piece of fluff.'

'Roger, don't be crude.'

'Well, she's what? Half his age?'

Anna took a breath, felt herself slide her shoulders down her back. 'She's my best friend actually. I think they're…' She glanced across in the direction of the benches and the village hall where her father was standing, his arm around Hermione's waist, the two of them laughing as Billy did a succession of back-flips across the cobbles. She paused, watched for a moment, watched the curl of Hermione's shoulders, the tilt of her head, the wide smile on her face that she usually refrained from because it could cause wrinkles. She saw the too-long flick on her dad's hair, the flip-flops, but the shirt that was ironed and the trousers that looked a touch more tailored, she saw how Hermione's hand wound round his at her hip. Saw the same smile on his face that he had had when he had stood beside her granny, waiting for Anna as she came out of the dressing room at the EBC. She turned back to Roger. 'I think they make each other really happy. And that's all you can ask, isn't it?'

Roger looked slightly taken aback for a moment, huffed a breath and then went to say something else. 'Well I don't know—'

'I do.' Anna cut him off. 'I know. And so do they. I think that's all that matters.'

She watched Hilary make a face at Roger, eyebrows raised, and both of them tuck this away for discussion later on in private.

The sun dipped behind a cloud and Anna felt herself shiver, the only jumper she had was fluorescent-green-and-yellow leopard-print and had been the last remaining in the box. She'd slept on it on the way back and it was now scrunched in her bag. As Hilary prattled on about God knows what to Seb, Anna put the champagne in her hand down on the floor, the celebration suddenly seeming over as reality slipped back in. She pulled out the jumper and pulled it on over her head.

'My my,' Roger snorted, 'wait while I get my shades.'

'Dressing like one of the kids now, Anne.' Hilary gave her a little shake of the head. 'Whatever next?' She raised a brow at Seb.

Anna swallowed, pushed her hands into the pockets of the jumper and didn't look up.

'Well, now all this nonsense is over I suppose you'll get back to the wedding planning,' Hilary soldiered on. 'I'm assuming you've done something? I still get calls every day and I still don't know what to tell them. I mean, I assume there is still going to be a wedding…'

Anna looked back over towards Hermione and her dad, wondered if she could just walk over and join them. Leave Hilary just standing there, her voice like a fist punching straight into the exhilaration of the day.

'Mum. Leave it,' Seb muttered.

Anna turned back to glance at him, wondering if she'd heard him right.

Hilary leant forward. 'I'm sorry, Seb, did you say something?'

Did he say something? Anna wondered. Had he actually said something to stop his mother?

'I said, just leave it,' he said again, through clenched teeth.

'Leave what?' Hilary asked, bemused. A little laugh on her lips.

'Just back the fuck off about Anna and the wedding. OK!' he snapped.

'Don't you swear at your mother,' Roger said sharply.

'I'll swear at who I like. At the moment your input isn't needed and it's not helping. We'll let you know what's happening and when. In the meantime—' Seb paused, some people near them had turned to watch. Anna couldn't breathe. 'I'd appreciate it if you took a step back and let Anna and me handle this. OK?' He looked at them like they were his pupils as he spoke with an authority Anna had never seen in her life before.

'Well, I…' Hilary started but then stopped. 'I'm shocked. Seb, I'm shocked by your tone.'

He held up a hand. 'That's enough. It's over, the subject is closed. That's it. We can discuss it again some other time.'

Roger's brows drew together in a frown. 'Indeed,' he said. 'Well, it seems you…have it under control.'

Anna could feel the people around them still half-listening as they pretended to carry on with their own conversations. Her heart was thudding in her ears.

'Very well, Sebastian.' Hilary straightened her blouse. 'You know best, of course. I wouldn't want to be thought of as someone who interferes. It's your and Anna's day. I look forward to getting my invitation.' Her cheeks had flushed under her rose cream blush. 'If, that is, we're still invited,' she added, and then touched Roger on the arm, their signal to leave.

As they stalked away to their car, Seb exhaled, ran his hand over his forehead. Anna just watched in awe.

'I shouldn't have sworn. Fuck.' He made a face. 'I just fucking wish I hadn't sworn. That's all she'll remember. I wouldn't have sworn with the kids. Argh, I'm so annoyed.'

Anna was still reeling. Filling up with adoration like a jug of orange squash. 'I thought…' she started.

'Why?' He turned her way, raking a hand through his hair. 'Why? Why did I have to swear?'

'I thought it was amazing,' she said, in almost a whisper.

'You did?' Seb said, taken aback.

She nodded.

'But it would have been better if I hadn't said fuck, yes?' he said.

She shrugged. 'I don't care either way. I thought it was amazing.'

She watched a little smile pull at the corners of his lips. 'You did?' He nodded his head. 'I suppose it was pretty good.'

'Miss!' Lucy shouted from across the square. 'Come and look at this.'

Anna glanced over to where Lucy, Matt, Peter and Mary were practising some balance formation that looked highly precarious. 'I'd better go,' she said, angling her head in their direction.

'Of course.' Seb nodded. 'Hey, have you seen who's with Jackie?'

'No.' Anna shook her head, looked across the square and saw Jackie, sipping champagne out of her plastic cup, standing with a tall guy, hands in his pockets, beaky nose and gold-rimmed glasses, but attractive in an Internet-millionaire type way. 'Who is he?'

'Smelly Doug.' Seb angled his head with a smile.

'Oh my God!' Anna held her hand up to her mouth. 'She met up with him?'

'More than once, apparently. He's seemingly seduced her with his Porsche and a day trip to Paris.'

'Wow.' Anna nodded, impressed. 'Maybe it's not all bad out there,' she said, looking back at Seb with a shrug.

'Maybe,' he replied, a little more serious.

'I'd better go,' she added, as she heard a shriek from the Razzmatazz quartet currently clambering over each other.

'Yep.' Seb nodded.

Anna started to walk away and then glanced back. He was watching her, his hands in the pockets of his jeans, the expression on his face unreadable.

She ended up staying in the square for ages, at least another hour, while Razzmatazz had photos taken and the journalist from *Nettleton News*, a fairly depressing man with bad skin and a terrible suit but a sweet smile, wanted an interview.

As the journo tucked his Dictaphone away and said, 'I think this'll make a nice piece,' Anna's dad walked over, his hands behind his back, and stood next to her.

'You did good,' he said.

'Well I suppose it was about time I did something right,' she said with a shrug.

'I told you it was there, didn't I? The bit you got from me.'

'OK, don't get too cocky,' she said with a raise of her brow.

He laughed. They stood side by side watching as Lucy and Clara tried to teach Hermione how to twerk.

'You still getting the money off your mother?' he said, as if it didn't really mean that much, as if this was just casual chat. 'You know, for the wedding?'

Anna turned to look at him. He stayed looking forward, smiling at Hermione's terrible attempts at twerking.

'Because I was thinking, I could sell my car. You know, if you wanted another option.'

She thought of her dad's red vintage Mercedes, his absolute pride and joy. The car that had been polished every week in the garage since before she was alive. The only thing he owned of any value whatsoever. She thought of the money she'd sunk into The Waldegrave wedding, the crap she'd racked up on her credit cards, the expensive wine she'd drunk in expensive bars in Bermondsey, the designer clothes she had wrapped in tissue at the back of her wardrobe. *And half that car, Anna, half that bloody car, that's mine. That's ours. Do you know that?*

She felt her face soften into a smile. 'I don't want you to sell your car, Dad.'

He glanced her way. 'You're sure?'

She nodded.

'I just…' He swallowed. 'I'd just like to be there. I don't have to give you away or anything, but I'd just like to be there, you know, to watch.'

She pressed her lips together, felt the prick of tears in the corners of her eyes and couldn't reply. So she just nodded. And he nodded. And they both went back to looking at Hermione.

Still dressed in her leopard-print sweatshirt, her gold lamé leggings stuffed into her bag, Anna finally made her way to her car. All the kids were still gallivanting about the square doing impromptu renditions of their act to whoever would watch, a couple of parents were standing around chatting, but most people had edged their way over to the pub and were standing outside, sipping bitter under the hanging baskets.

She'd been invited to join, officially welcomed into the abode by Babs who'd even said she'd bring the good wine out, but Anna had shaken her head. She was exhausted. 'Too much excitement for one day,' she'd laughed.

'Well we'll see you soon,' one of the parents had said, waving a hand. 'Loving what you've done to the shop, as well. Very nice. Very London,' he'd said with a joking drawl.

Anna had nodded, not quite sure what to do with all this pally chatter, and then turned away and walked towards her old hatchback.

There was a flier stuck under the windscreen wiper, which she leant over to pull out and scrunch up but, just as she did, she saw that it was written on lined paper with perforations down the side.

Sitting in the driver's seat, she flattened the paper ball out on her thigh and read it.

Man-cave-dwelling hero seeks stunning heroine for love, passion and possible marriage. I am a hugely intelligent, handsome, loyal lonely heart with GSOH and a very impressive Assassin's Creed score on PS4 (in some cultures this ranks high on the list of desirable attributes). Sometimes makes mistakes and occasionally poor at admitting when he is wrong, but handy in the bathroom, garden and recently prone to bouts of shockingly impressive machismo. WLTM girl of my dreams.

If interested, please join me for dinner. My current residence is just to the left of Primrose Cottage.

[for man-cave read shed]

[for mistakes read life-changing fuck-ups for which he will never be sorry enough]

[for impressive machismo read you ain't seen nothing yet!]

Chapter Twenty-One

The garden path twinkled with tea-lights, their flames flickering gently in the almost still air. The cherry tree to the side of the house sparkled with pinpricks of fairylight like a Christmas tree, the glistening unripe fruit shiny like baubles. Anna wondered whether she should go in and get changed, re-do her hair and make-up, but the door of the shed was ajar and she could just see a little table all set up, a candle burning down in the centre, and Seb sitting in a deck chair, reading a book with a glass of wine on the table in front of him, waiting.

She didn't go into the house to change, but instead followed the path of the fluttering flames and knocked gently on the wooden slated door.

'Hello?' she whispered, suddenly nervous.

Seb looked up from his book and seeing her, jumped up, shutting the paperback clumsily. 'Hi,' he said. 'I'm glad you could come.'

'Well, I—' Anna hovered on the threshold, peered round to see what he'd done with their common-or-garden shed. All the tools were pushed to one corner, a rusty hoe leaning against a spade and fork, the Flymo hanging from a hook above them. All the shelves had been cleared and swept, and held a mish-mash of his stuff – a couple of paperbacks, a cactus that he'd saved from her over-watering, his washbag, his teaching certificate in a frame and next to that a picture of her. A terrible photo of her on holiday, her shiny, sun-burned face smiling wide, that she always grimaced at because it made her face look fat but he loved because she looked so happy.

A pot was boiling on the Calor gas stove, plates were laid out on the summer table which he'd covered in an old sheet, one with tiny embroidered pink flowers on the edges, and wine was dribbling with condensation in a plastic bucket of ice. Next to the candle he'd filled an old mustard glass with wild poppies and ears of wheat from the field over the path, the wafer-thin petals bobbing and dancing iridescent in the flicker of the candle light.

'I'm Seb,' he said, tea-towel over his shoulder, hand outstretched. 'I can't believe you responded to my advert. Look at you! How lucky am I?' he smiled, denting the creases at the corners of his eyes.

Anna started to say, 'Don't be ridiculous.' But stopped herself. Instead she took a couple of steps forward so she was in reach to shake his hand. 'I'm Anna. I was really touched that you thought of me, you know, that you thought I fitted your criteria.'

'Well I've seen you around the village.'

'You have?' she said. Her hand was still warm in his.

'I could hardly miss you. You've created quite a stir. Seems suddenly everyone's buying vintage antiques and signing up to dance.' He let her hand go and turned to stir whatever it was simmering on the hob. 'I've even heard you're moving into adult classes.'

She snorted. 'Well, never say never.' She watched his shoulders rise and fall as he laughed at the very idea of it.

'I had heard that you were engaged,' he went on. 'But the wanker messed it up.' His back still to her, he shook his head. 'What a doofus, who'd let you go?' he said, turning and without meeting her eyes leant over to pick up the wine bottle. 'I only have white, I heard you don't drink red.'

'You certainly did your research.' She nodded as she took the small, chipped glass he proffered, then said, 'I was as much to blame, you know, for the break-up. I was in a funny place.'

He paused as he was topping up his own glass. 'You still there, do you think?'

She shook her head. 'I don't think so. I hope not.'

Seb nodded and took a sip of the white wine misting up his tumbler. Anna did the same, it tasted of elderflower and summer days by the river.

When he pulled out an orange-and-brown flowered deck chair for her, she sat down and waited a little nervously while he faffed about with the food. She felt self-conscious in her fluorescent jumper, worried that she might say something wrong and mess it up, but

287

then he turned round from the stove, looked at her, his lip caught between his teeth, slight panic in his eyes, and said, 'I made this soup thing and, to be honest, it tastes bloody awful. So I don't know… Do you want to maybe…' She wondered if maybe he was nervous, too. 'Just eat crisps and drink wine?'

Anna hid her smile behind her hand as she nodded. 'I really like crisps,' she said.

He put his hand on his chest and said, 'Me too!' And she laughed. Then she felt her body relax, her shoulders drop, her muscles lose their tension. She pulled a cardboard box over and put her feet up on it.

As he shook out a couple of packets of Walkers Ready Salted, a packet of Quavers and then, to his delight, found some cheese and Jacobs crackers at the back of the shelf, Anna realised what his diet had mainly consisted of out here in the shed. Laying the various bowls on the table, Seb paused and said, 'I'm sorry about the other day, when you asked me for dinner. I don't know why I turned you down. I think I was still angry and really ashamed of myself.'

She swirled her wine round in her glass, watched the liquid slosh to the rim, and shrugged. 'It was probably a good thing.' She looked up at him and went on, 'I don't think it would have gone very well.'

'Not like this.' He winked, holding out a flower pot of crisps.

'Nothing like this,' she said, stuffing a couple into her mouth. 'God, I've already had a Burger King today. What am I becoming?'

'Yeah, good job you're going to New York, you don't want to get fat in the country,' he said, and it was a joke but, as soon as he said it, they both paused, halted like startled animals.

'I don't know—' she started.

'No, wait.' He waved his hand. 'I've practised this, so let me say it. I've been thinking about it and I don't need to be here, Anna. I don't need to be anywhere. Christ, I don't care where I am, but the thing is,' he swallowed and said, 'I really care who I'm with. And I like being with you. You're a pain in the arse sometimes, but that's why I chose you.' He did a little laugh under his breath, like that was the favourite bit of his rehearsed speech. 'I don't want an easy life. I want an interesting life. And I want you to have the most interesting life you've dreamt of, so…if you would have me, I would very much like to come with you.'

'You would?' she asked, watching the way his mouth moved in the candlelight.

'Of course I would.'

Anna nodded into the silence that followed. Then she reached forward and ran her finger up the edge of the candle, picking at the globs of dried wax that had dribbled and set down the side.

'I suppose my main fear, Anna, is that I can never give you what you want.' Seb paused, as if summoning the courage for what he wanted to say next. 'That I'll never be enough.'

She paused. Felt the dribbles of warm wax gather and stop, bulging out where her finger halted their progress. Then, her eyes fixed on the flame, she took a breath in through her nose and said, 'I wasn't too tall to be a dancer.'

'I'm sorry, what?' Seb said, confused, as if his great admission had been misunderstood.

'I just said that I was. I made it up. It was the best excuse I could come up with for why I failed.' She plucked off the belly of wax drips and squished them between her fingers. 'But now I think I've finally realised that I was living someone else's dream and I never gave myself the chance to put it down and pick it up again and make it my dream.'

She glanced up, reluctant to look at him. Seb had leant forward, his elbows on the table and was watching her. 'I always thought you were about the same height as Darcey Bussell,' he said with a laugh.

Anna felt her lips twitch. Then she told him about Lucinda Warren and their dance off and her mother and the roses and he sat back, his arms folded across his chest, holding in a remark about her mother that he knew would annoy her because whatever happened she would always defend her because she knew the depth of how unhappy she had been and how deep the wound inflicted by her father had been.

'I loved it,' Anna sighed, 'I loved the ballet but, after that moment, those flowers all over the floor and the look on her face, I just completely severed it. I left.' She crossed her hands in front of her as if that was it. 'Left it completely. And now I find that Lucinda was shagging the bloody judge.' She laughed through her nose. 'I think that I have been trying to be better all this time, to be the best and I never really realised that good was good enough.' She looked up at him and smiled, plucked her leopard-print jumper away from her chest. 'That's something to thank Razzmatazz for!' She laughed and shook her head. 'A bunch of bloody misfits teach me what I've been legging it from all my life.' He snorted a laugh. 'I think though…' she said, going to fiddle with the candle again but he reached over and caught her hand, held it in his, 'I think I've finally caught up with myself.'

She looked at his hand over hers, his neatly trimmed fingernails, the smattering of hairs, the tan-line of where his watch usually was, the familiarity of the warmth of his palm.

'I'm glad to hear that,' he said.

'Me too,' she said, 'I think maybe I've been blaming the wrong things for my own unhappiness. And I'm not saying that we won't have any problems again in our lives but they won't come from the same place as they have before, for me anyway. And maybe I'll go to New York for a bit, or we can go or you could come out in the holidays, but I'll always come back, and maybe I'll start something completely new – a design arm of Vintage Treasure. God knows. But I feel like I can stop for a minute, and get my breath back.' Anna glanced up and looked at him, the warm chocolate-brown of his eyes sparkling in the candlelight. The corners of his mouth tipping into the start of a smile which she mirrored, feeling that shyness from earlier creep back in.

Then he pulled his hand away and she sat up straighter, startled, like maybe she'd said something wrong, that he'd processed what she'd said and it wasn't enough for him. She watched silently as he stood up and went over to the shelf with the books and the cactus and fumbled around at the back of it.

Then he turned back with a tatty brown leather book in his hands. 'I saved you this,' he said, holding her long-lost scrapbook out for her.

'You did…' she said quietly, unable to quite believe the sight of it, taking it from him with trembling hands. The feel of it between her fingers was like the touch of silk, like a familiarity of unpacking boxes from your childhood and only remembering what the things were once you saw them. Synapses flickering with recognition. The scratch across the front, the frayed pages, the smell of leather and glue. Leafing through all the glamorous shots of Cindy Crawford's Mexican holiday home, Maria Carey's walk-in wardrobe and Ivana Trump's swimming pool and she saw herself with her scissors and Pritt Stick, sitting on the edge of the bed dreaming of a future sparkling with glitter and riches and ambition. She laughed as she turned the pages. 'It's horrendous really, isn't it?'

Seb shrugged. 'I quite like it. I'd like my initials mosaic-ed in the bottom of my swimming pool.' He leant across the table to look at some of the gaudy images and then went over to the bucket on the floor to pull out another bottle of wine, ice and water clinking in the makeshift cooler.

As he searched for the corkscrew, Anna flicked back to the beginning of the book and saw where she'd printed her name and phone number so someone could get in touch with her if she lost it, the address of the poky London flat written neatly in fountain pen. She found the first two pages after that were stuck together, the glue melted and crisp, and as she prised them apart they unstuck with a crack.

There, before her, was the first picture she'd stuck in, right at the beginning, right at the start, from the first *Hello*! in the stack. It wasn't of ballrooms dripping with chandeliers nor was it of diamond-encrusted dresses and pearls as big as robin's eggs, it was a torn-out image of a patio, trimmed with olive groves and a setting Tuscan sun. Across the terracotta tiles were rows of trestle tables draped in white cloth and laid with mismatched crockery, lanterns strung up in the trees and wild flowers scattered in old oil cans. Along the centre of the table fairy cakes were tumbling in stacks of multi-coloured pastels, tiered on towering stands, and in the background was a band, the instruments leant up waiting for dancing under a sky twinkling with stars.

She traced the outline of the image with her finger and then closed the book and looked up at Seb.

'I would put you in my Yeses,' she said.

He paused mid-pulling of the cork, his mouth quirking up at the sides and his eyes crinkling as he tipped his head and said, 'I would put you in *my* Yeses.'

The feeling of her smile then went from the top of her head right down to her toes. She left the book on the table, pulled her sleeves down over her hands and sat back with her feet up on the box and watched him as he poured more white and watched her back.

And then they ate crisps and drank wine and talked about everything and anything and as the evening dipped into a blanket of darkness and all the birds fell silent, and they peered out to look at the glistening cherry tree and watch the last of the tea-lights flicker and fade, she said, 'This is the most fun I've ever had and I'm in the shed.'

He put his arm round her and turned her towards him as he leant back against the old work-bench, and said, 'Do you think you might want to marry me?'

'Steady on, I've only known you one evening.' She laughed, liking the feeling of his hands linked behind her waist.

He paused for a moment and then said, 'Well how about just sex, then? I've heard you've got some kinky new gold leggings.'

She shook her head. 'I can't have sex with you without knowing your intentions are honourable.'

'There you go,' he said, his hands held out wide as if his point was proved. 'It's a win-win situation.'

Chapter Twenty-Two

Anna woke up early to the sound of birds and maybe the distant rumble of a tractor, but it could have been a lorry on the M3. Her skin felt cooler than it had in months, the sheet that she usually kicked off just the right weight for the morning breeze. It felt though like something was missing, something wasn't quite as normal. She looked over at the pillow next to her and saw Seb, face relaxed with sleep, his hair all messy and skewiff, his arm flung out over the sheet and she let her hand rest on his wrist while she thought back to the night before, to the day before, and then she reached down and grabbed a big cushion from the floor and snuggled her shoulders back into it and sat, propped up, staring out the window at the bright-blue sky, the birds that she still had no clue what type they were swooping and hovering, at the butterflies and the wisps of morning cloud like streaks of paint, and she realised that in that moment, the only thing that was wrong was that she had the unfamiliar feeling of having nothing to worry about. Her mind, usually as frantic and cluttered as that hideous mess that once stood tangled at the back of

Mrs Beedle's shop, was empty and calm like a big balloon. A wide, cavernous space of nothing except the moment of sitting up in bed, the slow pulse of Seb's heart under her fingertips, and the disappearing clouds out the window.

When she turned back to look at Seb she saw that he was watching her. Both of them paused for a moment, hoping that the other wasn't going to say that last night had been a mistake.

'All right?' Seb said into the silence.

'All right.' Anna nodded with a smile.

Seb sat up with a yawn and a stretch, his hair all ruffled and skewiff and his face soft with sleep.

'So are you um, moving out of the shed?' Anna asked tentatively playing with the sheet.

'Ok, hold on a minute.' Seb held up a hand. 'Let's just sort this out. I'm glad you've got over the past and everything but I can't have this meek Anna in my life, it's not right. It's not you.'

Anna bit her lip. 'Sorry.'

'Stop it! That's exactly what I'm talking about. No lip biting or sheet fumbling. None of that. I need Anna back, just without the moody bits.' He laughed.

'I wasn't moody. I was emotionally scarred.'

Seb blew out a breath in mock disbelief. 'Give me a break. This isn't *Loose Women*.'

Anna made a face. 'When have you watched *Loose Women*?'

'It's on in the staff room sometimes. I find it very informative.'

Anna shook her head and then wiggled her way back down the bed. 'Go and make me a cup of tea.'

'Not if you ask like that.'

'You said you wanted the old me back.'

Seb lay back down again. 'Well I've now realised I was wrong. Off you go, my meek little girlfriend,' he said, and reaching over gave her a soft shove so she half tumbled out of the bed.

Scrambling up with affront, Anna spluttered, 'I can't believe you just did that.'

Seb looked a bit guilty. 'Neither can I actually.'

She laughed, yanking on Seb's old T-shirt, and said, 'I'll make you tea, but after that, meek Anna, she's gone.'

'Good. I don't want to marry meek Anna,' Seb said with a nod.

Anna paused in the doorway. 'But you do still want to marry normal Anna, without the moodiness slash emotional scarring?'

'Yes.' Seb sat up again, watched her for a second before adding, 'I really do.'

Anna nodded, took a couple of steps out into the hallway but then turned back, Seb was staring out of the window. His face looked less soft than a second ago, more anxious. He turned, surprised, to see her back in the doorway.

She knew what he was thinking.

'About the wedding… I don't need what I thought I needed, Seb,' Anna said, resting her head against the cool wood of the doorframe.

Seb narrowed his eyes. 'I can't work out if you're lying or not?'

Anna ran her tongue over her top lip and then smiled. 'I'm not lying. I promise. And from now on I promise that my promises are promises.'

Seb chuckled. 'I don't even know if that makes sense.'

'I honestly don't need it. Any of it. I'd marry you right now if I could. In fact you know, I can't imagine anything worse than a big do at The Waldegrave. I think I just want this—' She spread her hands wide. 'I want what I felt when I stepped into Mrs Beedle's lost garden.'

'Really?' Seb looked unconvinced.

Anna nodded. 'I think I'm going back to my roots, Seb. I think I might actually quite like vintage.'

'Well, bloody hell.' Seb ran his hand over his stubble. 'I never thought I'd hear you say that. Mastercard won't be happy.'

Anna laughed. 'Neither will your parents.'

'Well I suppose that's one reason to do it.'

She bit down on her smile.

'No lip biting, Anna, remember?'

She let the smile fill her face instead. 'OK. So it's a vintage wedding?'

'Looks like it.'

'We could see how cheap we could make it?' she shrugged.

'I like your thinking.'

298

'It'll still be expensive though,' Anna added, mentally thinking about how much even the cheapest wedding would cost.

'I thought you just said we were going to make it cheap?' Seb looked confused.

'I know but you have to feed people and give them somewhere to sit. And if we stick to the original date we only have—' She calculated the time in her head. 'Two weeks. Two weeks, Seb. Is that even possible?'

'Anna—' Seb laughed. 'This is Nettleton, if you ask for it, people will help you.'

'You think?' She paused, ran her finger along the grain of the wood she was leaning against. 'You think they'd want to help me?'

'I *know*, Anna. I know they would want to help you.'

She felt Seb watching her as her cheeks pinked half in embarrassment, half excitement and held his gaze even though she wanted to look away, suddenly shy at the emotion she couldn't hide.

'And anything they won't help us with, we'll just nab from the school,' Seb added, then leant back against the bedstead, arms crossed behind his head, the corner of his lip tilted up. 'So…two weeks.'

Anna bit her lip, then let it go as soon as she realised she'd done it. 'Two weeks,' she repeated with a flicker of a smile, the delicious flutter of butterflies in her tummy.

Seb nodded, his eyes dancing. 'Now, go and make me my tea.'

The bakery was just opening when Anna arrived in the square, Rachel had just unrolled the awning and laid out the tables and chairs. Anna walked over and followed her back into the shop as she piled hot chocolate croissants and pastries into wooden trays and bowls laid out over the counter.

'Blimey, you're here early,' Rachel said, shocked. 'Give me a sec to just get the rest of the croissants out the oven.'

Anna pulled up a stool on the edge of the counter and looked around as she waited. It was like walking into heaven. Cool and dark in contrast to the warm summer breeze just picking up outside. The glass counter to her right seemed to sparkle like the casings at Tiffany's. Blueberries burst out of erratically shaped muffins like ink, glazed apricots sat like half suns on sticky Danish pastries, swirling cinnamon buns were stacked precariously high with a dusting of snowy icing sugar, and raspberries just peeked out of the crisp dough on the drop scones. The shelf below bowed under the weight of jewel-coloured candid fruits, sugared almonds, tiers of strawberry creams and white chocolate thins. And then below that held what Anna was looking for, cakes with icing so thick it was like the froth on waves as they crashed. Slices were cut to reveal layer upon layer of sponge, multi-coloured or speckled with walnuts and shavings of carrot. There were dense chocolate gateaux as black as coal and then, her personal favourite, the Victoria Sandwich, two simple buttery tiers that oozed with jam and cream and, on the top, stencil patterns created in the coating of sugar. Her mouth watered at the very sight of it.

'What can I get you, then?' Rachel asked, heaping the last of the almond croissants, their centres plump to bursting like little fat bellies, onto a wooden tray.

'I'll have an espresso and…' Anna paused, glancing back to the glass counter. 'It's probably too early for cake, isn't it?'

'Anna…' Rachel rested her elbows on the counter. 'It's never too early for cake.'

Anna scrunched up her nose, thought about it, ummed and ahhed and then said, 'OK, go on then, the Victoria Sponge.'

'An excellent choice,' Rachel laughed as she banged about with the coffee machine behind her and then went to cut a great wedge of cake.

Once everything was laid out beautifully in front of Anna, and Rachel had got herself a cup of tea and a chocolate and almond croissant, she said, 'Did you hear about Jackie?'

'With Doug?'

'The one and only.' Rachel laughed. 'He makes her laugh out loud, she says.'

Anna made a face. Thought of the antagonism between her and Jackie from the moment she'd arrived back and then the realisation that she wouldn't be where she was without her, would never have taken Razzmatazz to London, would probably never have started on the journey of sweeping up her past if it hadn't been for her foray onto Tinder. 'I'm pleased,' she said with a nod, 'I'll be interested to see how it turns out,' she added, thinking that she actually, genuinely, would. And knowing she would most probably be around to see it play out.

'Won't we all?' Rachel laughed and took a bite of croissant, then added, with her mouth full, 'So, Anna, while it's a pleasure to have you here so early, I'm assuming this isn't just a friendly visit.'

Anna shook her head, her mouth stuffed full of light, fluffy sponge. When she finally swallowed, she said, 'I'm going to need a lot of cake.'

'Oh yeah?' Rachel looked a bit confused.

'But the problem is, I can't pay you very much for it, so I was hoping that maybe, you might let me make it with you.'

Rachel narrowed her eyes. 'You're going to bake?'

'I can try.' Anna raised her brows in encouragement. 'You're never too old to learn.'

'How about we do some kind of barter?' Rachel suggested. 'As much as I'm happy for you to be in the kitchen with me, I think you might be more of a hindrance than a help.'

Anna glanced away at the pictures of Paris on the wall so that Rachel wouldn't see her disappointment. 'But I don't think I have anything to barter with.'

'Yes you do.' Rachel frowned. 'You have your skill. Seb said something about adult dance classes. I would really like to dance. Philippe is great dancer and I'm terrible so—' Rachel shrugged. 'Maybe you could start a class? Jackie'd come. She's crap at dancing.'

'You really want a dance class?' It was Anna's turn to frown.

'You start a dance class. Let me come for free, and I'll make you your cakes.'

Anna toyed with her Victoria Sponge, pushing it around the plate with her fork. It would mean becoming a part of the community. It would mean sticking fliers up on noticeboards and renting out the hall. It would probably mean going to the pub afterwards, perhaps. It might even lead to a Nettleton Ball. Was she willing to become a real part of this community?

'Do we have a deal?' Rachel asked.

'Yes,' Anna said, spearing a piece of sponge onto her fork. 'Yes, we have a deal.'

Walking over to Vintage Treasure, Anna checked her eBay account on her phone. The 3G was crap in Nettleton so she had to sit on a bench and wait while it loaded. The sheepdog lifted its head as she sat down and then put it down again, just a little closer to her flip-flop. She pushed back her first thought of whether it had fleas, and instead gave it a little tap on the head, with just one finger, which she wiped on her top afterwards. It was a start, and the dog didn't seem to care either way.

Her eBay account loaded.

Six people watching.

Seeing as she'd only put it up an hour and half ago, that couldn't be half bad.

She thought of her beautiful Vera Wang wedding dress, of how she'd snatched it from Mr Mallory's hands on the first night, unpacking it at Primrose Cottage, how she'd hung it with such reverence at the back of the wardrobe, the dress-bag zipped up tight. She thought of standing in Selfridges and the assistant buttoning up all the tiny pearl buttons at the back and putting her hand to her mouth in a gasp as Anna had turned around and, while she probably did that with everyone, Anna had felt like a princess.

But of all the possessions that she had left, it was the only one actually worth anything. And what was the point of being a princess in off-white Vera Wang if the ball was full of all the people you didn't want to be there?

When she had held it up for Seb to take the photos that morning, he'd glanced up over his camera and said, 'Are you sure you're sure?'

Anna had felt the silk slip like water through her fingers, stifled the urge to clasp the dress as tight as she could against her chest, and said, 'Yes. I'm sure.' And once she'd said it, the urge disappeared because Seb had winked at her and that feeling was better than any dress.

Ooh, seven people watching.

Chapter Twenty-Three

Mrs Beedle was in the garden, sunning herself while reading an antiques magazine and drinking stewed tea.

'Someone said you were leaving to go to New York,' she said as she heard Anna step outside on the cracked cobblestones.

'I've had an offer. I don't know if I'm going to take it,' Anna said, swallowing, wishing she'd told her herself.

Mrs Beedle turned her head to look at her. 'If you do go, there are some wonderful flea markets. It could be your first buying trip. I don't want you to get any old crap though, if I can't sell it it'll be coming out of your pay packet.'

Anna laughed, leant against the doorjamb and plucked a sprig of lavender that was poking round the French windows. 'And if I don't go?'

Mrs Beedle took a sip of her tea, the marmalade cat winding its way round her ankles. 'I was thinking France. Hire a van. I haven't had any good French furniture for a while now and they love it here.' She paused and scooped up the cat, then said, all innocent–

'Your father's going with the lovely Hermione. I thought maybe we could all go together?'

Anna bit down on the start of her smile. 'If I'm going on buying trips, Mrs Beedle, I'm going to have to start earning more than £6.50 an hour.'

The old woman nodded, her bouffant grey hairdo bobbing. 'I'm sure we could come up with some kind of agreement. But I mean, if you're going to be swanning off to New York all the time it can't be fifty-fifty.'

'Oh no, I'd never expect fifty-fifty.' Anna shook her head, watched Mrs Beedle raise a brow at the hint of mocking in her tone.

'We'll think of something. But,' she pushed herself up off the chair, 'in the meantime there's work to do, while you've been off to London with your auditions I've sold half the bloody shop, so you need to get back to,' she waved a hand, 'whatever it is that you do that makes people buy all my bloody crap.'

Anna laughed, twirling the purple flower between her fingers. 'Mrs Beedle, do you think there's any chance I might borrow quite a lot of the chairs and those teacups out the back?'

Mrs Beedle paused and narrowed her eyes.

'It's for maybe, you know, something maybe to do with the wedding,' she said, feeling her cheeks go pink.

'Anna, my darling,' Mrs Beedle smiled, 'if in some way this brings your father into the picture, you can have whatever the hell you like. Try and sell them while you're at it.' She laughed and shrugged and ambled off out the back to make another cup of tea.

By the weekend, Anna had ten bids on the dress and fifteen people were watching. She had become obsessed with the eBay app, refreshing it every couple of minutes just to see if anything had changed. While the bids were creeping up, she would still be short of cash. Philippe had said that he could source her the wine from a friend's vineyard in the Dordogne and the champagne straight from the heart of the region, but it was still going to cost. And also, now the Vera Wang was going, she needed something to wear. Luckily the headmaster at Seb's school had said that if he didn't see the school trestle tables leaving the building, he wouldn't know that they were gone. And Billy and Clara's mum, she discovered when this time she stopped her in the pub to congratulate rather than chastise her, happened to work at The Rose Hotel and would happily sneak a whole bundle of white tablecloths out if she needed them.

Anna had arranged to meet Hermione outside Philippe's bistro at Saturday lunchtime. She rushed out of the shop late to find Hermione lounging back languidly on her little wooden chair, sipping a chilled glass of rosé and conversing with the waitress in fluent French. Her eyes were masked by huge black sunglasses and her hair had been shorn into a platinum crop.

'Look at you!' Anna shook her head. 'This is a very glam new look.'

Hermione shrugged a bony shoulder and threw the menu down on the table. 'I'm experimenting. I thought it was time for a change. You were doing all this putting the past behind you malarkey and I didn't want to be left out.' She raked a hand through the cropped layers and turned to look at herself in the bistro window. 'Do you think it's all right? Your dad said I look like a cabin boy.'

Anna held up a hand. 'He's an idiot. You look amazing.'

Hermione sucked in her cheeks and glanced at herself from different angles. 'Yes, that's what I thought. And you look marvellous, too, darling. Very pinched cheeks and rosy glow.'

'Yeah, I feel better.'

'Good. And you're talking to Lucinda about possibilities in New York? If you go for a month or so, I'll come out and visit. I haven't been this year and I need to get some more cranberry bubble bath from Saks, mine's got about an inch left.'

Anna rolled her eyes and Hermione laughed as she poured her a glass of rosé.

They enjoyed a perfect lunch of perfect food, crumbling chunks of blue cheese on endives dribbled with mustard dressing, flaky salmon and sugar snap peas that burst in the mouth with a crunch, followed by warm chocolate fondant that popped when cut with a spoon, oozing thick, melted chocolate out over the plate.

'It's not really as bad here as I always thought it was.' Hermione said, sitting back and patting her lips with a napkin. 'It has some plusses.'

'It has a couple,' Anna agreed.

'Not least its proximity to London.' Hermione guffawed a laugh and then drained the last of her wine. 'I have something for you.'

'You do?' Anna frowned. 'What?'

'Don't sound so suspicious. It's a gift.'

The last gift Hermione had given her was when they were sixteen and she'd pushed a condom into her hand and thrust her in the direction of where Luke Lloyd was standing by a chestnut tree in the park.

Anna watched as Hermione leant down to get something out of her bag and, then unable to find it amidst all the rubbish in there, hoisted it up on her lap and did a proper Mary Poppins-style search as things clinked and bashed and papers went flying. 'It's here somewhere,' she muttered, pulling out make-up and magazines. 'Ah, here!' she said finally. 'Here it is.' In her hand was a crumpled envelope, and she thrust it in Anna's direction. 'This is for you.'

Eyes narrowed, unsure about what the hell it was, Anna leant forward and took it tentatively, while Hermione beamed with delight.

Tearing the envelope open, inside she found a cheque, made out to Anna, for at least the cost of the wine, a couple of crates of champagne and maybe a bit else. 'You can't give me this.' Anna shook her head.

'Why ever not?'

'Because it's money. It's too much money.' Anna tried to push it back into Hermione's hand and when she waved her away tried to put it in her bag which Hermione swept to the side so Anna couldn't reach.

'It's not my money really,' Hermione said, exasperated, 'it's from the furniture.'

'What furniture?' Anna said, her mind distracted by the need to give the money back.

'The Hungarian furniture!' Hermione sighed. 'Mrs Beedle sold the lot for me at some flashy auction, it did phenomenally well. There's quite a market for it, apparently. I sent him some of the money and, well, my bit I didn't really want. I mean, what would I spend it on? Let's say I buy a lovely bag with it, I'd just walk around thinking, it's my Hungarian divorce furniture draped over my arm. But if I could put it towards something good. Something special that in some way might counteract the divorce, you know wipe it out so that it became neutral space, like a lovely wedding of my friend who I'm glad didn't listen to me too much when I said stupid things about PlayStation and rugby – you know, actually, I've played on that *Grand Theft Auto*, I'm quite good – anyway, if I could help my darling friend out and get to be something important at her wedding – that's a hint by the way – then that would make it seem worthwhile.' She paused, pulled her sunglasses back down over her eyes. 'That would make all the hideousness seem like it was worth it.'

Anna didn't know what to say. Just sat clutching the cheque between her fingers.

'Just take the bloody money, OK?' Hermione snapped in the end, and then laughed, trying to squeeze a few more drops out of the rosé bottle.

'Thank you,' Anna said.

'You're more than welcome.' Hermione nodded and then called to the waitress. 'Excuse me – could I have a glass of champagne? Can you have one, Anna? Surely you don't need to be sober to sell that stuff, do you? Two glasses, make it two.' Hermione sat back and raised her head to the sun, feeling the heat of it on her flushed cheeks.

Anna watched her and smiled, hit by the sudden realisation that she was glad she was dating her father, that she hoped that maybe it might last. 'If you two got married, would you want me to call you Mum?' Anna sniggered.

'Oh piss off.' Hermione shook her head and reached delightedly for the champagne the waitress brought out.

After a second, Hermione raised a brow and said, 'I'm still waiting, you know.'

'What for?'

'My important role at the wedding. But I don't want to be matron of anything.'

Anna sat back in her chair and took a sip of the sharp, bubbly champagne. 'You can be my best woman.'

Hermione pushed her sunglasses up onto her head and said, 'Yes, yes I like that. I like that very much.'

'What about invites?' Seb asked. They were standing in front of Presents 4 You staring at a limp-looking pack of notecards with the Paris, Milan, New York, Nettleton logo stamped on them. 'We could just email everyone, let them know it's back on?' he added with a shrug.

Anna shook her head. 'I'd really like to do it properly.'

'Well, remembering last time, anything we get printed professionally is going to cost.'

Anna nodded, and turning away from the shop window looked out over the square. 'Maybe we should just email then.'

A breeze flittered through the plane trees, their hedgehog seeds swaying, the sun dappling the pavement like a glitter ball.

An email just didn't feel right. When she thought of the old invitations, while personal, they felt like they were sent out by a different couple. She felt like this new wedding needed something of its own. To mark it as different.

'Do you want to write it today and I'll BCC it out to everyone this afternoon.' Seb was scrolling through the addresses in his phone.

As she surveyed the scene, Anna noticed Razzmatazz's Clara, Mary and Lucy sitting on a bench by the fountain drinking Diet Coke and flicking through a magazine while the boys messed about with their phones.

'What about new people we're going to invite? Do you they just get copied in to an email?' Anna turned and looked at Seb. 'It just doesn't feel right.'

Seb paused from his phone scrolling and frowned at her. 'Well what do you want to do?'

'I don't know.' Anna shook her head. 'I just feel that we need something that reflects the new us. Be a bit more this…' She did a sweep of the view with her arm, imagining some arty black and white photograph of the sun peeking through the plane tree branches or a line drawing of a bird sipping from the fountain.

Just then a song that Anna recognised from watching too much *X Factor* blared into the still air. They both glanced up to see Billy holding up his phone while Lucy and Clara danced to the tinny music.

Anna saw Seb narrow his eyes and as he shouted Clara's name she thought he was about to tell them off for making a racket. 'Clara!'

'What?' Clara yelled back over the music, clearly thinking the same thing.

'You're good at Art, aren't you?' Seb asked.

'What are you doing?' Anna hissed. She may be open to the whole vintage village theme but that didn't mean she was ready for some dubious GCSE art invitation.

Clara shrugged. 'I'm OK.'

'She's really good,' Mary said with wide-eyed admiration, shielding her face from the sun with her hand

313

to watch as Seb started striding over and Anna hurried to keep up.

'I'm not that good.' Clara shook her head. 'I can draw and stuff.'

'She says she's not that good, Seb,' Anna said, tugging on the back of his T-shirt.

'She's lying, Sir,' Billy piped up. 'She really wants to go to art college but Mum's not sure.'

'Shut up, Billy.' Clara whacked him on the arm.

Anna looked at Clara. Took in her wild orange hair, thickly painted make-up, the starburst tattoo on her wrist, fake-nails decorated with intricate black scrolls and tiny diamante.

'We need someone to design our wedding invites quickly and cheaply,' Seb said while Anna crossed her fingers hoping that she might say she was too busy. 'Do you think you could do it?'

Clara glanced up, her eyes not quite trusting. 'You don't look so sure, Miss.'

'I urm—' Anna swallowed, forced her lips into a smile, imagined the invite plopping onto Hermione's penthouse doormat. 'I'm certainly…intrigued.'

Billy sniggered.

'Don't think she can do it, Miss?' Lucy asked, one eyebrow raised.

Seb shook his head and had to hide a smile.

'No, it's not that—' Anna started.

'You're so obvious, Miss.'

Anna winced.

314

Clara tilted her head to one side, sizing Anna up, and not for the first time Anna thanked God that she wasn't sixteen again because this lot would eat her alive.

'You want to prove Anna wrong, Clara?' Seb goaded and Anna squeezed his hand to shut him up but he just squeezed hers back tighter.

She watched Clara's pout turn into the hint of a smile. 'Always, Sir,' she drawled and Lucy and the others sniggered.

Anna glanced heavenward, remembering the dreadful mixed-media collages and cross-hatched pencil drawings of Coke cans with wonky perspective that she'd always smiled fakely at when visiting Seb's school's end of term art exhibitions.

'Well I can't wait to see what you come up with.' Anna forced a brightness into her voice, already imagining how she was going to let her down gently.

'I'm sure you can't,' Clara smirked.

As they started to walk away, Anna muttered, 'Thanks for that.'

'I thought you were open-minded, new Anna,' Seb said, his eyes alight with mischief.

'I haven't lost my taste though,' she said with a roll of her eyes. 'And it'll be me that has to tell her no.'

'She might surprise you.'

'Hey, Sir,' Clara called before Anna could give a sarky reply to Seb, 'Do you have a theme or anything?'

'Not really.' Seb shook his head, turning to walk backwards as he talked to them. 'Everything is either begged, borrowed or stolen—'

'Vintage,' Anna cut in quickly. 'The theme is vintage.'

'That's very on-trend, Miss,' Lucy called.

'That's the kind of people we are, Lucy,' Seb shouted. 'Totes down with the kids.'

'Yeah right!' Lucy mocked.

As he walked away Seb did some manoeuvre that obviously he'd seen the kids do at school and all of them burst out into hysterics. 'You're so embarrassing.' Billy said.

'That's why I'm a teacher.' Seb said and, slinging his arm around Anna's shoulders, marched them back to the hatchback with a big grin on his face.

Chapter Twenty-Four

On Monday, when Anna came back in from lunch, Mrs Beedle pointed to an envelope on the counter.

It was crumpled from where it had been pushed through the letterbox and had Miss Whitehall written in block capitals on the front. The M of Miss had a familiar black scroll winding its way down and into a perfect curl.

Anna saw her fingers shake slightly as she went to tear open the flap. She'd been dreading this moment all weekend. As she'd sat in front of the TV cutting triangles for bunting while Seb had tied ribbons round jam jars and wired white paper lanterns with little LED lights, she'd tried to imagine what Clara might come up with and every possible option had made her grimace. She should have just asked Hermione to have something printed in town and sucked up the cost.

But then as she pulled the sheet of thick card from the envelope she knew immediately that her fears were unwarranted. There before her was a screen print in pink and blue and cream, tiny birds held up bunting across the top and the words, like a poster advertising a village fair, read *Anna & Seb's Vintage Summer Wedding*. All the elements of Nettleton were captured in the stencilling round the edge: the church spire, the plane trees, the sheepdog by the bench, the pigeons pecking by the fountain. And at the bottom, where she'd hand drawn the word Nettleton, Clara had adorned it with cut-outs of cakes, flowers, teacups and butterflies. It was stunning.

'Well isn't that nice?' Mrs Beedle said, from where she was looking at the design over Anna's shoulder. 'She's a clever girl, that Clara,' she added as she went off to make their afternoon cup of tea.

Anna nodded, she could feel the pressure of tears behind her eyes. There wasn't a cross-hatched Coke can in sight. She realised then that, if she let them, the people of Nettleton, or perhaps just people in general, would continue to surprise her every day.

She looked up when she heard a tap on the window and saw Clara peering in nervously. As they locked gazes, Clara gave her a tentative thumbs up and, as a smile spread wide across her face, Anna lifted a hand from where it clutched the invite to give her a very definite thumbs up in return.

She sent the invites out to everyone on the original list, hand-delivered the rest of them to half of Nettleton, and then stood in the queue at the post office to get stamps for Spain and New York.

Lucinda Warren emailed to say she wouldn't miss it for the world and would see if she could snaffle some jewels from the wardrobe department – there was a very lovely tiara worn just the other day by Odette in an outdoor performance of *Swan Lake*.

Her mother called as Anna was holding up a pale yellow summer dress she'd bought years ago and wondering whether, with some good jewellery, it could pass as a wedding dress.

'Anna, I can't be there,' was the first thing she said when Anna answered. 'I just can't.'

Anna hung the dress back in the wardrobe and walked over to the window. As she leant out, her elbows scratching on the chipped paint, she looked down at the honeysuckle that had started to weave its way over the front path. She had known this was what her mum was going to say. 'That's OK.'

'Why you have to have it there, I don't know. I could have paid for something back in London. I just can't go back there. The idea of even driving in… I can't.'

Anna closed her eyes and just felt the warmth of the afternoon sun and the sweet honeysuckle smell wrap round her, keeping her mind clear and her focus forward. 'I'm sad, Mum, but I understand. I think it would be OK if you came, I think it wouldn't be as bad as you think, but I understand.'

There was a pause on the other end of the line, she heard her mum cough. 'Well…' her mum said, but then didn't finish. Anna waited.

'At least you have the Vera Wang,' her mum sighed, skating easily over the emotional surface. Refusing to be embroiled in the possibility of putting the past behind her.

'I've sold it.'

'Oh Anna!' She sighed again as if the world had ended. 'How could you?'

'I needed the money.'

'I told you I could have paid, Anna.'

'I know.' Anna smiled as her dad walked up the front path with Hermione, a bottle of red wine under his arm. As they were nearing the front step, Philippe and Rachel pulled up, Rachel stepping out of the car balancing a huge box of cakes in one hand and a stack of bridal magazines in the other. They were coming round for a wedding planning barbecue. She heard Seb open the door and say, 'Welcome, welcome...'

Her mum was still talking. Anna wanted to go downstairs and join her friends.

Her friends she said under her breath.

'Mum, I don't need the Vera Wang dress and I don't need your money. I would far prefer you being here than any of that.'

Her mum paused.

Anna heard laughter downstairs.

'I can't be there, Anna, you know I can't.'

Anna nodded. 'You can,' she said. 'But I understand why you won't.'

There was another pause. Anna wondered suddenly whether her mum had hung up. Then she heard her say, softly, 'Thank you.'

Anna swallowed, opened her eyes wide to stop any moisture. 'You're welcome.'

'I'll send you something.'

'You don't need to.'

'No, but I want to.'

The girl who won the Vera Wang drove down from Nottingham to pick it up and almost cried with excitement when Anna unzipped the velvet-sheened bag to let her look.

A box arrived from her mum the very next day. Anna knew what it was just from the colour of the tissue paper when she took the lid off.

There, nestled in the bed of pale blue was the Chanel bag.

Quilted cream leather, a touch worn at the corners, gold chain handles and perfect interlocking CCs on the front. The flood of emotions that just touching it created made her think she'd close the top on the box and shove it to the back of the wardrobe.

But then she opened the card and in her mum's familiar flourish was written, *Always saved for the most special occasions.*

Anna clutched the card in her hand and thought, 'I did come back. I will be wearing Chanel. But I won't be better. I will be good enough.'

Chapter Twenty-Five

Anna had buried her head in the sand about the dress. Or lack thereof. Instead she had spent her time designing the cake menu with Rachel, talking to Philippe about the wine, discussing the seating plan with Seb and bickering about who should have to sit next to his parents.

'I'll sit next to the mother,' Hermione drawled as she sat in the tatty orange armchair in Vintage Treasure as Anna and Mrs Beedle sorted through the china, selecting the best teacups and side plates from the jumble to have at the wedding.

'No,' Anna shook her head, 'I don't think that would be wise.'

'It'd be funny though,' said Mrs Beedle, wiping the beads of sweat from her forehead. 'Hilary was a pain at school and she's a pain now. Oh look here's a whole box of teacups, well I never.' She ripped the gaffer tape off an old box in the storeroom and they both peered in to see an assortment of mint condition, duck-egg blue teacups with tiny silver flowers painted around the rim.

'They're lovely.' Anna's dad reached forward from where he was sitting on a stool rifling through an old chest packed with vintage Christmas decorations. 'And what about these?' He held up a mottled silver star and matching crescent moon. 'No one would have to know they're Christmas, would they?'

'You know actually—' Hermione said, stretching one long leg out to give Patrick a gentle kick, 'I saw in *Country Living* the other day that they'd tied little ornaments like that on string. Just simple old brown string and they looked phenomenal. Charging bloody two hundred quid a pop, which I thought was a bit much, but it was very simple and very effective.'

Mrs Beedle reached behind her and grabbed a ball of string off the shelf. She caught Hermione completely off-guard when she threw it in her direction and said, 'Well make yourself useful and start stringing.'

'Sounds kind of rude "stringing" doesn't it?' she said, nudging Patrick again with her foot.

'Cut it out,' Anna said. 'No sex talk of any kind while I'm with you. OK?'

'You're such a prude,' Hermione sighed as she started to unwind her piece of string.

Anna rolled her eyes. Then caught her dad watching her, his lips tilted into a half-smile, as if them all sitting together in the same room was the best thing he could have hoped for.

'Come on,' Anna said, embarrassed by the attention but also storing the look away to remember fondly later. 'Who can sit next to the dreadful Hilary?'

'What about Rachel's Philippe? He'd be good. Give her a run for her money.'

'Very true,' Mrs Beedle nodded.

'And I don't mind sitting next to Roger,' her dad shrugged.

'I want you to have fun.' Anna stood up and stretched. 'I was thinking maybe I'd put Kim next to Roger, at least he wouldn't be able to get a word in edgeways.'

Hermione laughed. 'Marvellous idea.' She was tying her little Christmas ornaments onto her string, measuring the distance between each one meticulously. 'Look, aren't these lovely,' she added, holding up what she'd done so far, the silver-leafed baubles glinting in the low light of the storeroom.

'That reminds me—' Mrs Beedle reached over to one of the big bags stacked against the wall. 'I've got some bunting somewhere around here. Silver Jubilee stuff.'

'Silver Jubilee?' Hermione scoffed. 'As in 1977, Silver Jubilee?'

'That's the one,' said Mrs Beedle, unzipping a huge plastic bag and hauling out some red, white and blue bunting, gold fringing clumped together on the edges of the flags and the white ribbon now a dirty cream. 'Silver Jubilee bunting.'

They all stared at it. Anna expected moths to circle the heap like a cartoon. Mrs Beedle looked up at them all, expectantly. 'Come on…' she said. 'This is good stuff.'

Hermione leant forward and lifted a pennant between finger and thumb. 'You'll have to hang it up high, mask the smell.'

'We strung it from the lampposts in '77,' Mrs Beedle shrugged.

'God, I actually remember that.' Patrick ran a hand over his face. 'Anna, were you even born?'

Anna paused from where she was wiping the dust off a couple of cups. 'Do you not even know my date of birth?'

Her dad looked sheepish. 'I have a vague idea.'

Hermione laughed. Anna opened her mouth in disbelief. Mrs Beedle changed the subject. 'So Anna, what *are* you going to wear?'

'I don't know,' she replied, leaning forward so she could run the bunting through her fingers. 'Maybe I should just wrap myself in this?' she joked. 'Very vintage.'

Just then the curtain to the stockroom pulled back and Seb appeared wearing one of the black tailcoats and top hats that Anna had added to the clothing display earlier in the week. 'Check me out, people, this is what I'm wearing,' he said, doing a semi-twirl and then plucking the hat from his head to take a bow.

'Very dapper,' Mrs Beedle said, sitting back in her chair and looking up at Seb admiringly.

'You look wonderful,' said Hermione, almost shocking herself as she admired the fit of the jacket. 'Like you've beamed in from the thirties.'

'Hang on,' said Patrick, jumping up. 'Let me have a go.' He nipped into the front of the shop and then came back in wearing his own tails and matching top hat, the velvet nap balding in places with age.

Hermione stood up and brushed down the shoulders of the coat. 'Fabulous. I want a go.'

Anna narrowed her eyes as Hermione disappeared out to the front of the shop and said, 'Are you serious?' to Seb. 'Your parents would flip.'

'I actually think my mother would quite like it,' Seb said as he tried to get a good look at his reflection in the cracked mirror above the sink.

'You're seriously going to wear that?' Anna said again.

Seb shrugged. 'Why not? I think I look pretty cool.' He struck a pose that made her laugh. 'And the rules seem to be out the window with this one. What is *that*?' he asked with a frown, pointing to the mouldy pile of material by Mrs Beedle's feet.

'Vintage bunting,' Anna replied, sheepishly, then put her head in her hands. 'Oh God, it's going to look like a car boot sale.'

Seb, unsure what to say, gave Anna's dad a look of slight panic who in turn deferred to Mrs Beedle.

Standing up from her chair, Mrs Beedle put her hand on Anna's shoulder and said, 'You have to pull yourself together. It's not going to look like a car boot sale, simply because you have so many people here with so much taste. Look.' She held up Hermione's string of decorations. 'Look how beautiful these are. And look at your fiancé – *look* at him! Forget about what you think this wedding should look like and enjoy what it does look like. *Look* at him, Anna!'

Anna glanced up, her eyes red. She saw Seb grinning where he stood in his top hat and tails, scruffy yellow T-shirt on underneath and board shorts.

'Handsome, huh?' Seb winked.

Anna found herself nodding.

'Now, Anna,' Mrs Beedle said, going over to the cupboard and bringing out a bottle of whisky and a stack of crystal tumblers.

'Blimey,' Patrick cut in, taking the bottle from her, 'where have you been hiding this? It must have cost about three hundred quid.'

'I keep it for special occasions.' Mrs Beedle grinned as his eyes widened at the twenty-five-year old single malt. 'Now Anna, listen to me. You have never been freer, my girl. Never been freer to do exactly what you like. Put all your expectations to one side and go and have some fun,' she said, thrusting a glass of golden firewater into her hand.

As Anna took a sip and winced, Hermione yanked open the curtain to the backroom and said, 'Da dah!'

She was dressed in the slinky black dress with the pearl choker. Where the seams had split she had copied Liz Hurley and pinned them together, using diamante brooches rather than safety pins. Over her shoulder she'd slung the hideous dead badger stole and on her head was a peacock feather fascinator. She'd slipped her feet into a pair of seventies patent black mules with an open toe and little pink bows on the front.

'Oh my God,' said Seb.

Mrs Beedle looked away and focused on pouring the whisky.

'Well what do you think?' said Hermione as she sashayed from left to right, doing a turn so they could see the trail of pearls that hung down the open back of the dress to her waist.

'It's er—' Anna didn't really know what to say. It was a cross between grotesquely hideous and catwalk model stunning. She was about to say as much but instead she looked at the dancing delight in Hermione's eyes, the laughter on her dad's face, the amused horror on Seb's, and said, 'It's bloody awesome.'

As she laughed she realised that Mrs Beedle was right, she had never been freer in her life.

Hermione giggled as she caught sight of herself in the dirty, cracked mirror. 'OK then,' she said, catching Anna's eye in the glass. 'Your turn.'

Chapter Twenty-Six

The village hall was filled with a variety of wooden school chairs, orange plastic ones they kept stacked in the store cupboard for bridge games, and the rest were mismatched antiques from Mrs Beedle's. Hilary and Roger looked uncomfortable perched on wrought-iron garden chairs, Philippe and Rachel lounged back on a pair of vintage cinema seats, while Billy was spinning round and round in a sixties bucket chair. To Anna and Seb it felt like they had chairs coming out of their ears, so it had never occurred to them that they might not have enough.

But it seemed that the whole village was coming to watch them get hitched. People were queuing up outside the double doors, cramming themselves into the standing room at the back. It was Razzmatazz Matt who took the initiative and compiled a crew to walk some gym benches from the school to the hall, so when Seb strode in he saw half his parents' friends perched as daintily as they could on the same wooden benches they'd been made to bunny-hop over as kids. He had to stifle a laugh as he watched them, knees practically up to their chins, making small talk while shifting uncomfortably.

He saw his mother's eyes widen as he strode the length of the makeshift aisle lined with big red geraniums in bright-coloured oil drums, his brothers loping next to him, wicked grins on their faces as they all savoured the shock on their parents' faces. They were dressed in matching top hats and tails, but as the coats were the only parts Mrs Beedle had of the suits, they'd had to improvise with the rest. One of his brothers had opted for shorts and Hawaiian shirt, the other had gone for cargo pants and a black vest, Seb was wearing his blue jeans, low-slung and faded with a raspberry pink T-shirt and matching poppy in his button hole. He wore his Converse on his feet and his top hat tilted jauntily on his head. He almost jogged down the aisle he was having so much fun.

Outside, the sun was teetering heavy and fat behind white clouds. The air just warm enough but not too hot, there had been a murmur of a chance of rain that everyone was choosing to ignore. The only patter of water at that moment was from the fountain, little sparrows perched on the edge drinking, the marmalade cat watching from one of the benches.

As Anna stepped out of the cherry-red Mercedes, Hermione reached over from the back-seat and handed her a bunch of wild poppies, raspberry stalks and golden ears of wheat, tied in a bow with white ribbon.

'I'm proud of you,' Hermione said, a slight hitch in her voice as she spoke. 'I don't know if I would have had the courage to do this.' When she said this she swept a hand over their outfits and up towards the hall where coloured lanterns bobbed in the breeze and the old bunting fluttered. 'Not doing what everyone expects, it's good. Just always make sure you remind yourself of this every time you feel yourself stifled by convention, because I will,' she said, her hand tightening on Anna's.

'Are you two going to chat all day?' Anna's dad asked. 'There's a wedding to get going.'

Anna smiled, squeezed Hermione's hand and then grinned. 'You're a good step-mum.'

'Oh shut up.' Hermione snatched her hand away with mock affront. 'I was trying to have a moment.'

'It was a moment,' Anna laughed.

'Come on!' Patrick crooked his arm so she could rest her hand at his elbow. He'd had his hair cut, but the back still brushed over the collar of his neatly pressed yellow-check shirt. She looked down and smiled when she saw his leather flip-flops.

They'd just started to walk when her dad stopped and said, 'Hang on, hang on, I've forgotten my hat.' Then dashed back to the car to get his top hat from the boot. When he put it on Anna had to close her eyes for a moment to remind herself that today was a day when anything went.

On his hat her dad had wired one of the taxidermy birds from the shop. A starling. Its black wings shimmering blue green in the sun, its beady eyes watching Anna from above.

'Nice bird,' she said.

Her dad puffed his chest out proudly. 'Thanks. I've grown quite attached to it, I might wear it all the time.'

'I'm sure Hermione will love that,' Anna laughed.

Then she heard one of the Razzmatazz girls shout, 'Miss!' and turned to see Hermione towering over Lucy in the doorway barking orders.

'What's the matter?' Anna called over to them.

'She doesn't like my outfit,' Lucy sneered, pointing at Hermione. She was wearing white New York Dance Academy tracksuit bottoms, a leopard print crop-top, Converse high tops and seemingly every necklace from Vintage Treasure she could find.

'She looks ridiculous.' Hermione pointed to the jewels piled round Lucy's neck.

'Speak for yourself,' Lucy huffed. 'It's ghetto.'

'Oh *please*,' snapped Hermiine. 'It's an eyesore.'

Anna looked at the giant pile of necklaces, the jewels and beads sparkling in the sun. Then she looked up at Lucy's jaw jutting out defiantly and Hermione standing with her hands on her hips, seemingly forgetting she had a dead badger on her shoulder and peacock feathers bobbing on her head.

'Hermione,' Anna started, feeling a little like her wedding was actually a giant fancy dress party, 'what did you just say about being stifled by convention?'

Hermione's lips pursed.

'Ha, see?' Lucy smirked. 'You can't tell me what to wear. Miss likes it.'

Anna watched as Hermione narrowed her eyes ready with a sharp reply, but then she saw her catch sight of her own reflection in the windows and do a double-take. 'My God, this badger looks terrible. Why did no one tell me?'

'It's meant to be freedom of expression,' Patrick said, his fingers reaching up to stroke the bird on his hat.

'Yes, but we still have to look good,' said Hermione, frowning. She peered down at her shoulder and started to unpick the fur stole. Without it she looked remarkably better, the neckline showed off her tanned shoulders, and the pearls round her neck were now free to wink in the sunlight.

'That is much better,' Lucy said, with a dismissive shrug.

Hermione turned to look at her. 'Do you think maybe I could just remove a couple of necklaces? Honestly, I think that would turn it from—' She paused, looking for the right words as she faced the ferocity of Lucy's scowl. 'Trailer trash to ghetto fabulous?'

Lucy eyed her, unconvinced.

'She might be right, Luce.' Clara took a step forward. She was wearing the Razzmatazz tutu, red Converse and the green Versace jumper with the fields on the front which clashed with her orange hair. Mary was standing back shyly, she'd somehow been persuaded into the gold lamé leggings.

Hermione did an encouraging little nod.

Lucy turned to Anna who was distracted by the glimpse of Seb she'd caught through the window, of him standing there, waiting for her. 'You can wear what you like,' she murmured. They could dance down the aisle in their bikinis for all she cared at that moment. As if sensing her watching, Seb looked up and, when he caught Anna's eye, touched the brim of his top hat, raising it a fraction from his head like a Regency gent. Anna felt her whole face light up.

When she looked back, Lucy was scooping handfuls of beaded necklaces from round her neck and, along with Mary and Clara, they were draping them over the low branches of the plane trees.

'Lovely,' said Anna. 'Can we get on with it now?'

Hermione nodded, smug that she'd got her way, and bustled the girls forward while checking all their bouquets of purple drooping buddleia, cut that morning from the Vintage Treasure garden, were in order.

When they got to the front doors of the hall, Clara gave the signal to the Nettleton High brass band to start up, but they weren't paying attention so she put two fingers in her mouth and wolf-whistled which made everyone turn. The boy conducting got the fright of his life, jumped up with a start and the music bellowed out with a clatter.

Seb hadn't taken his eyes from the door and when he caught site of Anna she thought he might, maybe, have had to wipe a tear from his eye.

As she started to walk, her hand curled tightly round her dad's arm, his smile as wide as she'd ever seen it, she glanced around the congregation. There was Rachel and Philippe, Babs from the pub wearing a bright cerise hat, Jackie in skin-tight leather leggings, Kim trying to discreetly put her Blackberry back in her bag, Lucinda looking perfect in some beige Calvin Klein number. Oh God, and there was Seb's mother in the front row, a brow raised with obvious distaste at the descending party, she caught Anna's eye and made her lose her confidence for a second but then she saw Mrs Beedle one row back, dressed in the vintage black smock with gold embroidery, giving her a beaming thumbs-up. Anna smiled and when she heard Kim do a whoop, suddenly she relaxed, this was her day. Her and Seb's day and it was damn well going to be the best day of her life.

While the Vera Wang was enjoying a lavish wedding in the heart of Sherwood Forest, Anna Whitehall got married wearing a vintage cream satin slip with lace trim. Draped over one shoulder and around into the crook of her other arm was a turquoise fringed Spanish shawl, the antique stitching of the big flowers on the back worn with age. Round her waist was a thick gold snakeskin belt that set off the sequins on a delicate net skirt to perfection. Where the fabric had been ripped and torn she'd darned it with zigzags of silver thread. As she walked the layers of tulle rustled softly, brushing the floor and sweeping wide against the pots of geraniums while the sequins flickered like little fish darting in water. Her hair was piled up under a tiara made especially for the Swan Queen, rows of tiny pearls, crystals and beads twisted and knotted into a shimmering white crown. On her feet were metallic green Jimmy Choos so high that she could barely put one foot in front of the other and clutched in her hand, along with the bouquet of wilting poppies, was a cream, quilted Chanel bag.

She looked sensational.

Seb choked up and had to take a moment before he could say his vows. Peter from Razzmatazz snorted at the show of emotion which made Matt giggle and Seb's mother, Hilary, shush them all.

Managing to compose himself by the time the registrar said the words 'For richer for poorer', Seb made a show of winking at Anna which made the crowd erupt into giggles and Hilary sit back, arms crossed and huff, 'Oh for goodness sake.'

As if on cue the sun streamed in through the window as they were pronounced husband and wife, the light dancing like a ball of fire as Seb stepped forward, wrapped one hand around Anna's back and, catching her completely off-guard, tilted her back for a movie-inspired kiss.

When she stood up her tiara had fallen off, her lipstick was gone, her cheeks flushed pink but the brightness of her smile rivalled the sunshine.

Seb leant down and kissed her on the tip of her nose before taking her hand in his so they could walk together past the smiling faces of their friends and family. The band started up and played them out completely off-key, Hermione tripped on her sky-high mules, Lucy and Clara had a row about who was meant to have brought the rose petal confetti which appeared to still be in Clara's dad's car, but nothing could wipe the smile from Anna's lips.

As they stepped out into the open, saw the whole square decked out in vintage jubilee bunting, Seb whispered, 'Thanks for marrying me – here, in Nettleton.'

Anna turned her head to face him, her eyes catching on the necklaces Lucy had laced over the branches earlier, and replied, 'I can't imagine anywhere better.'

Chapter Twenty-Seven

The trestle tables had been lined up all down the centre of the square in rows and as soon as the service was over all the Razzmatazz kids walked the chairs out from the hall in a giant chain. A stack of takeaway pizzas and a cooler of Coke bottles sat glistening in the sunlight waiting for them once the job was done.

Crisp white tablecloths had been smoothed over the battered tables and laid with a mismatch of crockery that had lived for years wrapped in paper in the storeroom of Mrs Beedle's shop. Frilled-edge plates with peonies in the centre sat with teacups covered in red rosebuds or hand-painted bumblebees. There were plates to commemorate royal weddings, best in shows, old crockery from The Savoy and The Four Seasons, cups stamped with Doulton and Wedgewood and others, decorated in black and white, with Woolworths printed on the bottom. Mrs Beedle had set up a discreet stand to one side, and if anyone wanted their plates and teacup, the set was theirs for a tenner.

More oil drums of geraniums in red, white and fuchsia lined the border of the square, the sheepdog had a red ribbon on its collar, and down the table were glass jugs from the storeroom over-flowing with wild flowers and weeds – dandelions flopped next to delicate poppies and pale yellow primroses. Mr Milton had come bearing bowls of fresh, sweet raspberries that dotted the tables like baskets of precious rubies.

On the floor they had laid old woven rugs scattered with toys for the babies and toddlers to play on, but they seemed more interested in the silk scarfs that had been tied to create more bunting around the makeshift bar.

Philippe's waitresses were waiting to serve champagne in an odd assortment of glasses – from ones lent by Babs from the pub to blue-rimmed retro Babycham ones that had been in the shop for yonks. Outside Rachel's bakery, her old blue bike had been leant against the brick wall and decorated with wild flowers, sprigs of raspberries trailed over the handlebars like tiny pink lanterns and two French loaves stuck out of the basket. Each guest had been asked to pose in front of it for a photograph and, when it was Anna and Seb's turn he hoisted her up on his lap so they wobbled precariously and she yelped when they almost toppled over, the Nettleton News photographer capturing it all for their album.

Along from the bar they had wheeled out the old fortune-teller who was scaring the kids and making the adults dare one another to put their hand in the slot for a painful stamp.

When it was time to sit down, everyone gasped with delight as they saw the little ornaments on their table settings (also available to purchase from Mrs Beedle) that held their name cards. Anna had taken a risk and put matching his and hers Toby jugs on Hilary and Roger's plates. Roger looked slightly wary as he picked his up, waiting to take the lead from Hilary to confirm his own reaction.

'Well really,' Hilary muttered, eyes narrowed as she lifted the round, rosy-cheeked jug up and turned it over in her hands. Then she seemed to be caught by the noise around her and glanced up to see all her friends laughingly comparing their little figurines with the person next to theirs. Smartly dressed women with big hats and floral dresses were delighting over marbled paperweights, horse-brasses and seventies table-lighters. Men who she usually saw pulling on a cigar, while expounding on the state of Europe, were bickering like children over who got the brass steam engine and who was left with the fake Staffordshire dog.

Hilary seemed momentarily lost for words. Anna watched her, waiting. Then she saw her look back to her jug, run her hand over the smooth varnish, take Roger's in her other hand and hold them up together, side by side. 'Well this one doesn't look anything like me,' she said, 'but I can see a bit of you in that one, Rog.'

And when Roger slapped her on the backside and said, 'Cheeky,' making them both snigger together, Anna decided that that was as near to hitting the jackpot as she would get.

When she walked round to her own chair, next to Seb's – on the back of which she'd tied a big bunch of honeysuckle from the garden – she saw that on the back of hers, to her surprise and absolute, heart-stopping delight, he had tied the ballet shoes that he had saved from the bin in London.

'Thank you,' she said softly, letting her hand trail over the familiar frayed satin.

Seb smiled. 'I will always be there for you, Anna. Always there looking out for you.'

She took a breath in to steady her emotions, then nodded and said, 'Me too.'

'Well then,' Seb said, pulling out her chair and gesturing for her to take a seat, 'let's eat.'

Menus had been perched against the flower arrangements at intervals along the table, all designed by Clara, with her beautiful blue and pink screen print acting as a backdrop to her hand-written words. As they sat and sipped tea and champagne, Rachel, Jackie, Philippe, Hermione and the rest of Razzmatazz brought thin finger sandwiches of cucumber and cream cheese and towering trays of cakes to the tables. Stands wobbled with every flavour of fairy cake, from dark-chocolate mint to red velvet, dusted with glitter and iced thick with pastel colours of the rainbow. Big four-tiered Victoria Sponges took centre spot on every table, some tipping precariously as the cream oozed out thick as the first slice was cut. Then came the Black Forest gateaux, booze-soaked cherries dark purple like bruises against black, bitter chocolate. Baskets of scones, squishy with sultanas, were passed up the rows as bowls of thick clotted cream glistened and fresh-made jam slithered off spoons. There was more tea served, and white wine hauled dripping wet out of buckets of ice and champagne corks popped, while plates of strawberries dipped in white chocolate were handed from one person to the next and then there were gasps as Rachel appeared with one dish that hadn't been ordered but prepared as a beautiful surprise. Anna's mouth hung open as she watched the teetering tower of profiteroles make the journey from the bakery to their spot at the centre of the table.

It was a giant cone of cream puffs, like a witch's hat. Rachel winked as she put it down on the table. 'Every wedding has to have a show-stopping cake,' she said as Philippe handed her a silver jug and she poured thick chocolate sauce from high above, letting it drizzle down over the soft, golden profiteroles.

Anna felt Seb take her hand under the table and give it a squeeze.

When it came to the speeches, Seb's pithy, well-rehearsed quips went down a storm. Anna's dad looked like the Mad Hatter, the starling wobbling on his top hat, as he stood and recited as many embarrassing stories as he could remember about Anna growing up. He ended it by saying, 'There was a moment when we thought she'd blown it. Anna inherited her pride from her mother so—' He held his hands out in a shrug.

Anna rolled her eyes.

'But luckily, the traits she inherited from me saved the day.' A wicked, wide grin spread across his face as he listed, 'Compassion, humility, a great sense of humour and goddamn fabulous good-looks!'

The crowd roared and her dad, smug on the attention, whipped off his hat to take a bow. When he did however the starling fell off into his profiteroles making everyone laugh even harder.

'Urm—' It was Anna who stood up next, to everyone's surprise. She had to tap the side of her glass to get the attention of the crowd who were still sniggering about her dad and the starling's little double act. 'Hi. Hi, everyone.' Anna started quietly, unexpectedly nervous. 'I know it's not tradition for the bride to speak, but—' She glanced around at the decorations. 'This hasn't turned into the most traditional of weddings.'

The crowd smiled.

'I don't want to say much, I just wanted to take the opportunity to say thank you for welcoming me back here. I know I haven't had the best history with this town...'

'You've made the Christmas play pretty funny though!' Jeff Mallory shouted.

'Yeah.' Anna cringed at the idea of her teenage strops being played out on stage every year. 'I'm kinda hoping that that part won't be reprised this Christmas.'

'I could play you, Miss,' Lucy shouted.

'No, I'd be better,' Billy yelled.

'OK, OK—' Anna waved her hands. 'This is not the way I had planned this speech to go—'

The crowd sniggered.

'Oh go on, let me play you,' Lucy called again.

'OK!' Anna sighed with a smile. 'As long as *I* can play *you!*'

'That shut you up, didn't it, Luce?' Seb shouted.

'Can I play you, Sir?' Matt yelled.

'Absolutely!' Seb said, sitting back with a grin.

Hilary raised a brow as it seemed the party had descended into chaos.

'Anyway,' Anna said, a little flustered and pink-cheeked. 'I really just wanted to say thank you. Thank you for helping me do this—' She did a sweep of her arm to take in all the decorations, the food, the wine. 'And thank you—' She swallowed nervously, felt Seb reach up and place his hand reassuringly in the small of her back. She looked down at her glass and said, 'Thank you for taking me back. Thank you, Nettleton.'

When she looked up again she saw that everyone was on their feet, glasses raised.

'To Nettleton,' Seb shouted.

'To Nettleton,' the crowd chorused.

And Anna saw Mrs Beedle wink at her as she took a sip from her champagne. She had made it, finally. And she had never felt better.

As the champagne flowed, the light turned to dusk and candles flickered in the jam jars and cut-glass jugs that Anna had found in the boxes at Mrs Beedle's. Strings of coloured lights that usually wrapped around the Nettleton Christmas tree had been strung between lampposts and danced with the bunting in the breeze above them.

When it was time for Razzmatazz to provide the entertainment, the little troupe amassed on the makeshift stage at one end of the square, huge speakers sort-of donated by the school rigged up so they could blare out the Rihanna. Behind them was the stage set of Manhattan from *Vintage Treasure*, the Empire State Building and the Statue of Liberty, a bit bent and broken, propped up with ladders and a bit of old scaffolding. Dressed in their NYC Academy outfits, Razzmatazz danced their *Britain's Got Talent* audition to perfection. Not a step out of place.

Anna clapped till her hands were raw and her cheeks hurt from smiling. She turned to look at Seb to see that he had enjoyed it, but found his place empty.

Glancing round the guests she couldn't see him anywhere.

'Where's Seb?' she whispered to Hermione across the table.

'How should I know?' Hermione said back, but wouldn't catch her eye and seemed to be on the verge of the giggles.

'What? What's going on?'

'Nothing's going on. Anna, you're so paranoid!' Hermione laughed.

But just then the sound system clicked over and a massive spotlight that usually lit the branches of the plane trees beamed out onto the centre of the stage.

Matt, Mary and Lucy remained on the edge of the stage while the rest of Razzmatazz had all moved down to the space just in front.

Anna glanced around, dubious. 'Hermione, what's going on?'

And then Seb appeared in the spotlight.

'Oh God.' Anna sucked in a breath. 'What's happening? Hermione, what's happening?'

The *Dirty Dancing* soundtrack kicked in, loud.

And there he was, dancing. Seb was dancing with Lucy and Mary with Matt. A full *Dirty Dancing* routine, and Anna could barely look, her eyelids narrowed as almost-shut as they could get.

'Oh my God!' she whispered, her hand over her mouth.

Seb's brothers were whooping and cheering from the crowd as everyone clapped along to the beat.

'But he doesn't dance,' Anna said to nobody in particular.

'He's been learning,' Hermione smiled gleefully.

Anna shook her head in disbelief. It was pretty scrappy, a hundred percent mortifying but, at the same time, somehow, magnificent. And, gradually, she allowed her eyes to open more than just a slit and let her face relax into a smile, and bit her lip watching with pride at his awkward, but enthusiastic, effort on stage.

It wasn't until it neared the end that she suddenly realised what was going to happen next. It dawned on her just as Clara and Billy ran round to grab her by the hands and pull her to the aisle between the trestle tables.

'No.' She shook her head. 'No, I'm not getting involved.'

Billy grinned. 'You have to, Miss.'

'No.' Anna shook her head vehemently. 'No I can't.'

'Yes you can.' Clara made a face. 'You made Mary do it.'

'No, this is different.'

'You should probably take those shoes off, Miss, you might break your ankle.'

'No.' Anna was rigid. 'No not in front of all these people.'

Clara glanced around. 'But they're your friends.'

'Fuck.' Anna put her hand in front of her eyes. 'Fuck, fuck, fuck.'

'Miss, you shouldn't swear.'

Seb had jumped down off the stage and was waiting for her while Razzmatazz were dancing away next to him. Anna glanced around at all the guests, all eyes on her, Hermione grinning delightedly, her dad nodding in encouragement, Hilary and Roger looking shocked, Jackie wiggling around waiting to dance, Philippe with a mocking smile and one brow raised, Rachel beaming, Kim already up on a chair dancing, a cigarette dangling from her lips, Mrs Beedle holding a smile in tight but looking on like a proud mother hen, swaying her ample bottom in time with the beat.

'Fuck,' Anna said again.

347

'Miss!'

Then she caught sight of Lucinda Warren, who had her hands resting on the edge of the table and was leaning forward watching, waiting and when she caught her eye, Lucinda winked and it felt like she was suddenly giving her back her moment.

It may not be The *Nutcracker* but, Christ, it was as good as the next best thing.

'OK. Fine. Right. Good,' Anna muttered, kicking off her shoes, handing her tiara to Clara, taking a really deep breath and suddenly she was running really, really fast and a second later she was jumping and Seb's hands were on her waist and then, the next minute, she was flying. She was flying and her sequins were shimmering and her hair had tumbled loose and she was up there, up there with the stars.

*We couldn't wait to sit Jenny Oliver down for a little Q&A session!
Read on to learn more about the fabulous author
of The Vintage Summer Wedding.*

Are your characters loosely based on real people?

Not consciously! I'm sure there are elements in there of lots of people that I know or stories I've been told that resonated, but otherwise they are entirely fictional. Philippe and Rachel appeared in my first book, *The Parisian Christmas Bake Off*, and I found that I missed them when the book was done, so it was really nice to bring them back for more—Philippe especially, he's a favourite of mine!

Would you personally prefer an extravagant wedding or a low-budget vintage wedding?

Low-budget vintage definitely, which is actually what I did have—lots of candles, bunting, geraniums in flower pots, mismatched china and lanterns hanging from the trees. I leave the big extravagant weddings to other people and really enjoy them when I'm invited! A friend got married at Babington House a couple of years ago, which was stunning—there were fireworks at midnight, big glinting candelabras on all the tables and trays of espresso martinis—it was as close as I've come to feeling like a celebrity!

What is your favourite wedding song?

Ooh, I don't know. When Dolly Parton comes on I head straight to the dance floor—does that count as a wedding song?

Did you learn anything from writing *The Vintage Summer Wedding*, and what was it?

I learnt an awful lot about ballet and the dedication it takes to be a star. I also reaffirmed the idea that good is good enough, which is something I often forget—you can only ever do your best. In the book Anna is taught that lesson by a bunch of school kids auditioning for *Britain's Got Talent,* which was really fun to write.

If you could meet any of your own characters, who would it be and what would you say?

Philippe definitely—he really makes me laugh and he's so good-looking that I'd just gaze at him across the table. I would also quite like to have lunch with Hermione from *The Vintage Summer Wedding,* because she's so brash and I think would be great fun to be around (although I'd never want to cross her!).

What has been the best part about writing *The Vintage Summer Wedding*?

I wrote it in the depths of winter, so it was lovely to feel the sun. I love the ending as well—that was probably the most enjoyable part to write—I don't want to give it away, so you'll have to read it to find out why!

Give us an interesting fun fact about your book.

Nearly all the antiques in it are things that someone in my family owns, I've bought, been given or nearly bought over the years.

Who is your favourite character from your book and why?

Hermoine, definitely. She's a fab secondary character, because she breezes in all audacious and causes trouble. I love her (and her clothes!).

Are you a good dancer?

No. I think I'm more enthusiastic than good.

If you had the chance to be part of a reality TV show, which would it be and why?

Good question. I'd quite like to pop into the *Big Brother* house just for a night to see what it's like (I'd be terrible on the show though, because I'd get caught gossiping about the other contestants!) and I'd swing by the King's Road to have a glass of champagne on *Made in Chelsea*. At the moment I'd quite like to go on the Bear Grylls Island programme with all the men trying to survive in the wild, because I think it'd be good to see how a group of women would fare in the same position.

Jenny Oliver's Wedding Tips

Jenny Oliver talks brides, grooms and wedding dresses…

So, I am no more qualified to give wedding tips than anyone else—I thought my own wedding was brilliant, but I'm sure there were things that went wrong, not least my own crippling nervousness before walking down the aisle, because I was certain I might trip (I didn't). The only thing I'd do differently would be my wedding car—I opted for just a simple black taxi when I wish I'd hired a great big pink Cadillac for the pure indulgent fun of it. *C'est la vie…* Maybe I'll hire one the second time round (fingers crossed hubby isn't reading).

Anyway, here goes…

For a bride—Don't get nervous! It's the most fun day you'll ever have, so enjoy. And take a moment, five minutes is enough, to spend with just the groom and bask in the joy of it all. That's the five minutes that may just become your clearest memory.

For a groom—Urm. Get a good suit and a good haircut!? There is nothing like a good suit, I think, to make a man.

Dream wedding gift list—We weren't going to have a list until my aunt demanded it of us and so we spent an afternoon in John Lewis picking out fun things we would never have bought ourselves. Things like bright red toasters, a yellow bread bin and a juicer. We even had his and hers electric toothbrushes on the list. When the man came to deliver it all after the wedding, it was like Christmas! Boxes and boxes of presents piled up in our kitchen. I'm ashamed to admit it was one of the best bits of the whole thing! So I can't tell you what to get or ask for, but make sure it's something that will make you smile. Even now when I use my red toaster I'm reminded of the friend who bought it for us.

The Dress—In *The Vintage Summer Wedding* the dress is quite a contentious issue. It becomes more important than the marriage itself. I'd say that whatever the bride wears she invariably looks stunning, so don't bankrupt yourself and don't necessarily go white just because tradition dictates. If you like a cream trouser suit or a hot pink maxi dress, then go for it. Like Anna in TVSW, though, if I had all the money in the world, I'd choose Vera Wang.

Finally, try and get a couple of photos on your phone or e-mailed to you, because they are all you'll want to look at on the plane or in the car to the honeymoon! Happy days! xx

Jenny Oliver's next book

THE LITTLE CHRISTMAS KITCHEN

is out now

(Turn the page for a sneak peek…)

THE LITTLE CHRISTMAS KITCHEN

by Jenny Oliver

CHAPTER ONE

ELLA

The meeting was tedious. The air conditioner was broken and whirring too loudly, so it muffled the execs calling in on the speaker phone. The stuffy air smelt of aftershave and strong coffee, with a hint of the marker pen that kept running out on the flip chart. Big bushy garlands of tinsel were looped along the wall, baubles hung in bunches like grapes on the windows and a white fake Christmas tree with glittered branches twinkled in the corner.

Ella was having to look anywhere but the new account assistant, Katya, who was presenting and nerves had made her voice catch and her cheeks flush a blotchy red. She couldn't stomach the embarrassment she felt for her.

Their boss, Adrian, was tapping frustratedly on his

BlackBerry, not listening. She knew he was getting the presentations out the way before he brought up the accounts they lost last week and what it would do to revenue. As she glanced around the room, taking in the glazed faces and the distracted looks of her colleagues all wired on too much coffee and bourbon biscuits, her gaze stopped on the building opposite where an aerobics class was in full swing. As Ella watched the women jumping up and down in their Sweaty Betty lycra, she wondered when the last time she'd had time to do any exercise was. She'd cancelled her gym membership alongside her last promotion when she realised she rarely left work before eight.

Tonight she was leaving early though. Tonight she was being wined and dined. Tonight they were going to Fera at Claridge's and she had a brand-new Stella McCartney chocolate silk dress hanging on the back of her office door ready to team with her nude Manolo Blahniks and an Aztec print scarf. It was all from Net-a-Porter—she'd ordered the entire outfit that the model was wearing. Shamefully, she always ordered exactly what the model was wearing. The grey pencil skirt she had on at the moment, and the cerise mules, was a case in point. Occasionally, when she went completely off-piste and gave her own eye a go, Max would walk into the bedroom, himself dressed like a Ralph Lauren model, and say something like, 'Really?' or 'I don't think that's quite right for…' whatever event they were off to—Ascot or Henley or the Hunt Ball. Then he'd pinch her bottom and kiss her cheek and say, 'I'd love you in anything, but you know what the girls are like…'

The girls. Ella narrowed her eyes at the baubles. The girls...

Friends since school, Max's tight little gang were ferocious. A terrifying mix of confidence and boredom that came with being too good-looking and having too much money. All caramel highlights and butterscotch tans, they had ample time on their hands to be as vicious as they were whip smart and wickedly hilarious. Ella was like a fish gasping at the surface of a puddle when she was with them, not that she'd ever admit it to Max. What perplexed her the most was that she could handle the hardest CEO in the boardroom, present to rooms of the coolest, most guarded clients without breaking into a sweat, but those girls...they could pierce her with a look, undermine her with a laugh, leave her flustered and blushing and wanting to cling on to Max's hand when he was wandering off with the boys to check out a new sports car or racehorse and reminisce about boarding school.

At the front of the room Katya was ploughing on through the presentation. From the way she was stumbling and relying so heavily on her notes, Ella knew she'd be packed off on a presentation course before the day was out. She glanced at her watch. She was booked in for a blow dry in forty minutes. *Come on*, she thought, *this is child's play, we all know this stuff, why do we need a bloody meeting about it?*

Tonight was their anniversary—her and Max—seven years. Seven years and look how far she'd come. If she was the kind of person to put stuff on Facebook, then she'd plaster it with pictures of the diamond bracelet he'd given her that morning. Almost just to reaffirm to them all that he loved *her*. Even after all this time she still heard the whispers behind the smiles. But, if she ever mentioned it, Max would squeeze her tight and lift her in the air and say, *they're all just jealous*. Burying her face in his neck, she would close her eyes and breath him in and hope this life lasted forever.

She glanced down at the gems sparkling on her wrist. She loved it. Or at least she thought she loved it, was it her taste? Yes, it was her taste. It was a bit thin and delicate for her wrist, but yes, no, she loved it. *I love it*, she thought, as it winked under the strip light.

Her BlackBerry vibrated where it sat on top of her iPad on top of her laptop on the boardroom table. She let the bracelet tip forward over her hand as she reached forward, wondered if anyone else had noticed it sparkle, and slipped her phone off the table, holding it under the desk, out of sight, as she opened the new e-mail.

'This is all very wel—' Her boss said, sitting up and stretching his back in an arch. 'But I can't see anything different here. I can't see what you'll be offering the client that every other firm won't be offering. We've seen all this before. And if I've seen it, they've seen it.' He frowned, frustrated. 'Come on, people. We need a bit more blue sky thinking. A bit more oomph.' He sat forward. 'Basically, we need this new business. It's Christmas, for crying out loud. Wow them with a bit of sparkle. Ella, can you take charge of this one—' He paused. 'Ella…are you with us?'

Ella wasn't with them at all. Every ounce of her concentration was caught by the e-mail she'd just opened on her phone. Her mouth had hung open of its own accord. Her right eye, that had recently developed a tiredness tick, was flickering. Her stomach had tightened like she'd forgotten to exhale.

Subject: *I just thought you should know.*
Your husband is having an affair with my wife. Photo attached confirms. Suggest you get yourself a good lawyer. I'm going to annihilate her in court.

Ella recognised Prague in the background of the photograph. Saw the ornate buildings dark and dirty and snow speckling the canopies of the market stalls. She recognised it because she'd been there with him. Last Christmas. His company had an office there, he could get business class flights and a room in the Mandarin Oriental on expenses.

'Ella?' Her boss repeated.

'Yes, sorry.' She pressed her phone off and cleared her throat. 'Sorry, I just…' She shook her head. 'Yes, absolutely, I totally agree. Great presentation, Katya. Just fabulous, exactly what we were looking for. Really, really great. Good, let's get started then.' She said, her mouth stretched into her work smile as she started to stand up, gathering her iPad, notebook and pen to her chest and pushing her chair back.

She felt everyone in the room watching her. Mark, her colleague who sat to her right, whispered, 'There are still three more presentations.'

'Oh, sorry.' Ella paused. Felt her cheeks begin to pink.

'Ella?' Her boss sat back, put his hands behind his head. 'Is everything all right? Did you hear what I was saying?'

She looked around the room as she sat down, everyone seemed suddenly distracted by their notepads, or the wood grain of the table top.

'Yes.' She lied quietly.

He made a face. Ella was his secret weapon. Ella was the reason he'd been promoted. Her work, his leadership. Ella had won them the last four accounts and was possibly the single reason they were still in the black. Ella, who worked twenty-four/seven and never took her eye off the prize. Award-winning Ella. 'Let's talk afterwards,' he said, and she nodded vaguely. Her hand burning like her phone was on fire.

CHAPTER TWO

MADDY

'If I tell my mum about the job, then she won't let me go because she won't approve. If I don't tell her that I have a job, then she won't let me go because she'll say that I'll just be bumming it round London wasting my life when she needs me to work here.' Maddy wiped her oily hands on the old rag hanging out her jeans pocket and then took the hand Dimitri was offering to haul herself out of the boat and up on to the jetty.

'Maddy.' He said, bending down to pick up the board of his windsurfer, the sail already propped up by the side of the taverna. 'You're twenty-four. Don't you think it's about time you just went anyway?' He raised a dark brow and looked at her with a fairly patronising smirk on his lips, but then got distracted when he noticed a scratch on his board. 'Shit, when did that happen? It's those kids, isn't it? Oi, you lot—' he shouted at the gaggle of little kids who were messing around at the end of the jetty, dangling bits of rope into the sea with worms on hooks to try and catch the millions of silver fish that darted around the wooden posts. They looked up all big-eyed and terrified when Dimitri yelled. 'Did you mess with my board?'

'No, Dimitri,' they all chorused in unison, faces pale and perfectly innocent.

He glared at them for a second. Six foot with shoulders like the Ark, black shaggy hair and at least three days stubble, he knew he could terrify them.

'Don't.' Maddy rolled her eyes. 'They're only little.'

'They've messed with my board. Look at it.'

'You're mean. Stop being mean to them. Look at them.' She turned to wave in their direction, all four kids huddled together, their fishing rods clutched in their hands, their cheeks pink, waiting for their telling off.

Dimitri sighed. 'You stay away from my board. Yes!'

'Yes, Dimitri,' they chorused again.

'And while you're at it, stay away from my bike as well. I saw you the other day sitting on it. Yes. I did, don't shake your heads, if it fell on you it could do some damage. Don't sit on my bike.'

'Can we ride on it again with you, please?'

He narrowed his eyes and shook his head. 'What have I started?' he said to Maddy. And she shrugged a shoulder.

'You shouldn't have been so keen to show off your new toy, should you?' she said, nodding to where his beautiful Triumph Bonneville T100 sat gleaming on the cobbled slipway.

Dimitri followed her gaze, paused for a second to admire his bike and then said with a shrug, 'I was excited.'

Maddy shook her head and turned away with a laugh. She stuffed the rag in her pocket, turned around to the kids and said, 'I'll take you out on this, if you like.' *This* was the sleek white forty-foot yacht she'd just repaired the engine of.

'Are you sure, Maddy?' Dimitri questioned, dubious, as the kids all whooped and, chucking down their rods, ran over to jump on the deck of the boat, their shoes leaving tiny, dusty footprints on the gleaming surface like a cat's.

'Yeah, it'll be fine.' Maddy said, pulling on a big red, oil-streaked jumper that came down to just above the frayed edge of her shorts and then, sweeping away the wisps of hair that the wind was blowing in her mouth, said, 'And with my mum, I just don't want her to *not* want me to go, I want her to approve, I suppose. Stupid, huh?' She laughed, husky and dry like a granddad.

'It's pretty windy out there, Mads.' Dimitri shielded his eyes from the low sun and looked out to where the waves were starting to pick up.

'Can you focus on what I'm saying about my mum.' She frowned. 'And—it's OK for you take your windsurfer out, but I can't handle the boat? Are you kidding?'

'It's got worse in the last few hours. I would never dream of implying you couldn't handle the boat. But let's look at the facts, Maddy, it's really bloody windy and it's not your boat.'

'Well, he'd want me to test the engine as well as fix it, wouldn't he?' She kicked one of the posts with her old Nike hi-top trainer.

'You can test it by turning the key in the ignition. Not taking a bunch of seven-year-olds for a joyride into a mistral.' Dimitri shook his head, tendrils of black hair wobbling like a sea anemone.

'It'll be fine. And anyway—' Maddy jumped down on to the stern, taking the rope she'd looped into one of the jetty rings with her to cast off. 'I can't say no now, look at them…'

The kids were all sitting crossed-legged at the bow like tiny figureheads, watching expectantly.

'See, this is probably what your mum's talking about. In your desperation to please people, you don't think things through.'

'Oh please,' Maddy scoffed as she pressed the button to haul up the anchor. 'She just doesn't want me to go off to London and leave her alone.'

'I think she worries that you've been too sheltered,' Dimitri yelled over the wind and the sound of the two hundred and fifty horsepower engine as it sprang to life.

'Bullshit,' Maddy shouted back. 'That's the most patronising thing I've ever heard, Dimitri. You're so annoying.'

'Good come-back,' he said, raising a brow. 'My case in point.'

Maddy snorted a laugh and then turned her back on him to steer the boat out of the little harbour. The kids were clinging on to the tinsel-wrapped railing at the front, dangling their feet over the edge and laughing as the spray bounced up into their faces.

As Maddy looked past them, out at the wide blue sea, dark like sapphires, the white horses jumping like skittish foals, rays of low winter sun darting off each wave like silver fish, all she could think was, *God, I wish this was London*.

CHAPTER THREE

ELLA

Ella threw her BlackBerry on the sofa. Bloody holiday. She didn't need a bloody holiday. She needed to curl up into a little ball and hibernate like a hedgehog. She needed to talk to Max.

Adrian had called her into his office directly after the meeting and asked her what was wrong. She'd shown him the e-mail and he'd sucked in his breath.

'Do you want a cigarette out the window?' he'd asked.

'I don't smoke, Adrian.'

'I know, but sometimes moments call for a cigarette. If you don't want one, I might have one.' He pulled open his desk drawer and fumbled around at the back for a hidden packet of Marlboro Reds and a box of matches. Hauling up the sash window, he leant on the sill and inhaled half the cigarette in one. 'Christ, I've missed this.' Exhaling he shook his head. 'Max, Max, what are you doing?'

'I think maybe it's been photoshopped,' Ella said, crossing the room to perch on the edge of the big leather-covered desk. Outside it had started to sleet, watery white flecks cascading down like a snowglobe. A couple of mangy pigeons on the roof opposite were shaking out their feathers, huddled up together next to a light-up Santa Claus, plump and wet and depressed.

Adrian raised a brow, the creases on his forehead deepening. Ella frowned. 'You don't think so? You think he's having an affair. I don't think he's having an affair. Especially not with her. I really don't. Look—' She held out her arm, where the bracelet slipped forward over the back of her hand. 'Look,' she said again, a little quieter.

'It's very pretty.' Adrian nodded. Took another drag and then flicked the cigarette out on to the roof top. The pigeons scattered. 'Do you want me to see what Anne thinks?'

Anne was Adrian's wife. Anne had been friends with Max since childhood and it was through a dinner at their house that Ella had met Adrian and he'd given her a job. They had garden parties in the summer in their huge dilapidated mansion and their wild, adorable children ran around in slightly dirty clothes and no shoes while everyone else drank Pimm's and adored the roses. They were the antithesis of Max's other friends. So rich they could bypass into shabby and boho and not care in the slightest. But they were all so inextricably linked. Like a web. Or Kerplunk. One stick pulled out and it all falls down.

'No.' Ella shook her head. 'I trust him. Of course I trust him. There will be an explanation. There's always an explanation for things like this. It's not bloody *East-Enders,* is it? She's one of his friends, for God's sake. If he was going to have an affair, would he really do it on his own doorstep?' She felt her voice catch in her throat. She thought of Max—gorgeous, funny, beautiful Max, with his arm casually draped round the waist of a woman who wasn't her—a woman with lovely hair and eyes that tipped up at the corners. Amanda. One of his 'girls'. The one who had taken Ella aside when they'd first got together and taken her shopping and bought her champagne and linked her arm through hers and managed to get her to tell all her secrets about Max.

Max, whom she looked at every morning as he slept on their cream linen sheets and wondered how she'd managed to get that lucky. The sleet had turned to rain. It was pouring down the window and making a mockery of the Christmas decorations strung across the street. Little white lights trying to sparkle like her diamonds.

Max was actually having an affair. No longer did she need to worry about it or imagine it. Because it was actually happening.

No, he couldn't be.

Adrian went over to his Nespresso machine in the corner of his office. 'Do you want one?' he asked and Ella shook her head.

As it rumbled out the dark, glossy liquid in a thick white cup, Adrian said, 'I've got some eggnogg from that Christmas hamper we were sent last week. Do you want me to pour you a glass of that?'

'No, I'm fine. Honestly, I'll just have some water.' As Ella leant over to the carafe on his desk, her eye caught the photo that sat next to it of him and Anne and their kids. She thought of the amount of times she'd stared at that picture and imagined having one on her desk of her and Max and a couple of kids with his bright blue eyes and her dark hair. If Max was having an affair, then he might want to split up and they'd never have children. And that might mean that she'd never have children because she'd have to get over Max, meet someone else and fall in love with them enough to want to have kids with them before she ran out of time. She was thirty-three. If Max was having an affair, then not only would he have battered her heart, he would have snatched at her chance to have a family photo on her desk.

Please God, she thought, *please don't let him be more in love with the woman with the shiny hair and the eyes that tip up at the corners than he is with me*.

She felt Adrian watching her over the rim of his coffee cup.

'OK,' she said after a pause.

'OK what?' he said.

'OK, ring Anne,' she said, when really she just wanted to ring Max and hear him say something funny down the phone and then walk into Claridge's tonight looking all shiny and satiny in her new dress and him to whistle and then grin and pull her chair out for her the way they'd taught him at Eton.

But instead they were going to ring Anne. Anne wouldn't lie.

And that was why she was standing in her bedroom

now, hauling her wheelie case from under the bed, chucking in whatever was in front of her. Not her packing style at all. No rolled clothes and shoes in their own little bags, and travel-sized toiletries. No outfits laid out on the bed, making sure that she hadn't missed a vital top or pair of shoes. This was more Max's style of packing. Ella was the organised one, he was the haphazard fun one. That was how they complemented each other. That was why they worked so well. She succeeded, he charmed. They were the perfect unit. They were 'Maxwella' his friends joked.

Going over to the wardrobe, she yanked out everything closest to hand—a pair of Jimmy Choo flip-flops, Ralph Lauren shorts bunched up next to the top half of her Missoni bikini and the bottom half of a Stella McCartney one. Record temperatures across southern Europe this winter was all the news could talk about. Violent thunderstorms and above average hours of sunshine were creating flood havoc alongside flocks of holidaymakers jetting off for cheap winter sun. But, as she threw in some white Victoria Beckham jeans that she'd bought just because all 'the girls' had them, a kaftan and a huge woolly cardigan that she usually wore to watch TV on her own, she didn't actually think she'd be wearing any of it. Her subconscious knew it was all for show. The case, the holiday, the fleeing just before Christmas. Because her knight would come home, throw his sword to the ground, scoop her up and carry her off into the rainy London sunset while declaring it was all lies.

She chucked in toiletries, scattered in loose. Half pots of Eve Lom moisturiser and her specially mixed shampoo clattered alongside her hairdryer, straighteners, trainers. The crisp shirts she'd paid a fortune to have pressed at the dry cleaners were stuffed in willy nilly. She stopped for a second and called a taxi—*to the airport? Which one? I don't know. Heathrow? Yes, madam*.

She caught a glimpse of herself in the mirror as she hung up the phone. Hair uncharacteristically skew-whiff. Eyes that someone who knew her well might say had been crying. The trace of mascara stains on cheeks that she'd scrubbed already with cold water and while telling herself to get a grip.

Adrian hadn't had to say anything. She'd just watched the expression on his face when he'd asked Anne if Max 'might be perhaps being unfaithful'. She'd heard the cough he'd done to try and buy himself some time. Then the nod as if he were pretending that Anne was saying something completely different.

'Shit. What am I going to do?' Ella had said without thinking when he'd put the phone down.

'Talk to Max.' Adrian had said. He'd looked worried, like a boy watching his mother cry. Ella couldn't break down. Ella didn't show her emotions. Ella was always the strong, confident one.

'Yes, good idea.' She'd swallowed, pulled herself together. 'There's bound to be a rational explanation.'

Perhaps Anne didn't know Max that well.

But instead of calling Max she had gone home and rifled through his drawers. Discovered nothing. Wondered if that was because their style was so minimalist or because it wasn't true.

As Ella was just zipping up the overstuffed bag she heard the click of the front door, the pad of Gucci loafers on the beige carpet, and turned to see Max standing in the doorway, one hand pulling his tie loose.

'I thought you were going to Claridge's straight from work?' he said, his beautiful face innocently perplexed. Arrow-straight eyebrows drawing lightly into a frown, blond hair casually dishevelled.

'Are you having an affair?'

Welcome to the most celebrated patisserie competition in Paris

The search for Paris's next patisserie apprentice is about to begin! And super-chef judge Henri Salernes is an infamously tough cookie. But Rachel Smithson isn't about to let her confidence (or pastry) crumble. She's got one week, mounds of melt-in-the-mouth macaroons and towers of perfect profiteroles to prove that she really is a star baker.

But as well as clouds of flour, and wafts of chocolate and cinnamon, will there be a touch of Christmas romance in the air…? It is Paris, after all.

Marianne Baker is happy.
Sort of.

She's worked at the same job for years, lives at home
with her mum and her love life is officially stalled.
Playing the violin is her only real passion—but
nobody like her does that for a living.

But when the father who abandoned Marianne as a
child turns up on her doorstep with a shocking secret,
suddenly her safe, comfortable world is shattered.

If her father isn't the man she thought he was, then
who is he? And, more to the point, who is *she*?

It's time to find out who the real Marianne Baker is.

HARLEQUIN®MIRA®
www.mirabooks.co.uk

COMING SOON

The fantastic new read from rom–com queen Fiona Harper

Claire Bixby grew up watching Doris Day films and yearned
to live in a world like the one on the screen—sunny,
colourful and where happy endings were guaranteed.
But recently Claire's opportunities for a little 'pillow talk'
have been thin on the ground. That is, until she meets Nic.

Sparks soon start to fly, but Claire's now questioning
everything Doris taught her about romance.

Can true love can ever really be just like it is in the movies?
Perhaps, perhaps, perhaps…

COMING APRIL 2015
Pre-order your copy today

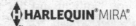